MW00757522

Lord of the Privateers

"What is it?" Her tone suggested she was perfectly aware he was harboring some…inner turmoil.

"I feel as if, after eight years of emptiness, I've only just got you back, just long enough to glimpse heaven again—my version of it, at least—and here I am happily or, as it happens, not at all happily, risking you and everything between us, and all hope for our future, again." He let his chin drop to her shoulder; from beneath his lashes, he watched her face in the mirror. "I know it's what needs to be—that you need to do it, and all the reasons why—and yet…" He closed his eyes, fractionally shook his head.

Isobel heard the words he didn't say and turned in his hold. Instantly, he straightened, raising his head and opening his eyes. She met his gaze, searched, and saw what he allowed her to see in the roiling gray. "What do you think I felt knowing you would lead the attack in the compound? That you would be the first of our men to drop inside an enemy-held perimeter? And that I could be nowhere near—not even within sight of you, let alone close enough to step in should anything unexpected occur…" Her eyes on his, she tilted her head. "Isn't that the same thing?"

He held her gaze, then bluntly said, "It might be, but you're a woman—you handle it better."

Other titles from Stephanie Laurens

Cynster Series
Devil's Bride
A Rake's Vow
Scandal's Bride
A Rogue's Proposal
A Secret Love
All about Love
All about Passion
On a Wild Night
On a Wicked Dawn
The Perfect Lover
The Ideal Bride
The Truth about Love
What Price Love?
The Taste of Innocence
Temptation and Surrender

Cynster Sisters Trilogy
Viscount Breckenridge to the Rescue
In Pursuit of Eliza Cynster
The Capture of the Earl of Glencrae

Cynster Sisters Duo
And Then She Fell
The Taming of Ryder Cavanaugh

Cynster Special
The Promise in a Kiss
By Winter's Light

Cynster Next Generation
The Tempting of Thomas Carrick
A Match for Marcus Cynster

Medieval
Desire's Prize

Novellas
"Melting Ice"—from *Scandalous Brides*
"Rose in Bloom"—from *Scottish Brides*
"Scandalous Lord Dere"—
from *Secrets of a Perfect Night*
"Lost and Found"—from *Hero, Come Back*
"The Fall of Rogue Gerrard"—
from *It Happened One Night*
"The Seduction of Sebastian Trantor"—
from *It Happened One Season*

Bastion Club Series
Captain Jack's Woman (Prequel)
The Lady Chosen
A Gentleman's Honor
A Lady of His Own
A Fine Passion
To Distraction
Beyond Seduction
The Edge of Desire
Mastered by Love

Black Cobra Quartet Series
The Untamed Bride
The Elusive Bride
The Brazen Bride
The Reckless Bride

Other Novels
The Lady Risks All

The Casebook of Barnaby Adair Novels
Where the Heart Leads
The Peculiar Case of Lord Finsbury's Diamonds
The Masterful Mr. Montague
The Curious Case of Lady Latimer's Shoes
Loving Rose: The Redemption of Malcolm Sinclair

Regency Romances
Tangled Reins
Four in Hand
Impetuous Innocent
Fair Juno
The Reasons for Marriage
A Lady of Expectations
An Unwilling Conquest
A Comfortable Wife

The Adventurers Quartet
The Lady's Command
A Buccaneer at Heart
The Daredevil Snared
Lord of the Privateers

STEPHANIE LAURENS

Lord of the Privateers

Recycling programs for this product may not exist in your area.

ISBN-13: 978-0-7783-1973-3

Lord of the Privateers

For questions and comments about the quality of this book, please contact us at CustomerService@Harlequin.com.

www.MIRABooks.com

Printed in U.S.A.

First printing: December 2016
10 9 8 7 6 5 4 3 2 1

Lord of the Privateers

CAST OF CHARACTERS

Principal Characters:

Frobisher, Captain Royd	Hero, oldest Frobisher brother and captain of *The Corsair*
Carmichael, Isobel Carmody	Heroine, only child of James Carmichael and Anne Carmody, and heiress of the Carmichael Shipyards, Aberdeen

In Aberdeen:

Frobisher, Captain Fergus	Royd's father
Frobisher, Mrs. Elaine	Royd's mother
Carmody, Mrs. Iona	Isobel's maternal grandmother and matriarch of the Carmody clan
Carmichael, Mr. James	Isobel's father and owner of Carmichael Shipyards
Carmichael, Mrs. Anne Carmody	Isobel's mother
Carmichael, Mrs. Elise	James's mother, Isobel's paternal grandmother
Featherstone, Miss Gladys	Royd's secretary at the Frobisher Shipping Company office
Jeb	Head groom at Carmody Place

On board The Corsair:

Stewart, Lieutenant Liam	First mate
Kelly, Mr. William	Master
Williams	Quartermaster
Jolley	Bosun
Bellamy, Mr.	Steward
Various other sailors	

In London:

Family:

Frobisher, Captain Declan	Royd's brother and captain of *The Cormorant*
Frobisher, Lady Edwina	Declan's wife, Royd's sister-in-law
Frobisher, Captain Robert	Royd's brother and captain of *The Trident*
Hopkins, Miss Aileen	Robert's intended and sister of Lieutenant William Hopkins, West Africa Squadron

Staff in Declan & Edwina's town house:

Humphrey	Butler

Government:

Wolverstone, Duke of, Royce aka Dalziel	Ex-commander of British secret operatives outside England
Melville, Lord	First Lord of the Admiralty

Society:

Wolverstone, Duchess of, Minerva	Royce's wife, society grande dame, major ton hostess
St. Ives, Duke of, Devil (Sylvester)	
St. Ives, Duchess of, Honoria	Devil's wife, society grande dame, major ton hostess
Cynster, Mr. Harry	Devil's cousin
Cynster, Mr. Rupert (Gabriel)	Devil's cousin

Dearne, Marquess of, Christian	Ex-member of the Bastion Club, ex-operative of Dalziel's
Dearne, Marchioness of, Letitia	Christian's wife
Warnefleet, Jack, Lord	Ex-member of the Bastion Club, ex-operative of Dalziel's
Warnefleet, Lady Clarice	Jack, Lord Warnefleet's wife
Trentham, Earl of	Ex-member of the Bastion Club, ex-operative of Dalziel's
Hendon, Jack, Lord	Owner of Hendon Shipping, ex-operative, ex-army
Hendon, Kit (Katherine), Lady	Jack, Lord Hendon's wife
Carstairs, Major Rafe	Army officer, covert liaison, involved in Black Cobra incident
Delborough, Colonel	Ex-army officer, involved in Black Cobra incident
Clunes-Forsythe, Mr.	Power broker, wealthy member of the haut ton
Deveny, Lord Hugh	Indolent member of the haut ton
Risdale, Marquis of	Wealthy member of the haut ton
Cummins, Sir Reginald	Wealthy member of the haut ton
Rundell, Mr. Phillip	Jeweler, part owner of Rundell, Bridge, and Rundell
Bridge, Mr.	Jeweler, part owner of Rundell, Bridge, and Rundell

In Southampton:

Higginson	Head clerk, Frobisher Shipping Company office

At Sea:

Frobisher, Captain Lachlan	Captain of *Sea Dragon*
Frobisher, Captain Catrina (Kit)	Captain of *Consort*

In Freetown:

Holbrook, Governor	Governor-in-Chief of British West Africa
Satterly, Mr. Arnold	Governor's principal aide
Eldridge, Major	Commander, Fort Thornton
Decker, Vice-Admiral Ralph	Commander, West Africa Squadron
Winton, Major	Commissar of Fort Thornton
Babington, Mr. Charles	Partner, Macauley & Babington Trading Company
Macauley, Mr.	Senior partner, Macauley & Babington Trading Company
Ross-Courtney, Lord Peter	Wealthy and influential visitor
Neill, Mr. Frederick	Well-born and wealthy associate of Ross-Courtney's
Undoto, Obo	Local priest
Muldoon, Mr. Silas	The Naval Attaché
Winton, Mr. William	Assistant Commissar at Fort Thornton
Hardwicke, Reverend	Minister of Church of England
Hardwicke, Mrs.	Minister's wife
Sherbrook, Mrs.	Lady-employer of Katherine Fortescue
Dave	Cockney coachman

In the Mining Compound:

Mercenaries:

Dubois	Leader of the mercenaries, presumed French
Arsene	Dubois's lieutenant, second-in command, presumed French
Cripps	Dubois's second lieutenant, English
Plus twenty-eight other mercenaries	Of various ages and extractions

Captives:

Frobisher, Captain Caleb	Youngest Frobisher brother and captain of *The Prince*
Fortescue, Miss Kate (Katherine)	Ex-governess of the Sherbrooks' and Caleb's intended
Quilley	Quartermaster of *The Prince*
Foster, Martin, Ellis, Quick, Mallard, Collins, Biggs, Norton, and Olsen	Experienced seamen from *The Prince*
Lascelle, Captain Phillipe	Longtime friend of Caleb's, privateer captain of *The Raven*
Ducasse	Quartermaster of *The Raven*
Fullard, Collmer, Gerard, and Vineron	Experienced seamen from *The Raven*
Dixon, Captain John	Army engineer
Hopkins, Lieutenant William	Navy, West Africa Squadron
Fanshawe, Lieutenant	Navy, West Africa Squadron
Hillsythe, Mr.	Ex-Wolverstone agent, governor's aide
Frazier, Miss Harriet	Gently bred young woman, Dixon's sweetheart
Wilson, Miss Mary	Shop owner/assistant, Babington's sweetheart

McKenzie, Miss Ellen	Young woman recently arrived in the settlement
Halliday, Miss Gemma	Young woman from the slums
Mellows, Miss Annie	Young woman from the slums
Mathers, Jed	Carpenter
Watson, Wattie	Navvy
Plus eighteen other men	All British of various backgrounds and trades
Diccon	Young boy, eight years old
Amy	Young girl, six years old
Gerry	Boy, eleven years old
Tilly	Girl, fourteen years old
Simon Finn	Boy, twelve years old
Plus sixteen other children	All British, ranging from six to ten years old
Plus three other boys	All British, ranging from eleven to fourteen years old

On board The Trident*:*

Latimer, Mr. Jordan	First mate
Hurley, Mr.	Master
Wilcox	Bosun
Miller	Quartermaster
Foxby, Mr.	Steward
Various other sailors	

On board The Cormorant*:*

Caldwell, Mr. Joshua	First mate
Johnson, Mr.	Master
Grimsby	Bosun
Elliot	Quartermaster
Henry, Mr.	Steward
Various other sailors	

On board The Prince*:*

Fitzpatrick, Lieutenant Frederick	First mate
Wallace, Mr.	Master
Carter	Bosun
Hornby, Mr.	Steward, carries information to London and returns on *The Corsair*
Various other sailors	

On board The Raven*:*

Reynaud	Bosun, on ship, but returns to the jungle compound
Plus four other seamen	On ship, but return to the jungle compound
Various other sailors	

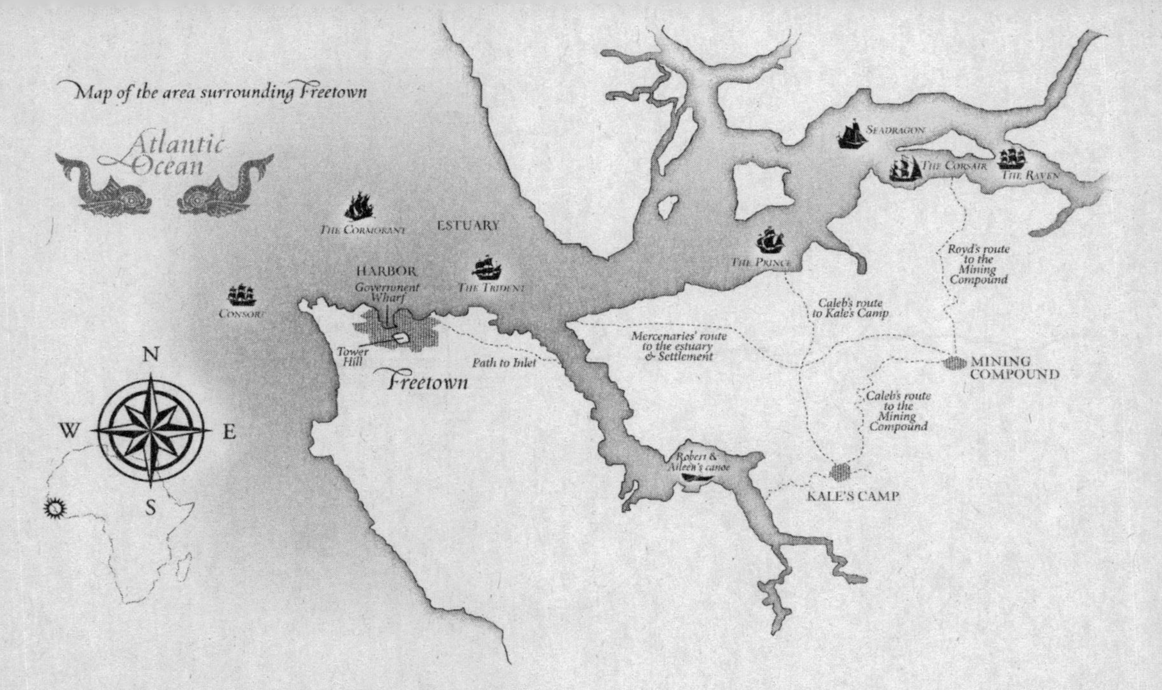
Map of the area surrounding Freetown
Atlantic Ocean
The Cormorant
ESTUARY
HARBOR
Government Wharf
The Trident
Consort
Tower Hill
Freetown
Path to Inlet
N
W
E
S
Seadragon
The Corsair
The Raven
The Prince
Royd's route to the Mining Compound
Caleb's route to Kale's Camp
Mercenaries' route to the estuary & Settlement
MINING COMPOUND
Caleb's route to the Mining Compound
Robert & Aileen's canoe
KALE'S CAMP

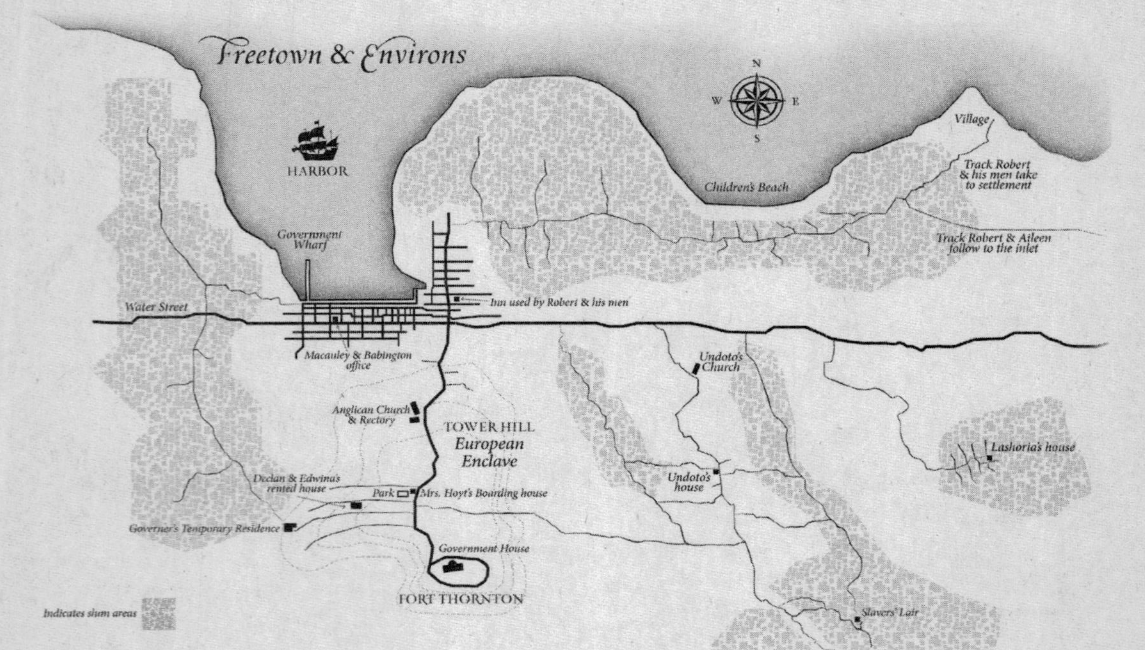

Freetown & Environs
HARBOR
N
W
E
S
Government Wharf
Children's Beach
Village
Track Robert & his men take to settlement
Track Robert & Aileen follow to the inlet
Water Street
Inn used by Robert & his men
Macauley & Babington office
Undoto's Church
Anglican Church & Rectory
TOWER HILL
European Enclave
Lashoria's house
Declan & Edwina's rented house
Park
Mrs. Hoyt's Boarding house
Undoto's house
Governer's Temporary Residence
Government House
FORT THORNTON
Indicates slum areas
Slavers' Lair

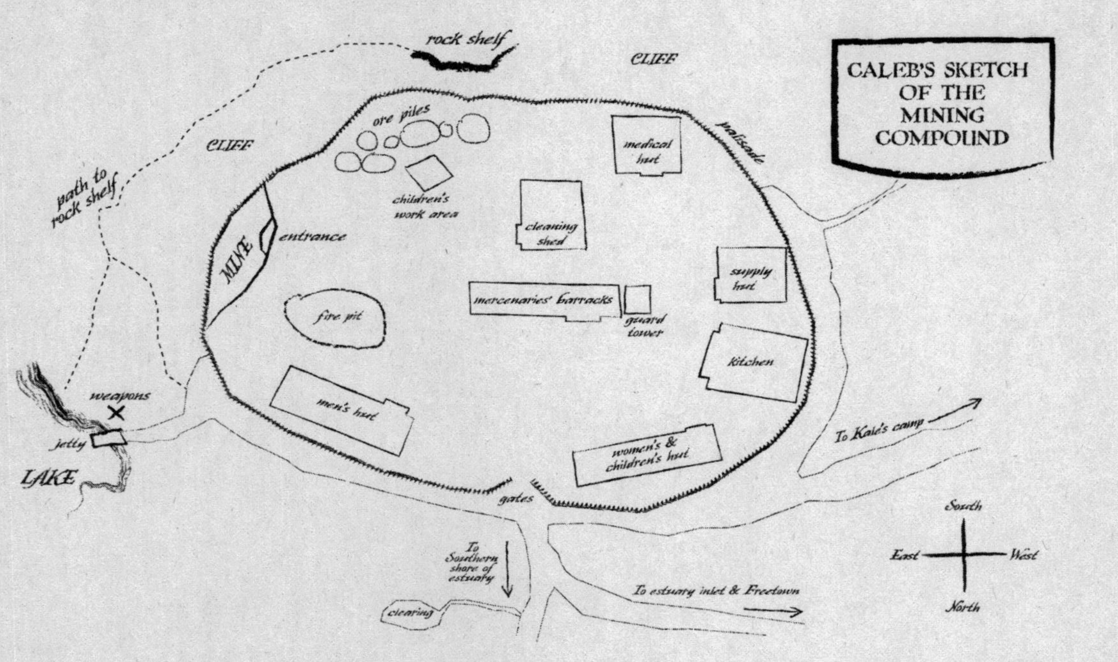
CALEB'S SKETCH OF THE MINING COMPOUND
rock shelf
CLIFF
CLIFF
path to rock shelf
ore piles
children's work area
medical hut
palisade
cleaning shed
entrance
MINE
supply hut
mercenaries' barracks
guard tower
fire pit
kitchen
men's hut
weapons
jetty
LAKE
To Kale's camp
women's & children's hut
gates
South
East
West
North
To Southern shore of estuary
To estuary inlet & Freetown
clearing

Prologue

Aberdeen
August 9, 1824

Royd Frobisher stood behind the desk in his office overlooking Aberdeen harbor and reread the summons he'd just received.

Was it his imagination, or was Wolverstone anxious?

Royd had received many such summonses over the years Wolverstone had served as England's spymaster; the wording of today's missive revealed an underlying uneasiness on the part of the normally imperturbable ex-spymaster.

Either uneasiness or impatience, and the latter was not one of Wolverstone's failings.

Although a decade Wolverstone's junior, Royd and the man previously known as Dalziel had understood each other from their first meeting, much as kindred spirits. After Dalziel retired and succeeded to the title of the Duke of Wolverstone, he and Royd had remained in touch. Royd suspected he was one of Wolverstone's principal contacts in keeping abreast of those intrigues most people in the realm knew nothing about.

Royd studied the brief lines suggesting that he sail his

ship, *The Corsair*, currently bobbing on the waters beyond his window, to Southampton, to be provisioned and to hold ready to depart once news arrived from Freetown.

The implication was obvious. Wolverstone expected the news from Freetown—when it arrived courtesy of Royd's youngest brother, Caleb—to be such as to require an urgent response. Namely, for Royd to depart for West Africa as soon as possible and, once there, to take whatever steps proved necessary to preserve king and country.

A commitment to preserving king and country being one of the traits Royd and Wolverstone shared.

Another was the instinctive ability to evaluate situations accurately. If Wolverstone was anxious—

"I need to see him."

The voice, more than the words, had Royd raising his head.

"I'll inquire—"

"And I need to see him now. Stand aside, Miss Featherstone."

"But—"

"No buts. Excuse me."

Royd heard the approaching tap of high heels striking the wooden floor. Given the tempo and the force behind each tap, he could readily envision his middle-aged secretary standing by the reception desk, wringing her hands.

Still, Gladys Featherstone was a local. She should know that Isobel Carmichael on a tear was a force of nature few could deflect.

Not even him.

He'd had the partition separating his inner sanctum from the outer office rebuilt so the glazed section ran from six feet above the floor—his eye level—to the ceiling; when seated at his desk, he preferred to be out of sight of all those who stopped by, thinking to waste the time of the operational head of the Frobisher Shipping Company. If callers couldn't see him, they had to ask Gladys to check if he was in.

But he'd been standing, and Isobel was only a few inches shorter than he. Just as the glazed section allowed him a view of the peacock feather in her hat jerkily dipping with every purposeful step she took, from the other side of the outer office, she would have been able to see the top of his head.

Idly, he wondered what had so fired her temper. Idly, because he was perfectly certain he was about to find out.

In typical fashion, she flung open the door, then paused dramatically on the threshold, her dark gaze pinning him where he stood.

Just that one glance, that instinctive locking of their gazes, the intensity of the contact, was enough to make his gut clench and his cock stir.

Perhaps unsurprising, given their past. But now…

Nearly six feet tall, lithe and supple, with a wealth of blue-black hair—if freed, the silken locks would tumble in an unruly riot of large curls about her face, shoulders, and down her back, but today the mass was severely restrained in a knot on the top of her head—she stared at him through eyes the color of bittersweet chocolate set under finely arched black brows. Her face was a pale oval, her complexion flawless. Her lips were blush pink, lush and full, but were presently set in an uncompromising line. Unlike most well-bred ladies, she did not glide; her movements were purposeful, if not forceful, with the regal demeanor of an Amazon queen.

He dipped his head fractionally. "Isobel." When she simply stared at him, he quirked a brow. "To what do I owe this pleasure?"

Isobel Carmichael stared at the man she'd told herself

she could manage. She'd told herself she could handle being close to him again without the protective barrier of any professional façade between them, too—that the urgency of her mission would override her continuing reaction to him, the reaction she fought tooth and nail to keep hidden.

Instead, just the sight of him had seized her senses in an iron grip. Just the sound of his deep, rumbling voice—so deep it resonated with something inside her—had sent her wits careening.

As for seeing that dark brow of his quirk upward while his intense gaze remained locked with hers…she hadn't brought a fan.

Disillusionment stared her in the face, but she mentally set her teeth and refused to recognize it. Failure wasn't an option, and she'd already stormed her way to his door and into his presence.

His still-overwhelming presence.

Hair nearly as black as her own fell in ruffled locks about his head. His face would make Lucifer weep, with a broad forehead, straight black brows, long cheeks below chiseled cheekbones, and an aggressively squared chin. The impact was only heightened by the neatly trimmed mustache and beard he'd recently taken to sporting. As for his body…even when stationary, his long-limbed frame held a masculine power that was evident to anyone with eyes. Broad shoulders and long, strong legs combined with an innate elegance that showed in the ease with which he wore his clothes, in the grace with which he moved. Well-set eyes that saw too much remained trained on her face, while she knew all too well how positively sinful his lips truly were.

She shoved her rioting senses deep, dragged in a

breath, and succinctly stated, "I need you to take me to Freetown."

He blinked—which struck her as odd. He was rarely surprised—or, at least, not so surprised that he showed it.

"Freetown?"

He'd stiffened, too—she was sure of it. "Yes." She frowned. "It's the capital of the West Africa Colony." She'd been sure he would know; indeed, she'd assumed he'd visited the place several times.

She stepped into the office. Without shifting her gaze from his, she shut the door on his agitated secretary and the interested denizens of the outer office and walked forward.

He dropped the letter he'd been holding on to his blotter. "Why there?"

As if they were two dangerous animals both of whom knew better than to take their eyes from the other, he, too, kept his gaze locked with hers.

Halting, she faced him with the reassuring width of the desk between them. She could have sat in one of the straight-backed chairs angled to the desk, but if she needed to rail at him, she preferred to be upright; she railed better on her feet.

Of course, while she remained standing, he would stand, too, but with the desk separating them, he didn't have too much of a height advantage.

She still had to tip up her head to continue to meet his eyes—the color of storm-tossed seas and tempest-wracked Aberdeen skies.

And so piercingly intense. When they interacted professionally, he usually kept that intensity screened.

Yet this wasn't a professional visit; her entrance had been designed to make that plain, and Royd Frobisher was adept at reading her signs.

Her mouth had gone dry. Luckily, she had her speech prepared. "We received news yesterday that my cousin—second cousin or so—Katherine Fortescue has gone missing in Freetown. She was acting as governess to an English family, the Sherbrooks. It seems Katherine vanished while on an errand to the post office some months ago, and Mrs. Sherbrook finally saw her way to writing to inform the family."

Still holding his gaze, she lifted her chin a fraction higher. "As you might imagine, Iona is greatly perturbed." Iona Carmody was her maternal grandmother and the undisputed matriarch of the Carmody clan. "She wasn't happy when, after Katherine's mother died, we didn't hear in time to go down and convince Katherine to come to us. Instead, Katherine got some bee in her bonnet about making her own way and so took the post as governess. She'd gone by the time I reached Stonehaven."

Stonehaven was twelve miles south of Aberdeen; Royd would know of it. She plowed on, "So now, obviously, I need to go to Freetown, find Katherine, and bring her home."

Royd held Isobel's dark gaze. Although he saw nothing "obvious" about her suggestion, he knew enough of the workings of the matriarchal Carmodys to follow her unwritten script. She viewed her being too late to catch and draw her cousin into the safety of the clan as a failure on her part. And as Iona was now "perturbed," Isobel saw it as her duty to put matters right.

She and Iona were close. Very close. As close as only two women who were exceedingly alike could be. Many had commented that Isobel had fallen at the very base of Iona's tree.

He therefore understood why Isobel believed it was up

to her to find Katherine and bring her home. That didn't mean Isobel had to go to Freetown.

Especially as there was an excellent chance that Katherine Fortescue was among the captives he was about to be dispatched to rescue.

"As it happens, I'll be heading for Freetown shortly." He didn't glance at Wolverstone's summons; one hint, and Isobel was perfectly capable of pouncing on the missive and reading it herself. "I promise I'll hunt down your Katherine and bring her safely home."

Isobel's gaze grew unfocused. She weighed the offer, then—determinedly and defiantly—shook her head.

"No." Her jaw set, and she refocused on his face. "I have to go myself." She hesitated, then grudgingly confided, "Iona needs me to go."

Eight years had passed since they'd spoken about anything other than business. After the failure of their handfasting, she'd avoided him like the plague, until the dual pressures of him needing to work with the Carmichael Shipyards to implement the innovations he desperately wanted incorporated into the Frobisher fleet and the economic downturn following the end of the wars leaving her and her father needing Frobisher Shipping Company work to keep the shipyards afloat had forced them face-to-face again.

Face-to-face across a desk with engineering plans and design sheets littering the surface.

The predictable fact was that they worked exceptionally well together. They were natural complements in many ways.

He was an inventor—he sailed so much in such varying conditions, he was constantly noting ways in which vessels could be improved for both safety and speed.

She was a brilliant designer. She could take his raw ideas and give them structure.

He was an experienced engineer. He would take her designs and work out how to construct them.

Against all the odds, she managed the shipyards and was all but revered by the workforce. The men had seen her grow from a slip of a girl-child running wild over the docks and the yards. They considered her one of their own; her success was their success, and they worked for her as they would for no other.

Using his engineering drawings, she would order the workflow and assemble the required components, he would call in whichever ship he wanted modified, and magic would happen.

Working in tandem, he and she were steadily improving the performance of the Frobisher fleet, and for any shipping company, that meant long-term survival. In turn, her family's shipyards were fast gaining a reputation for unparalleled production at the cutting edge of shipbuilding.

Strained though their interactions remained, professionally speaking, they were a smoothly efficient and highly successful team.

Yet through all their meetings in offices or elsewhere over recent years, she'd kept him at a frigidly rigid distance. She'd never given him an opportunity to broach the subject of what the hell had happened eight years ago, when he'd returned from a mission to have her, his handfasted bride whom he had for long months fantasized over escorting up the aisle, bluntly tell him she didn't want to see him again, then shut her grandmother's door in his face.

Ever since, she'd given him not a single chance to reach her on a personal level—on the level on which they'd once engaged so very well. So intuitively, so freely, so openly. So very directly. He'd never been able to talk to anyone, male or female, in the same way he used to talk to her.

He missed that.

He missed her.

And he had to wonder if she missed him. Neither of them had married, after all. According to the gossips, she'd never given a soupçon of encouragement to any of the legion of suitors only too ready to offer for the hand of the heiress who would one day own the Carmichael Shipyards.

It had taken him mere seconds to review their past. Regardless of that past, she stood in his office prepared to do battle to be allowed to spend weeks aboard *The Corsair*.

Weeks on board the ship he captained, during which she wouldn't be able to avoid him.

Weeks during which he could press her to engage in direct communication, enough to resolve the situation that still existed between them sufficiently for them both to put it behind them and go on.

Or to put right whatever had gone wrong and try again.

In response to his silence, her eyes had steadily darkened; he could still follow her thoughts reasonably well. Of all the females of his acquaintance, she was the only one who would even contemplate enacting him a scene—let alone a histrionically dramatic one. One part of him actually hoped…

As if reading his mind, she narrowed her eyes. Her lips tightened. Then, quietly, she stated, "You owe me, Royd."

It was the first time in eight years that she'd said his name in that private tone that still reached to his soul. More, it was the first reference she'd made to their past since shutting Iona's door in his face.

And he still wasn't sure what she meant. For what did he owe her? He could think of several answers, none of which shed all that much light on the question that, where she was concerned, filled his mind—and had for the past eight years.

He wasn't at all sure of the wisdom of the impulse that gripped him, but it was so very strong, he surrendered and went with it. "*The Corsair* leaves on the morning tide on Wednesday. You'll need to be on the wharf before daybreak."

She searched his eyes, then crisply nodded. "Thank you. I'll be there."

With that, she swung on her heel, marched to the door, opened it, and swept out.

He watched her go, grateful that she hadn't closed the door, allowing him to savor the enticing side-to-side sway of her hips.

Hips he'd once held as a right as he'd buried himself in her softness…

Registering the discomfort his tellingly vivid memories had evoked, he grunted. He surreptitiously adjusted his breeches, then rounded the desk, crossed to the door, and looked out.

Gladys Featherstone stared at him as if expecting a reprimand.

He beckoned. "I've orders for you to send out."

He retreated to his desk and sank into the chair behind it. He waited until Gladys, apparently reassured, settled on one of the straight-backed chairs, her notepad resting on her knee, then he ruthlessly refocused his mind and started dictating the first of the many orders necessary to allow him to absent himself from Aberdeen long enough to sail to Freetown and back.

To complete the mission that Melville, First Lord of

the Admiralty, had, via Wolverstone, requested him to undertake.

And to discover what possibilities remained with respect to him and Isobel Carmichael.

* * *

Dawn wasn't even a suggestion on the horizon when Isobel stepped onto the planks of Aberdeen's main wharf. In a traveling gown of bone-colored cambric with a fitted bodice, long, buttoned sleeves, and full skirts, with a waist-length, fur-lined cape over her shoulders, she deemed herself ready to sail. A neat bonnet with wide purple ribbons tied tightly beneath her chin, soft kid gloves, and matching half boots completed her highly practical outfit; she'd sailed often enough before, albeit not usually on such a long journey.

She paused to confirm that the five footmen, between them carrying her three trunks, were laboring in her wake, then she turned and strode on.

Flares burned at regular intervals, their flickering light dancing over the scene. The smell of burning pitch and the faint eddies of smoke were overwhelmed by the scent of the sea—the mingled aromas of brine, fish, damp stone, sodden wood, and wet hemp.

The Frobisher berths were already abustle—a veritable hive of activity. Stevedores lumbered past with kegs and bales balanced on their shoulders, while sailors bearing ropes, tackle, and heavy rolls of canvas sail clambered up gangplanks. Accustomed to the noise—and the cursing—she shut her ears to the crude remarks and boldly walked toward the most imposing vessel, a sleek beauty whose lines she knew well. *The Corsair* was one of two Frobisher vessels making ready; over the gunwale of the company's flagship, Isobel spied Royd's dark head. She halted and studied the sight for an instant, then turned and directed her footmen to deliver her trunks into the hands of the sailors waiting by *The Corsair*'s gangplank.

She was unsurprised when, on noticing her, the sailors leapt to assist. All the men on the wharf and on the nearby ships knew her by sight, much as they knew Royd. Throughout their childhoods, he and she had spent countless hours in these docks and the nearby shipyards. At first unacquainted with each other, they'd explored independently, although Royd had often been accompanied by one or more of his brothers. In contrast, she had always been alone—the only child of a major industrialist. In those long-ago days, these docks had been Royd's personal fiefdom, while the shipyards had been hers.

In that respect, not much had changed.

But when Royd had hit eleven and his interest in shipbuilding had bloomed, he'd slipped into the shipyards and stumbled—more or less literally—over her.

She'd been a tomboy far more interested in the many and varied skills involved in building ships than in learning her stitches. Although she'd initially viewed Royd's incursion into her domain with suspicion and a species of scorn—for she'd quickly realized he hadn't known anywhere near as much as she had—he'd equally quickly realized that, as James Carmichael's only child, she had the entree into every workshop and vessel in the yards, and no worker would ignore her questions.

Despite the five years that separated them—an age gap that should have prevented any close, long-term association—from that moment, Royd had dogged her footsteps. And once she'd realized that, as the eldest Frobisher brother, he had access to the entire Frobisher fleet, she had dogged his.

From the first, their relationship had been based on mutual advancement—on valuing what the other brought in terms of knowledge and the opportunity to gain more. They'd both been eager to go through the doors the other could prop wide. They'd complemented each other even then; as a team, a pair, they'd enabled each other to intellectually blossom.

They'd encouraged each other, too. In terms of being single-minded, of being driven by their passions, they were much alike.

They still were.

Isobel watched her trunks being ferried aboard and told herself she should follow them. This was what she'd wanted, what was necessary—her traveling with Royd to Freetown so she could fetch Katherine back. That was what was important—her first priority. Her second…

When she'd informed Iona of her intention to ask Royd to take her to Freetown—to browbeat him into it if she had to—Iona had looked at her for several seconds too long for comfort, then humphed and said, "We'll see." When she'd returned from Royd's office and told Iona of her success, her grandmother had scrutinized her even more intently, then said, "As he's agreed, I suggest you use the hiatus of the journey there and, if necessary, the journey back to settle what's between you."

She'd opened her mouth to insist that there was nothing to settle, but Iona had silenced her with an upraised hand.

"You know I've never approved of him. He's ungovernable—a law unto himself and always has been." Iona had grimaced and clasped her gnarled hands on the head of her cane. "But this state you're both in—as if a part of your life has been indefinitely suspended—cannot go on. Neither of you have shown the slightest inclination to marry anyone else. For both your sakes, you and he need to settle this before you become too set in your ways—I wouldn't want that for the Frobishers any more than I would wish it for you. Living your life alone isn't a state to aspire to. The pair of you, together, need to decide what is and what isn't, accept that reality, and then move on from there."

Iona had held her gaze, and Isobel hadn't been able to argue. Despite settling things between Royd and her being much easier said than done, she had to acknowledge that Iona had it right—for multiple reasons, the current situation couldn't go on.

But Iona's reaction to Royd agreeing—and when Isobel had reviewed the exchange, she'd realized he'd agreed without any real fuss—had raised the question of why he had. Did *he* have some ulterior motive in mind with respect to her? Just because she'd seen no sign of any such ambition on his part didn't mean it wasn't there—not with Royd.

She glanced up at the ship, then nodded a dismissal to the waiting footmen, hauled in a breath as if strengthening invisible shields, raised her skirts, and started up the gangplank. She couldn't understand why Royd hadn't married someone else; once he did, her way forward would be clear. But he hadn't, so now she was faced with the necessity of exorcising their past and putting it to rest once and for all.

That was her secondary objective for this trip—to kill off the hopes that haunted her dreams and prove to her inner, still-yearning self that there truly was no hope of any reconciliation between them.

He'd handfasted with her, warmed her and her bed for three weeks, then disappeared on some voyage for the next thirteen months with no word beyond his initial assurance that the trip would take a few months at most.

And then, without warning or explanation, he'd returned.

He'd expected her to welcome him with open arms.

Needless to say, that hadn't happened—she'd told him she hadn't wanted to see him again and had shut the door in his too-handsome face.

"Handsome is as handsome does"—one of Iona's maxims. To Isobel's mind, she'd *lived* that, and as witnessed by the past eight years, it hadn't gone well. But for some godforsaken reason, her fascination with Royd had still not died. She needed to use this journey to convince that naive, yearning self who had once loved him with all her heart that Royd Frobisher was no longer the man of her dreams.

She needed to use this journey to eradicate every last vestige of buried hope.

To extinguish the kernel of her once-great love.

She'd been walking upward with her eyes on the wooden plank. She reached the gap in the ship's side, raised her head—and looked into Royd's face. The very same face she would dearly love to strip of its power over her witless senses.

She was a long way from succeeding in that. Her heart performed a silly somersault, and her nerves came alive simply because he was close.

Then he added to her difficulties by extending his hand.

She was quite sure he did it on purpose, to test her. To try, in his usual challenging way, to discover what she intended on the voyage—whether she would insist on the rigid distance she preserved while sailing with him when testing their latest innovation or whether she was going to acknowledge that this voyage was different. That this was personal, not professional.

In for a penny, in for a pound. If she was going to use

the journey to resolve what lay between them, she might as well start as she meant to go on.

Steeling her nerves and every one of her senses, she placed her gloved fingers across his palm—and clamped down on her reaction as his fingers closed firmly—possessively—over hers.

"Welcome aboard, Isobel." Inclining his head, he handed her down to the deck.

He released her, and she could breathe again. She nodded regally. "Again, thank you for agreeing to let me sail with you." She raised her gaze and met his. "I know you didn't have to."

A quirk of his black brows spoke volumes.

"Capt'n—" Royd's quartermaster, who'd been backing toward them while relaying orders to crew in the rigging, swung around, saw her, grinned, and bobbed his head. "Miss Carmichael. Always a pleasure to have you aboard, miss."

"Thank you, Williams." She knew and was known to all of Royd's crew; all had sailed with him for years. She glanced at Royd. "I'll get out of your way."

He waved to the stern deck. "If you want to remain on deck until we're at sea, you'll be least in the way up there."

She assented with a nod and walked to the ladder. Royd followed, but he knew her well enough to allow her to climb unaided; she was more than accustomed to going up and down ladders while wearing skirts.

She felt his gaze on her back until she gained the upper deck. She stepped away from the ladder, then glanced back and down. Royd had already returned to Williams, and they were discussing which sails Royd thought to deploy for sailing out of the harbor.

Once they hit the open seas, he'd fly most of his canvas, but negotiating the exit from the basin and the mouth of the Dee required a fine touch and much less power. Courtesy of the improvements she and Royd had made, when under full sail, *The Corsair* was the fastest ship of her class afloat—another reason she'd petitioned him to take her to Freetown. Quite aside from the assured speed, she was eager to see how the alterations she'd tested only on short forays into the North Sea performed on a much longer journey.

Lifting her gaze from Royd's dark head, she looked along the main deck. From all she could see, they were almost ready to cast off.

Turning, she saw Liam Stewart, Royd's lieutenant, standing ready at the wheel. He glanced her way and smiled.

She smiled back and nodded. "Mr. Stewart."

"Miss Carmichael—welcome aboard. I hear you're sailing south with us all the way to Africa."

"Indeed. I have business in Freetown." She realized that where Royd had been, so, too, had Stewart. "I take it you've visited the settlement before."

Stewart nodded. "We've sailed into the harbor there several times, but not in the past…it must be four years." He cast her an apologetic glance. "Being a relatively new settlement, it will have changed significantly since last we were there."

She grimaced, but Stewart wasn't the man who would be by her side when she ventured into the settlement in search of her cousin.

"I need to run through the checks on the rudder. Royd and I normally do that together, but"—Stewart nodded down the ship—"he's busy resetting those rigging lines. Would you like to stand in for him?"

"Nothing would give me greater pleasure." She walked

purposefully toward him. Meeting his widening eyes, she smiled sweetly and reached for the wheel. "But if you think I'm going to be the one hanging over the stern, you're sadly mistaken."

He grinned sheepishly and surrendered the wheel. While she swung the wheel, halting at the usual positions, he checked that the rudder responded freely and swung to the correct angle.

By the time they were done, Royd was calling for the lines to be cast off. He strode down the deck and came up the ladder in rapid time. Straightening, he saw her standing behind the wheel.

She savored his blink of surprise—then she stepped aside and gestured to the vacated position. "Your wheel is yours, Captain."

He cast her a look as he strode forward, but the instant his hand touched the polished oak, his focus shifted. One glance confirmed that the lines had been freed. He glanced at Stewart as he came to stand by the rail on the other side of the wheel. "Very well, Mr. Stewart—let's get under way."

Stewart grinned. "Aye, aye, Captain."

Isobel gripped the rail and watched as, with Stewart acting as his spotter, Royd eased *The Corsair* from her berth, working with only a jib.

As he feathered past the ships anchored in the basin, he called up more sail, but gave the canvas only enough play to have the hull gliding forward. Then they were through the narrows and turned, and the mouth of the Dee lay ahead, unobstructed by any other vessel, and Royd called for full mainsails. Topsails and topgallants followed in rapid order, then he called for the royals… and the ship lifted.

Literally lifted as the wind caught the unfurling sails and powered the vessel on.

Feeling the wind buffeting her bonnet, Isobel pushed it back so it lay across her nape, the better to appreciate the ineluctable thrill of speed.

And yet more speed as the skysails unfurled.

She listened with half an ear to the rapid-fire instructions as this sail was drawn in, that eased, and the ship, now well out from the shore, heeled to the south.

She couldn't stop smiling.

As he had several times since they'd left the wharf, Royd glanced at Isobel's face—let his eyes drink in the sheer joy displayed there, openly, for anyone to see. Emotionally, it was like looking into a mirror; this was something they'd always shared and patently still did—this love of the sea, of racing over the waves, of harnessing the wind and letting it have them.

Yet another strand in the net that still linked them.

Usually on a voyage, after steering the ship past the river mouth and into the ocean swells, once he felt the hull riding smoothly and was satisfied with the set of the sails, he would hand the wheel over to Liam, who normally stood the first watch from port. Today, when his lieutenant sent him a questioning look, he shook his head and remained where he was, with his hands on the wheel and Isobel beside him.

When she sailed with him during the testing of their improvements, she rarely stood anywhere near him; if she came up to the stern deck, she would stand at one rear corner where, from his position at the wheel, he couldn't see her.

So although she'd sailed with him often in recent years, this was different. He wanted to prolong the moment, to wallow in the connection, in the shared passion that still linked them, in the magic that still reached to their souls. To experience again the mutuality of the sensitivity that had them glorying at the feel of the wind in their hair and of the deck surging beneath their feet.

She didn't look at him—he would have felt her gaze—so he looked at her frequently. He drank in her delight and felt the same joy move through him—and felt closer to her than he had in years.

Patently, this element of their togetherness was still there, alive and very real, strong, and apparently immutable.

If this aspect of their long-ago connection—the plethora of shared needs and desires that had urged them to the altar and seen them handfasted—had survived the years unchanged…what else remained?

He had to wonder—and wonder, too, about the past eight years of being so very definitely apart.

Why had she turned from him?

And why had he allowed it?

The latter wasn't a question that had occurred to him before, yet…standing alongside her again, aware of all he felt for her still, it was a valid question.

Eventually, their tack took them farther from land, and he reluctantly brought the magical moment to an end. With a few words, he surrendered the wheel to Liam, stepped back, and turned to Isobel.

Instinctively, Isobel swung to face Royd; her senses leapt, and she realized remaining close had been a tactical error…then again, wasn't this what she wanted? To explore what remained between them, put whatever that was into some more mundane context, and, hopefully, cauterize her ridiculous sensitivity to his nearness. She couldn't retrain her senses if she didn't allow herself to dally close to him.

That said…she pushed away from the railing. "Perhaps someone can show me to my cabin?" From long experience, she knew that the only way to deal with Royd was not just to keep the reins in her hands but to use them.

His face was always well-nigh inscrutable; she could read nothing from his expression as he inclined his head. "Of course." He waved her to the ladder.

She walked across, turned, and went quickly down.

He followed and dropped lightly to the deck beside her.

She'd assumed he would summon one of his men—his steward, Bellamy, for instance—and consign her into their care. Instead, he stepped to the companionway hatch, pulled it open, and waved her down. "I've moved my things out of the stern cabin. It's yours for the duration."

"Thank you." With a haughty dip of her head, she went down the stairs. She stepped into the corridor and started toward the stern. "What cabin are you using?"

Having worked on *The Corsair* over the past years, she knew the ship's layout. Unlike most vessels of this class, Royd's personal ship had fewer cabins, but each cabin was larger; his captain's cabin took up the entire width of the stern and was unusually deep.

"I've taken the cabin to the right."

The captain's cabin had doors connecting to the cabins on either side, creating a multi-roomed stateroom. She'd gathered such spaciousness and the luxurious fittings were a reflection of the quality of passenger Royd occasionally ferried to and fro; he rarely did anything without calculation and some goal in mind.

She walked unhurriedly along the corridor, striving to appear entirely unaware, even though, with him prowling at her heels in the confined space, her every nerve was alert and twitching.

Clearly, she had a long way to go to eradicate her Royd sensitivity.

The door to the stern cabin neared, and she slowed. Then she stiffened as, in one long stride, Royd closed the distance between them, reached past her, grasped the knob, and sent the door swinging wide.

Ignoring the warmth washing over her back, tamping down her leaping nerves, she inclined her head in thanks and swept through the door.

Her gaze landed on the figure kneeling on the window seat.

She halted.

He'd been staring out at the dwindling shore—she raised her gaze and saw the last sight of land vanishing into the sea mist—but he'd turned his head and was looking at her.

Panic gripped. *Hard.*

Every iota of air left her lungs. She swung on her heel, slammed both palms to Royd's chest, and tried to shove him back so he wouldn't see…

Too late.

He'd halted in the doorway. He didn't move, didn't shift an inch. One glance at his face confirmed that he was staring across the cabin, transfixed.

Her pulse hammered. Unable to—not daring to—shift her gaze from his face, she watched as realization dawned, as he grasped the secret she'd hidden from him for the past eight years…then shock stripped all impassivity from him.

He dropped his gaze to hers. Fury—*fury*—burned in his eyes.

Mingled with utter disbelief.

She couldn't breathe.

Through the roaring in her ears, she heard the thump as Duncan's feet hit the floor.

"Mama?"

Royd's breath caught, and he wrenched his gaze from hers. He looked across the room, then his eyes narrowed, his features set, and he looked back at her.

She stared into his eyes. So many emotions roiled and clashed in the gray...anger, accusation, hurt. She couldn't take them all in.

Her senses wavered, then swam. Her vision grayed...

Royd was already reeling when Isobel's lids fell, and her head tipped back, and she started to crumple—

With a muttered oath, he caught her. It took a second for him to register that she truly had fainted, that she was limp and unconscious. He'd never known her to faint before—panic spiked and swirled into the cauldron of emotions surging through him.

He juggled her, then hoisted her into his arms and straightened.

He felt as if he was swaying, but the sensation owed nothing to the motion of his ship.

A rush of footsteps neared. "What did you do to her?" The boy skidded to a halt an arm's length away. He looked up at Royd, sparks and daggers flashing from eyes that were all Isobel, his young face pale—Isobel-pale—but his jaw setting in a way Royd recognized. Fists clenching, the boy glared up at him. "Let her *go*."

The command thrumming in the words was recognizable, too.

Royd dragged in a breath. Looking into a face so like his own was only adding to his disorientation. "She fainted." At present, that was the most critical issue. He hefted her more securely against his chest. "We should lay her down."

The boy's glare barely eased. "Oh." He glanced around. "Where?"

"The bed." Royd nodded to the bed hidden behind its hangings. "Draw back the curtains."

The boy rushed to do so; he grabbed handfuls of the heavy tapestry fabric and hauled the curtains to the bed's head and foot, revealing the sumptuously plump mattress and large pillows.

Royd knelt on the bed and laid Isobel down with her head and shoulders on the pillows. He'd never dealt with a fainted female before, and that it was Isobel only added to his near panic. He undid the ribbon holding her bonnet in place, then raised her head, pulled the now-crushed bonnet from under her, and flung it aside. He eased her back to the pillows, loosened the ties of her cape, then smoothed her hair back from her face.

She didn't wake.

The boy scrambled up from the foot of the bed and crawled to kneel on her other side. He peered at her face. "Mama?"

Royd sat on the side of the bed. He picked up her hand, drew off her glove, then chafed her hand between his; he'd seen someone do that somewhere.

The boy studied what Royd was doing, then picked up Isobel's other hand, tugged off her glove, and roughly rubbed her hand between his own. His gaze locked on her face as if willing her to wake.

Royd found his gaze drawn to the boy's face, his profile, but the strangeness of looking at himself at an earlier age was too confounding. He forced his gaze to Isobel. He frowned. "Does she often faint?"

The boy's lips set. He shook his head. "I've never seen her do this before. And the grandmothers have never said anything, and they yammer about such things all the time."

Grandmothers, plural. Royd made a mental note to investigate that later.

"Will she be all right?" The boy's quiet words held a wealth of anxiety.

Royd wanted to reassure him, but wasn't sure what he should say. Or do. After flailing through the clouds of distraction in his mind, he reached for Isobel's wrist, checked her pulse, and found it steady and strong. Relief flooded him. "Her heartbeat's steady. I doubt there's anything seriously wrong."

The boy had watched what he'd done, but wasn't sure…

"Here. Let me show you." Royd reached across and lifted Isobel's hand from the boy's. He traced the vein showing through her fine skin. "Put your fingertips just there. Press a little and you'll be able to feel her heart beating."

He waited while the boy tried; the lad's face cleared as he felt the reassuring thud of his mother's heart. "What's your name?"

The boy glanced briefly his way. "Duncan."

Royd forced himself to nod as if that wasn't an earth-shattering revelation. The firstborn sons of the Frobishers bore one of three names in rotation—Fergus, Murgatroyd, and Duncan.

He let his gaze skate over the lad—all long skinny limbs and knobbly knees, gangly like a colt. He'd been the same; so had Isobel. "How old are you?"

"I'll be eight in October."

He could have guessed that, too.

He looked at Isobel's still-unresponsive face. He had so many questions for her, he could barely think of where to start. But first...what did one do to revive a woman who had fainted? "I don't have any smelling salts." Bellamy might have some somewhere, but Isobel would hate the crew learning of such uncharacteristic weakness. "A cold cloth on her forehead might help." He rose, crossed to the washstand, and dipped a small towel in the pitcher. After wringing most of the water from the cloth, he returned to the bed. Duncan helped him drape the cold compress across Isobel's brow.

Royd stood back and watched. Duncan sat back on his ankles, waiting expectantly.

Isobel didn't stir.

"Let's try raising her feet." Royd grabbed two of the extra pillows and handed them to Duncan. "I'll lift her ankles—you push those underneath."

Once that was done, they waited another minute, but Isobel remained comatose.

Royd frowned. "I'm certain she's only fainted." She'd been so stunned, so shocked, to find Duncan there. He looked at the boy. "She's safe here—she can't roll out of the bed." It was a ship's bed; it had raised sides. "I suggest we leave her to recover in peace. Meanwhile, we can get some air."

He needed to breathe. Deeply. He needed to feel the wind in his face, to let it blow the fog from his mind.

Then he needed to grapple with the reality of the son he hadn't known he had.

At the mention of getting some air, Duncan's attention had deflected to him. "You mean go up on deck?"

Royd held his son's gaze—so much like Isobel's. "You're too young to go into the rigging, so yes—on deck."

For a second, Duncan wavered; he looked at Isobel again, then he shuffled back down the bed and hopped off. He straightened and tugged the short jacket he wore into place.

After one last glance at Isobel, Royd led the way to the door.

Duncan trailed after him.

When he reached the door, Royd glanced around and saw Duncan staring back at the bed.

"She will be all right, won't she?" he asked.

"Is she often ill?" Royd would have wagered on the answer being no.

"Hardly ever."

"Well, then." He opened the door and led the way out. "Let's leave her to rest." More quietly, he added, "Perhaps she needs it."

She was going to need to be very wide awake when next he got her alone.

* * *

Fifteen minutes later, among other startling revelations, Royd had learned that this was Duncan's maiden voyage. Small wonder he was so eager to see and try everything. Royd had taken him up to the stern deck and reclaimed the wheel, to Duncan's transparent delight. He clung to the forward railing, peering down the deck and peppering Royd with questions.

Then the companionway hatch flung back and Isobel emerged.

Erupted from the depths was nearer the mark. Royd had seen her "wild" many times before, but he'd never seen her this…frenzied.

Her gaze landed on him and Duncan, then, her expression curiously blank, she strode for the ladder. Despite her skirts, she was up in a blink. She stepped onto the deck, her gaze already locked on Duncan.

Royd clenched his jaw. From Duncan's prattle of the

past minutes, it was plain the boy had been starved for all things nautical, yet the desire to be on the sea, to sail, ran in his blood. What had Isobel been thinking to keep him landlocked?

But that question would keep until later. First, he would stand by and listen to her deal with their son. Aside from all else, she was focused on Duncan to the exclusion of literally everything else. Even him—yet another surprise for him to assimilate.

Duncan released the railing and swung to face her; from the corner of his eye, Royd saw the boy straighten, stiffen. He didn't hang his head. Rather, he tilted it upward a touch—to an angle Royd recognized. He struggled not to grin.

Sea, meet granite crag.

He'd had enough clashes with Isobel to recognize the signs. He shifted his stance so he could keep mother and son in view without being obvious.

Isobel halted before Duncan, her hands rising to grip her hips. "What are you doing here?" Her tone was low but unsteady, a warning of imminent explosion.

Evenly—fearlessly—the boy replied, "You said you were off on this voyage—that it was just a trip, and there was no danger involved." He cut a glance Royd's way, for all the world as if, having now met Royd, he was re-evaluating her veracity. Then he looked back at her, and his features set. "I'm on summer holidays for weeks and weeks yet, and you know I've always wanted to sail. If there's no danger, then there's no reason I can't sail with you."

Royd kept his eyes forward and his expression noncommittal, but he rather thought Isobel had been hoist with her own petard.

Her gaze boring into Duncan's, she folded her arms across her chest. "So you stowed away. How?"

"In your trunk—the brown one."

From the corner of his eye, Royd watched her stiffen.

"What happened to the clothes and shoes I had in there?" Her normally low voice rose an octave. "Good God—where are they?"

"In your other trunks. I just squished things a bit more than they already were, and they all fitted—there was plenty of room."

Isobel stared at her errant offspring and didn't know what to say—not with his newly alerted father standing behind him. But at least Duncan had had the sense not to jettison her clothes; wrinkled clothes could be ironed—given her height, replacing clothes was much more difficult. She eyed him. "What about your clothes?"

"I brought two other sets in my satchel—and my comb."

The most horrible thought struck. "Heaven help us—what about those at home? Did you think—"

"I left a note to be delivered to Great-grandmama." Duncan's tone was the one normally accompanied by a glance heavenward, but he was clever enough not to add the action. "She'll have it by now."

Her wits were still giddily reeling. Her breathing hadn't yet steadied—she was still too easily pitched off kilter by the revelations that just kept coming. She drew in a deep breath, exhaled, then determinedly drew in another; she was *not* going to faint again.

Refocusing, she discovered that two pairs of eyes were watching her closely—with near-identical looks suggesting their owners were poised for action, such as catching her if she swooned again. Lips setting, she fixed Duncan with a commanding stare. "Go down and wait for me in the cabin"—she saw his expression harden and close, and rashly relented—"or down there, if you prefer." With a wave, she indicated the main deck. "I need to talk to Captain Frobisher—"

"Tell him."

She inwardly started at Royd's dictate—his tone made the words exactly that. Her eyes leapt to his face, and she met his hard gray gaze.

Before she could even begin to think, he reiterated, "Tell him now."

She stared into Royd's implacable gaze, felt the brutal force of his will… She could stand against him, but at what cost—to them both, and to Duncan, too?

And given Duncan had almost certainly guessed… was there any point in putting off the moment?

Given the timing of his birth, Duncan's paternity had never been in doubt, but she'd steadfastly refused to name his father, to confirm or deny, which had made it easier for others to let matters lie and treat Duncan as solely hers. But she'd never lied to Duncan—and she couldn't lie to Royd.

And the look in his eyes made it clear that he wasn't going to allow her to quit his deck without making a clean breast of it.

She drew in a long, deep breath. Ignoring the way her heart thudded, she clasped her hands and lowered her gaze to Duncan's now-curious face. She looked into his eyes—her eyes in a young Royd's face. "I've always said I would tell you who your father is one day. It seems that day is today." Her voice threatened to quaver—so much would change the instant she said the words—but she firmed her chin and forced her voice to an even tone. "Your father is Captain Royd Frobisher."

Duncan didn't even blink. His gaze swung to Royd,

taking in his features, not so much noting the similarities—he'd already done that—but confirming them. "Truly?" The question—laced with inquisitive interest and a touch of hope—was directed at Royd.

He shifted his gaze to meet Duncan's. "Yes. And no—I didn't know, either."

With that, father and son looked at her, and she found herself the focus of twin gazes carrying a wealth of unspoken accusation.

She had no idea how to counter it, how to respond. She felt as if she was swaying entirely out of time with the rolling of the deck. Breathing grew difficult again. She cleared her throat. "I'll leave you two to get acquainted. I believe I need to lie down again."

With that, she cravenly turned tail, walked stiffly to the ladder, and started down.

Royd watched her go, a frown in his mind if not on his face. He'd never seen her run before, certainly never from a potential confrontation. She thrived on drama and challenge—and what could be more challenging and dramatic than this situation?

He glanced at Duncan and saw much the same perturbation openly displayed on the boy's—his son's—still-expressive face. Clearly, Duncan knew his mother's proclivities and also thought her retreat somewhat strange.

Royd looked down the length of his deck. He noted the crew members here and there; none were close enough to overhear conversation on the stern deck. Yet it was true that what Isobel and he had to discuss would be better addressed in private—away from eyes as well as ears, and without the object of their discussion standing between them. Perhaps her retreat had been strategic.

Duncan had remained beside him, his hands lightly

resting on the forward railing, his gaze—as far as Royd could tell—fixed forward, most likely unseeing.

Royd waited, expecting that, with their relationship confirmed, Duncan would have questions.

When the silence from that quarter continued, he glanced, faintly puzzled, at the boy.

Just as Duncan turned to look up at him. The boy's features had grown stony; Royd realized Duncan's expression was now closed, forming not just a screen for his thoughts but a shield.

When Duncan continued to study his face as if trying to make up his mind about something, Royd arched a brow in unspoken invitation.

Duncan straightened, squared his shoulders, then drew in a breath and asked, "Are you married, then? To someone else, I mean."

Royd blinked. "What?" For a second he was at sea—what had prompted Duncan to ask that?—then he realized. "Good God, no!" His tone underscored the denial in an entirely convincing way.

Even as the words left his lips, light dawned, and reality struck.

He paused to let his mind trace the connections that had suddenly become so very clear. Rapidly, he reviewed the scenario revealed and checked his understanding, then, as much to himself as Duncan, said, "Now I think of it, I believe I'm married to your mother."

He was as good as, wasn't he?

And that, in large part, was why she had never told him about Duncan.

* * *

Royd spent the rest of the day fielding eager questions from his son. Most of the barrage concerned ships and sailing, but here and there a query about the Frobishers crept in. For his part, when he could get a query in, he learned that Duncan lived at Carmody Place and had been schooled with the rest of the children on the large estate by governess and tutor, but that discussions were being held about him going to a grammar school next year.

Royd and his brothers had attended Aberdeen Grammar School; he made a mental note to inform Isobel that Duncan would be attending there, too. No need to send the boy away—a decision that found ready favor with Duncan. Once he'd extracted an assurance from Royd that he would always be welcome to explore any Frobisher ship in port, Duncan wasn't going to readily accept any circumstance that would prevent him from taking up the invitation.

Royd didn't get a chance to discuss anything with Isobel until after night had fallen. Until after he and she sat down to dinner in the main cabin with their son. Just like a normal family. As it happened, the meal went off without even one awkward moment; Duncan led the way, leaving his parents to follow. Later, Isobel put Duncan to bed in the cabin to the left of the captain's cabin. Royd watched from the main doorway, noting all the signs of mother-son affection that, regardless of the situation, were evident. When Isobel reached to turn down the lamp, he tipped his head toward the companionway. "I'll wait for you on deck."

She met his gaze and nodded.

He went up to the stern deck to check with his navigator, William Kelly, who presently had the wheel. They exchanged comments about their route southward, then fell into a comfortable silence.

Royd leaned against the stern railing, looked up at the night sky, and waited. As the hours had passed and his new reality had taken shape and taken hold, his fury had abated, replaced by a powerful need to examine, learn, reassess, and then reform and rebuild—if he could.

If she would.

Several minutes later, Isobel emerged from the companionway hatch. She'd thrown a shawl about her shoulders. Knotting it against the breeze, she saw him heading for the ladder down to the main deck. She crossed her arms, holding the shawl close, and led the way to the bow.

When he joined her, she was leaning against the starboard gunwale, staring out at the darkness ahead.

The ship was running hard before the wind; he and his men knew this route like the backs of their hands, and he needed to reach London with all speed. Although clouds had blown up and now covered the moon, sufficient starlight remained to paint the occasional crest phosphorescent bright, creating flashes of brilliant white on the rolling night-dark sea.

He halted behind Isobel and, with a hand on the smooth upper rail, braced himself against the irregular pitching. None of the watch was close enough to hear them, and the wind would whip away their words regardless. The stance she'd deliberately taken meant he couldn't see her face, but at this point, that might make the discussion they had to have easier. Certainly easier to keep on track.

She remained silent, but he'd expected that—that it would be up to him to lead. He started with what was, to him, the most pertinent question. "Why?"

He sensed rather than heard her sigh, but her head remained high, and her voice, when it reached him, was strong.

"You weren't there. You'd left and hadn't come back."

"But I did come back. Why didn't you tell me then?" *Why didn't you tell me I had a son?*

"Because if I had, you would have taken him from me. Given Duncan was a child born of a failed handfasting, all rights regarding him would have rested with you as his father. I would have had no say in his upbringing or his life—no right to keep him with me."

He frowned. Why would he have taken…? His perception whirled like a kaleidoscope; when the facts settled again, they formed a different pattern—one altered to accommodate what he'd just heard. What she'd just revealed.

The only reason for her hiding Duncan's existence was if she had decided she didn't want to marry him.

Yet there was still something out of alignment; the pieces still didn't fit. In all the years since, she'd never even encouraged any other suitor.

"Isobel—"

"You would have."

There was so much conviction underlying the words, he felt forced to consider…and he had to admit, if she'd wanted to marry another, and he had known about Duncan…

In a rush of emotion, he remembered how he'd felt when she'd told him to go away and had shut the door of Carmody Place in his face. She was the mercurial one, but in truth, he wasn't far behind her when it came to temper, although he burned cold while she flamed hot. He'd been frigidly angry and hurt—a dangerous combination. She'd been one of the few people who could truly hurt him—he'd given her his heart, after all—and she had. She'd crushed his heart and flung it back at him. Or so he'd thought.

She was right. Regardless of what she'd intended to do, if he'd known about Duncan then…he couldn't say what he might or might not have done.

She shifted fractionally and tightened her grip on the shawl. "Know one thing—I will *never* allow you to take him from me. Remember that. *Believe* that."

He had no trouble doing so. He knew her nature, how passionate and devoted to her causes she became. How she gave her whole heart, and even her soul, to protecting and nurturing those she loved—like Duncan. Like Iona. Like Katherine Fortescue.

More than any other, he'd been the recipient of her passion and devotion once upon a time.

And he missed that, too; he had every day since she'd slammed that damned door.

Looking back…he couldn't explain, even to himself, why he hadn't tried harder. He had attempted to talk to her in the days that followed, but after twice meeting a blockade—manned by her family, admittedly; he hadn't succeeded in speaking directly to her but had assumed they'd acted with her blessing—he'd ended in an even fouler temper and had walked away and never gone back.

He'd given up on her, on them, and on all the promise that he'd thought they'd had.

And he'd felt righteous and entirely justified in doing so. She had rejected him, after all.

Pride had risen up, sunk its claws deep, and ridden him.

To his mind, he'd returned a conquering hero, albeit one not publicly acknowledged; that mission had been covert first to last. He'd been riding high, sailing home with his ego inflated by the immense satisfaction of a job done better than anyone could have hoped. It had been a quiet triumph. Regardless of her not knowing the details, he'd expected her—his handfasted bride—to welcome him with one of her brilliant smiles and open arms. Instead...the reality had been so very different, he'd struck back by turning and walking away.

She hadn't lived up to his dreams—the dreams that had kept him alive, his skills and talents honed and focused, through all the preceding hellish months.

He'd wanted to hurt her as she had hurt him—so he'd walked away and left her.

He hadn't appreciated then what he'd been walking away from—not just a son but the one woman—the only woman—with whom he would ever contemplate sharing his life. His soulmate. His younger self hadn't understood the magnitude of all that title encompassed, but he'd always known that she was his—his other half, his anchor in life's storm.

He'd been adrift from the moment he'd turned his back on her.

With the benefit of the years and the wisdom of hindsight, he could admit that, if she hadn't behaved as he'd expected, equally he hadn't lived up to her expectations—what most would consider entirely reasonable expectations—of a handfasted partner, either. But because they were soulmates, he'd expected her to overlook his shortcomings and for all between them to be exactly as it had been when he'd sailed away.

He hadn't known about Duncan—hadn't known she'd borne his child alone. She would have been surrounded by her family, but she hadn't had him.

And he knew her well enough to comprehend that more than anything else, his absence then was a large part of what had pushed them apart.

He wanted her back—he'd already decided that. Learning of Duncan only strengthened his determination. Duncan was his. He wanted the boy openly acknowledged and legitimate. Reclaiming her would achieve that, too.

Reclaiming Isobel was the route to the future he was now adamant he wanted and needed.

He—they—had wasted eight years; he wasn't about to waste any more.

But getting her back wasn't going to be easy. She would be prickly, barricaded; he would need to undermine her defenses one by one.

A sliver of her profile was all he could see. He studied it, then said, "Tell me what happened eight years ago from your point of view. What happened after I left?"

Over her shoulder, she threw him a brief, frowning glance.

After fleetingly meeting his eyes—and confirming he was, as she'd supposed, in earnest—Isobel faced forward. Why had he asked that? Long inured to his silences, she'd waited, every nerve tense, ready to engage and defend in whatever way his attack, when it came, might require…but that?

She'd jettisoned any notion of keeping him at a distance while she re-evaluated their situation. Duncan's appearance had put paid to any chance of not explaining all to Royd. She couldn't in all conscience refuse to answer his questions, not when even she recognized that he had a right to know.

Yet the question he'd asked wasn't one she'd been expecting. Not phrased in that way. And she knew him; if he wasn't reacting quickly and instinctively but rather after considered thought, then he would have some goal in mind.

What that goal might be…in the circumstances, she couldn't even guess.

But he was being reasonable, so avoiding the question wasn't an option; he was far too canny to give her an excuse to take refuge in her histrionic side. She couldn't get away with enacting some drama and distracting him, as she could with almost anyone else.

Not with him and not with Iona. All others she could manage, but not those two.

"Very well." If that was the tack he wanted to take, she would follow and see where it led. "You left three weeks after our handfasting. You told me you expected the voyage to last for a month, two at the most. You sailed away. I went to live with Iona at Carmody Place—she wanted the company, and as we'd handfasted, I no longer needed to live with Mama and Papa and attend balls and dinners. It suited me to go to the Place and not have to bother with society—you know I was never enamored of the social round." An understatement, yet in drawing back from society, she'd unwittingly laid the groundwork for what came later.

"I settled with Iona, then realized I was pregnant. I was thrilled and so happy." She'd been over the moon. "I didn't tell anyone. I thought to wait for you to return to tell you first." She couldn't stop her tone growing colder. "But you didn't return. At first, I just waited, but after three months had passed with no word from you, I went to the Frobisher office and asked when they expected you back. I was told they didn't know. They smiled and assured me you would return as soon as you could. I left, but went back a week later and asked if there was some way to contact you. I wanted to send you a letter, but they explained that there was no way to get any message to you at that time. And they confirmed they hadn't heard anything from you anymore than I had."

She paused, feeling the memories draw her back and pull her into the roiling vortex of emotions she'd experienced then. "A week later, I went back and asked them how, given they'd heard nothing from you or any others on your ship, they knew you were still alive. They hemmed and hawed and, ultimately, admitted that they didn't precisely *know*, but as they hadn't heard otherwise… In short, they couldn't confirm that you still lived. All they would say was that they were sure you would eventually turn up. Needless to say, I wasn't reassured."

"You didn't speak to my father or any of my brothers?"

"Your father was out of town at the time, and I think Robert, Declan, and Caleb were at sea." She hesitated, then asked, "Would I have got a different answer if I'd asked them where you were?"

She shifted her head enough to, from the corner of her eye, catch his grimace. After a moment, he replied, "Probably not from my brothers. But my father might have…understood enough to reassure you."

"Hmm. Well, he wasn't there." She looked forward again. "And while I did think of speaking to your mother, she was off with your father. And later… By the time your parents were back in Aberdeen, I'd rethought things."

"What things?"

If he'd sounded demanding, she might have found it more difficult to go on. As it was, he was still Royd, the one person in all the world she'd unreservedly shared her thoughts, wishes, and dreams with, once upon a time. The link—the connection—was still there; she could tell him anything. Even this. "Things like why you'd wanted to marry me. I realized that it wasn't as I'd supposed—that I'd been naive in ascribing to you the same motive that applied to me."

Even though she now viewed that time from the insulating distance of eight years, and she had—she firmly believed—come to accept the reality, the surge of remembered devastation still swamped her. Not having to meet his eyes helped. Allowed her to draw breath and reasonably evenly say, "I always knew I was an unlikely princess to your prince. I was too tall, too...unfeminine in so many ways. Not least in my aversion to feminine pursuits and my determination to succeed in being allowed to build ships."

She paused, then, as calmly as she could, went on, "As you know, I was told from an early age by supporters and detractors alike that the only reason any man would seek to marry me was to gain control of the shipyards." She raised one shoulder in a slight shrug. "I'd thought you were different, but when you stayed away and didn't even write, I realized I'd misread things. I'm sure you recall it was Iona who insisted on us handfasting and not formalizing a marriage immediately. She'd seen the truth that I hadn't." Blindly, she gestured toward him. "And of course, you, as the future head of Frobisher Shipping, had the greatest incentive of all to want to gain control of the Carmichael Shipyards." Despite her best efforts, the breath she drew shook, but she clung to her dignity and went on, "As I wanted more from marriage than you were able to give, I realized I couldn't go forward and formalize our marriage. Once I'd reached that understanding, there was no reason to do anything other than wait to tell you if you ever got back."

Royd stood behind the woman who, despite the years, still held his heart, and felt as if he'd been turned to stone. He'd known of her belief that she wasn't attractive, and that her temperament made her unsuitable to be any gentleman's wife—ergo that no gentleman would offer for her hand other than to gain control of the shipyards. He vividly recalled the day he'd gone to meet her at the yards, but hadn't been able to find her. He'd been certain she was there somewhere, so he'd hunted, and eventually, he'd found her hidden away on a perch overlooking the ribs of a hull in production. She'd been hunched in on herself and had been, if not actively crying, then deeply upset; he'd had to tease the reason for her uncharacteristic downheartedness from her, but in the end, she'd told him—gifted him with—the raw truth. The truth as she'd seen it—the same truth she'd just handed him, but then, she'd been all of fourteen.

Despite the difference in their ages, at that time, she'd been as tall as he, all long limbs and bony elbows and knees. He remembered that girl quite well.

He'd talked her around, convinced her that she didn't need to worry about any gentleman marrying her—that everything would change by the time she was ready to walk down the aisle.

Even then, he'd intended to be the man waiting to meet her at the altar.

It had never occurred to him that that fragile and vulnerable girl of long ago still existed inside the confident, exuberant twenty-year-old young lady he'd handfasted with, much less inside the woman she now was.

Didn't she have a mirror?

But no—he knew perfectly well that if one was convinced of a truth, one didn't necessarily see reality. He'd used that human failing to his advantage many times over the years. He'd been actively doing exactly that—letting people think they saw what they expected to see—while she'd been giving birth to his son.

How to open her eyes...especially given that Iona would have held up his behavior of eight years ago as proof of his motives for marriage? Her grandmother had always viewed him and his involvement with Isobel askance. And he couldn't argue that he wasn't the prime candidate for wanting control of the shipyards; he was.

Yet that had never figured in his determination to

marry Isobel. If she had nothing whatsoever to do with the shipyards, he would still want to marry her.

Intellectually at least, he—with the help of others—could convince her that, even by the age of twenty, her ugly duckling had transformed into a swan. But with her, that was only half the problem, and over the years, the other half—her unfeminine behavior and her devotion to and passion for the active practice of shipbuilding—had only grown more real, more confirmed, more blatantly a part of her.

And for the very same reasons she'd believed he'd wanted to seize the shipyards via marriage, he would never urge her to change her involvement in shipbuilding. Put simply, she and her talents and skills were far too vital to his and Frobisher Shipping's future.

He wanted her as she was—on every count.

All those thoughts reeled through his brain at mind-numbing speed. He felt pummeled by realizations, but he was too experienced to leap into actions that might prove counterproductive.

Winning Isobel again—claiming her again—was a battle he needed to approach with all due caution.

He focused on the sliver of her face that he could see, faintly lit by the ship's running lamps. Simply telling her the truth—his version of the truth, the real truth of why he'd wanted to marry her...would she believe him? He doubted it; putting himself in her shoes, based on what she currently knew, he didn't think he would believe him, either.

When she'd dismissed him so decisively and refused to see him again, he'd walked away and done his damnedest to appear unaffected and unconcerned, especially in ways he knew were likely to be reported back to her. Behaving openly as if her dissolving their handfasting hadn't bothered him had been his way of striking back, and he had a lowering suspicion he'd succeeded all too well. He usually did.

He'd screened his true feelings from everyone—too hurt and, yes, too *wounded* not to. Attempting to rewrite the truth he'd encouraged not just her but everyone else to believe wasn't going to be any easy matter.

One fact, however, was now crystal clear. She'd hidden Duncan from him as a direct consequence of him knowingly concealing a significant section of his life from her.

The eight years they'd spent apart, the nearly eight years of Duncan's life he'd missed, were the price he—and unwittingly she and Duncan—had paid for him keeping a secret mission secret.

He could swear and rail against a Fate that had conspired to so tangle them in their own strengths and weaknesses, their own vulnerabilities, but to what end? They were where they were now and had to go forward from there.

The past was the past. They needed to put it behind them and move forward.

In that order.

She was comfortable with his silences; few were, but she remained patiently waiting—one of the few things about which she'd learned to be patient.

She knew him better than anyone else in the world. He was fairly certain she still felt something for him, but he didn't feel confident as to what that something was. Not now. Still, she was a passionate woman, yet she hadn't encouraged any other man. As far as he'd heard—and when it came to her, he'd kept his ear to the ground—she'd never taken any other man to her bed. Why was that if not…?

An alternative answer came with his next heartbeat.

She hadn't taken up with any other man because of Duncan. Because, according to the laws under which they'd handfasted, she was still plighted to him—Royd—even if he hadn't known it.

Another realization buffeted him.

He narrowed his eyes on her face. "You've been waiting for me to marry."

"Obviously."

He managed not to snort. As if that was going to happen. He'd long ago accepted that he wouldn't be marrying anyone else; for him, it had always been her or no one.

As things stood, that also meant that for her, there would be no one. Or at least, no one else.

Not unless he agreed to release her from their troth.

He couldn't imagine doing that, certainly not while any hope of rewinning her remained.

Had she really believed…?

As if reading his mind, she added, "Once you married, I intended to approach either you or your wife and petition you to release Duncan formally into my care."

He bit his tongue against the impulse to inform her that, regardless of the circumstances, once he'd learned of Duncan's existence, he would never have let the boy go; he'd known his son for only a few hours, yet he knew he'd fight anyone who thought to separate them again. Yet although she wasn't normally skittish, this unexpectedly vulnerable Isobel required careful handling. Even under normal circumstances, her ability to surprise knew few bounds.

Insistently, his mind returned to her earlier words—*I'd been naive in ascribing to you the same motive that applied to me*—and the revelation by implication buried therein.

What had been her motive in handfasting with him?

Was it what he'd always believed it to be?

And did that mean she still loved him?

He couldn't be certain and was long past taking anything about her as a given. Regardless, could she come to love him as she once had?

He reviewed the tangled skeins of their lives and had to believe that there was a real chance of that—that it was definitely a possibility. But the human heart was such a complex organ, and love could be impacted by so many other factors.

One conclusion stood out, one absolute in the morass of uncertainties. He wanted her to love him again with the same wholehearted—wild and open-hearted—passion she'd once lavished on him. And he wanted that with a desperation that reached to the bottom of his soul.

He was a renowned strategist. This might not be his usual sort of mission, but he had to believe he could pull it off.

He had to believe she hadn't ceased loving him, but rather, his behavior as she'd interpreted it had caused her to lose faith in him, trust in him, and she'd drawn back. His behavior, all unwitting on his part, had caused her old vulnerability to rise up, and she'd withdrawn and barricaded herself against him.

His behavior as she'd perceived it was his first problem—the first issue he needed to address.

Inwardly, he grimaced. She'd trusted him implicitly, from the bottom of her heart, from her earliest years. In acting as cavalierly as he had, he'd taken that trust for granted; he hadn't honored the reality that trust needed to be reciprocated, needed to be earned and deserved. By not telling her the truth of where he was going and why, and never explaining his prolonged absence, he'd broken her trust.

Irreparably?

He hoped not. Had to believe not.

Where trust had once been, surely it could be built again.

He had to believe that; he had no other choice and no other way forward. He needed to rebuild her trust in him before he would have any chance of reclaiming her love.

And in rebuilding her trust, he had to ensure he never, ever led her to imagine that he might assert his rights and effectively force her into marriage. Another man less wise in her ways might use the hold he now had over her via Duncan to force her to the altar, but any step in that direction would result in immediate resistance—she would fight him every step of the way, and so would her family—but more critically, such a move wouldn't gain him what he wanted. He wouldn't regain her love and all that went with that.

He pushed away from the ship's side, caught her hand, and drew her around. "Come below. There's something I want to show you. Something you need to read."

He didn't have to glance at her to know she frowned at him—but she obliged and, despite her start, instantly suppressed, when his hand had closed around hers, didn't pull away but allowed him to tow her back to the aft hatch. He opened it and, releasing her, waved her through, then followed her down the stairs.

He nodded past her as he joined her in the narrow corridor. "The main cabin."

Isobel led the way into the stern cabin. Immediately, she crossed to the connecting door to the cabin on the left. She looked in, saw Duncan's face faintly flushed in sleep, and gently shut the door.

"Will our voices disturb him?" Royd had paused by the side of the desk.

She shook her head. "He's a sound sleeper." *Even more so than you.*

As if he'd heard her unvoiced comment, Royd humphed and continued to the large, glass-fronted bookcase built into the wall to the right of the desk. He opened the doors and reached to the second-highest shelf. His long fingers skimmed the spines of the narrow volumes packed along the shelf's length, then his hand halted, and he eased one slender volume from the rest.

He closed the bookcase doors, turned, and held out the book. "I believe you'll find the contents of interest."

Premonition tickled her spine. She approached and took the book from him. It appeared to be a journal. "What is it?" She turned the book in her hands and opened the cover.

The date leapt out at her, inscribed in his strong, blatantly masculine hand. *February 24, 1816.* The day after he'd fatefully sailed away. She stilled. She sensed—knew—that he'd put the answer to her most vital question into her hands.

"It's an account of the mission I sailed on, the one that unexpectedly kept me from home through 1816 and into 1817. It's all there—just bare bones, but if you want to know more on any point, ask, and I'll explain."

When she looked up at him, feeling again as if the world was rocking independent of the waves, he met her gaze, but she could read nothing at all in his expression.

He tipped his head toward the desk. "Sit. Read. Once you've finished, if you wish to read any of the others"—he gestured to the bookcase—"feel free."

Returning her gaze to the journal, she sank against the front edge of the desk.

He crossed to the main door, but paused with his hand on the latch. When she glanced at him, he said, "It just occurred to me...the mission that separated us is similar in many ways to the one we're presently on." Before she could ask what he meant by that, he nodded at the book in her hands. "Read that first. I'll tell you the rest later."

With that, he opened the door, stepped out, and quietly shut the door behind him.

She stared at the panel for several seconds, then looked down and refocused on the journal's first page.

Royd entered the cabin he'd moved into. He shrugged off his coat and hung it up, then started unknotting his cravat.

With something this important—the rescripting of their pasts with a view to shaping a shared future—a wise man would take his time and set each foundation stone properly and securely in place.

She didn't yet know it, because he hadn't yet explained, but they would be stopping in London for several days—possibly as long as a week. Then would come the voyage to Freetown, whatever action awaited them there, and the voyage back to London, and eventually, the journey home to Aberdeen. He had weeks—possibly as many as five or even six—in which to execute his campaign.

His quest to win Isobel Carmody Carmichael again.

* * *

Isobel read far into the night. Royd's journal didn't just cover the events of his long-ago mission but also included snippets of his personal life. As well as learning what had kept him from her for more than thirteen months, she read of his frequent wish to send word to her, an act he drew back from again and again.

Finally, she reached the end of the volume and laid it aside. Having her world as she'd known it turned upside down for a second time in one day was exhausting; she fell into a deep, dreamless sleep.

She didn't re-emerge onto the deck until the morning was well advanced. On waking late, she'd been unsurprised to find herself alone in the stern cabins; she'd breakfasted in solitary state while sampling some of the other volumes in the bookcase—some earlier, some later.

Most of Royd's missions—for the voyages detailed in the journals were transparently that—had been short, only a month or two. A few had stretched for nearly a year. Some had occurred during the late wars, while others had been more recent—after she'd ended their handfasting.

Of those later missions, certain of the details he'd jotted down in nonchalant vein would have induced panic if she hadn't known he was still hale and whole. He'd always harbored a certain disregard for danger—a trait she in large part shared—yet some of his actions in those later missions seemed ridiculously risky, even for him.

Via the logs filling the third shelf of the bookcase, she'd confirmed that, in between missions, he'd sailed on Frobisher company business, ferrying personages of wealth and influence—often royalty—across various seas. Those were the voyages she and others in Aberdeen, and no doubt elsewhere, knew of and associated with Royd Frobisher.

The missions were something else entirely.

She'd led a relatively sheltered existence, yet even with her limited knowledge, she could imagine just how dangerous some of the undertakings he'd been involved in must have been.

Last night, he'd intimated that this voyage was a mission similar to the one that had disrupted their handfasting.

Even more than a need for fresh air, curiosity sent her up on deck. She took several of his journals and logs with her. One glance confirmed that he was at the wheel, and that Duncan stood by his side, the wind whipping his hair about his eager face. She returned her son's wave—and returned Royd's sharp look with a noncommittal nod—then headed for the bow.

A triangular bench filled the bow's tip; the spare anchor was stored beneath it. She climbed up, wedged her shoulders between the gunwales, and settled to read; the more she learned about the man she'd thought she'd known but evidently hadn't, the better.

Eventually, Bellamy came forward to speak with her. "If you're ready for luncheon, miss, I'll summon the captain and the young master."

"Thank you." Isobel allowed the old sea dog to gallantly assist her off the bench, then she gathered the journals and logs. "I'll go down directly."

Young master. She wondered whether Royd had made any announcement regarding Duncan. Then again, he wouldn't have had to say a word for his crew to know exactly whose son Duncan was; just seeing father and son together was declaration enough.

Bellamy accompanied her to the aft hatch. While he went on to the upper deck, she went down the stairs and back to the main cabin. She returned the journals and logs to the bookcase; she was closing the doors when she heard Duncan's feet pattering down the stairs, then thundering along the corridor.

She turned in time to catch him as he hurled himself against her.

"Mama!" He flung his arms around her waist, tipped his head back, and smiled delightedly up at her. "We saw *seals*—big ones! And lots of gulls."

She couldn't resist that smile. She ruffled his hair. "And have you been asking lots of questions?" She knew her son.

"*Endless* questions." Royd followed Duncan in; his tone was long-suffering, but his face was alight—as alight as Duncan's.

The large desk was their table; Isobel sat at one end while Duncan took the place at the front of the desk, facing Royd, who settled in his accustomed chair.

While she smiled at Bellamy and complimented him on the finely sliced corned beef he set before them, she wondered what tack Royd's calculating mind was taking with respect to Duncan. And herself. In the instant Royd had set eyes on Duncan, their lives—Duncan's, hers, and Royd's—had irreversibly changed.

What she didn't yet know was where that change had landed them. While she would have infinitely preferred to control everything to do with Duncan, now Royd knew of his existence, there was no point imagining she could sit back and hope that Royd would grow bored with the demands of parenthood and lose interest in his son.

She'd told him she would never let anyone take Duncan from her, but from what she'd seen of their interactions, of Royd's protectiveness and the patience he displayed in dealing with Duncan's incessant questions, Royd releasing Duncan to her sole care was not going to happen, either.

They—she and Royd, and Duncan, too—were going to have to find common ground, but exactly what such ground might look like, at this stage, she couldn't begin to guess.

Duncan didn't speak but applied himself assiduously to taking the edge from his ever-present hunger. Royd watched his son, studying Duncan while he, too, ate.

Isobel watched them both, curious as to how they were getting on—curious to see how Royd managed. She'd definitely thrown him into deep water in terms of dealing with a son.

Then again, in all contexts, Royd was an excellent swimmer.

With the worst of his hunger assuaged, Duncan looked at Royd and started asking about ropes and knots.

Royd answered easily.

Isobel kept her attention on her plate.

But eventually, Duncan looked at her. She felt his gaze, looked up, and, for once, couldn't define the expression in his dark-brown eyes. Then he transferred his gaze to Royd. "You said you're married to Mama. So what's my name? My proper full name?"

Royd's gaze swung her way.

She met it, but not knowing what he'd said to Duncan—and unable to dispute that, in a way, they were, indeed, married—she didn't know what to say.

Royd looked at Duncan and met his gaze levelly. "What name have you been going by?"

"Duncan Carmody."

Royd nodded as if having expected that; he probably had. "Your full name is Duncan Carmody Carmichael Frobisher." He glanced at her and arched a brow.

When Duncan looked at her, she forced herself to nod. "Yes. That's correct." She met her son's gaze. "That is your full name."

Silently, Duncan repeated the four words, then grinned. "Good."

He'd finished his meal; he set his cutlery down and reached for the apple Bellamy had left for him. Duncan crunched into the fruit, chewed, swallowed, then asked, "Can I go back on deck?"

She'd eaten enough. Royd had cleaned his plate and was sitting back in his chair, observing. A touch unnerved by the apparent domesticity, she pointed to the glass in front of Duncan. "Finish your milk, and then we'll go up."

Duncan seized the glass, drained it, then he grabbed his napkin and wiped off the resulting milky mustache. "I'm ready."

She rose; so, too, did Royd. She followed Duncan from the cabin, and Royd followed her.

Once again, she retreated to the bench in the bow, and while watching Royd and Duncan, revisited the questions to which she still lacked answers.

Royd opted to leave the wheel in Liam Stewart's care and spent the next half hour teaching Duncan a set of basic nautical knots. Eventually consigning Duncan to the tutelage of his bosun, Jolley, to learn more about where and when the different knots were used, Royd strolled to the bow.

On reaching Isobel, he met her dark gaze, then turned and sat by her feet. He rested his forearms on his thighs and clasped his hands. "Well?"

He was perfectly sure she had questions.

"The mission you were sent on after we handfasted. You originally expected it to last only for a month or so. Why did it take so long?"

He knew what he'd written in his journal. He'd reread it many times over the years, whenever the question of whether he could have done anything other than what he had—and thus not lost her—became too insistent and had to be, once again, put to rest. "The original mission was to infiltrate the court of the Dey of Algiers and confirm that he was capturing, holding, and eventually selling Europeans as slaves. In order to do that, I had to pose as a half-French emissary of an Arabic slave trader. I succeeded in getting access to the Dey's slave pens—where I discovered over three thousand Europeans. That was a far larger number than anyone had imagined. Originally, I was supposed to simply learn the number and then get out and report to Exmouth, who was supposed to be at Gibraltar. But Exmouth came in early and stood off the port of Algiers, thinking to intimidate the Dey into releasing his European captives."

"And instead, the Dey dug in his heels."

He nodded. "Rather than report to Exmouth in person, I sent Liam Stewart—I wasn't all that sure I could keep a civil tongue in my head, but more importantly, I couldn't risk being seen and recognized boarding Exmouth's ship. And with Exmouth flying the flag in such a bellicose fashion, I couldn't risk taking *The Corsair*—which was masquerading as a corsair's vessel—out of the harbor. But sending Liam turned out to be a miscalculation. Unknown to me, Exmouth had demanded and been given command over my mission. I hadn't expected that, but it was around the time Dalziel—my previous commander—was pulling back. Whitehall assumed Exmouth would deal with the Dey without any great problem, and I was, after all, a privateer—giving an admiral command over my mission seemed appropriate to them. By sending Liam, I missed our only chance to retake the reins of the mission, at least as related to me and *The Corsair*. Liam was in a position to receive orders, but he wasn't in a position to refuse orders, as I might have done."

"So it was Exmouth's orders that kept you in Algiers?"

"Initially. But the longer the stalemate went on, the more essential it became that I remained in position in the Dey's court. Without the intelligence I provided, Exmouth had no way of knowing what was going on inside the walls—what was happening to the slaves, and what the Dey was planning." He paused, then added, "It became impossible for me to pull back."

She'd read his notes; now she had the broader context. He waited, knowing the most critical of her questions was yet to come.

Eventually, she said, "You dithered over sending me a letter. You never dither."

He snorted. She was right. But over that… "Once I realized I was stuck, and the negotiations between the Dey and Exmouth looked set to drag on for months, I wanted to write, at least to let you know that I was unavoidably detained. But by then the blockade was increasingly tense. I couldn't leave the city—by then, I couldn't easily leave the palace. My men were running messages out to Exmouth. While *The Corsair* could slip out of the harbor—the fleet knew her and would have let her past—she wouldn't have been able to sail in again, not without being marked as an enemy, along with all those on her." He paused, remembering. "Several of my crew—Stewart, Bellamy, Jolley, and others—offered to take a letter and, using a rowboat, slide around the blockade in order to get the letter out to you. They would have had to go to Gibraltar. But the French were hanging off, beyond the fleet, looking to make mischief. They didn't dare bother Exmouth, especially as he had the Dutch fleet at his back, but if the French had intercepted a letter from me, as me, to you…they would have taken great delight in informing the Dey as to whom, exactly, he was entertaining."

"The risk was too great."

He looked at his clasped hands. "My life, my crew's lives, and the lives of over three thousand captives—that was what hung in the balance." He wasn't overstating the matter. "I had to let all notion of contacting you go."

And he'd believed she'd loved him enough to overlook his silence.

In retrospect, that had been his biggest miscalculation, but even now, he couldn't imagine doing anything other than what he'd done.

"Exmouth bombarded Algiers in late August." He may as well give her the complete picture. "All the targets in the city that were hit were ones I'd identified—the armory, the magazine, the barracks. The Dey capitulated and surrendered the European slaves. But he sent out only just over a thousand—those from one set of pens. So I had to remain until we got all the Europeans released. It took until March the following year. Only once that was done was I free to drop my disguise, reboard *The Corsair*, and sail home."

In what had turned into a very bitter victory.

Minutes ticked past. Neither of them spoke. The bow rose and fell; water susurrated against the sides as the prow cleaved through the waves.

She stirred. "Looking back at what happened…it was inevitable in the circumstances. It was no one's fault."

A few days ago, he wouldn't have agreed, but after hearing her version of events… "Inevitable because you didn't know why I'd stayed away."

"Yes." Isobel hesitated, but she'd always wondered about what had happened next. "And you didn't try to explain. After I told you to go away, you walked away and left it at that."

"No." For the first time since he'd sat by her feet, he turned his head and, frowning, met her gaze. "I tried twice to see you—precisely to explain."

She frowned back. "When?"

"The first time was two days after. It took me that long to…convince myself I had to speak to you." He faced forward. "That I needed to make you understand." He paused, then said, "I was met at the door by one of your older cousins. She told me in no uncertain terms that you didn't want to see me."

A chill touched her heart. In a low voice, she said, "I never knew you'd come."

He looked down at his clasped hands. "I thought perhaps you were still in a snit—I tried again a week later. Another cousin turned me away with a flea in my ear."

She looked at Duncan, sitting cross-legged beside Jolley and busily knotting rope. "They were trying to protect me—they knew about Duncan."

A shudder ran through Royd's large frame. She glanced at him; he was staring at his linked hands. His fingers were gripping hard, then abruptly they eased. In a low, almost tortured voice, he said, "I'd been the central cog in a long and difficult mission—I'd saved three thousand lives and got away with my crew and myself unharmed. I was…a hero by anyone's standards, yet you didn't want to know. That's how I saw it."

His chest swelled.

Her gaze locked on his profile, she didn't expect him to say more, yet she waited, breath bated…

"I was so damned *hurt*! No, worse—it felt like a wound, a stab wound more deadly than any I'd ever taken." His voice was raw, his tone harsh. "You were the only one I'd ever let so close—you were the only one who could ever have hurt me like that. And you did."

The sounds of the sea—of the wind, the waves, the sails, and the gulls—surrounded them and held them in a cocoon of remembered pain.

Then he drew a huge breath and, raising his head, exhaled. "So yes, I walked away. From you, from us. From everything we'd been to each other." More evenly, he stated, "There was no other way for me to go on."

She didn't need to think to know that everything he'd said had been the literal truth. His expression might be unreadable, impenetrable, but this was Royd; she'd always been attuned to his moods, his emotions. His feelings rippled over her awareness; she sensed them in the same way a blind person used touch to read.

"I thought then," he went on, once again gazing at his clasped hands, "that while I'd been away fighting for king and country, you'd fallen out of love with me. That you'd changed your mind. That whatever had been between us, it hadn't been love, the sort that never died—that that hadn't been a part of our equation at all." He lifted one shoulder. "What else was I to think?"

Rocked by the intensity of his feelings—she'd forgotten how powerful his emotions were—she felt as if, once again, she was reeling.

Then he turned his head and looked at her. The unshielded emotions in his gray gaze sliced effortlessly through her defenses; they might as well not have been there. Then he said, his tone hard but even, "You didn't fight for us, either."

She held his piercing gaze. "I didn't know there was an 'us' worth fighting for."

Royd held to the contact, to the steadiness in her dark-brown eyes; she'd ever been his anchor, his safe harbor through any storm. But this storm raged between them, created of them, yet it seemed they now stood at the eye, with the past behind them, but no clear view of what might lie ahead. Of what future they might have.

Your future will be what you make of it.

His father's words. Oh, so true.

"Now we both know the truth of what happened eight years ago, is there an 'us' worth fighting for now?"

The critical question.

She didn't look away; she felt the weight of the moment as acutely as he.

After several silent seconds, she drew breath and simply said, "I don't know, but there might be." Her gaze flicked past him, down the deck. "And then there's Duncan."

He followed her gaze to where their son was diving headfirst into his heritage.

He considered the sight, then replied, "As there is, indeed, Duncan, I suggest 'might be' is a possibility you and I need to explore."

She returned her gaze to his face.

He turned his head and met her eyes.

Her gaze was steady and unwavering.

He realized he was holding his breath.

Then she nodded. "To confirm or eliminate—we can't go forward without knowing…what might be."

* * *

Royd spent the rest of the afternoon with William Kelly, going over charts and plotting the fastest route from Southampton to Freetown. He made no attempt to advance his position with respect to his de facto wife and his son until, seated about his desk in the main cabin, the three of them had dined, and after having cleared their plates, Bellamy produced a blancmange for Duncan.

How his steward had managed to concoct such a thing while at sea, Royd couldn't imagine, but as he watched Duncan's eyes light, he couldn't help but smile. Duncan babbled his thanks, then attacked the treat. Satisfied, Bellamy withdrew.

Duncan glanced at Royd and—predictably—posed another question; having learned of knots and ropes to his immediate satisfaction, his interest had shifted to sails.

Royd dutifully listed the sails *The Corsair* flew, expounding on when each set was deployed and what weather conditions limited their use.

Throughout, his senses remained trained on Isobel.

The task of rewinning her was going to be a great deal more demanding than winning over Duncan, even though he suspected that more of what she'd once felt for him remained in her heart than she'd yet let him see. As far as he could tell, he had reason enough to hope that, under her prickly carapace, she still loved him.

God knew, he still loved her.

After their discussion in the bow—which he didn't want to revisit even in his mind; just the thought of what had fallen from his lips left him feeling naked and vulnerable—she'd retreated somewhat. Just half a step, enough to think things through. That was her way. She tended to stand back and assess before stepping forward, while he forged on, assessing as he went.

That was why, in all their childhood adventures, she'd always followed rather than led. Not because she was any less adventurous but because she possessed at least one cautious instinct.

He wasn't sure he possessed any such instincts at all. Any caution he brought to bear derived from a single-minded drive to succeed, to win—a recognition that sometimes winning required caution. In pursuit of a prize, he could be cautious. He could be patient.

He was going to have to be patient to win the particular prize he'd set his heart on. Dealing with Isobel had never been easy. Challenging, exhilarating, and satisfying, undoubtedly. Easy, no.

But she'd admitted to a "might be," and at present,

that was enough. He wasn't going to push her; that way lay dragons.

That didn't mean he couldn't shore up his position. Not sharing all aspects of his life with her had been his critical misstep in the past; that wasn't a mistake he would make again.

By the time Duncan had scraped every skerrick of blancmange from the bowl and downed the last of his milk, Royd had decided on his next step.

He waited while Isobel oversaw Duncan's nighttime ablutions, then tucked him into the bed built out from the ship's side and dropped a motherly kiss on his forehead. Royd stepped back from the doorway as she returned to the main cabin. Once she'd shut the connecting door, he tipped his head toward the door to the cabin he was using. "Now you've caught up with the past, perhaps you'd like to learn what I know of what's going on in Freetown."

Curiosity flared in her eyes.

His words hadn't been any real question; he didn't wait for an answer. She followed readily as he walked to the connecting door, opened it, and went in. He'd left a lantern burning. She hesitated on the threshold, then her gaze fixed on the documents he'd left on the bed's coverlet.

He waved her to them. "That's all the information I've received to this point. The letters are in order."

She walked in, picked up the sheaf, sat on the bed, and started reading.

He leaned against the washstand and indulged himself by watching her. The decision to show her the letters hadn't been a difficult one. He'd unwittingly taught her she couldn't trust him to be entirely open with her; it was therefore up to him to demonstrate that he'd changed his tack and that she could henceforth have confidence that he would share all with her.

Fifteen minutes later, she reached the end of the last missive—Wolverstone's recent summons. She set the sheet down on top of the inverted pile, then raised her head and met his gaze. "You said you were on a mission that echoed that one eight years ago. I can see why—it's white slavers again. And in Africa, although a different part." Her eyes searched his face. "In the letter from Declan, he said his wife, Lady Edwina, believed several young women had been taken by the slavers. Do you think Katherine might be among them?"

He caught her gaze. "It's possible—perhaps even likely—but with luck, we'll learn if your quest and my mission are one and the same soon enough." He paused, only then realizing she might not be all that keen to meet his brothers again, not in his company, not in the present circumstances. Regardless… "*The Corsair* is headed for Southampton to provision for the voyage to Freetown, but I have to go to London—to receive my orders, learn everything Declan and Edwina, and also Robert and Miss Aileen Hopkins, can tell me, and most important of all, to be there when Caleb gets back, so I can hear his report firsthand and glean the most detailed information on the slavers and the suspected mining camp. If I'm to successfully take the camp, I need to learn as much about it as I can."

She gestured at the letters. "They don't spell it out, but I take it your mission will be to rescue those taken and capture the villains behind the scheme."

He nodded. "In that order, at least in my mind. As you no doubt noted, there's political pressure building over bringing the perpetrators to justice, and from the tone of communications thus far, I expect to be charged with securing evidence sufficient to convict whoever's involved. I will if I can. However, *my* overriding objective will be to get the captives—however many there are and whoever they are—to safety."

"Indeed." She folded her hands in her lap and met his gaze challengingly. "I'll accompany you to London."

She expected an argument. He hid a grin and inclined his head. "We'll leave the ship tomorrow morning. I'll have Liam lay in to Ramsgate so we can go ashore, then the ship will proceed to Southampton, provision, and stand ready."

She frowned. "Duncan." After a second of staring into space, she refocused on his face. "Do you think there's any viable way to send him back to Aberdeen?"

"Quite aside from the battle you would have to pry him from the ship, I can't imagine any way I would want to risk it." He paused, then said, "He stowed away. From what I gathered, he managed the feat of escaping Carmody Place and all those who no doubt keep an eye on him there and managed to get himself to the docks and aboard *The Corsair* all by himself. If you try to send him home now, after he's had his boots on my deck, what do you think is most likely to happen?"

She grimaced.

Dryly, he added, "You only need to consider how his parents would react in the same situation. He is, after all, both of us combined. Attempting to send him home at this point will be wasted effort—and, incidentally, effort and time neither you nor I have to spare."

Isobel stifled a sigh. "You're right. If we try to send him home in the care of anyone but you or me, I wouldn't put it past him, glib-tongued and quick-witted as he is, to slip his leash and board some other ship bound for Freetown...and the risks of such an action don't bear thinking of." She paused, then refocused on Royd. "So what do you suggest?"

He told her.

Of course, he'd already seen the potential problem and had worked out a solution.

She had to admit it was a workable plan, one that would assuage her motherly concerns while at the same time allowing Duncan to do what he now needed to do—namely, to get to know his father. And that was best done on *The Corsair*. Regardless of what happened between her and Royd, Duncan's relationship with Royd was now a nascent reality, one that needed to be given time to develop and evolve.

She'd always felt deeply guilty over denying Duncan the father he'd desperately wanted. Now that, viewed through his ship-mad boy's eyes, he'd discovered his father far surpassed most normal mortals, she couldn't in all conscience deny him more time with Royd. And she harbored no doubts that on *The Corsair*, Duncan would be safe.

"All right." She thought, then added, "If you can convince him to stay aboard while we go to London, we'll follow your plan."

That plan hadn't specifically covered what to do with Duncan while they detoured to London, but Royd nodded. "While in London, I'll need to focus on the mission, on learning everything I can and dealing with Wolverstone and Melville. Especially Melville and his political pressures. I assume you'll be similarly involved in pursuing all pertaining to Katherine and her whereabouts. Leaving Duncan in the care of people he doesn't know, and with whom he shares no affinity, would be senseless, and neither you nor I will need the additional distraction of having to explain his existence to Declan, Edwina, and Robert at this time."

As usual, he saw the situation as she did. She was well acquainted with his natural protectiveness; she could rely on him to ensure their son was safe. Truth be told, it was something of a relief to have someone she trusted with whom to share parental responsibility—a lightening of the burden she'd carried entirely by herself since Duncan was born.

Although Royd had remained leaning against the washstand, as far from her as he could reasonably be in the confines of the cabin, even though she'd left the door to the main cabin open, she was nevertheless intensely aware of him, his physical presence—that he was just a yard or so away and she was sitting on his bed. A sort of sensual fluster, a tempting distraction, had risen inside her, but she'd be damned if she let him see any hint of her abiding susceptibility. She fought to maintain her expression of calm focus. "Very well." She raised her gaze and met his eyes. "When in the morning will we reach Ramsgate?"

He almost gave her the time in bells; she saw the fractional hesitation as he worked out the hours. The instant his boots hit a deck, he converted to ship's time, but she'd never been able to keep ship's bells in her head.

"About ten o'clock. It depends on the tide."

Deliberately regal, she inclined her head and rose. "In that case, I'll start packing." She walked to the door to her cabin. She paused in the doorway; without looking back, she said, "Thank you for telling me about the mission." She tipped her head. "Good night."

She walked into her cabin and closed the door on his low-voiced, darkly sensual "Good night."

And only then allowed a reactive shiver to course

through her. His tone had evoked memories of sliding sheets, naked skin, hot hard muscles, and bone-deep pleasure.

Frowning, she banished the images and busied herself getting one of her trunks ready for a short sojourn in London. She wished she'd asked Royd how long he thought they would be there, but suspected even he didn't know. If they were waiting on Caleb and *The Prince* to return from Freetown, there was no telling how long that might be.

Later, after she'd changed into her nightgown, turned out the last lamp, and slid between the sheets, she lay on her back and stared at the starlight washing across the cabin's coffered ceiling.

She didn't try to stop her mind from replaying their recent exchanges. In looking back over the years, at a past she now knew a great deal more about, it seemed as if their handfasting had attracted the notice of some malignant Fate—one that had arranged for the mission that had called him away and ensured he hadn't been able to come home or to contact her. His absence had allowed her doubts to rise and gain strength. And because she had doubted herself so much, she hadn't believed in him. She'd lost faith in what had been between them, had convinced herself the link was too weak to sustain a marriage.

But what lay between them had been far stronger than she'd thought—it had sunk its claws into him as much as it had her—and it had never eased its grip. It certainly hadn't died. It hadn't even withered from neglect.

That bond still thrummed and thrived—in every glance, every touch. In every meeting of their minds.

And now there they were, setting off on a different yet similar mission, this time together with their son by their side and her cousin, by all accounts, among the captives they would fight to free.

"Fate," she murmured, "moves in decidedly cynical ways."

But it wasn't Fate that occupied the center of her mind. It wasn't even Duncan.

Royd was there again. He'd never slipped from her mind entirely, but he hadn't commanded that central position for the past eight years. Now he'd reclaimed it, becoming the lynchpin in the wheel of her existence.

And the revelation of his other life—of the missions he'd run, the dangers he'd faced, the risks he'd taken for king and country—had only repainted her long-ago, somewhat-faded picture of him in bright, intense hues. The Royd of now was infinitely more vibrant, vital, and virile than her memories.

He was everything she'd dreamed he might grow to be, and more. He now possessed dimensions that hadn't been there before, and they called to her even more powerfully.

He'd reclaimed that place at the center of her soul as if by fiat—by right.

The irony of it was that it had been she who had marched into his office and insisted he deal with her on a personal level again—she who had invited him to resume that dominant position, not that she'd imagined he would reclaim it, much less so effortlessly.

That hadn't been a part of her calculations at all.

Thinking of calculations…she wasn't at all sure what his were—exactly what steps he had in mind. He'd made her privy to his past, something he hadn't needed to do, yet had. He'd allowed her to see more than anyone would have expected him—a man like him—to reveal of how their fraught past had affected him. Then he'd shared all he knew about his current mission before she'd asked, and topped it off by readily acquiescing to her accompanying him to London and—although they hadn't specifically discussed the point—insinuating herself into the mission, by his side.

She was intimately acquainted with how his mind worked. He always had a goal in mind. With respect to her, to them, she didn't yet know what his desired goal was—he hadn't yet shared that detail with her. Perhaps he didn't yet know himself; the Lord knew she was still at sea as to what the possibilities were, what options they might have.

From her point of view, what lay between them was a sea of uncertainty. Yet as he'd suggested, there might, even after eight years apart, be something between them worth fighting for.

A proper marriage and a shared future?

That had been the goal that, once, had glowed ahead of them, almost within their reach.

But they'd stumbled at the last, courtesy of Fate.

Now they'd come around again…but were they on the right tack to secure the same goal, or had they lost their way entirely and were sailing on some other sea?

Her thoughts merged into dreams before she caught even a glimpse of an answer.

* * *

Isobel stood at the starboard rail and watched Ramsgate draw nearer. The headland to the north of the town slid smoothly past; flocks of seagulls rising into the air and settling again marked the harbor just beyond.

The day had dawned fine, the sky clearer now they were farther south. The seas were running reasonably smoothly—no impediment to them being rowed into the harbor and to the main wharf.

Earlier, over breakfast, she'd sat back and let Royd

break the news to Duncan that they would be leaving the ship to go to London while he remained aboard and traveled on to Southampton.

If she'd thought more about it—if she'd put herself in Duncan's shoes—she might have realized that his reaction would be one of relief; at his age, London held little allure, while the prospect of spending more time aboard *The Corsair*—under Liam Stewart's wing and with unlimited access to the rest of the crew—was Duncan's idea of heaven.

Royd—in typical Royd fashion—had immediately capitalized on Duncan's rapture to address the next stage of the adventure. Royd had made his expectations clear; once he and she rejoined *The Corsair* in Southampton, Duncan could decide whether he wanted to return to Aberdeen in the company of one of Royd's men or sail on with them to their destination. However, if he chose the latter, once they reached Freetown, Duncan would have to remain on board—without complaint—throughout the time they were in the tropics.

"Your choice," Royd had concluded. "Think about it during the days you're in Southampton. While there, you can accompany the crew onto the docks and into the town, as long as you first get Liam's approval. While I'm absent, Liam's word is law on *The Corsair*. But once we return, if you elect to sail on with us, I will need your word that you will remain on board until we reach Southampton again."

Duncan was clever enough not to rush into making a decision. He'd nodded soberly. "All right."

So matters with Duncan were as settled as they could be.

Which left her able to focus on her quest to find and

rescue Katherine. And on the more immediate and distinctly fraught question of how to deal with Royd.

Of deciding what to do about him, her, and their future.

Courtesy of Duncan stowing away, Royd and she clearly now had a future, but what shape it might take…

Despite all she'd learned over the past days, rescripting beliefs held for years couldn't, she'd discovered, be accomplished overnight. Even though she now understood the why of Royd's behavior eight years ago, her emotions—her feelings—hadn't yet seen the light.

Hadn't yet let go of their entrenched resistance, much less lowered the shields she had, for nearly a decade, deployed. In time, that might come, but meanwhile, she still felt very much on guard around him—still instinctively kept her heart shielded.

She'd once been utterly open to him, and he'd hurt her. That was a truth, too, one her emotions hadn't yet accepted could be excused and forgiven.

Rescripting emotions appeared akin to resetting a building's foundations—difficult, and once done, other things needed to be changed to keep the building stable. Similar to altering a ship's hull and having to change structures throughout the vessel to compensate. In short, such a change was not a simple one.

And Royd was rarely patient, not over anything he'd set his mind to achieving, but presumably, he, too, would be struggling with similar inner difficulties.

As Ramsgate harbor came into full view, and Liam swung the wheel and called for the wind to be spilled from the sails and for all canvas to be lowered, she turned to look back along the deck—and saw Royd pacing toward her. His eyes were fixed on her; although his features told her little, the intensity of his gaze suggested he'd already moved past any difficulties he might have had.

For an instant, she felt bathed in the force of his will, the invincibility of his intent. It took effort to drag her gaze from his—to look to where the crew were readying the tender to swing it over the side.

To remember how to breathe.

He halted beside her and looked at the tender. "I had them load your bandbox and the brown trunk. That was the right one, wasn't it?"

Surreptitiously, she cleared her throat. "Yes." Where did this fluster come from? She knew this man, had for years, yet… She glanced around. "Where's Duncan?"

"By the winch."

The sight of her son—*their* son—calmed her. He was standing beside Jolley, listening intently to the bosun's crisp orders and avidly watching every move the sailors made.

His gaze on her face, Royd said, "I told him he couldn't go in the tender—not this time—but that he'd have plenty of opportunity to ride in it and learn to row while in Southampton."

As usual, their minds traveled on similar lines. "No telling who might be on the wharf to see him farewell us."

"Indeed. But in Southampton, the wharves will be so crowded it's unlikely anyone will pay much attention to one boy, even if he's with my crew."

"Even if they did, they'll assume he's a cabin boy."

The tender had been swung over the side and steadily lowered; it landed in the sea with a small splash. Four sailors slid down the ropes to land in the bobbing vessel, followed by Williams, Royd's quartermaster. In the gap where the ship's side had been opened, Jolley—assisted by Duncan—sent a rope ladder unrolling toward the tender.

Together, Isobel and Royd walked to the gap. Isobel peered out and was relieved to see that the end of the ladder reached the tender's side; she could drop the last yard easily enough.

She turned to Duncan—and he flung himself at her and hugged her.

"Goodbye, Mama!" He tipped his head back and looked into her face, and the delight that radiated from him slayed any whisper of worry that he was secretly bothered by them being parted, however temporarily. He grinned exuberantly. "I'll see you in Southampton!"

Her heart twisted a little as she smiled back, then she hugged him close and bent to press a kiss to his forehead—the only sort of public bussing he would currently permit. "Be good." She released him and stepped back.

Royd briefly met Isobel's eyes, then hunkered down beside Duncan, bringing his head level with his son's. He caught and held Duncan's gaze. "Remember—on board ship, the captain's word is law, and Mr. Stewart is captain while I'm ashore. If you break the law, then you won't be able to remain aboard. If that happens, we"—with a brief glance, he included Isobel—"will be forced to send you back to Aberdeen with an escort." He returned his gaze to Duncan's now-sober dark eyes. "That's what happens when someone breaks ship's law. They don't get to board that ship again."

Entirely serious, Duncan shook his head from side to side. "I won't break ship's law."

Royd grinned—man-to-man—and rose. "I know you won't—you're too clever for that."

Duncan's brilliant smile bloomed again. "Goodbye." He held out his hand.

Royd grasped it, but instead of shaking hands, pulled Duncan into him. He hugged Duncan's slight body and ruffled his hair, then when Duncan squealed with laughter, let him go. "As your mother said, be good."

With that, he turned to Isobel. "Let me go down first."

He suited action to the words. She'd elected to wear an ivory carriage dress, severe and form-fitting. When they met in office or shipyards, she routinely wore darker colors, most likely to better withstand the inevitable dust and grime. Although no hue could mute her vivid coloring, certainly not in his eyes, the ivory outfit, with its matching hat, gloves, and half-boots, made her a cynosure for all eyes, male and female alike. And although he knew she could swim, he would rather she didn't get dipped in the drink; his men wouldn't be able to catch her, but he knew her weight and could.

He dropped into the tender, caught his balance, and looked up. She was already more than halfway down.

Accustomed to going up and down ladders, she knew the knack of accomplishing the feat in skirts. He'd never worked out how she did it, but her skirts never flared, nor did they tangle her feet.

She slowed as she neared the end of the ladder and stopped on the last rung, leaving her swinging just above the tender's side.

He reached up and grasped her waist. She clung to the ladder for an instant—whether to allow him to adjust to their combined weights or simply from surprise—then she released her grip on the ropes, and he swung her inboard and set her on her feet before the middle bench.

"Thank you." She looked down, brushing her skirts.

Royd glanced up at the deck and saw Liam Stewart looking down, a grin on his face. Royd sketched a salute. "Command is yours, Mr. Stewart."

Liam snapped off a salute in reply. "Aye, aye, Captain. We'll see you in Southampton."

The opening in the ship's side rattled back into place. Duncan's face appeared over the top edge. He waved energetically. "Goodbye!"

Royd grinned and waved back. He glanced down and saw Isobel, seated on the middle bench, smiling and waving, too.

One set of hurdles cleared.

At his nod, Williams, at the tiller, barked an order, and the four sailors seated on the benches fore and aft bent to the oars. Royd sat beside Isobel, and the tender came smoothly around and set off for the harbor and the inner basin beyond. "We'll use the water stairs before the Castle Hotel. It has the best stables in town—we'll be able to hire a carriage and four there."

She nodded. A moment later, she murmured, "What you said to Duncan—that was...clever, too."

His gaze on the hulls ahead of them, instinctively plotting the course Williams would take through the maze, he replied, "As we both know, there's no point hoping he won't have wild impulses. The best we can do is teach him to think through the consequences—that there always will be consequences—before he gives in to the wildness."

She snorted softly. "Spoken as one who knows all about wildness?"

He nodded. "Just like you."

* * *

Apparently, Frobisher captains used the Castle Hotel on the Harbour Parade frequently enough to not just be recognized but welcomed as princes. The landlord greeted Royd effusively and, immediately on being informed of their need, showed them to a small, well-appointed private parlor where they might wait in relative peace while his ostlers scrambled to harness the house's very best team to their fastest, most recently acquired carriage.

That exercise didn't take long. Having declined an offer of tea, as soon as the head ostler looked in to report that their conveyance stood waiting, Isobel declared herself ready to depart.

She'd spent the fifteen minutes in the parlor mentally listing all the subjects on which she needed to quiz Royd in an attempt to force her mind and her witless senses from dwelling on the recent scintillating moments when he had touched her—when he'd lifted her from the ladder to the rowboat in a potent display of mind-numbing strength, then later, when he'd handed her from the boat to the water stair and had to seize her and steady her when her boot slipped on the slimy stone. In that case, she'd landed flush against him, breast to chest, and had lost her breath. Then she'd tumbled into his gray eyes and nearly lost her wits entirely; she'd only just resisted the urge to haul his head down and kiss him.

She knew perfectly well what caused such reactions—there was no sense pretending they had never been intimate—but the effect of such moments was proving to be more intense, more distracting, and indeed, more discombobulating than she'd foreseen.

Of course, he had to hand her into the carriage, but that much touch, she could deal with; even though there was no escaping the undercurrent of possessiveness that imbued even that minor gallantry, she could ignore it.

After the head ostler shut the door and the coachman cracked his whip, the carriage—excellently well-sprung and obviously new—rocked out of the inn yard and wound its way out of the town and onto the highway.

She waited as long as she could—as long as she could bear the impact of his nearness without reacting in any way. They were bowling along, the repetitive thud of the horses' hooves a steady, reassuring rhythm, when the sense of being private and alone with him at close quarters grew too intense, and she surrendered and broached the first topic on her list. Or, at least, the first point she thought it safe to address.

The implication underlying Royd's discussion with Duncan over breakfast that morning had been that, when in Freetown, she would accompany him off-ship. While that was precisely what she wished, she had to wonder how far his new policy of including her in his mission would stretch. Now, however, wasn't the moment to examine that issue; better to wait until she knew more about Katherine's whereabouts and the details of his mission.

That said, he would know she would have noticed the change in his tack.

"I'll admit that while I'm"—*reassured? appeased?*—"impressed by your willingness to take me into your confidence with respect to this mission, I'm unsure as to whether you will be, for instance, interested in my opinions on the matter."

He was sitting opposite her; across the carriage, he met her eyes. "I am. I expect to hear your opinions." His lips twitched. "Indeed, I feel supremely confident that I'll hear your opinions whether I invite them or not."

She sent him a distinctly unimpressed look.

His smile deepened, and he settled more comfortably against the squabs. "But yes, I expect us to work together on this. Unless your cousin has fallen prey to some other scheme entirely—which, frankly, is unlikely, not in such a relatively small settlement—then I expect our goals will align, and our paths forward will be intertwined."

She studied him for a full minute, trying to see, to

imagine… "You're no more likely to invite a woman to share command than the next captain."

"But I'm not inviting just any woman to join me—I'm inviting you."

The intensity in his gray gaze assured her he meant exactly that with full knowledge of the consequences. She couldn't stop herself from baldly asking, "Why?"

"Because despite all the storm water under our joint bridge, we've always—since I was eleven and you were six, for heaven's sake—worked well together. Our characters are similar, so we understand each other instinctively, often without the need for explanations—which we both find boring—and our talents are astonishingly complementary." He hesitated, then went on, "You might not realize how rare that is, but as a team…we're blessed."

"Together we're more than each of us separately?"

"Exactly." He paused, then said, "You know my mother often sailed with my father—more or less whenever she could. When she was on board, she was Papa's first mate in every sense, except the actual sailing. That wasn't an interest of hers, but everything else to do with his voyages was as much her domain as his." He held her gaze levelly. "So in my family, having the captain's wife aboard, functioning more or less as an equal partner, is not a novel concept."

She wasn't his wife…except she was. Rather than venture into that quagmire—one topic she was definitely not ready to discuss—she inclined her head and turned to the next item on her list. "Speaking of your family, who can I expect to meet in London?"

"Declan and Edwina—we'll stay at their house. And Robert's there at present, along with Miss Aileen Hopkins, who returned from Freetown with him. Robert and

Miss Hopkins intend to marry, but because of the ongoing mission, they haven't announced their betrothal yet."

She'd heard of Declan's wedding, held at a ducal estate somewhere in England. "I gather Lady Edwina visited Aberdeen after their wedding, but we didn't meet. She's a duke's daughter, isn't she?"

Royd nodded. "As you'll have noted, that didn't prevent her from sailing with Declan to Freetown and immersing herself in his leg of the mission. It seems her contribution was significant—she manages social situations very well."

Declan had always struck her as the most conservative of the brothers; she found herself rather more interested in meeting his wife than she had been. "What do you know of Miss Hopkins?"

"I've never met her, but she's the younger sister of two navy men I know. They have an even younger brother who's a lieutenant with the West Africa Squadron, and like your cousin, he, too, has inexplicably disappeared."

"He was one of those sent to look for the army engineer who vanished, wasn't he? That was in Declan's and Robert's letters."

"Indeed." Royd paused, then grimaced. "While I understand why Caleb took Robert's journal, I wish he'd left a copy."

"By the sound of it, there wasn't time."

Royd humphed. "He didn't waste time setting sail so no one could stop him."

Why did he want Robert's journal? "Is Robert's journal like yours?"

He shook his head. "Mine's more like a captain's log. Robert keeps a much more detailed record. There'll be lots of descriptions and sketches. It's a habit he picked up from my mother, and in circumstances like this, it's a godsend."

"Presumably Caleb will bring Robert's journal back. You'll have time to read it before we reach Freetown."

He nodded absentmindedly, his gaze shifting to the trees flashing past.

The carriage was rocketing along; they'd passed onto a properly macadamed stretch, and the pounding of the horses' hooves resembled thunder.

After the coachman took a curve at speed, forcing her to steady herself with a hand against the side, she looked at Royd. "Did you say something to the coachman about being in a rush?"

"I offered him ten guineas if he got us to Stanhope Street before three o'clock."

She considered that as the reckless, unquestionably risky pace continued unabated. The sooner they reached Stanhope Street—presumably where Declan and his Edwina lived—the sooner she'd be able to put some space between Royd and her, and the sooner her nerves, tense in a way she recognized from long ago, would ease.

After weighing the risk against the reward, she concluded it wasn't in her best interests to protest. She sat back and, like Royd, stared out at the scenery whizzing past and waited for journey's end.

One

The carriage slowed and drew up outside a town house in a typical Mayfair street. Royd glanced out. He didn't have to check the house's number—the door stood open, and as he looked, Robert and Declan appeared in the doorway.

They hadn't known he was on his way; he had to wonder what had brought them to the door—with, he noted, papers in their hands. He glimpsed Edwina beside Declan, and a lady with hair of a brassy shade that suggested she was a Hopkins peering over Robert's shoulder. "It appears we've arrived at an opportune moment. For some reason, we have a reception committee." He leaned forward, opened the carriage door, and stepped down to the pavement.

He looked up at his brothers and their ladies for a second, then turned to the carriage and gave Isobel his hand. She put her fingers in his—such a simple, mundane thing, yet he felt possessiveness surge as he closed his hand about her slender digits and assisted her down the carriage steps.

Once on the pavement, she straightened. With her hand still in his, she, too, looked up at the group filling the doorway. Then she smoothly drew her hand from his and turned to look up at the postboy and direct him to hand down her bandbox.

By the time the postboy had retrieved the box, three footmen had emerged from the house. Isobel consigned the box into the hands of the youngest, along with Royd's traveling bag. Leaving the two older, burlier footmen to wrestle with her trunk, she turned to Royd, just as, having paid off the coachman and postboy, he turned to her.

He met her eyes, offered his arm, and quirked a brow. "Shall we?"

Shall we operate as a couple? Shall we try it again and remind ourselves what it feels like?

She looked into his gray eyes and read the challenge therein. Given that they would pursue his mission together—given the decision they would face when the mission was over and they returned to Aberdeen—seizing the opportunity to see how well they managed in this more social sphere was arguably wise. She arched a brow back, then, sternly suppressing her leaping senses, calmly laid her hand on his arm.

Side by side, they faced his family, then she raised her skirts, and they climbed the steps to the narrow front porch.

Swiftly, she surveyed the "reception committee"; she maintained a serenely assured expression, but inside, she couldn't help but grin. While Declan and Robert were glad to see Royd, they were uncertain how to interpret her presence. They'd been at sea for most of her and Royd's handfasting; she had no idea what they thought was the reason for the failure of the relationship. As they, of all people, knew, Royd rarely failed at anything. Yet knowing him, she sincerely doubted he'd explained anything at all about her; in the few seconds it took to reach the porch, she decided to assume that Robert and Declan knew nothing beyond the bald facts.

In stark contrast to the wariness evident in the men, the fairylike blond beauty peering around Declan and the brassy-haired lady by Robert's side appeared intrigued and keen to make her acquaintance.

"Royd." Declan held out a hand.

Royd smiled, and the brothers clasped hands and buffeted each other's shoulders.

"Robert." Royd and Robert repeated the process.

Isobel struggled to suppress a grin; both Lady Edwina and Miss Hopkins were all but jigging with impatience—not to meet Royd but to be introduced to her.

Declan turned to her. "Isobel."

She smiled and held out a hand. "Declan. It's good to see you again."

He bowed over her fingers, then turned to his wife. "My dear, this is Isobel Carmichael, of the Carmichael Shipyards in Aberdeen. Isobel—my wife, Lady Edwina."

Lady Edwina's cornflower-blue eyes widened fractionally as she made the connection; she would have heard of the shipyards when she'd visited Aberdeen. She beamed and held out her hand. "Miss Carmichael. Welcome to London and to our home."

Isobel clasped Edwina's fingers and returned her smile. "Lady Edwina—it's a pleasure to meet you. And please, call me Isobel. I understand we're throwing ourselves on your hospitality, at least until Royd learns what Caleb has found and receives his orders."

Declan blinked, then he turned to Royd and Robert, who were exchanging news.

Edwina brightened even more. Rather than release Isobel, she tugged her forward. "Do come in—you must meet Aileen." She glanced frowningly at the trio of males, but they'd moved sufficiently to allow Isobel to slip past.

She stepped into an elegant front hall.

The brassy-haired lady had fallen back and stood waiting to offer her hand. "I'm Aileen Hopkins. I met Robert in Freetown, and I returned to London with him on *The Trident*."

Isobel clasped Aileen's fingers. "I'm delighted to meet you, Miss Hopkins."

"Aileen, please. It seems we all have an interest in what's been happening in Freetown." The statement was a poorly disguised question, a transparent invitation to share.

Apparently, neither Edwina nor Aileen was at all slow in observing and deducing. Isobel sobered. "Indeed. I'll be traveling there with Royd in pursuit of one of my cousins. I understand both of you have been in the settlement, so I'm particularly keen to speak with you." She glanced from Aileen's hazel eyes to Edwina's encouraging blue gaze. "I need to learn everything you can tell me about a Miss Katherine Fortescue."

"Miss Fortescue!" Edwina's expression grew concerned. She put a hand on Isobel's arm. "I greatly fear, Isobel, that Miss Fortescue has been captured by slavers. Possibly taken to work in a mine."

She compressed her lips and nodded. "Royd and I agree that her disappearance is very likely linked to his mission."

Edwina and Aileen swung their gazes to the men, still standing on the porch.

Isobel looked, too; the three brothers were holding various papers and notes, shuffling, reading, and exclaiming.

"You've arrived at the perfect moment," Edwina said. "Hornby—one of Caleb's men—arrived not five minutes ago with that satchel Robert's holding. It's full of reports and maps." Edwina met Isobel's gaze. "It seems Caleb has found the mine and has remained to keep watch over the captives."

"He might have sent a list of said captives." Aileen narrowed her eyes on the three men. "But we haven't had a chance to see."

Edwina exchanged a steely glance with Aileen, then looked at Isobel. "Do you need to go up and refresh yourself and rest or…?" She gestured toward the men.

Isobel met Edwina's eyes. "I'm not the wilting sort. Let's get those papers and see what Caleb's sent."

Edwina nodded once. Her chin firming, she bustled forward. Aileen followed in support.

Isobel nodded to the butler, who was supervising the footmen as they ferried her and Royd's luggage inside. She removed her hat, laid it on a side table, and pulled off her gloves. By the grace of God, she'd fallen in with like-minded women. Edwina might be a slip of a thing, a petite, delicate-looking, golden-haired damsel with bright-blue eyes, but she possessed a great deal of energy and—for Isobel's money—a spine of steel. Like recognized like, and Aileen Hopkins seemed of similar disposition. Isobel watched with approval as, with a ruthless efficiency the Frobisher brothers had no hope of resisting, Edwina and Aileen herded the three off the porch, into the hall, and into a cozy drawing room.

Tucking her gloves into her skirt pocket, Isobel joined the women as, bringing up the rear, they swept into the room. Edwina paused on the threshold to instruct the butler—Humphrey—to prepare rooms for Isobel and Royd. Isobel grasped the moment as they arranged themselves on sofas and chairs to exchange greetings with Robert—like Declan, he viewed her with wary trepidation, but cloaked it better—then she sank onto a sofa beside Aileen.

Royd claimed the armchair to her left. Edwina made a spirited bid to commandeer the satchel, but in that, she didn't succeed. Royd had taken possession and stared her down. Then he leaned forward and spread the satchel's contents on the low table between the twin sofas. "There's no sense attempting to discuss anything while each of us knows only bits of the whole. I suggest we each take a portion of these documents, read and assimilate, then pass what we have to the right. Once we've all absorbed what's been sent, we'll see what we can make of the current situation."

No one argued. Royd divided the papers into six roughly equal piles, distributed them, and they settled to read.

Silence descended, broken by the rustling of papers and the occasional "humph." Accustomed to reading screeds of reports, Isobel reached the end of her pile first. She sat and let all she'd learned settle in her mind—like a jigsaw for which she was still missing too many pieces to even guess the shapes. Robert raised his head and tidied the stack of papers on his knee. Like her, he said nothing; from the slight frown on his face, she suspected he was adjusting some view he'd previously held.

Aileen was the last to finish her documents—which included Robert's journal. She humphed and passed her pile to Robert. They all handed on what they'd read, received the next batch from the person on their left, and settled to read again.

By the time each of them had read all the documents, the afternoon was well advanced. Edwina rang for tea, and Humphrey and a footman brought in trays loaded with two teapots, cups, saucers, and plates, and a selection of cakes, including a heavy fruitcake sufficient to satisfy manly appetites.

Royd waited until the ladies had sipped and nibbled, and he and his brothers had demolished the fruitcake—and their minds had had at least that much time to absorb all they'd just taken in—before, with the documents once again piled on the satchel before him, he said, "We should summarize what we've learned to this point, revised in light of what Caleb has sent."

His brothers nodded. The ladies directed alert gazes his way, but didn't speak.

Good.

He set down his teacup. "We now know that three instigators—for want of a better label—living in Freetown devised the scheme. Somehow they learned of a deposit of diamonds deep in the jungle. It doesn't matter how they learned of it, only that they did. Consequently, they set up a mine to operate in secret—presumably to avoid all fees and excise and any government intervention. Also so they could use slave labor, thus increasing their profits."

"That much seems clear," Robert said. "We know that Muldoon, the naval attaché, and a man named Winter, who has access to mining equipment and supplies, are two of the three instigators."

"And the third," Declan stated, an edge to his tone, "is someone on the governor's staff, but as yet, we don't have a name."

Royd nodded. "Initially, Lady Holbrook was a player in the scheme—whether by choice or under duress is immaterial as she's taken herself out of the picture."

"Just as well," Edwina muttered direfully.

"In order to establish the mine," Royd continued, "the instigators needed capital, so they contacted people willing to finance illicit ventures. The captives call that group 'the backers,' and there are several of them—how many we don't yet know. The backers are most likely in England, and they are the ultimate perpetrators, as it's unlikely the scheme would have come to anything without their support."

He paused, then went on, "Dreaming up villainous schemes is not a crime. Putting them into action is, and enabling such an action is equally a crime—arguably a greater one. As the backers are presumably wealthy men well able to finance such a scheme, it's likely the bulk of the profits is flowing to them—which is raising the ire of the government, for various pertinent reasons."

Robert made a derisive sound. "The government had to make all sorts of reparations after the Black Cobra incident last year. In the aftermath, they made slews of rash promises, as governments are wont to do, assuming any repeat of a similar nature would be too far in the future to trouble them. Instead, they're now facing a different but equally horrendous situation likely to stir the public to anger, scorn, and protest." Robert met Royd's eyes. "Given the current state of the government, given the dissatisfaction with the monarchy, they can't risk another situation where the public sees them failing to act against perpetrators who are wealthy and influential."

Royd nodded. "Judging by the tone of Wolverstone's communications, the government is *exceedingly* keen to have this scheme dismantled, the captives restored to the bosoms of their families, and the villains—instigators and backers alike—brought to justice. I've a strong suspicion my orders will focus on that last item, but once there, I'll be in charge and, as usual, we'll do things my way." After a moment, he went on, "Our priorities should be, first, to rescue the captives and get them to safety, second, to dismantle the scheme—we don't want it starting up again later—and third, to gain evidence to convict the backers."

Firm nods and murmurs of agreement came from the others.

"Aside from all else," Declan put in, "said backers are almost certainly here and not there. The best evidence you're likely to get will come from the three instigators, and we'll be seizing them anyway. Once they're shown the noose, I imagine they'll be only too happy to implicate the backers."

Robert grunted. "I can't imagine there'll be any honor among such vermin."

Again, all agreed.

A moment's silence followed, then Royd shifted in his chair. "Returning to the mechanics of what happened in the settlement, a local priest, Obo Undoto, was involved in helping a group of slavers identify adults from the European population with skills needed for the mine. As with Lady Holbrook, we don't know whether Undoto was willing or acting under duress, and given Caleb's success in eliminating the slavers entirely, at this point, we can ignore Undoto. By removing the slaver Kale and his men, Caleb has disrupted the supply of slaves to the mine and, from what Aileen had earlier learned, also the delivery of mining supplies. While those at the mine have alternative routes for delivery available, it will take time for them to realize they've lost Kale completely and put new procedures into place." He paused, then added, "Having no immediate supply of new captives will increase the incentive to keep those they have in good health."

"Which can't hurt," Aileen put in.

Royd nodded. "Viewed from all angles, Caleb's action in eliminating Kale's gang in the manner he did was inspired. As he himself wrote, not having to guard against the slavers supporting the mercenaries at the mine will be a significant advantage when it comes to seizing the compound."

After a moment, he went on, "To return to how their system operated—Undoto identified the adults, and Kale and his men kidnapped them and transported them to the mine. Acting directly, the slavers lured children into becoming captives, too. Although a heartless and ruthless man, Kale treated his captives well, apparently under orders from the mercenary captain actively overseeing the mine."

"The major cost in running the mine would be the mercenaries," Robert said.

Royd considered the papers piled before him. "The mercenary captain is called Dubois. In taking the compound and freeing the captives, he will unquestionably be our biggest obstacle."

Declan had tilted his head the better to study Royd's face. "You've used the terms 'we,' 'us,' and 'our' several times. Does that mean you intend us"—with his gaze he included Robert—"and our crews to be actively involved in your leg of the mission?"

Royd met Declan's gaze, then his lips curved. "Did you expect to remain here and enjoy"—he waved—"the social whirl?"

"Good God, no!" Declan looked appalled. "But I wasn't sure if our ships would form a part of your plan or if we'd just be following, tagging along."

Royd nodded at the documents before him. "Judging from the numbers Caleb has sent, even though my crew are unquestionably the most experienced in such exercises, I'm going to need far more men. Even more telling, we'll need to go in simultaneously at two different locations—the mining compound and the settlement. I can't see any way around a two-pronged approach. And while it's helpful that Caleb recruited Lascelle on his way down there, if we're to get the captives out safely, we're going to need overwhelming numbers."

His gaze on the papers, he went on, "Between them, Caleb and Lascelle have given us a detailed account of the threats, dangers, and obstacles we'll face. Add in the reports from inside the compound—from Dixon and Hillsythe—and the need to ensure that, once we initiate an attack, the mercenaries cannot reach the captives is clearly paramount. Exactly how we'll accomplish that is impossible to say, not without viewing the compound ourselves and assessing the possibilities, but one thing is clear—we'll need significant numbers, more than Caleb's, Lascelle's, and my crews combined."

Royd glanced at Robert and Declan, then waved the point aside. "We can discuss numbers and how we get them later. The first thing we need is the basic framework of a plan to successfully carry off this mission."

Isobel's gaze rested on his face. "You've already got a framework in mind. So tell us."

She knew how his mind worked—that he was quick to process information and define the necessary steps to achieve his desired goal. He looked around the group, then told them the outline of his plan.

He wasn't surprised by his brothers' enthusiasm, but their ladies' enthusiasm almost made him renege. Then he noticed Isobel regarding him with a certain light in her eye—as if she could read his thoughts—and he decided his brothers were transparently able to look out for their ladies themselves.

"How soon can we leave?" Isobel asked, and the others looked his way.

"As soon as possible, which means after getting my

orders from Melville—he has to formally request my assistance and give me a letter of authority, which he won't want to do." Royd glanced at Robert and Declan. "It's one thing to direct Decker to render all possible support—quite another to put the vice-admiral directly under my orders."

Robert smiled cynically. "Melville will give you whatever you ask."

Royd tipped his head. "As well as dealing with Melville—and Wolverstone, too—we need to sit down and work out those numbers. Most likely, I'll need to call in some others, and that means at least a few days to learn who's available, where they are, and get any new orders out to them."

"Lachlan would be an obvious choice," Declan volunteered.

"I checked before I left Aberdeen," Royd said. "With luck, he should be sailing into Bristol any day."

"Who else are you thinking of?" Robert asked. "Are you going to reach further than our own fleet or…?"

Royd grimaced. "The problem with reaching to others is that I can't be sure of command. Lascelle and Caleb have worked together before, so I foresee no problems there. But with others, especially of the caliber we need? I'd rather stick with our own captains."

"Kit?" Declan asked.

Royd pulled a reluctant face, but nodded. "For one particular aspect of this exercise, she and her crew are the best suited, so yes. I'm not sure she'll reach Bristol in time to leave with Lachlan, but that won't matter—she can follow and come in behind the rest of us."

Isobel knew of whom they spoke; Kit Frobisher was an anomaly in the seafaring world—a female who commanded a ship and had for the past eight years. Isobel had met Kit several times on the Aberdeen docks and had always found her—and her rather startlingly direct way of dealing with the world—quite fascinating.

Edwina was staring at Isobel. "Have you met Kit?"

When Isobel nodded, Edwina glanced rather pointedly at the clock on the mantelpiece, then declared, "It's nearly time to change for dinner. Aileen and I will take Isobel up and show her to her room."

Edwina rose, bringing the three men to their feet, along with an eager Aileen. Perfectly willing, Isobel rose, too. It was time she learned more about the other two ladies. Regardless of what eventuated between her and Royd, these ladies were, or would shortly become, Frobishers, and therefore Duncan's aunts-by-marriage.

Aside from any friendship she might strike up with ladies who, on the basis of just the past hours, seemed of similar bent, they might also be of additional support—even mutual support—whatever their future relationship became.

After waving Isobel and Aileen to precede her, Edwina stated, "Dinner will be at seven, gentlemen. Don't be late."

Royd watched Edwina sweep out of the room in Isobel and Aileen's wake and resisted the urge to shake his head. Declan was never going to rule his roost, not with such a force of nature as his wife…

When it came to forces of nature, Isobel had all the others trumped, even her scarifying grandmother.

With that reflection sinking into his mind, he looked at his brothers and arched a brow. "We need to send word to Wolverstone and Melville that Caleb's report has reached us. The sooner I can meet with Melville and get the orders I want from him, the sooner we'll be able to get down there, join Caleb, and get those people out."

Declan exchanged a glance with Robert, then waved to the door. "Come to the library—you can write your missive to Wolverstone there."

Composing a note to Wolverstone, stressing the need for an immediate meeting and holding out the lure of information just received, was quickly done—Royd knew how to pique the ex-spymaster's interest. Once the missive was dispatched via Declan's senior footman, Royd leaned back in the chair behind the desk and waited for the inevitable interrogation.

It commenced the instant the door clicked shut.

Robert fixed Royd with a direct look. "What the devil is Isobel doing here?"

In his mildest tone, Royd replied, "She's searching for one of her cousins—Katherine Fortescue." Briefly, Royd outlined Katherine's story as Isobel had related it to him. "When Isobel and Iona finally got word of Katherine's disappearance, Isobel presumed on our past to ask that I take her to Freetown. I'd just received Wolverstone's summons, so…" He waved. "Here we both are."

Neither of his brothers knew quite what to make of that.

Eventually, Robert humphed. "A happy coincidence, then, that Caleb actually met Katherine, so he could report that he spoke with her and heard directly from her that she was well." Robert grimaced. "As well as could be in such circumstances."

Royd nodded. "Which, of course, means that Isobel knows where Katherine is."

Declan stared at him—whether in horror or shock, Royd wasn't sure. "You're not going to take Isobel into the jungle with you? To the compound?"

Royd opened his eyes wide. "Do you think I could stop her? Or that I'm fool enough to waste time and effort trying? Now she knows her cousin's in that compound, she's going to be by my side every step of the way." Because of Katherine, and for another reason entirely, but his brothers didn't need to know about that. They'd be taken aback, but for Royd's money, they should look to their own ladies before concerning themselves with Isobel.

He would lay odds that, at that very moment, the three women were exchanging confidences. And once the other two learned that Isobel would sail with him—and would go into the jungle to the mining compound, too—he seriously doubted Edwina and Aileen would settle for any more-restricted roles. From their reactions to his plan, he'd gathered they, too, were committed to the mission—that like his brothers, they felt a burning desire to see the captives released and justice done. Although he'd met Edwina before, those encounters had perforce been on a social stage. Now he'd learned of her contribution during Declan's leg of the mission, he was leaning to the view that although Edwina and Isobel were very different women, they shared significant similarity under the skin.

And if he was any judge, Aileen Hopkins was another cut from the same cloth.

Which meant the last leg of this mission, run according to his plan, looked set to be exceedingly interesting for the three oldest Frobisher brothers. He wished Robert and Declan luck; he was going to have his hands full leading the mission and dealing with Isobel.

Neither Declan nor Robert had discovered any further comment they wished to make on the subject of Isobel. While Royd appreciated that a significant part of their concern was driven by a wish to support and—yes—protect him from a woman they believed had run roughshod over his heart, there was far more between him and her than his brothers knew. Than he wished them to know. The time for revelations—including Duncan—was not yet.

Declan stirred and threw him a puzzled look. "One thing—you don't seem overly perturbed by Caleb filching the reins as he did."

Royd shrugged. "Given he'd learned of the ongoing mission, I wouldn't have expected him to do anything else. And for once, he seems to be behaving with the gravity due command."

Robert snorted. "Taking on Kale and his men like that?"

"It was a bold move, but a highly strategic one." It was almost certainly what Royd would have done had he been in Caleb's place. "And judging by Lascelle's comments, Caleb behaved with the right blend of caution and forcefulness. He covered every contingency and had everything in place before he went in." Royd shrugged. "Our little brother is finally growing up." His lips twitched. "Thank God."

"Amen to that," Declan murmured.

Robert still looked unconvinced.

But Royd had been waiting for just such a sign of evolving maturity in his youngest brother; he felt vindicated that his faith in Caleb was proving well founded. Aside from all else, he had a strong suspicion he was going to need a more mature Caleb in order to steer his own future in the direction he wanted.

Robert glanced at the clock. "Edwina said seven, didn't she?"

It was just after six.

Declan sighed and rose. "We'd better get ourselves washed and brushed."

It was an old saying from their childhood. Royd grinned, rose, and joined his brothers on the trek up the stairs.

* * *

The conversation over the dinner table was revealing. Seated at Edwina's left with Royd beside her, Isobel ate, listened, and learned.

She wasn't surprised by the assessing glances Robert and Declan directed her way when they thought she wasn't looking. Both knew her temper—and Royd's—well enough not to directly engage her on the point, but they were clearly wondering what was going on between her and Royd. She took a certain delight in pretending to be oblivious to their curiosity.

As she'd expected, she'd got on well with Edwina and Aileen. The pair had accompanied her to the room Edwina had assigned her. Declan and Edwina's bedchamber lay to the left of the upstairs drawing room, which faced the head of the stairs. Aileen had mentioned that she and Robert had rooms along the corridor to the right of the stairs. The room to which Edwina had steered Isobel lay to the left of the stairs, had a lovely view over the rear garden, and, as Edwina informed her, was next door to the room she'd given Royd.

Isobel hadn't reacted, but Edwina hadn't appeared to expect her to. Her hostess had sat in the chair by the fireplace, Aileen had sat in the window seat, and while Isobel had prowled the room, checking to see where her things had been put, the pair had engaged in a quick-fire exchange, not about Isobel and Royd but about the mission, the likely weather, and the necessity of commencing their packing forthwith.

Isobel had found it impossible to keep a straight face. She had a strong suspicion that Robert's and Declan's views regarding their ladies' involvement in the mission did not match that of said ladies. She knew whom she favored to win the upcoming arguments.

When Edwina had declared they would leave her to change and had pushed up out of the chair, Isobel had realized her hostess was pregnant; until that telltale move, the fall of Edwina's gown had hidden the evidence.

"Five months," Edwina had confirmed, with a smile the quality of which would have made her condition plain to the most undiscerning eye. "But I'm entirely well, and if I wasn't ill on the way back from Freetown—and I wasn't—then I doubt I will be on the way down again." She'd nodded at Aileen. "And we think Aileen might be increasing, too, but she's decided not to tell Robert yet."

"I daresay he'll want to wrap me in wool like some delicate porcelain, which I am most definitely not." A militant gleam had shone in Aileen's eyes. "No power on earth will keep me from getting to that compound and finding Will."

Isobel had bitten her lip against the impulse to share that she'd largely ignored the supposed restrictions of pregnancy, too, at least until she'd grown too heavy to easily move; thankfully, Duncan had had the good sense to make an appearance two weeks later.

She had grown up in what was essentially a matriarchy; she was accustomed to having other women—cousins of all degrees and others Iona drew under her wing—about her all the time. She had many women she would class as friends, yet none had had the freedom to chart her own life that she had had, and that factor in many ways set her apart.

She wasn't entirely sure how the freedom she enjoyed had come about; certainly, being the only child of James Carmichael had been a critical factor, but if she hadn't seized the opportunities that status had afforded her and *pushed*—hadn't been such a tomboy and scrambled all over the shipyards and fallen in with Royd Frobisher—

she would never have attained the uniquely unfettered position she now held.

That was a point to ponder. Would taking up with Royd again change anything—anything critical to her work, to who she now was?

They'd reached the last course.

"Having experienced the climate in Freetown once, I must have a closer look at my wardrobe." Edwina popped a grape into her mouth, chewed, and swallowed.

Isobel helped herself to several nuts, then passed the platter to Royd.

"I was glad of my half-boots when we were trekking through the jungle," Aileen added. "And while bonnets or hats are to be recommended in the settlement—certainly if one is going anywhere on foot during the day—there's really no need for them in the jungle. The trees block well-nigh all the light." She glanced at Robert. "From Caleb's and Lascelle's descriptions, it seems the mining compound is in jungle of a similar type to Kale's camp."

Reluctantly, Robert agreed. After a moment, he shot a look at Declan, then said, "The jungle's exceedingly oppressive. You really don't have to venture into it. It'll be much cooler waiting on board."

"Oh no." Aileen's hazel eyes widened to a remarkable degree as she faced Robert. "I absolutely have to go to the compound. Quite aside from finding Will, I couldn't live with myself if I didn't check on those five children—the four boys and that girl. We had to let them be taken for the greater good—that, I was forced to accept. But I won't rest easy until I know they're safe—and I see that they are with my own eyes. I have to be there when we get them out—you must see that."

Robert pressed his lips tightly together, then dipped

his head in a gesture that might be interpreted as agreement, and wisely declined to argue.

Having carried her point, Aileen happily returned her attention to peeling a fig.

Declan looked down the length of the table at his delicate, fairylike wife. He hesitated, but clearly felt forced to ask, "Am I to take it that you intend to march to the compound, too, despite..." With a nod, he indicated her expectant state.

Edwina grinned. "Yes, of course. I'm only increasing, you know—something women have done for millennia. Even Dr. Halliwell has said I may go about as I please—indeed, he quite recommends it."

"I doubt he had the African jungle in mind," Declan grumbled.

"Possibly not, but I'm accustomed to walking for miles at Ridgware, and even on the moors when we were in Aberdeen, so as long as I take care not to overexert myself, it will all be perfectly fine." Edwina looked down the table and watched Declan's jaw set. "Besides," she continued, a note of steel sliding into her voice, "you wouldn't want me to regret that I'm carrying your firstborn at this moment, would you?"

Royd swallowed the bark of laughter that nearly escaped him. There was absolutely no possible answer Declan could make, other than...

Declan shifted in his chair. "No, of course not." He concentrated on peeling the pear on his plate.

Shortly after, in sunny good humor, Edwina rose, and the company adjourned to the drawing room. The room had a pleasant ambiance; Royd approved of his sister-in-law's taste, which apparently ran to comfort rather than the latest fashion.

The women sat on one sofa and the nearby armchair.

He claimed the armchair he'd previously occupied, leaving the other sofa for Robert and Declan. They sprawled, relaxed and at ease. Isobel asked Edwina if she had any social engagements planned over the next days, and from there, talk turned to more general topics.

Royd learned that, on their ultimate return from Africa, Robert planned to visit Aileen's family in Scarborough. Royd asked about Aileen's brothers, which led to a discussion of the situation in the Americas. Royd contributed to the debate, but for the most part, remained focused on Isobel. He listened to her opinions—which, of course, she had; she knew nearly as much about global shipping as he did. What he learned suggested that the past eight years, while not altering anything fundamental about either of them, had nevertheless expanded their knowledge and experience in ways the other might not yet appreciate.

That was a point he decided to bear in mind.

The ringing of the doorbell was, minutes later, followed by the entrance of the butler, Humphrey. He bore a silver salver on which resided a letter opener and a white envelope. Humphrey paused by Royd's chair. "For you, Captain."

Royd lifted the envelope, glanced at the writing, and straightened in the chair. "Wolverstone." He picked up the letter knife, slit the envelope, then returned the knife to the salver. "Thank you, Humphrey."

Humphrey bowed and departed.

From the envelope, Royd drew out a single sheet. He unfolded it and read.

"Well?" Robert asked.

"We have an appointment with Melville at Wolverstone House tomorrow afternoon at two o'clock. Apparently, that's the earliest Melville can absent himself from the Admiralty."

"Excellent!" Edwina looked at Isobel and Aileen. "That means we'll have the morning free to further our own plans."

Royd looked at Edwina, then at Isobel's and Aileen's faces—and deduced that the males of the party weren't included in Edwina's "our."

Which suited him. He had arrangements of his own to make, and his brothers would have, too.

Against that, of course, lay the undeniable fact that the three women were fast connecting in a way that would forge them into a formidable supportive force; Royd knew all about the power that females in plural could bring to bear—witness Isobel's grandmother and her largely female clan.

Yet when he considered what the outcome would likely be, it wasn't concern he felt but an odd form of contentment. Anything that helped bind Isobel into his family was to be encouraged.

He sat back and smiled at Edwina. He was appreciating his sister-in-law more and more.

Two

Early the following afternoon, Isobel found herself seated on an elegant sofa in the large drawing room of Wolverstone House. Beside her sat Minerva, Duchess of Wolverstone, who had welcomed them and, somewhat to Isobel's surprise, had remained to hear Caleb's report; although Minerva was only a handful of years older than she, Isobel hadn't expected the calmly serene duchess to have any involvement in her powerful husband's intrigues.

In that, she'd erred; judging by Edwina's response to the duchess, Minerva was of a similar mind to Edwina regarding a wife's role in her husband's business, which left Isobel feeling unexpectedly at ease. Edwina had introduced her to the duke and duchess, blithely explaining that she hailed from Aberdeen and was sailing with Royd to Freetown in pursuit of a cousin they now knew to be among the captives held at the mine. Both duke and duchess had accepted the explanation at face value, but Isobel had seen Minerva's gaze divert to Royd in a considering fashion—Royd on whose arm Isobel had arrived.

He was seated in a straight-backed chair to her right; Edwina sat on Minerva's other side, and Declan, Robert, and Aileen were in possession of the sofa opposite.

The two key figures sat in armchairs angled away

from the hearth to face the company. Wolverstone wielded stillness like a weapon; with coloring much like Isobel's own—dark hair, dark eyes, pale skin—neither his expression nor any movement of hands or body indicated his thoughts, much less his feelings.

In sharp contrast, Melville, a corpulent figure with his corsets over-laced and his balding head sheening, fidgeted and fussed, his pudgy hands rarely still. He had the pasty-pale complexion of someone who spent all his life indoors. Despite his ancestry, his features were coarser than those of any other in the room, and the expression on his face was overtly fretful. The expression in his washed-out brown eyes was, Isobel considered, closer to hunted.

She listened while Royd presented Melville, Wolverstone, and Minerva with a concise summary of Caleb's findings. He concluded with "Armed with Caleb's and Lascelle's information, as well as the reports from Dixon and Hillsythe, we have all we need to seize the compound."

His fingers steepled before his face, Wolverstone nodded. Although his gaze remained on Royd, Isobel got the distinct impression it was Melville Wolverstone addressed when he said, "To adequately lay this matter to rest, we need to achieve three distinct objectives. The first must be to rescue the captives, to preserve their safety and return them to Freetown, with whatever compensation is feasible. We also need to dismantle the mine and subsequently ensure such an enterprise cannot flourish again—the latter will require changes to the settlement's governance, along with consequent oversight, neither of which is of immediate concern. Of more relevance to all here is the capture of those involved—the three local instigators and, through them, the mysterious backers."

Wolverstone finally glanced at Melville. "I believe we're in agreement that the backers are almost certainly English and of an ilk that means their exposure will provoke considerable scandal." Wolverstone's voice didn't rise, but his tone hardened. "In the current circumstances, it's imperative we gather sufficient evidence to convict the backers—identifying them alone will not be enough to take them down, and unless we do, the populace will howl."

The First Lord's expression had grown almost petulant, his fingers agitatedly plucking his sleeve. When Wolverstone spoke again, his voice was milder, yet his tone remained implacable. "I suggest that the government's best way forward will be to give Captain Frobisher whatever he needs to successfully complete this mission."

Melville frowned peevishly and irritatedly waved. "Yes, yes—whatever is necessary. We have to have this settled—have to have those damned backers in our hands with evidence enough to convict—before the infernal news sheets learn of it."

Royd and Wolverstone exchanged a glance, then Royd calmly stated, "I need a directive from you to Decker."

Melville's frown turned confused. "I gave a letter to your brother here." He waved at Declan.

"Caleb kept that letter in case of need—the correct decision in the circumstances. But even if he'd sent it back, it wouldn't be enough." Royd met Melville's gaze. "I don't need a letter directing Decker to give me all assistance. I need a directive placing Decker under my command. In order to complete this mission, it's imperative that I be able to give Decker orders that I can have confidence he will obey without question."

Melville looked aghast. "You're asking me to give

you—a privateer—command of a naval squadron? Over a vice-admiral?"

Royd let a heartbeat go past. "Yes." When Melville huffed, Royd said, "It's essential that I be able to give Decker one particular order, and that he obeys immediately and without question or alteration. If he doesn't—if he vacillates—it will put the success of the entire mission at risk."

At that, Melville's gaze turned wary. After a second, he glanced at Wolverstone.

The duke met his gaze imperturbably and arched one dark brow as if to say: What did you expect?

Melville looked down, then he humphed. From beneath his pale brows, he shot a look at Royd. "Very well. I'll have the orders prepared and sent over this evening." Melville glanced at Declan. "Stanhope Street, isn't it?"

Declan nodded. "Number twenty-six."

Melville swung his gaze back to Royd. "Anything else you need?" The First Lord's tone was sarcastic.

Royd nodded. "I'll need a similar letter from the Home Office, sufficient to guarantee Governor Holbrook's compliance with any orders given to him by whoever presents it, and another such missive from the War Office for the Commanding Officer at Fort Thornton. Don't make the latter specific. We need to ensure whoever's in charge at the time acts as required."

Melville's jaw had fallen slack. Again, he looked at Wolverstone; again, he received no support from that quarter, leaving him to shut his mouth, humph, and fidget, and ultimately agree with a terse, tight-lipped nod.

Wolverstone took pity on the First Lord and asked Royd, "When will you sail?"

"*The Corsair* will have reached Southampton this morning. She'll already be provisioning. Once she's ready, she'll stand off, and *The Trident* and *The Cormorant* will provision as well—we'll send orders down tomorrow. After that...we'll need a day or so to get out further orders and complete our preparations." Royd met Wolverstone's dark gaze. "I'll be taking at least two other Frobisher ships down in support—so, all told, five ships' complements to join with Caleb's and Lascelle's. At this point, I anticipate departing on Monday's tide."

"Monday?" Melville grumped. "This is urgent. Can't you set out sooner?"

"I could," Royd calmly replied. "But because *The Corsair* is faster than the other ships, there's no point me setting out in advance—after initiating Decker's action, I would have to skulk close to Freetown, waiting for the others to arrive before going farther down the estuary, and the more prolonged that stage, the greater the risk of one of the instigators learning of our presence and guessing our intentions. I need Robert and Declan to get into Freetown as soon as possible after I arrive and deal with Decker. That timing works best if we leave on the same day."

Melville's face tightened. "Very well. The more important question is when you'll be back." His voice strengthened. "When can I expect this all to be over, everything resolved and finished with, heh?" Agitated aggression colored the demand.

Royd held the First Lord's gaze for several seconds, then stated, "This will end when we have the backers in our hands and evidence enough to send them to the gallows."

The meeting broke up after that. Melville left first. As Wolverstone walked with Royd and Isobel to the front door, he murmured, "As you saw, the prospect of political ramifications has the First Lord rattled. He knew this matter was a grave threat to the government the instant it came to his attention—that was why he called me in. For all his fluster and bluster, his instincts are sound. But he didn't expect it to be this bad."

Isobel leaned forward and, across Royd, fixed Wolverstone with her gaze. "Exactly how bad is it?"

Wolverstone slowed. The three of them halted a little way from the front door. Wolverstone held her gaze as he considered his answer, then said, "It's not this incident in isolation but the compounding effect of this coming on top of last year's disaster with the Black Cobra cult. While the Black Cobra and her associates were finally tracked and brought to justice—public justice—the ramifications continued long after. The government is struggling to maintain order—we have an ostentatiously profligate king, while the coffers are low, and the country as a whole has yet to emerge from the dark days after the war. Against that background, the demands for reparation from the colonies over the atrocities of the Black Cobra cult fueled anti-government fury on several fronts. In response, the government adamantly promised such a situation would never be allowed to occur again—and now they have this." He paused, and they resumed strolling toward the door. "The only saving grace is that the news and scandal sheets have yet to get wind of it. If we can end the situation in the settlement and deliver the backers to public justice, it will avoid an incendiary public reaction and demonstrate the government's resolve to no longer turn a blind eye to those of the elite who believe they are above our laws."

The butler had opened the door, and the others had gone ahead. Royd paused on the threshold to arch a cynical brow. "And *is* the government so resolved?"

Wolverstone's lips quirked in an equally cynical expression. "For the moment, yes. Let's take what we can get."

Royd grunted. He and Isobel exchanged farewells with the duchess, then he escorted Isobel down the steps.

* * *

They elected to stroll back to Stanhope Street. Her arm looped with Royd's, Isobel was glad of the chance to stretch her legs and breathe. While the smells of the city and the bustle and constant noise were a far cry from crisp sea air and the quiet shush of waves, she was equally at home in the clatter and clang of the shipyards, with the smell of tar and the tang of sawn wood and varnish surrounding her.

By the time they turned the corner from South Audley Street into Stanhope, she had heard enough of Edwina's and Aileen's comments—floating back from where the other two couples walked just ahead of her and Royd—to appreciate the slightly grim, resigned expressions on Robert's and Declan's faces. It appeared they'd finally accepted that their ladies would be sailing with them.

Isobel wasn't so certain that Declan and Robert had as yet agreed to what would happen when they reached Freetown, but she had every confidence that when it came to the point, Edwina and Aileen would carry the day.

Royd was also watching the interplay between Declan and Edwina, and between Robert and Aileen. He knew his brothers were pinning their hopes on persuading their respective ladies to remain in relative safety in the settlement while they led their men to meet with Royd's forces. He didn't give much for Robert's and Declan's chances, but he'd resolved to say nothing to burst their bubble; he had no intention of calling attention to, much less inviting questions about, his own tack with Isobel.

In the not so distant past, *he* would have been the one

most rigidly holding the line against allowing the women to endanger themselves in even the most minor way. But not this time. Not with Isobel.

Sharing all with her was too vital to his long-term goal.

They reached Declan and Edwina's house and trooped up the steps. In the front hall, Royd caught Robert's and Declan's eyes. "Now we've got Melville's agreement, we need to get all our orders out, then put our minds to anything extra we might need." They'd spent the previous afternoon and all of that morning working through lists of men, stores, weapons, and munitions; they didn't expect to have to use any cannon, but that didn't mean they would sail unprepared.

The other two nodded and followed him to the library. The ladies, he noted, already had their heads together as they headed for the drawing room.

In the library, he, Declan, and Robert sat around Declan's big desk—Declan had surrendered the chair behind it to Royd—and wrote detailed orders to their lieutenants. Declan had already requested Humphrey to call in two couriers; as soon as all the orders were complete, they were sealed and on their way to the Frobisher Shipping Company offices in Southampton and Bristol.

With the most crucial aspects of their preparations in train, they settled to scan their lists again and work through the details.

* * *

Royd retreated with his brothers to change for dinner. The ritual gave him a few minutes alone in which to review his plans—all his plans.

Everything to do with the mission itself was as it needed to be.

As for his plans for Isobel…

He could hear movement in the room next door, the one she'd been given; the sounds focused his senses as well as his mind. He didn't need much thought to conclude that, with respect to reclaiming her, he needed to continue as he'd started. He harbored no doubts that the surest way to win her to his side again—to confirm her as his wife in all ways—was to treat her as if she occupied that position.

In many ways, she did, and always had. That was why their handfasting had come about, and why she remained so very definitely the only wife for him.

The reality of *them* was that the position of his wife was uniquely crafted for her; she slipped into it instinctively, entirely without thinking, and the more she grew accustomed to doing exactly that and the more comfortable with him she became, the better.

That was already happening in the social sphere and in their day-to-day life. But there was one aspect of their relationship neither had yet broached, even though the mutual impulses remained active, very much there.

As he settled the fresh cravat he'd tied and anchored it with his gold pin, he thought back to all that had gone before, how that particular aspect had come about before…

He frowned at his reflection in the mirror.

He'd never wooed her. He'd never seduced her—they'd fallen into each other's arms as naturally as rain falling from the sky, without any effort whatsoever on either of their parts.

"Huh." He stared into his own eyes, then softly stated, "But that was then, and this is now, and that's not going to happen again."

Especially not when she was watching him so closely and keeping such a tight guard on her senses—over all her responses.

He refocused on his face and slowly smiled. They had one day and two nights more in London before they reboarded *The Corsair*—before they returned to more limiting surroundings and the inhibiting presence of their son.

"Obviously, it would be wise to engage on that front now."

* * *

Isobel was instantly aware of the change in Royd—not in him, himself, but in his focus. The intensity in his gray gaze was back, along with a certain calculation in his expression and a speculative glint in his eyes.

If she had any sense at all, she would pull back and erect a barricade of haughty, chilly politeness beyond which he couldn't reach; she was perfectly capable of doing that…with any other man.

With Royd…there had always been something about him that called to her. Inevitably, invariably, she would join him in any game.

Even one as potentially dangerous as she knew this particular game might be.

She knew from the outset where it would lead. Did she really want to go there again?

To her inner befuddlement, no clear answer to that question appeared in her brain.

Meanwhile…she allowed Royd to lead her in to dinner. That was hardly surprising given the other two couples went ahead, and just as they had the previous night, the pair of them brought up the rear. But this time, he closed his hand over hers where she'd rested it on his sleeve, and his thumb stroked over the sensitive skin on the back of her hand.

Her breath hitched. Her diaphragm tightened. Her heart thudded just a touch harder.

They reached her chair, and he released her; he waved the footman back and drew the chair out for her. She sat, and he pushed the chair in, then he moved on to the chair beside hers.

His fingertips trailed over her bare shoulder, lightly tracing a path from the outer tip of her collarbone to her nape.

She had to clamp down hard to stop herself from shuddering.

She still felt the shivery sensation to her marrow.

She waited until he sat, then she slowly turned her head—and smiled into his eyes.

After that, the dance was on. And it was a dance of sorts, something like a cotillion, with them metaphorically circling each other, choosing to let their hands and fingers touch—here, there—accompanied by glances that were apparently innocent, but in reality were anything but.

She'd forgotten how heightened her senses could become, how those glances and the flaring sexuality investing each otherwise mundane little touch could provoke her. Could wind her nerves tight and ratchet anticipation to such a degree it was a battle to breathe, let alone maintain any semblance of rational conversation.

But that was the challenge—and she'd never backed away from one in her life.

The final outcome, she suspected, could be scored as a draw.

She might have babbled in response to several questions from Aileen and Edwina, but when they returned to the drawing room, he, distracted by the surreptitious drift of her fingertips across his wrist as she lifted her teacup from his hand, completely missed a comment-cum-question from Robert, who called him to order.

Royd shook his head as if to break a spell, then frowned and turned to answer.

It was only as she was swallowing the last of her tea that it occurred to her to wonder why—why had he taken it into his head to institute such a game now?

Tonight.

They retired all at once, climbing the stairs in a group with the ladies in front and the gentlemen following.

Awareness skittered up and down her spine as, on reaching the head of the stairs, the three couples parted, going their separate ways. Declan and Edwina entered their room and shut the door; Isobel heard the snick of the latch as she strolled with wholly assumed nonchalance toward the door to her room.

Royd prowled at her heels.

She'd swept her hair up for the evening, leaving her nape exposed; she could feel his gaze on the sensitive skin, the sensation growing more intense with every step.

She reached her door and swung to face him. To confront him.

He halted mere inches from her—so close she had to tilt her face up to meet his eyes.

In the shadows of the corridor, he appeared predatory, or so her senses informed her.

He looked down at her for three seconds, then his gaze slowly lowered to her lips—and held there.

She couldn't help herself; the tip of her tongue slid past her lips and cruised slowly over the lower…

He caught her hands, drew them up and wide, and pressed them against the wood as, with the grace of a dancer, he stepped closer and backed her against the panel of her door.

He gave her plenty of time to avoid the inevitable.

Of course, she didn't. That had always been her problem with him—where he led, she unfailingly followed.

Always.

His head dipped, and their lips met.

Sensation as precious as her fondest memory rolled over her. Sank into her.

Oh God, yes! How she'd missed this, ached for this—this simple communion of the senses. Driven to taste, to savor again, she parted her lips, and he angled his head, and his tongue found hers.

Stroking, heavy and wet, heated and so welcome.

She curled her fingers in his and kissed him back—long, slow—and he answered in the same vein, with a banked hunger that called to her own.

Passion surged, but they skirted it, senses whirling, yet together, still so much in tune—attuned to each other as they always had been.

So easy. It had always been so; in this sphere as in any other, they moved with one mind, with one aim, one goal.

She couldn't hold back—she'd never learned the knack. Had never seen the sense in muting her responses, not when they so patently pleased him. Not with the scintillating web of sexual attraction spinning about them—fed equally by her as by him; slowly it enclosed them, then tightened and ensnared them.

As the kiss spun on and spun out into pleasure.

Pleasure of a type, a kind, a depth Royd had forgotten could be. He hadn't expected the allure of the past to blossom and bloom so easily, to surge through them both so effortlessly in response to a simple kiss.

He'd intended to take just a taste—just a teasing of their senses. But he couldn't draw back, pull back from the promise inherent in this kiss—their first in eight long years. Neither were who they had been. And who they now were, on this plane, remained to be defined.

Their hunger for each other needed no definition. No permission.

Entirely beyond his control, that hunger rose, then slipped its leash and roared.

He plunged into her mouth, intent on taking more, and she met him as she always had. Met, matched, and brazenly encouraged—

He was reaching for the handle of her door when instinct abruptly yanked on his reins.

Not yet. Not yet!

It was too early for them both—they couldn't plunge over that cliff before either had made the decision to fly.

His head pounded with the effort—and other parts of him throbbed, too—but he wrestled his long-denied impulses down, locked them behind the wall of his will. And managed, step by step, to draw back from the glorious temptation of the kiss.

Eventually, he raised his head, and their lips parted.

From under heavy lids, he looked into her face, waited until her lush lashes rose and revealed her dark, lustrous eyes.

At the sight—a sight he hadn't seen for too long—his libido howled and rattled its cage, but he clung to control and held firm.

And saw awareness bloom in her gaze.

Her eyes swiftly scanned his face; he had no idea what she could see—what might show to her educated scrutiny. But no words need be said; they both knew the danger. Knew the power of what existed between them, of the compulsion that, if they let it loose, could and would overwhelm them.

Years ago, it hadn't mattered—they had indulged

without restraint. But now…they were estranged, and the consequences for them both were real, if undefined.

Even as he registered the light flush in her cheeks, the faint swelling of her luscious lips, even as awareness of that dangerous compulsion swelled, a small voice in the depths of his mind asked: When had either of them ever drawn back from danger?

But his strategist's mind had reasserted control. Yes, he could push, and she would yield. Yes, he could lead, and she would still follow, but it was too early for this, not with so much still unresolved between them. This was definitely not the way to persuade her to trust him again.

He shackled his instincts in iron, eased his hold on her hands, and edged back.

Her gaze locked with his, she tilted her head, trying to read his thoughts even as, reaching blindly, she found the doorknob and turned it. The door swung open behind her. She held his gaze for an instant more, then stepped back through the opening.

Immediately, he missed her warmth. He fisted his hands to stop himself from reaching for her.

Although her eyes didn't leave his, he would have sworn she knew.

A lilting smile curved her lips, and her gaze locked with his to the last, she softly closed the door, and finally the contact was cut.

He exhaled. His gaze on the door, he drew in a deep breath, then turned and walked the few yards to his room.

He opened the door, walked inside, and—as quietly as she—shut the door. His gaze fell on the bed. The empty expanse of coverlet mocked him.

Feeling decidedly sour, he shrugged off his coat.

He seriously doubted he would get much sleep.

Three

"The tide tomorrow will run in the afternoon." Royd attacked his breakfast, attempting to appear as hungry as he usually was. What sleep he'd managed had been wracked by dreams the like of which he'd not suffered in years.

A humbling experience to discover that one particular woman still held the power to so command his psyche.

Then again, this was Isobel.

"Should we leave here today?" Edwina asked. "Or will tomorrow morning be soon enough?"

The men looked at each other, then Robert shrugged. "I can't see any advantage to going down today. Our crews know what they're doing, and there's nothing we can do to speed the provisioning."

"All we would do is get in the way." Declan glanced around the table. "I vote we stay until tomorrow morning." He glanced at Royd. "We can leave as early as you like."

Isobel felt torn; this was the longest she'd been away from Duncan, yet she was perfectly certain he would be enjoying himself hugely. Today or tomorrow would make no difference to him.

As the others added their voices to the call to leave tomorrow, she felt Royd's gaze and looked across the table.

He faintly arched a brow. She hesitated for another second, then shrugged. "Tomorrow, then."

He looked at Declan. "I agree, but we should order fast carriages."

Declan nodded. "I'll get Humphrey on to it. Consider it done."

Robert was scanning a list he'd set beside his plate. "I've been reviewing the number of men—we'll definitely need Lachlan's crew and several men from Kit's as well to be certain of having adequate numbers." He glanced at Royd. "What do you estimate their sailing times will be?"

"I've told them to provision from the Bristol stores, then head directly south. They shouldn't be that far behind *The Trident*." Royd looked at Declan. "I'm assuming that, the winds being equal, *The Cormorant* will be the first into Freetown after *The Corsair*."

Declan pushed aside his empty plate. "Exactly how are you imagining the arrivals will go? How will they align with what needs to be done?"

Edwina glanced swiftly around the table; everyone had finished eating. "Perhaps"—she pushed back her chair and rose, bringing the men to their feet—"we should repair to the drawing room and allow the staff to clear the table." She shooed them toward the door. "We can sit in comfort and go over the plan step by step."

They did just that. Ensconced in one corner of the sofa, Isobel listened as Royd, standing before the fireplace in a typical seafaring captain's stance, his legs braced and his hands clasped behind his back, listed the major stages of the mission as he saw them.

"*The Corsair* will leave Southampton first and reach Freetown first. *The Trident* should follow *The Corsair* out of Southampton Water, with *The Cormorant* following. I expect *The Cormorant* will overtake *The Trident* on the way down, but I need you to arrive as close together as possible, so bear that in mind. Once there, I'll slip into the estuary at night and stand well out from the harbor. I'll locate Decker's flagship and pay him a visit. We need him to act as soon as possible." Royd glanced at Declan. "Expect to find your way barred, but the squadron will have orders to allow all Frobisher vessels through, so be sure to fly the right colors."

Declan dipped his head. "Duly noted."

"In addition to that," Royd went on, "both of you will need to sail into the estuary under the cover of darkness. Assuming *The Cormorant* gets in first, we'll rendezvous and see where we are."

"You're likely to get in at least a day if not more in advance," Robert pointed out.

Royd nodded. "After I've dealt with Decker, I'll use the time to learn what I can regarding the situation in the settlement, although obviously I can't stride up to the governor's residence, knock on the door, and ask."

"So who will we ask?" Isobel had an excellent memory for details; if he was going to slip into the settlement incognito, she wanted to know where he—and she—would be headed.

Royd's gaze rested on her, on her face, for a moment, then he replied, "I don't yet know. We'll see how the land lies once we're there."

He'd been using the pronoun "I" too much for her liking, a fact she was certain he now understood.

"Once you arrive and we rendezvous"—Royd looked at Declan—"I'll fill you in on anything pertinent we've learned and hand over the settlement side of the action to you and Robert. Your objective is simple enough"—with his gaze, he included Robert—"but achieving it might not be so straightforward. You'll need to bail up Holbrook and also the commander at the fort, and using the orders that should arrive this morning, convince both that it's in their best interests to place an effective perimeter guard around the eastern side of the settlement. We need to ensure that, once your presence in the settlement becomes known, no communication goes via land from the settlement to the mining compound."

"So those at the compound won't know we're coming, that rescue for the captives is imminent." Robert looked at Declan. "You've met Holbrook—better I leave him to you and take on the commander at the fort."

Declan slowly nodded. "You spent more time in the settlement, especially on the eastern side. You'll have a better understanding of where the pickets should be placed." He glanced at Royd. "While we're doing that, I assume you'll be off up the estuary?"

"As soon as I hand over to you, I'll use the rest of the night to push up the estuary. We should find Lascelle's ship standing off—a marker for where we need to go ashore. I anticipate making directly for the mining compound."

"What about Lachlan and the reinforcements from his and Kit's crews?" Robert asked.

"The men left aboard *The Corsair* and *The Raven* will direct Lachlan to the right path." Royd paused, his gaze growing distant as if envisaging the action, then he refocused on Robert. "I need to reach Caleb and to spend some time reconnoitering and assessing the possibilities, so that by the time you and Declan arrive, we'll have some idea of how to pull off the rescue."

His expression tending grim, Robert growled, "You and Caleb will wait for us, won't you?"

Royd grinned a pirate's grin, but then sobered. "In this

case, yes, unless something forces our hand." He paused, then added, "If our aim is to rescue the captives with least risk to their lives, then it's imperative we attack with the strongest force we can muster." He glanced at Declan. "So we'll wait for you to join us outside the compound. For obvious reasons, you shouldn't dally in the settlement longer than absolutely necessary to ensure all communication between Freetown and the compound is cut off."

Declan nodded. "Which brings us to the critical action—the taking of the compound. From all the information Caleb sent, unless he's discovered some way to get us inside prior to hostilities breaking out, us getting through a palisade like that without alerting the mercenaries isn't going to be easy."

"Indeed." Royd's lips thinned. After a moment, he stated, "The greatest weakness in our position is that, even with numbers sufficient to overrun the mercenaries, with our forces all outside that damned palisade, and too few men with fighting skills inside it, there's no effective way to keep the mercenaries away from all potential hostages—away from the women and children—long enough to cut our way inside."

"And any such entry point is going to be obvious," Robert pointed out. "We'll just set ourselves up for an ambush that way."

The ladies had been paying close attention, their gazes switching from one brother to the other as they spoke.

Isobel stirred. "The palisade." She met Royd's gaze. "I studied Caleb's drawing and read Lascelle's description. I agree with their assessment that trying to cut through the palisade as part of the attack isn't feasible. But what if we could weaken it ahead of the attack—enough to be able to quickly bring down multiple parts of it when the attack is launched? Some breaches might act as gates to get the captives out—Caleb has already established a way to let those inside the compound know what we're planning, so they could be ready and waiting. Other gaps, opened simultaneously, could let your men stream in."

Royd's gaze, locked on her face, sharpened. "Is there a way to achieve that?"

"I don't know." After a moment's thought, she grimaced and glanced at the others. "I can't be certain until I see it for myself—until I examine the construction." Frowning, she looked back at Royd. "But there's something familiar about that construction—the lashing and binding—and once I remember where I've seen it… Anything I can put together, I can also take apart."

Declan leaned forward and opened his mouth—

"No." Royd held up a hand. "Leave her to think—it'll come to her if we let her mind work on it in peace."

He did, indeed, know her well. She looked at the others. "It will come to me—I just need to give it time."

Robert grumbled under his breath about not having that much time, which earned him a slap on the arm from Aileen.

Royd grinned at the byplay, then sobered again. After a moment, he said, "There's really not anything more we can plan—not until we reach the compound and can see and gauge the possibilities for ourselves."

The general, somewhat disgruntled agreement was cut short by Humphrey, who entered to announce that luncheon was served.

They were surprised to realize the entire morning had passed. In a loose group, they made their way to the dining room, where the talk turned to Frobisher company business and the short-term impact of having the pride of their fleet pulled away on a government mission.

The three ladies listened avidly. All three put questions, establishing that, although the company derived no direct payments from the government for their services, they were covered for any losses of men or vessels, were not restricted with respect to any commercial activities they might engage in at the same time, and most important of all, in return for the provision of said services whenever required, the company was the mandated first choice for shipping contracts from a wide range of government departments.

Immediately after the meal, the three ladies retreated to their rooms to pack, while the men retired to the library to revisit their lists and go over their sailing plans yet again.

With the problem of the compound's palisade revolving in her brain, Isobel absentmindedly headed for her room—only to realize that, as she'd been living out of her trunk, packing took no time at all. After establishing that everything that could be packed had been, she wandered down the corridor to Edwina's room and stuck her head around the door.

Aileen was already there, perched on one side of Edwina's big bed, while their hostess pondered a selection of gowns spread over every piece of furniture in the room.

Edwina glanced at Isobel and invited her in with a smile, then returned to her pondering. "It's August. I'm not going to need heavy fabrics for the temperature, but in the jungle, from what you've said, I'll need my sturdier skirts." She arched her brows at Aileen, then appealed to Isobel. "Won't I?"

Isobel glanced at Aileen, then looked at Edwina. "Breeches," she said. "And a lightweight jacket and riding boots."

Edwina blinked. Then her expression cleared. "Of

course!" Almost immediately, her face fell. "But I don't have any breeches, and Declan's certainly won't fit."

Aileen grimaced. "I don't have any, either, although you're perfectly correct—lightweight breeches and a jacket would be the ideal attire for the sort of jungle we'll need to tramp through."

Edwina looked at Isobel. "I suppose you have a pair?"

"Several." Isobel pushed aside two confections in silk and sat on the dressing stool. "I came prepared—I usually wear them when climbing over hulls and rigs in the shipyards. As for jackets, summer riding jackets will work well enough."

"The jackets, I have. And the boots." Edwina whirled to her armoire. She hauled open the doors and started hunting. "But breeches…" Her muffled words trailed away into silence, then she popped upright and swiveled to face Isobel and Aileen; the delight in her face made it clear she'd solved the problem. "I know just who to appeal to."

She bustled across the room to her escritoire, sat, and pulled out a sheet of paper. "My brother's secretary, man of business, account-keeper, or whatever his title—Jordan Draper. He's a magician when it comes to problems like this—he'll wave his magic wand and voila! We'll have breeches."

Edwina scribbled madly, pausing only to survey Aileen—"You're much the same height as my sister-in-law, Miranda"—and three minutes later, her note had been dispatched. Edwina shut the door on the footman. "I do hope Jordan isn't out prowling Julian's clubs. If he's in Dolphin Square, I expect he'll send something suitable around by the end of the day."

Isobel thought that estimation a trifle optimistic, but she held her tongue and allowed herself to be beguiled by a discussion as to the likelihood of them requiring evening gowns while in the settlement or if they might need to attend a church service.

"And then there's the matter of the right gown to appropriately impress Governor Holbrook to ensure he toes our required line." Edwina held up two elegant walking gowns, one in jonquil, the other in blue, displaying them to Isobel and Aileen. "Which do you think?"

"The blue," they said in unison.

* * *

By early evening, they were packed—even the men, who, in Isobel's experience, always left such things to the last moment. Trunks had appeared at the bottom of the stairs, along with traveling bags and seabags; she noted the pile as she descended the stairs and the clocks in the house struck six o'clock. The only items missing were Edwina's and Aileen's smaller cases and Isobel's bandbox, which would join the pile come morning.

Footsteps on the stairs behind her had her lifting her head. The sensation that swept down her back told her who it was.

She reached the last stair, stepped onto the tiles, and turned to watch as Royd descended the last flight.

He, too, glanced at the luggage, then he looked at her and arched a brow. "Ready?"

For what? But she was too wise to ask such a question of him. "I gather the carriages have been ordered for five o'clock in the morning."

He nodded. "Even with four fast horses to each carriage, it'll take seven hours to reach Southampton, and we can't afford to miss the tide." He waved her to the drawing room.

She turned and walked that way. He followed close behind. Determinedly ignoring the phantom sensation due to his hand hovering at the back of her waist, she asked, "When, exactly, is the tide?"

"Half past three. We'll make it."

They passed into the drawing room and found the others already there. Edwina had arranged for dinner to be served at six so they could retire early with a view to their pre-dawn departure. Humphrey appeared almost immediately to announce the meal.

Royd caught Isobel's hand and wound her arm in his. She permitted it; there seemed no sense in attempting any distance. Not when they both found a certain…comfort with each other.

Much in the way she sensed Declan and Edwina did; they'd been married for months, yet still shared private smiles, still touched in that unobtrusive yet telling way of established lovers.

Robert and Aileen were heading down the same road.

As for Royd and herself…as he sat her at the table, she owned to the truth that they had always been each other's "other half." That was undeniable, but whether they could find their way to some place—some workable relationship—that satisfied them both remained to be seen.

Inevitably, they returned to the subject that dominated their minds.

"Do we try for Holbrook first or the fort's commander?" Declan mused.

"We do it simultaneously," Robert said. "I'll go to the fort while you go to the governor's residence."

"One thing," Royd put in. "Send a group of men to block the path from the settlement to Kale's camp first. I'd rather not have any unexpected surprises wandering up to the compound from that direction."

Robert nodded. "Easy enough. I'll send a small squad.

They can guard the path until we're ready to march out that way, then fall in with us."

When the discussion turned to the arguments most likely to make the situation—and how they were expected to respond to it—clear to Holbrook and the fort's commander, Edwina and Aileen made several excellent suggestions.

However, when attention shifted to the logistics of the subsequent trek through the jungle to the mining compound, several comments dropped by Declan and Robert made it clear both were still laboring under the misguided notion that their ladies might be persuaded to remain in the settlement.

Edwina ruthlessly put an end to their delusions with a cheery, "Did we mention Aileen and I have acquired breeches? So just like Isobel, we'll be able to tramp easily down the jungle paths." She smiled brightly at Declan. "Jordan had them delivered an hour ago—such a sensible fellow. He didn't even ask what they were for but just sent a note saying: 'Wear these in good health.'"

"Given the short notice," Aileen said, "I hardly dared hope, but the pairs he found for me fit perfectly. With my boots and the jackets I had made for my earlier visit, I'll have no trouble keeping up." She looked at Robert and opened her eyes wide. "Or even running, as we had to last time. Without skirts, it will all be much easier."

After a second's silence, Robert and Declan exchanged a glance and subsequently said nothing—at least at that point.

Isobel suspected they would pursue the matter with their ladies in private, but if they asked her opinion, she would advise saving their breaths. There was no way either woman would consent to being left in the settlement. Edwina might be pregnant, but she was carrying the babe well and was not as yet encumbered by her increasing girth. As for Aileen…what was Robert thinking?

That question raised another in her mind, one she resolved to address later, when she and Royd were alone in the corridor outside their rooms.

Meanwhile, he and she continued to play their subtle game of mutual enticement. Of minor, unexpected touches and suggestive glances that spiked the inevitable tension between them.

Where such actions would lead, she didn't, at that moment, wish to dwell on. Time enough for that when they were back on *The Corsair*.

It was mid-August and the pavements were baking, but Edwina's cook had excelled in providing a refreshing and delicious meal. Vichyssoise had been followed by jellied eels and trout in aspic, then slices of roast turkey and chilled baked quail had been served with a medley of boiled vegetables, eventually giving way to sorbet. The meal ended with a platter of freshly cracked nuts and fresh fruit.

As she helped herself to a fig, Isobel made a mental note to ensure the supply of fruit aboard *The Corsair* was sufficient to see Duncan through the journey. The market in Southampton wasn't far from the wharves, and she'd already decided she needed to make a quick visit to the local shipyards; the solution to the problem of the palisade was still nagging in the back of her mind. If she could see the things she normally saw, perhaps that would jar the required snippet of memory loose.

"Here." Royd handed her a fruit knife with which to peel the fig.

She reached out and took it, allowing her fingers to glide over the back of his hand as she did.

From the corner of her eye, she saw awareness spark

in the moody gray of his eyes and contented herself with a small smile. She peeled the fig, then made a fine production of savoring the plump fruit in a way she knew would make him distinctly uncomfortable.

For several moments, his gaze was locked on her face, on her lips; only when she had to swipe juice from her lower lip with the pad of her finger did he manage to tear his eyes from the sight.

He shifted in his chair, swung his gaze to Declan, quietly cleared his throat, and asked about *The Cormorant*'s crew.

Isobel swallowed a laugh. Royd would find some way to pay her back; her reckless side was looking forward to it.

Sure enough, when half an hour later, after deciding against wasting any time in the drawing room and dismissing any need for tea, the group climbed the stairs and, at their head, separated with goodnights and reminders of the early hour of their departure, instead of letting his hand hover at the back of her waist, Royd set his palm firmly in place—as if reclaiming the right that once had been his to possessively guide her before him.

She had too much control to overtly react; she smiled at the others and returned their goodnights. But inside, waves of warmth spread from where his hand burned through the two layers of fine silk separating his hard palm from her skin. One wave rose to fill her breasts, leaving them heated and swollen. A second wave sank to her hips, infused her womb, heated her thighs, and made her knees weak.

Her lungs constricted. As with outward serenity she walked before him down the corridor to their rooms, longing flooded her. A yearning for him. Deep and abiding, that yearning had never left her. Over all the years, it had remained, dormant perhaps, yet always there, immutable and unchanging.

As it rose and crashed through her, shaking her to her core, she realized that, if anything, the power of that yearning had only grown.

But she wasn't the girl-woman she'd been eight years ago, and he wasn't the man with whom she'd naively handfasted.

She halted before her door and turned to face him, and finally his hand fell from her back.

The temptation to reach out and re-establish contact surged, but she suppressed it and met his eyes. "Just so we're clear, you're not imagining I won't accompany you to the compound."

He'd halted when she'd turned; they were standing far closer than mere friends would—a wordless declaration of sorts.

He studied her for a second, as if tracing her train of thought back to what had given rise to the statement-cum-question. Then his lips twisted wryly. "I'm not my brothers."

"No, you aren't." She'd never been the least intrigued—and even more importantly, challenged—by them. They were, if not typical, then reasonably predictable. He was not. With him, one assumed at one's peril.

He confirmed that by stating, "Just so we're clear, from now on, I intend to share everything—every aspect of my life—with you." He held her gaze. "Nothing held back—not anymore."

The promise in his eyes shivered through her. She arched a brow as if unimpressed. "Just as well."

His gaze roved over her face, an intimate exploration all on its own. His eyes returned to hers; he held her gaze for an instant, then, his voice low, said, "We should get what sleep we can. Tomorrow will be a very long day."

She didn't take her eyes from his. Couldn't. "Indeed."

A pregnant second followed, then they surrendered. Whether she stepped to him or he to her, she had no clear idea. Once she was in his arms and his lips were on hers, all rational thought faded. Fled.

She slid her hands up to his shoulders, gripped and clung as he surged into her mouth, and she gave herself over to sharing this moment, to giving and taking what she needed *now.*

With his lips on hers and hers on his, her senses drew in to focus on the kiss.

On the exchange, on the rioting sensations and the storm of feelings the simple communion unleashed.

There was, Royd thought, drawing her deeper into his arms, angling his head to deepen the kiss yet further, nothing simple about what erupted between them—what still simmered, so hot, so vital, so demanding, within them.

It claimed them both—effortlessly. Caught them and trapped them in this world in which they'd played before, in which their reckless, highly sensual natures instinctively reveled, freed to experience, to seize, to wonder.

Together, to explore every pleasure.

He plundered the dark haven of her mouth, savored the lingering hints of fig on her tongue, while she moved into him, shifting sensuously against him, wordlessly urging him on.

The kiss drew them both deep. More heated, more steeped in promise—because the very action of seizing the kiss, of giving in to the compulsion of the moment as they had, said something.

Quite what, he wasn't yet game to define; with her, that would be premature. But that they'd both stepped forward meant they both were ready to go further.

He was entirely as one with her as they did precisely that, their mouths melding, tongues tangling and inciting in ways far more potently evocative than they'd deployed eight years before.

Eight years before, they hadn't wanted with this much frustrated, pent-up desperation.

The surging, swelling, tumultuous need was very much there, coloring each foray, driving them further.

Her lips demanded, commanded, and he responded by ravaging her mouth, plundering her senses, and satisfying his.

As always, her responses—her blatant wildness and her unscreened wanting—captured him and drew him on.

Her passion had always been a siren's song to him, an elemental call to the male inside him, an irresistible beckoning.

But he couldn't let her lure him on.

Not yet.

He knew just when to draw back—when her hunger had flared and her desire surged.

The effort nearly staggered him, but he raised his head and all but ripped his lips from hers.

Ignoring the harsh rasp of his breathing and the rapidity of hers, he looked into her face, into the sultry depths of her eyes, and managed a smile, although he suspected it was crooked.

She blinked at him dazedly.

Her grip on his shoulders had eased. He grasped her upper arms and gently set her back from him. He held her until she caught her balance, then forced himself to release her.

Her eyes, fixed on his face, slowly narrowed.

At the sight, his smile grew more genuine and deepened. He stepped back and saluted her. "Until tomorrow at four thirty."

He didn't wait for her reaction but turned and walked the few paces to his door.

He heard no sound from behind him. Curious, on reaching the door, he grasped the knob, then paused and looked back.

In the soft light of the corridor lamps, he saw her eyes had narrowed to dark slits. They remained locked on him.

Isobel waited a heartbeat, sensing—assessing—the heightened tension between them, then softly said, "Two can play at that game, you know."

Her tone made the words a sultry challenge.

Across the ten feet that separated them, his eyes held hers; the intensity of the connection was so weighty, so real, she would have sworn sparks flashed and smoldered.

Then his lips curved slightly, tauntingly, and his deep voice reached her, dark and low. "Feel free to take me on anytime."

Then the damned man opened the door and went into his room.

She heard the door softly shut.

Leaving her struggling to breathe deeply enough to steady her whirling senses.

And to wonder if the water in her pitcher would be cold enough to douse her fire.

* * *

At four o'clock the following afternoon, Isobel stood beside Royd on the upper deck of *The Corsair* and, with a sense of excitement she'd never felt before, watched the sails unfurl.

The ship surged. The wind whipped her hair; fine spray stung her cheeks. She drew in a deep breath, her smile distinctly giddy.

Still high in the western sky, the sun beamed down

upon them and the other ships following in their wake—an omen, a benediction.

They'd led the departing ships out of the basin. *The Corsair* was well known—larger ships gave way to her speed and agility, while smaller ships stood in awe of her power. The wind was brisk, and Southampton Water already lay largely behind them. Ahead, the waters of the Solent glimmered and beckoned.

Then the royals unfurled, and the ship literally lifted on the wind. Clinging to the forward rail beside her, Duncan cheered.

Grinning, she looked down at him, drinking in the sight of his hair ruffling over his forehead, of the bright-eyed delight in the face beneath.

As she'd expected, although he'd missed her, his life aboard ship had been filled with activities—the sort of activities he'd long dreamed of. When she'd finally come aboard an hour ago, a mere half hour before they'd slid away from the wharf, he'd been waiting to greet her with hugs and smiles and endless chatter about all he'd done.

He was happy.

And she was content.

She cut a glance at Royd; standing behind the wheel, he was currently engaged in steering *The Corsair* into the Solent. She didn't know how much he'd already heard of his son's exploits; he'd come aboard before she had. She was sorry to have missed seeing how Duncan had greeted him; it might have told her more of how their son now saw his father.

She looked ahead—and again felt a surge of exhilaration and knew she wasn't the only one so affected.

By the time they'd gathered for their early breakfast, they'd all been impatient and eager, gripped by a sense of needing to get on, to plunge into this mission—to get on the waves. Promptly at five o'clock, three carriages had arrived, and they'd piled in and set out.

They'd rattled down the highway at a breakneck pace. On arriving outside the Frobisher Shipping office, the three ladies had consulted while the men had paid off the carriages. Subsequently, with Royd, Robert, and Declan needing to get aboard their respective ships, Edwina and Aileen had accompanied Isobel on a visit to the local shipyards. Over breakfast, she'd explained her notion of visiting the yards in the hope the sight of familiar construction would jog her memory regarding some method of breaching the palisade.

Royd had wanted to come with her, but he'd had too much to do aboard; he'd taken charge of her trunk and bandbox, squeezed her hand, wished her luck, and let her go.

As a Carmichael, she was assured of being granted instant access to the yards; the name was synonymous with excellence in shipbuilding and revered in such circles throughout the British Isles.

The foreman at the yard had gabbled a welcome and immediately sent for the owner, but before that worthy appeared, she'd spied what she—their mission—needed. When the owner had come hurrying up, the tails of his coat flapping, she'd smiled, complimented him on his yard—which had, indeed, appeared well run—and asked to borrow the special saw.

The owner hadn't hesitated, pressing her to borrow whatever she needed; the tool wasn't expensive, although it was of a very particular design. After assuring the owner that the saw was all she required and that she would return it to the yard on her return to the port, she'd parted from him in excellent humor.

As they'd hurried back to the wharf, Aileen had asked, "Will it work?"

"It's used to cut through tarred ropes, large ones that have been in position for years and are hardened and solid." She'd glanced at the oilskin-wrapped saw. "I'm as certain as I can be that it'll cut through those vines locking the palisade's planks together. To my mind, the only question remaining is how best to wield it."

The satisfaction of having found the answer she'd been seeking buoyed her. The desire to reach the compound and find out if her hunch about the saw would prove correct only added to her innate impatience.

Royd rapped out an order, drawing in a sail—getting just that touch more power from the wind angling at their backs. She glanced at his face and grinned. If she was impatient, he was equally so. And he'd infected his crew with the same keenness; they were looking ahead, all eager to get on.

The Corsair was running hard before the wind.

She turned and looked back at the flotilla of vessels departing on the tide, strung out behind them and dwindling in size as *The Corsair* leapt ahead. A moment sufficed to identify *The Trident*, graceful as a swan as she eased into the Solent's deeper waters. *The Cormorant* lay not far astern, sails billowing as Declan kept to the script and followed, rather than jockeyed for the lead. Neither ship had yet gone to full sail; as there were other ships around and before them, they would have to wait for the more open waters of the Channel before they unfurled more canvas.

She faced forward as Royd called another change and saw Duncan's lips move as, gazing raptly at the sail in question, he parroted Royd's words. No doubt committing them and their effect to memory.

Raising her gaze from her son's face to his father's, she reflected that Duncan's wholehearted plunge into life on the waves was only to be expected—his inheritance, as it were. She now accepted she'd been wrong to keep him from sailing, not when the activity gave him so much pleasure.

After a moment, she stepped back from the railing. When Royd glanced at her, with her eyes, she directed his attention to Duncan. He looked, then looked back at her, a question in his eyes: Was he interpreting her intention correctly? With a dip of her head, she consigned Duncan to his care and headed for the ladder.

She went down to the stern cabin, checked her brown trunk, and put the brushes, combs, and pins from her bandbox back into the drawer in the washstand. Then she sat on the bed and gave herself over to her thoughts.

Later, when they were well out in the Channel and *The Corsair* was slicing through the waves, having achieved a modicum of mental clarity, she returned to the deck.

Instead of climbing to the upper deck, she strolled down the ship, making for the bow. One glance to the rear informed her that they were already far ahead of the other ships; she couldn't even see them.

Idly ambling along the side, she realized that, out of instinct rather than intention, she was noting lines and checking ropes. Then she spied Duncan skipping down the opposite side of the deck; when he turned and called something to someone behind him, she looked and saw Royd pacing forward. He was, rather more deliberately, doing as she had been—checking that all was right on his ship, all as he wished it to be.

He saw her and changed tack, unhurriedly crossing the deck and ducking under a boom to join her.

She leaned back against the ship's side and watched as Duncan danced on, with Williams, the quartermaster, stepping into Royd's place and shadowing Duncan. Keeping him safe.

Royd settled against the upper rail beside her, his shoulder brushing hers.

Her gaze on Duncan, she said, "I had to keep him away from the docks. If given the chance, he would have crawled and climbed all over, but everyone there knew of our handfasting, and he was instantly recognizable as your son."

Royd considered the comment and why she was making it now, at that moment in time. While his immediate reaction was one of deep-seated anger, it was a useless emotion, one with no outlet—one that wouldn't help him attain his goal.

He let the hurt flow from him, too…then thought to ask, "Does he know of your work?"

She shook her head. "He knows I help his grandfather manage the shipyards—I suspect he thinks I'm some sort of secretary."

Royd snorted. It was tempting to feel that Duncan not knowing of her work—her worth—was a small penance for her having hidden the boy from him, yet…that seemed wrong, too—equally wrong. Something else that needed to be rectified. Their son deserved to properly appreciate the brilliance of his mother.

Who'd borne him alone, birthed him alone, and raised him alone, until now.

His gaze, like hers, following Duncan, he said, "I understand why you hid him from me. Now tell me how you managed it." It was important, he realized, that he learn the whole truth, and the only source of that whole truth was her.

"It wasn't as hard as you might think. Back then, Papa was doing everything himself—brokering the deals, handling all the details, and overseeing the design and construction as well. He was rarely home, and even less frequently did he visit Iona—if you recall, he and she don't often see eye to eye, and after we'd handfasted and you'd sailed, I'd moved to Carmody Place to live with her."

He narrowed his eyes against the sun's glare. "Are you saying your father doesn't know?"

"He didn't know—not when Duncan was born, not as he grew. Not until recently." She paused, then went on, "About two months ago, Papa came to see me at Carmody Place. It was Sunday, and I wasn't expecting him—there was an urgent issue with a build on which he needed my opinion. It was a sunny afternoon in June. All the children were playing outside, and I was in the kitchen with most of the other women. Iona had gone upstairs for a nap, so she wasn't about. The footman knew Papa, of course, and with no one around to direct him, he showed Papa into the parlor."

"Let me guess. The parlor overlooks the area where the children were playing."

She nodded. "By the time I was summoned and reached the parlor, Papa was standing by the window, and he'd already noticed Duncan. Had already guessed he was a Frobisher." She drew in a breath, then exhaled. "But he still didn't know."

She glanced at him, her eyes searching his face; he felt her gaze, but didn't meet it. "From a distance, Papa couldn't see me in Duncan, so he still hadn't realized Duncan was ours. I breathed a sigh of relief and shut the parlor door."

He glanced at her in time to see her lips quirk resignedly.

"We were discussing the problem at the yards when

Duncan burst in to tell me something." She gestured with one hand. "I still don't know what, but he flew across the room and flung himself at me—you've seen how he does—and yelled, 'Mama! Mama! Guess what?'"

He could see the scene clearly. He shook his head. "Your poor father."

"Indeed. I believe he came closer to fainting than he ever has in his life. I had to push him into an armchair. I sent Duncan to fetch a glass of whisky. He brought a full glass. Papa drained it."

Royd was struggling not to laugh, but in that moment, he truly felt sorry for James Carmichael. The man had never been entirely happy about Royd wanting to marry his daughter, and as things had turned out, his reservations had appeared well founded. To then stumble on Duncan in such a way and discover all Isobel had concealed…

He glanced at her. "So what happened next?"

"Papa insisted we tell you, but we convinced him to hold his tongue, at least for the moment."

"By we, you mean you and Iona?"

"And Mama, and my Carmichael grandmother—Papa's mother, Elise—and his sister and Mama's sisters." She shrugged. "Virtually all the women on both sides of the family."

"They *all* knew?"

"Only Iona and Mama actually *knew*, so to speak, but of course, the others all guessed." She glanced at him as if that should have been obvious. "A baby—let alone a child like Duncan—is rather hard to hide."

Yet you managed for eight years. But the rancor he'd expected to feel wasn't strong enough to register over all the other thoughts and attendant feelings whirling through his head. Several thoughts clicked into a whole.

"That's why, in our recent meetings, your father's been… uncomfortable and oddly short with me."

"Yes. He's distinctly uncomfortable about the whole thing."

"Hardly surprising."

"No—it's worse than that. It's not just you. Mama and Papa know your parents, too. And Duncan is—possibly—your heir."

There was no "possibly" about it; as his firstborn son, Duncan *was* his heir.

Of course, he and she still had to tie that up in a legally acceptable way.

Her gaze tracking Duncan as he rounded the bow and headed toward them, she sighed. "Papa has hated every minute of not being able to tell. Bad enough what you'll think, but he worries more about your parents—he and your father go back a long way."

Initially as businessmen operating in allied spheres, but as she'd noted, the connection had remained as James and Fergus had aged. It was one of the reasons many had deemed a marriage between him and her an inspired alliance.

It still was.

He pushed away from the ship's side as Duncan neared. "Once we get back, we'll have to tell my parents. I've no idea how they'll react—I doubt Mama will forgive you for keeping Duncan from her anytime soon—but that's something we don't need to concern ourselves with now."

Isobel didn't disagree. She watched as Royd crouched as Duncan ran up. Watched as their son gabbled excitedly about the fish he'd spotted from the bow. Watched as the man she still loved rose and tousled their son's dark hair, then he glanced at her, met her eyes, briefly nodded, then headed off to his stern deck with Duncan skipping alongside, still peppering him with questions.

She folded her arms, leaned back against the side, and let her thoughts flow with the roll of the waves and the rise and fall of the deck.

She knew Royd prioritized. He always had; it was the way his mind worked. A large part of his success was due to the intensity he could bring to bear on any goal. And that intensity stemmed from his ability to focus on that which he wished to attain, excluding well-nigh everything else.

Right now, his focus was on the mission, specifically on the mission's goals. Which was, in the wider scheme of things, well and good—how things should be.

That said, while she didn't disagree with his consigning telling his parents about Duncan to an unspecified date in the future—a date when he and she no longer had higher claims on their time and wits—there were several other matters unconnected with the mission that, in her opinion, would be better dealt with over the next days. In the hiatus before they reached Freetown and plunged into the heart of the action.

She knew Royd well enough to be certain that, with the mission now fixed as top priority in his mind, he would leave those other matters unaddressed and unresolved.

Men had one-track minds. She, in contrast, was all woman, and she was unwilling to wait until after the mission to bring those other matters to a head.

Four

She bided her time, waiting until they'd dined, and she'd put Duncan to bed and watched over him until he slept, before making her way above deck. As she'd expected, Royd stood at the wheel, guiding *The Corsair* into the twilight.

While at sea, he dined at six with the men of the first dog watch. Then at eight, he went on deck and took the wheel for the first four bells of the first watch. Occasionally, he claimed the wheel at other times, either to steer the ship through some tricky situation or simply to spell Liam Stewart or William Kelly.

She'd heard the second bell of the first watch rung some time ago. Now she'd made up her mind as to her next step, she had no difficulty drawing patience to her.

After wrapping her shawl more tightly about her shoulders, she walked down the deck. She felt Royd's gaze touch her back, but a snapping sail high above diverted his attention. He barked out orders, and two sailors leapt to the rigging.

She reached the bench across the bow and sat. After a moment, she drew her legs up, knees bent, wriggled around, and set her back to the gunwale.

They were still in the lower reaches of the Channel, or so she assumed; evening skies and steel-blue waves looked much alike to her. Although the first stars were already glimmering in the darkened sky, she wasn't sailor enough to use them to determine their position.

In recent years, she'd sailed with Royd more times than she could count—when they took the ships they'd worked on out to test their modifications—yet even when they were testing for speed, they never went this fast. This consistently fast. The sense of power, of unstoppable momentum, as *The Corsair* leaned before the wind still made her catch her breath.

The sensation thrilled her, stirred the wild side of her, and she could readily understand why Royd worked as he did to achieve this—this triumph of harnessing the wind.

She drew her legs close, wrapped her arms about her calves, and rested her chin on her knees.

And rode the waves and listened to the wind whisper.

She was still sitting, simply being, at one with the wind, the sky, and the sea, when the fourth bell of the first watch was rung.

A few minutes later, Royd walked out of the shadows cast by the running lights.

She raised her head and swiveled to set her feet on the deck. "Are you going down?"

He gave her his hand and drew her to her feet. "I'm done for the day. I thought you would have already retired."

She tugged her shawl into place and shrugged. "I was thinking." *Plotting and planning.*

Royd turned and walked beside her to the aft hatch. She'd been "thinking." Sometimes, she sat and thought and the result was some new design or improvement. But at other times, her thinking was a prelude to danger.

As he followed her down the steps and into the corridor leading to their cabins, he wondered in which direction her recent thoughts had taken her.

He was tempted to ask, but they'd reached the doors to their cabins, hers dead ahead, his to the right.

Her fingers closed about her doorknob; she released the latch and turned to face him.

Instead of the simple "good night" he'd expected, that he'd planned on deflecting long enough to steal another kiss, she studied him for a heartbeat, then said, "There's an issue we need to address."

They were standing mere inches apart; the unique perfume he associated with her—a combination of the herbs in her soap and the elemental scent of woman—was wreathing around his brain. With his senses and a good portion of his wits already distracted, he tried but couldn't imagine what she meant. He arched a brow. "What issue?"

Her dark eyes locked with his. "This."

She closed the distance between them, slid a hand behind his nape, drew his head down, and pressed her lips to his.

Before he could react, she took one last step—and her body met his, her breasts to his chest, her hips to his, her firm thighs riding against the length of his.

His brain seized. His senses flared.

She parted her lips, and he was already falling.

No power on earth could have prevented his arms from locking about her, his hands from splaying over her back and seizing, his lips and tongue from surrendering, avid and greedy, to her invitation.

Then, quite deliberately—with a deliberation that was statement, declaration, and challenge rolled into one—having seized their reins, she let them go.

Let them fall.

And there was nothing left—no restrictions, no reservations, no reason at all—to stop them from plunging into the maelstrom of a passion too-long denied.

It erupted and swallowed them whole.

Heated hunger rose. Need flared, far more visceral and demanding than mere desire. His arms tightened, crushing her to him. Her fingers speared through his hair, and her nails pricked his scalp like spurs. He angled his head and ravaged her mouth. Her other hand clutched his shoulder, while with her lips and tongue, she taunted and provoked, dancing in the flames they'd invoked.

Without warning, she pivoted, pulling him away from his door.

Trapped in the kiss, he moved with her, obligingly swinging around.

His shoulder hit her door. Already unlatched, it swung wide.

With them still locked in the kiss, in their ever-tightening embrace, she surged against him, and he stepped back into the cabin.

She followed in a heated rush of feminine curves. Of demanding lips, greedy hands, and commanding, demanding desires.

Understanding bloomed in his lust-fogged brain; she really did mean what her scorching kisses, her urgent hands, and her flagrantly blatant actions were telling him.

She wasn't interested in any slow, step-by-step wooing.

Had he really thought she would be?

The point was moot given she showed every intention of waltzing them to the bed.

He reached back and managed to shut the door without slamming it.

The recollection that Duncan lay sleeping in the next

cabin rose through the sensual haze, but he was certain she wouldn't have forgotten that; if she saw no reason to conduct this elsewhere, he could, he felt, safely follow her lead.

That was the last rational thought he entertained. Her busy fingers had opened his shirt. She gripped the sides and yanked them wide, then her hands were on his skin.

Sensation seared him, fracturing all thought.

Passion ignited; between one heartbeat and the next, it flared into an inferno that engulfed them both.

She pulled back from the kiss, tipping back her head on a throaty moan as her splayed hands clutched his naked skin.

His fingers had found the laces of her gown. He hauled in a tight breath that did nothing to steady his whirling senses. Her urgency had infected him; he wrenched the laces free, then reached for the shoulders of her gown.

She came at him again, and he dove into her mouth. With one hand, he framed her jaw and held her face immobile as he ravaged and plundered.

She'd never been one to yield; there was nothing tame or compliant, much less submissive, in her hungry—nay, *ravenous*—response.

Stripped of all civilized restraint, the kiss had transformed into a communion of hunger.

Of need already raging and passion too hot to endure.

He set his hands to her shoulders and pushed down the bodice of her gown.

Through the kiss, she muttered incoherently and released him long enough to free her arms of the sleeves—then immediately fell on him, gripped his shirt and yanked and tugged, until he let her go, stepped back and shrugged out of his jacket and stripped off the shirt.

From under heavy lids, her eyes locked on his chest;

the corners of her lips kicked upward, and she uttered a distinctly feminine purr. Then she stepped to him, her hands reaching to explore.

The intensity of her touch seared him, but he had a goal of his own before him. Her translucent chemise barely screened her breasts; the sight of the lush mounds had his mouth watering and evoked memories of the rosy peaks—and a sharp stab of desire to see if anything had changed now she'd suckled his son lanced through him.

It was the work of a few seconds to unravel the ribbon-ties, then the shimmering fabric slid down.

Revealing a bounty he remembered very well. He reached for her. The instant his hands closed about the firm mounds, she shuddered and stilled, her lids falling, and her lips, now lusciously swollen, parting on a shaky breath.

He squeezed and watched passion flood her face. It was like stepping into the past, yet a past that had subtly altered.

So much was the same, yet the changes were real.

Her nipples were a darker shade of rose. He bent his head and took one into his mouth, and pleasure, exquisite, exploded on his tongue.

He suckled, and her knees weakened. He locked one arm about her waist and held her to him, and with renewed devotion, pandered to her senses and his.

Gripping his head with both hands, Isobel shuddered under an onslaught infinitely more potent than anything in her memories. His body, the heavy musculature of his chest and arms, was, her giddy senses informed her, significantly more powerful than previously—back then, when they'd been younger, not yet fully mature. Now they were both in their prime.

In this sphere, that made a difference.

A lot of difference.

A lot more…everything.

But that was what she'd wanted to know—or, at least, a part of it. She'd needed them to step into this arena to see if they still reacted to each other as they had—if the depth of desire and passion they'd once shared was still there. Still theirs to command.

She had her answer on that score. But it wasn't as it had been; now it was more.

So much more.

She dragged in a broken breath, raised her lids enough to look through her lashes and watch as he circled one damp nipple with his tongue, then licked. The long, slow rasp shot sensation to her core. She gasped, then gripped and tugged until he raised his head enough for her to duck hers and press her lips to his.

He straightened, and she flung herself against him. Her aching breasts pressed flush to his hot skin—and for one instant, their hands gripping blindly, their mouths merged, their senses swirling, they both stilled…teetering.

The dam burst and swept them away.

Tossed them into a tumultuous sea of aching needs and piercing wants that utterly consumed them.

Nothing mattered but getting her hands on more of his skin. Than filling her reeling senses with him.

He came at her with equal fervor, as driven, as desperate, as she.

Boots hit the floor. Clothes flew.

Somehow, they made it to the bed and fell across the silk coverlet in a wild tangle of naked limbs and grasping hands. Of skins so heated, they burned.

So hot, they branded each other with their passion, snared each other with their desires and needs.

He liked to stretch the moments out; so did she.

They tried.

They fought.

He to hold her back enough to taste her skin, to devour her and feed both their hungers.

She to relearn the contours of his body, to explore, caress, and drive him wild.

But in precipitating this exchange, she'd let some genie out of a bottle, and it wasn't going to release its grip on them until they'd sated it.

They were both breathing hard, their breaths coming in ragged pants, their skins slick with desire, their bodies tortured with wanting, when he finally broke, tossed her on her back, and covered her.

Then he was inside her.

They froze. Caught by a moment of exquisite sensation they'd both forgotten held such power.

She raised her lids and looked into his eyes. Saw all she felt—every emotion roiling inside her—reflected back at her. The yearning, the never-ceasing longing—the sense of loss and of wasted time and of confusion that it had all gone wrong and they'd lost their way.

They'd found it again—found each other again.

Now they had to hold on.

He withdrew—muscles in his arms flickering as he tried to control the pace—then he thrust in again, deeper, burying himself inside her.

She let her lids fall and felt her lips curve—felt her body unfurl and take him in and hold him.

The feel of him inside her, so hard, so real, filling her and completing her and making them one again sent heat laced with joy flushing down every vein.

With an ease born of their past, they fell into a rhythm as old as time, as ancient as the sea. They rode from crest to crest, the landscape of intimacy unfolding before them as memories surged, and they adjusted here, shifted there, and built on what they knew.

She wrapped her legs about his hips and tilted hers to take him deeper.

He pushed back on his elbows, altering the angle of his thrusts, the better to pleasure her.

They gave, they took, they clung and surrendered, and journeyed ever on.

Until they reached the ultimate peak and she flew.

A starburst of pleasure, more intense than she recalled, flared, burned bright, and shattered her. Her nerves unraveled, her senses imploded, and she lost touch with the world as she soared.

He joined her in that second, thrusting deep and muffling his roar in the pillows by her shoulder.

Ecstasy claimed her. Claimed them. Rocked, shattered, and remade them.

Linked and fused them anew. Forged them once again.

Then flung them, hearts thundering, breaths sawing, into the void. Into an oblivion that had never felt so deep, so profound.

So blissful.

They sank slowly, tension flowing from their limbs.

Subtle awareness seeping into their hearts.

Royd sensed the silent reality and accepted it. He'd always known it might come to this. This reforging of a link that, now, would be too strong to ever be broken, to ever be put aside.

So be it. If he was irrevocably linked to her, then likewise, she would be irrevocably linked to him.

She'd softened beneath him, around him. Long minutes passed before he could summon the strength or the will to ease from the haven of her body and lift from her.

She murmured and reached for him—calming the

primitive male inside, wordlessly reassuring him that releasing her didn't mean she would pull back from him again.

Unsettled by that unexpected glimpse into his own psyche, he wrestled the covers from beneath them, then slumped beside her and drew the sheets and silken counterpane over their cooling limbs.

And was rewarded when, all but asleep, she turned and snuggled against him, until he closed his arms about her and settled her with her head on his chest and her body tucked along the length of his. One of her legs strayed across his thigh, and she sighed, then the last vestige of tension left her, and she tumbled into sleep.

He tipped his head to look past the tousled mane of her hair. For long moments, he let his gaze caress her face, drinking in the flushed beauty of her satiation.

Eventually, he righted his head, settled it on the pillows, closed his eyes, and followed her into slumber.

* * *

She woke to darkness and the sound of the ship's bell. For several minutes, she lay unmoving, taking mental stock.

Royd lay sunk in the bed beneath her; judging by the rhythm with which his chest rose and fell beneath her cheek, he was still asleep.

Which gave her a chance to think. At least, about them. While lying naked together with his arms wrapped about her, she wouldn't trust herself to think worth a damn about anything else, thinking about them—about what was taking shape between them—that, she could manage.

Her wits circled, almost wary, but eventually settled to the task. Had she achieved her objective? Had the issue she'd identified been sufficiently addressed?

Gradually, the answer solidified in her brain.

They hadn't clarified all she needed clarified. They might have exorcised the past enough to put it behind them, but she hadn't sufficiently exercised her passions of today to feel confident of where they now were. The interlude had been too driven, too fiery, too impossible to control to allow her to explore where she—the woman she was today, with today's wants and needs—stood with him, the man he'd grown to be.

She'd remained relaxed in his embrace, staring unseeing across his chest into the softly shadowed room.

Moonlight and starlight glimmered and shimmered; dawn seemed hours away.

And the object of her thoughts lay beneath her, and the key to the knowledge she sought lay in her hands.

And her mouth.

Silently, she eased up, sliding sinuously from his loose hold to lean on one braced arm and survey her battlefield. She plotted her course, her plan of attack.

Then she put it into action.

Royd woke to the sensation of silken tresses sliding across his chest. At first, his sleep-fuddled brain assumed she was simply shifting her head, then he registered the warm, open-mouthed kisses she was pressing to his skin, and his nerves leapt and tightened.

Then she shifted and straddled his thighs, and her lips trailed lower.

Eyes still closed, he shifted to lie fully on his back beneath her. He realized he was smiling as he wondered how far she would go…

They'd never ventured in this direction before, so he doubted she'd go much farther.

Two minutes proved him wrong.

When she closed her long fingers about his erection—

already rock-hard—he sucked in a breath. His sharply tensing muscles had his spine arching, stretching.

The caressing slide of her hair over his abdomen gave him an instant's warning before he felt her warm, wet tongue stroke—slowly—from root to tip.

Then, delicately, she swirled her tongue about his broad head and gently blew across the hypersensitive surface…

Of their own volition, his hands reached for her, but before his fingers tangled in her hair, she parted her lips and took him in. She enveloped his erection in the heated darkness of her mouth and sucked.

His hands spasmed; his fingers gripped her head—only to discover that he was helpless to do anything other than hold her to him.

While she toyed with his libido and ripped every last shred of resistance from him.

Isobel gloried in the sense of power that ministering to him, holding him a sensual captive as far as he allowed, gave her.

She'd waited to do this for eight long years. Even back then, she'd known of the act, but the girl she'd been then hadn't had the courage to try it—to press for the chance.

But the woman she now was knew what she wanted, and she hadn't been prepared to wait any longer.

His erection was too large for her to take completely into her mouth; fully engorged, it was thicker than her wrist, a rod as solid as iron with the flexibility of steel and corded with huge pulsing veins, the whole gloved in peach silk—a tactile contradiction that had always amused her. Instead of attempting the impossible, she drew back repeatedly to lick, to lave—lured by the complex taste of him. If wildness had a taste…and the tangy saltiness reminded her of the sea. The lingering musk of their earlier engagement added another note to the symphony.

Yet the physicality of the act was the true lure—the drag of her tongue over the finest, most delicate, most sensitive skin on his big body, the feel of his fingers gripping her head, the restless shift of his limbs as she drew him deep and sucked, and his muscles tensed and tightened.

To her mind, the moment embodied the confirmation that what had been was their past, and this—him and her together in this bed—was their now. Where they now were. Who they now were.

They would go on from here.

This was about establishing their current position in this sphere, on this plane, before they set any compass for the future. With increasing assurance, increasing abandon, she gave herself over to defining their coordinates.

Royd had closed his eyes—tight; he didn't need to see what she was doing to feel the blatantly sexual tug all the way to his marrow. He was fast nearing the point of losing his mind and losing all hope of staving off release, yet he couldn't make himself stop her. The pleasure she was lavishing on him was simply too great.

Suck by lick, she reduced him to chest-heaving, teeth-gritted, near-mindless desperation as he clung by his fingertips to control…then she released him.

Cool air washed over his burning flesh. He slitted open his eyes; she'd raised her head to examine the results of her handiwork. As he watched, she tipped her head, studying…

He hauled in a massive breath, surged half upright, and seized her, then he rolled and came up on his knees. Smiling in triumph, in keen anticipation, he tossed her back on the bed, her head on the pillows. Before she could react, he closed his hands about her thighs, spread her legs wide, then looked into her startled face.

He smiled.

Then he slid down the bed, bent his head, and settled to return the pleasure she'd pressed on him—with interest.

Despite the raging of his cock, he was not of a mind to rush. He took his time savoring her as he never had before; this, too, had been one of those experiences that, eight years ago, he'd left for later.

Later hadn't come then, but the opportunity was here now, and he seized it with reckless abandon.

And pleasured them both by reducing her to arching, sobbing, utterly witless abandon, too.

Her honey flowed freely, as tart as apples in the first flush of summer; it lured him like ambrosia, a nectar to which he could easily grow addicted.

One addiction he would readily claim.

And her responses—the shrieks she fought to smother, the way she bucked under his hands—only fed his determination to prolong this and push her as far as he could.

His shoulders wedged between her thighs, his palms cruising their silken outer curves, he lapped at her softness and listened to her breathless gasps, then raised his gaze and surveyed the rosy flush of desire that now tinted her alabaster skin.

He reached up and claimed one breast. After kneading the swollen flesh, with a fingertip, he circled the tight peak, then closed his fingers about the distended tip and tweaked.

She only just managed to muffle her shriek. Her eyes were opened wide; they locked on his.

He'd never seen her quite so wild, so utterly unrestrained, so frantically needy…this was an Isobel he'd never had before.

The realization sank in—and drove him.

With passionate ruthlessness, he took her up and over one jagged peak, waiting only until her sobbing breaths had reduced to panting before taking her up and over again, sending her soaring into mindless ecstasy.

When she fell back to the bed, limp and wrung out, he knelt between her widespread thighs. She was tall, and most of her extra length was in her long, glorious legs. He slid his hands beneath the globes of her bottom and raised her hips, leaving her knees draped over his elbows.

He entered her on one long, slow thrust and saw her breasts rise on a shuddering breath.

Then he settled to find his own release in the scalding slickness of her welcoming sheath.

He hadn't expected her to join with him again.

Again, she proved she wasn't the woman of his memories.

The lust that blazed between them now seared hotter and flared more fiercely; the conflagration caught them both, cindered all restraint, and left them riding through a raging firestorm of unadulterated need.

It shattered them again. Ripped them from this world in a blast of brilliant ecstasy that wiped their minds and left them floating on oblivion's sea like hollowed-out shells.

Left them clinging to each other in the aftermath, cleaving once more, each to the other, as they had so long ago.

No. The simple denial echoed in his mind as, limbs and bodies still tangled, they slumped together in the cocoon of the sheets. A detached corner of his mind confirmed it—they were no longer those people who had handfasted years ago.

This time, he didn't immediately fall asleep, and neither did she.

As they disentangled themselves and settled once more as they preferred, with him on his back and her against his side, he was conscious of a calmness, a steadiness inside that hadn't been there before.

Cathartic. The exchange had been that; the heated moments of passion had made them let the past go—they'd had to in order to engage with each other as they now were.

But some things hadn't changed. Like the physical joy of having her beneath him, the deeply sensual pleasure he found only with her, and the sense of completeness that lingered long after the act.

How important she was to him—she and no other—hadn't changed. If anything, the imperative to reclaim her had just grown significantly more pressing.

Satiation had sunk to his marrow. Sleep tugged, but rather than surrender, he set his mind to replaying the encounter, like a cat reliving the wonders of an entire bowlful of cream.

He refrained from licking his lips, although he did start to smile—then a less welcome thought doused his smugness. How had the girl he'd known years ago come to be the woman in his arms? The siren who had so recently tortured him with pleasure.

He told himself he shouldn't ask—that he had no right to do so. Yes, technically, they'd been plighted all that time, and she was the mother of his son, but if he asked her, she might ask the same question of him, and what could he say?

He certainly hadn't been celibate for eight years.

The risk in asking was too great. If he had any sense at all, he would let the matter lie—

"Where did you learn to do what you did to me?"

For several seconds, she didn't react, then she raised her head from his chest and, through the shadows, looked him in the eye. Her eyes were so dark, he had no hope of reading any expression in them, but the sheer weight of her gaze had him tensing.

Especially when her eyes slowly narrowed. "Where do you think I learned about it?"

And that was an even worse question than the one he'd feared. Her tone had been rigidly even, giving him no hint at all… He took refuge in a frown. "If I knew, I wouldn't be asking."

She continued to stare at him for five silent heartbeats, then she humphed. "If you must know, women talk—and there are a lot of women at Carmody Place." She lowered her head to his chest, then shuffled to get comfortable and ended somewhat huffily turning so her back was to him.

She yawned, and he almost missed her next words. "I knew all about the theory eight years ago. I've been waiting to try it out ever since."

Ever since?

By the time he'd convinced himself that her last sentence meant what he wanted it to mean, she'd fallen asleep.

Through the dimness, he stared at her, then he slowly smiled. She was lying on his arm. He turned and gently drew her to him so her back was nestled against his chest, then he spooned his body around hers and closed his eyes.

He continued to grin smugly; he fell asleep planning his next move.

* * *

He woke her as dawn was streaking the sky.

With slow, drugging caresses, he led her onto a plane

where every touch sparked magic, and the subtlest pressure of a palm wrought exquisite delight.

He'd searched his repertoire for a special gem, and this was what he chose to offer her. In reparation for his gaucheness, he gave her devotion and worship.

Flushed, heated, awash with desire, Isobel floated in the mists of pleasure he conjured, barely able to breathe through the clouds of sensation he wrapped her in. Trapped her in.

But he kept hold of her. He pleasured her until she was aching—*aching*—then joined with her, and while the warmth built and overflowed, as it surrounded them, enveloped them, and flooded them, the pace remained slow.

Exquisitely, excruciatingly slow.

All the way to that moment of peaking sensation, where pleasure scintillated and glory beckoned. He held her even then, his fingers locked with hers as their bodies strained in naked harmony.

And then came apart.

Later, when their breathing slowed and their hearts no longer thundered, she lay slumped by his side and languidly reviewed their present. One point was clear—their today wasn't going to be the same as their yesterday.

This—the resumption of their intimacy—had been inevitable, unavoidable, something she, at least, had had to broach before she—they—could move on.

Into whatever future awaited them now he was back in her bed.

Or she in his, as the case actually was.

Now the step had been taken, and they'd discovered that, if anything, their physical connection was even more intense than memory had painted it—or perhaps the people they now were needed with a greater intensity than their younger selves had—the next question on her list was simple. *What now?*

They were both awake. She shifted her head on the pillows so she could see his face. "Where do you intend this to go?"

He would have a goal in mind; he always did.

He glanced sideways and met her eyes. "I would have thought that was obvious."

Waspishly, she retorted, "If I knew, I wouldn't be asking."

His lips twitched, but almost immediately, he sobered. His eyes remained on hers. After several seconds, he said, "I want you as my wife. As my partner in life. As my helpmate in all things."

All things? Yet his tone, his expression, what she could read in his steady gray gaze said he meant it. Every word.

The realization shivered through her, and yet…

"And Duncan?" She asked more to give herself a moment to think than from any real doubt.

"Will formally become my son and heir." He paused, then added, "He already is, regardless."

She didn't dispute that. But when she'd boarded his ship, even though she'd accepted that he and she needed to resolve their relationship, she hadn't anticipated this situation. So she hadn't yet asked herself the vital question, much less found an answer.

His declaration, however, required some response.

Obviously, the woman she now was had no reservations over trusting him with her body. That was one question answered, one critical issue resolved.

What she didn't yet know was whether the woman she now was could ever again trust him with her heart.

She had once, and he'd crushed it. Unintentionally,

perhaps, yet pain was pain, and pain of that magnitude raised defenses that weren't readily susceptible to logic.

She no longer blamed him for what had happened; that didn't mean she could erase the remembered pain. Nor could she recalibrate her reaction to the thought of making herself vulnerable to such pain again.

He'd articulated his goal clearly, and she knew him well enough to know he spoke truly. And his mention of *all* things—of sharing his life with her, all the varied aspects without limitation—had sparked a deep-seated, instinctive recognition that such a complete sharing was exactly what she wanted. It was the only prospect she would actively reach for—and he'd known her well enough to offer it.

He was an excellent strategist and an even better tactician. And he was sincere in offering her what she wanted, what she needed.

Today.

It was easy to say the words, easy to intend to keep their promise.

But just as she appreciated that the offer he—the man he now was—had made was a major, well-nigh unprecedented concession, one that cut across instincts and deeply entrenched preferences, knowing that it did, she had to wonder whether, when some unforeseen situation arose, he wouldn't find sharing too hard and, instead, convince himself she didn't need to know.

That had been his attitude before.

She continued to hold his gaze as realization dawned; there was only one way to see if this particular leopard could indeed change his spots.

Like her, he wasn't unnerved by long silences. He'd waited, patiently, for her to come to a decision.

With a fractional dip of her head, she said, "Let's see where the winds take us."

It wasn't the answer he'd hoped for; she saw that in the sharpening of his gaze, the faint hardening of his features. But then he inclined his head in graceful acceptance.

They weren't going to get any more sleep. Moving together, they flipped back the covers and got up to meet the day.

Five

Twelve days later, Isobel stood beside Royd as, under the cover of darkness, he steered *The Corsair* into the wide mouth of the estuary on the southern shores of which the settlement of Freetown sprawled. Peering across the dark water, Isobel could just detect glimmerings of light on the distant shore.

It was imperative that *The Corsair* shouldn't be identified, preferably not even seen; they couldn't risk someone in the settlement realizing another Frobisher ship had arrived and alerting the instigators, who in turn might send word to the mercenaries at the mine. Isobel had been intrigued to discover that the ship carried false name boards and extra flags; she was currently *The Pelican*, and her pennants identified her as Dutch.

Flying three black sails, the ship glided forward with barely a whisper. Isobel was impressed by how Royd finessed the onshore breeze to keep their forward momentum low so the ship slid rather than splashed through the waves.

They were breaking maritime law by sailing without running lights. Although it was overcast and the moon had yet to rise, there was enough starlight to see that their way was clear, and they weren't going into the harbor.

Royd wasn't calling orders, either; the members of the

watch were standing ready to act on his signals. All had sailed under his command for years; they understood the need for silence. Sound traveled all too well over water.

She glanced at Royd. Eyes narrowed, he was gauging the distance to the harbor, some way off to starboard. As she watched, he swung the wheel, bringing the ship slowly around.

They sailed on for ten minutes. As the harbor drew nearer, a sense of expectation gripped her. Tonight would be the first real test of Royd's commitment to sharing all aspects of his life with her.

Since that first night out of Southampton, they'd shared the bed in the stern cabin, more or less as a matter of course. That side of their present was now well established—stronger and more intense than it had been before, and something they both valued and enjoyed. All was serene on that front.

And while she'd wondered how Duncan would adjust to the change, that hurdle had been surprisingly easily overcome. He'd woken early one morning and found them both in her bed. They'd roused to find him staring at them, a frown in his eyes. Then he'd asked the obvious question of Royd: "Why are you in Mama's bed?"

She had to give Royd credit; he'd replied without hesitation, "You know I'm your papa. Sharing a bed is one of those things mamas and papas do."

Duncan had thought about that for all of two seconds, then he'd smiled sunnily and asked when they were going to get up.

She'd given thanks he hadn't seemed to notice that she hadn't been wearing a nightgown.

Her mind shifted to where Duncan was now—fast asleep in his bed below deck. She was rather relieved he wouldn't witness the reckless adventure his mother and father were about to embark on.

Assuming, of course, that Royd held to his declaration.

Finally satisfied with their position, he steadied the wheel and pointed at the men standing ready at the mizzenmast. With very little rattling, the sail on the mizzen was lowered. In similar silence, the other two sails were successively taken in, and the ship slowed, then bobbed on the waves, drifting slightly on the incoming current.

Royd handed the wheel to Kelly, picked up the main spyglass, and walked to the starboard rail, the better to survey the harbor.

Isobel followed. At this distance, to her unassisted eye, the vessels in the harbor were distinguishable only by their relative size and, in some cases, their shape. She could guess how many masts each had, but she couldn't be sure.

With the glass to his eye, Royd scanned the dark shapes, eventually focusing on one. After several moments, he murmured, "Our luck's in—it looks like Decker's at home." His tone conveyed satisfaction and no small amount of anticipation.

"Which is his ship?"

He handed over the glass and pointed. "The seventy-four anchored to the right of the rest of them."

Although she'd never worked on navy ships, she knew what the designation meant—seventy-four guns. She put the glass to her eye and located the ship in question. "You assume he's there because there's a light in the stern cabin?"

"I can't imagine anyone else being in that cabin at this hour, and the light's steady—a lamp, not a candle." A moment later, he said, "It's already after ten o'clock.

We should get moving. I'd rather not have to roust the man from his bed."

"Good God—the thought." She handed back the glass and headed for the ladder.

Royd returned the spyglass to Kelly, paused to signal Jolley to lower the tender, then followed. As he went down the ladder, then trailed Isobel through the aft hatch, down the companionway stairs, and along the corridor to the stern cabin, he reviewed his plan for reaching Decker. If all went as he wished, there should be no danger, yet…

His campaign to win Isobel was proceeding, if not as he'd planned, at least very definitely in the right direction. He'd assumed a slow wooing would work best, but he'd failed to allow for her innate impatience—or his. So she'd filched the reins and rescripted his plan—and he certainly wasn't about to complain. The past twelve days—and nights—had been…like finding port after an eight-year-long storm.

That side of their relationship was now rock solid. But, of course, everything came with a price. Namely, now that he had her in his bed again, his aversion to allowing her to face any sort of danger had also rekindled and grown.

How to balance the competing claims—two opposing compulsions, one an instinct, the other a need—he hadn't yet worked out.

Walking into the stern cabin, the first thing he saw was Isobel bending over his armory trunk. He paused, distracted by the sight of her luscious derriere outlined beneath the thin fabric of her skirt, but after a second, he shook free and walked over to see what she was about.

Testing the weight of knives was the answer. He had a good selection of various sorts in the trunk, and she was busy comparing the heft of two short blades.

"This one, I think." She put the other knife back in its scabbard, then straightened, her selection in her hand. She glanced at him. "You don't mind, do you?"

"No." That much was true. He'd taught her to use knives himself, to throw and defend, but he doubted she'd ever had reason to use the training. He watched as she headed toward the bed, her full skirts swaying. "You're not going to be able to board Decker's ship, you know." When she swung to face him, he nodded at her legs. "Your skirts will make climbing up impossible."

The tight-lipped, narrow-eyed smile she threw him suggested she'd been waiting for the quibble. "Indeed." She waved, directing his attention to the bed—to what lay on the coverlet. "That's why I won't be wearing skirts."

He looked and inwardly swore. She presented a powerful enough distraction in skirts. In breeches? The only saving grace was that at least they weren't skintight.

She'd set down the knife and was busy unlacing her gown. He left her to change and swung his gaze to the armory trunk and his attention to arming himself.

His gaze, he could control; his attention proved more problematic. He heard the rustles as she dispensed with her gown, then the sliding *shush* as those long legs with which he was now intimately reacquainted were sheathed in sturdy cotton.

Unlike most girls, she'd frequently worn breeches throughout her childhood; as he'd heard it, her grandmother had advised her daughter—Isobel's mother, Anne—to accept the fact that Isobel would always be a tomboy, that that was her nature, and as she was destined to inherit the shipyards, perhaps that was no bad thing, and if wearing breeches allowed her to safely scramble over the ships being built and learn what she would later need to know, it was a small and, indeed, sensible price to pay.

Sensible because there were many places in a working shipyard where skirts would constitute a hazard. As Isobel spent considerable time in the yards, he wasn't surprised to learn that she still occasionally wore breeches. He hadn't, however, seen her in breeches for over eight years.

After securing several knives about his person, he shut the trunk and turned to see her repinning her long hair into a tight bun on the top of her head. Standing as she was, with both arms raised and the long lines of her body displayed in short jacket, breeches, and riding boots, the impact of her appearance was every bit as bad as he'd feared.

How in all the hells was he going to corral his thoughts into sufficient coherence to argue rationally with Decker while she was standing beside him looking like that?

How was he going to react to Decker seeing her like that?

Or his crew?

With a final pat to her last pin, she lowered her arms and swung to face him. "Ready." Her expression was plainly eager, but steely determination infused her eyes and informed the set of her lips.

Faintly disgusted with his own susceptibility, he mentally gritted his teeth and waved her to the door. "Let's get going. We need Decker to move before morning."

* * *

Half an hour later, the tender slid all but soundlessly into the deep pool of shadow beneath the prow of Decker's flagship. They'd approached via various stealthy tacks, using the bulk of other ships to screen them, then timing their crossing of the last short stretch, when they'd been on open water and clearly visible, for the moment when Decker's watchmen were as distant as possible.

No challenge had yet come their way. All remained silent on the deck of the big ship.

The plan was to board and reach Decker in his cabin without being seen and challenged by the watch—and preferably to leave equally secretly. The fewer to know of their visit, the better.

As most naval commanders would when in their home port, Decker had only two men on watch, pacing slowly around the deck. Even from the tender, the pair were easy to track by their footfalls; given the usual clutter on the deck of any ship, let alone a navy vessel of this size, avoiding being seen by the watchmen wouldn't be difficult.

Reaching the deck was a different problem. They couldn't risk the clatter of a grappling hook. That left the anchor chain. As usual with a ship of such tonnage, there were two anchors out, both chains attached at the bow. With the current in the harbor running as it was, both anchors had been set to starboard, the chains angling into deep water about ten feet apart, helpfully within the shadow cast by the prow.

Royd glanced at Isobel, seated on the middle bench beside him. She'd studied the ship and the anchor chains and was listening to the watchmen pace. He leaned close and whispered, "You take the left chain. I'll take the right. We climb when the watchmen reach middeck, pause when we get to the top and wait for the watchman to pass, then we go over."

She nodded, then glanced at him, met his eyes, and grinned—all reckless delight. Then she breathed, "Let's go." She rose fluidly and, without rocking the tender, stepped to the left chain.

He mirrored the movement. Grasping the chain, he looked at her. They held each other's gazes as they listened, waiting… "Now," he mouthed.

She swung onto the chain and started swiftly climbing, hand over hand, feet bracing on the chain.

She was fast. Stifling a curse, Royd swung onto his chain and started to climb.

Isobel had more difficulty suppressing the impulse to laugh with sheer exhilaration than she had with the climbing. She'd climbed ropes, chains, netting, and webbing all her life, and the chain's links were large enough for her boots to slide in.

A glance to her right showed that Royd wasn't catching up to her; his larger boots didn't fit into the links, and he was having to work to gain purchase on the chain.

She reached the side of the deck first and swung on the chain to lean her shoulder and hip against the ship's side; protected by the overhang of the deck, she wouldn't be seen unless the watchman leaned right over the side. She was breathing faster than she had been, but was by no means out of breath.

Several seconds later, Royd wedged himself into the same position on the other chain, less than a foot away.

They waited, listening; the footsteps of the approaching watchman were clearly audible.

The man paused in the bow, more or less directly over their heads, then walked on, pacing down the deck.

They waited for two heartbeats, then Royd shifted—but she was quicker. She tipped back on the chain, got the sole of one boot onto the sill of the slot where the chains left the ship, then she pulled up, flung one arm over the upper rail, and hauled herself up so she was standing on the slot, her head well above the rail. One swift glance showed the watchman's back steadily retreating. Courtesy of the bulkheads, masts, furled sails, hatches, capstans, winches, and other equipment that filled the center of the deck, the other watchman, pacing toward the bow along the port side, had no clear view of them.

She tipped forward and flipped over the side, landing silently in a crouch.

Half a second later, Royd joined her. She didn't wait for him to take the lead but darted from the shadows of the raised side and melted into the deeper shadows cast by a bulkhead. From there, she flitted to the cover afforded by a sail locker. The differences between commercial and navy vessels weren't sufficient to give her pause; she barely needed to think to know what structures lay ahead and which would afford them the best protection from the watchmen.

With Royd on her heels, she reached one of the ship's companionways; they slipped into the cave-like cowling shielding the entrance from rain and spray just as the bored watchman neared.

They barely breathed as he plodded past, but as soon as he had, she slipped out and hurried on. They had to take cover again, this time crouching behind a winch casing, as the first watchman passed them again, then they reached the aft companionway.

She'd opened the door by the time Royd joined her. They paused and listened, but no sound reached their ears. With a touch on her back, Royd urged her on. She went silently down the stairs. In the corridor, she turned to the door that led deeper into the ship. As she'd expected, there were two bolts, mounted high and low, so the door could be secured; she slid both into place, then swung around and followed Royd as, soft-footed, he led the way to the door of Decker's cabin.

On reaching the door, Royd put his ear to the panels. She squeezed in and did the same.

No talk. No footsteps or hint of anyone moving. But

there—the sound of paper being shuffled, followed by the scratch of a pen.

Royd straightened and reached for the doorknob. He flicked her a hand signal: *Me first.*

She had no argument with that; she stood back and watched him open the door and walk boldly in.

Decker glanced up, a peevish frown on his face—then he saw who it was who had dared disturb his peace. His eyes widened, and his jaw slowly dropped; an expression equal parts horror and outrage infused his features.

Battling a grin, she slipped into the room and quickly shut the door.

In the next instant, Decker surged to his feet and all but bellowed, "What the devil's the meaning of this?"

Calmly, Royd replied, "Keep your voice down. I've been sent to discuss a certain laxity on your watch."

Decker blinked. The vice-admiral wasn't unintelligent; he caught the implication of "I've been sent" and probably guessed that there was some double meaning in the "laxity on your watch." Regardless, Decker scowled. "What's the meaning of this?" The words came out in a low growl.

Royd reached into his jacket and drew out a folded sheet. He tossed it on the desk. "New orders from Melville. Read, then I'll explain."

Decker eyed the folded sheet as if it were a serpent, then, reluctantly, reached to pick it up. As he unfolded the sheet, from under beetling brows, he glanced at Royd—and that was when he saw her, standing before the door.

His first glance showed him what he expected to see—one of Royd's crew. But although she wore breeches, she never pretended to be a man, and something in her stance, or perhaps her shape, made Decker look again.

His eyes widened, and he straightened. If he'd been shocked to see Royd, he was stunned to see her.

His mouth opened. "Ah…"

"Please sit," she said. "I prefer to stand." When Decker simply stared, she nodded at the missive in his hand. "You need to read that."

Her tone earned her a suspicious look from Royd.

Decker blinked, then he tore his gaze from her, refocused on the orders—and then he slumped into his chair.

His face grew pale. He read the orders twice.

Neither she nor Royd showed any sign of impatience while he did.

When Decker finally looked at Royd, his face had set in belligerent lines. "This is preposterous!"

Royd merely arched his brows. "You saw the signature."

"Pshaw!" Decker's lip curled, and he flung the offending order on the desk. "Melville wouldn't know the first thing about commanding at sea."

His calmness unimpaired, Royd tilted his head. "That might well be true. However, in this instance, although it falls within your bailiwick, the problem doesn't lie at sea but here." With a wave, Royd indicated Freetown and the harbor. "In the settlement and beyond." He caught and held Decker's gaze. "If you knew what's been happening, you wouldn't be surprised to see me here or to receive those orders."

That Decker did not have the first clue about any problem in the settlement could not have been plainer. He humphed and fidgeted, then, with a frustrated gesture, waved Royd to one of the chairs before the desk. "For God's sake, sit down—and tell me what the devil this is about."

Royd reached for a chair. He looked at her and arched

a brow—there was a second chair—but she shook her head. She was too tense to sit. As she watched him draw back the chair and, with nonchalant ease, settle, she had to wonder how he did it. How he concealed—or was it controlled?—his emotions so well during such an engagement. This was a side of him—the secret side—she'd never before seen; she shifted so she could watch his face as well as Decker's.

With an economy of words and, indeed, facts, Royd told Decker what he needed to know to comprehend the enormity of what had been occurring in the settlement—as Royd had phrased it, under Decker's watch. At least in part.

To give him his due, Decker didn't flinch from accepting responsibility, or at least his portion of it. He asked several pertinent questions, which Royd answered candidly.

Avidly, she watched the exchange. In some respects, it might be seen as the old meeting the new, but she thought it more correctly cast as the reckless but effective meeting the hidebound conservative. Decker was certainly the latter.

He was specifically charged with holding the line against slavery of all kinds, but most especially slavery involving His Majesty's citizens; although his remit primarily concerned the shipping lanes, that such a crime had been committed in his home port, literally under his nose, would be a blot on his record he wouldn't easily expunge.

Doubtless, Decker saw all that. Regardless, when Royd reached the end of his explanation, which stopped well short of revealing their plans, Decker's jaw set pugnaciously. With his hands clasped on his desk, Decker viewed Royd through hard blue eyes. "I don't need you to tell me how to handle this." The words were uttered with rigidly entrenched resistance. Decker pushed to his feet, one hand rising to the cord of a bell mounted on the wall. "I'll contact Holbrook. He and I will have this matter contained—"

"You will do no such thing."

The power in Royd's voice reverberated through the cabin; Isobel had never heard such a tone from him. The intensity in the words—the unvoiced promise—gave even Decker pause. He froze with his hand several inches short of the cord.

Royd held Decker's gaze mercilessly. His voice flat, his tone invincible, he said, "Make no mistake. If you attempt to act in any way that might endanger my mission, I will be forced to assume command of this vessel, and I will clap you in irons in your own brig."

As ruthless threats went—threats the one threatening had the power to carry out—that, Isobel felt, took the cake. If Decker forced Royd's hand, and he did as he'd said, Decker's career would be over. Ignominiously over, at that.

A full minute ticked past as the men—one past his prime, the other very much in his—stared at each other. She could almost *see* their wills clashing—Royd's fueled by his commitment to the mission, Decker's by his clearly deep-seated resentment at being placed under Royd's command. Royd, who she'd heard referred to as the lord of the privateers. No real wonder Decker was finding his new orders hard to swallow. That said, although she knew who would ultimately win, they didn't have all night.

She folded her arms, shifted her stance, and focused on Decker. "For God's sake, Ralph! Do you *want* my grandmother to write to you? And to your wife and Admiral Harte?"

Startled, Decker looked at her.

She walked forward, holding his gaze; it wouldn't help for Decker to notice Royd's surprise. "Do you?" She halted. "Because although you might have missed the reference, there's a Carmody involved here, and no, I do not mean me. My cousin Katherine Fortescue is in that mining compound." She pointed to the east. "She was kidnapped off the streets of the settlement—on her way to the post office, no less!—*months* ago. And she's been held against her will by the villains behind the scheme and forced to work in the mine ever since!"

No one had ever accused her of failing to extract the maximum drama from situations such as this. Her delivery had Decker reeling. She narrowed her eyes on his and reached for her ultimatum. "If you don't think Iona can make that your fault, you've obviously been out of her immediate orbit for too long. Trust me, if I do *not* report back that you did everything—absolutely everything within your power without any contemptible protecting of your own dignity—to aid the rescue of my cousin, Grandmama will hang you out on a *very* long yardarm." She held Decker's now-horrified gaze for a final fraught second, then more quietly said, "You know Iona. You know she will." She tipped her head at Royd. "Perhaps you'd better do as he says."

Royd fought to quash the impulse to applaud and worked at keeping his expression neutral.

When, shell-shocked after Isobel's broadside and paler than ever, Decker finally glanced his way, he met the man's gaze with a nonthreatening expression. The notion of Decker viewing him as the lesser of two evils made it exceedingly hard not to grin.

Decker swallowed, then, slowly, he lowered his hand and resumed his seat. He looked down at the order from the First Lord, then raised his gaze to Royd's face. "Very well. What..." He drew in a tight breath and managed a more conciliatory, "What do you want me to do?"

Royd told him. He stressed the timing and the need to ensure the action was passed off as a routine exercise. "We can't afford anyone in the settlement guessing there's a rescue afoot. That means you'll need to keep this from your officers. Give them the information they need, but no more."

Decker nodded. He glanced at the clock mounted on the wall. "I'll send out the orders immediately." He paused, then said, "I'll say we've grown complacent and need to practice those maneuvers we don't regularly use but might, at some point, be required to execute." He met Royd's gaze. "Some of my captains will think I've grown senile, but"—he shrugged his heavy shoulders—"they'll do as they're told."

"That's all we need." Royd pushed out of the chair, glancing at Isobel as he did. She nodded and moved to the door.

Decker came to his feet. He tugged his waistcoat into place. "Is there any...ah, assistance I can offer? I take it you intend to depart as...clandestinely as you arrived?"

Royd hesitated, but the man was offering—which, in his experience, was a first. "For all concerned, the fewer to learn of this visit, the better. If you could accompany us on deck and, once we're under cover, engage your watchmen and keep them at this end of the ship for two minutes, we'll be over the side and gone."

Decker nodded. He waved them to precede him.

Royd led the way, Isobel behind him, with Decker in the rear. As they reached the stairs, Isobel pointed to the corridor door. "Don't forget to unbolt that later."

Decker humphed.

But he followed them onto his deck and did as Royd had asked.

In the bow, Royd reached for Isobel to help her over the side and onto her chain. He grasped the second when their heads were close to whisper, "Ralph?"

She shot him a narrow-eyed glare.

When they were both on the chains and, much more slowly than they'd come up, making their way down, she murmured, "It helps to remember first names—sometimes they're useful, especially to order people about."

The glance she threw him confirmed she wasn't talking about only Decker.

Immediately, he quipped, "And sometimes, they're not." Like most people in his life, she'd never used his full first name, to order him about or anything else.

He saw the flash of her teeth as she grinned, then she went more quickly down the chain and beat him back to the tender.

She dropped into the boat without assistance. When he joined her, she turned to him with a radiant smile.

He looked into her face and couldn't help but smile back. He'd forgotten this—the camaraderie, the way they pitted themselves against each other, challenging each other over just about anything in good-natured rivalry, yet always closing ranks and standing shoulder to shoulder against any outsider.

Another aspect of having her in his life that he'd missed.

He sat beside her on the middle bench and gave Williams the signal to steer the tender back to *The Corsair*. Facing forward, reaching in the darkness, he found her hand, and their fingers twined.

He held her hand as they glided across the night-dark waters.

Six

After they'd returned from visiting Decker, Royd had taken the helm, called up a few sails, and steered *The Corsair* as far toward the northern shore of the estuary as the reefs lining the coast allowed. Finally satisfied, he'd murmured, "Only someone high on Tower Hill with an excellent spyglass and reason to search will be likely to spot us here."

He'd ordered the anchors dropped, and he and she had retired to the stern cabin for the rest of the night.

Now, with dawn lightening the sky, she stood beside him at the stern rail and, through a second spyglass Bellamy had found for her, watched the ships of the Royal Navy's West Africa Squadron depart the harbor and take up station in a long line across the entrance to the estuary.

As the last two ships tacked into position, Royd humphed. "If nothing else, Decker is efficient." He paused, then, his voice low, said, "Incidentally, while I appreciated your assistance with Decker last night, if I'm sharing all the information I have relevant to this venture, do you think you could return the favor?"

She lowered her spyglass and looked at him. After a moment, he lowered his glass and met her gaze. When she didn't say anything, he arched a brow and waited.

She studied his face, then evenly said, "All right."

When he widened his eyes, she smiled and looked out at the blockade taking shape on the waves. "Truth be told, I wasn't sure he would recognize me. Once I realized he had, I decided to gauge his reaction to you and your approach before attempting to use the connection."

Royd grunted. "It's a basic tenet of command to know all the weapons at one's disposal before taking the field. And obviously there are benefits to having a dragon-cum-harpy for a grandmother."

Isobel laughed, then added, "If there's anyone else in this mission against whom I have a lever we might use, I will let you know."

Appeased, he inclined his head, then put the glass to his eye again.

But there was little more to be seen. The navy ships, mostly frigates, were well placed to effectively control ingress and egress from the estuary. No communication from Europe would reach the mine, or vice versa, through the blockade. If a messenger was truly desperate, they might try to come in or go out of the settlement via the coast to the west, south of the estuary, but Kit would soon move into position to block that route as well.

"Thus far"—he lowered the spyglass—"all is going to plan."

Isobel lowered her spyglass, snapped it shut, and turned to lean against the stern rail. "So what have you planned for today?"

He glanced at her and grimaced. "We have to lie low. There are too many who would recognize me to risk going into the settlement, at least not in daylight." He braced a hand on the rail, looking toward Freetown. "I can't even send any of the crew—one sighting of any of us, and the news will flash around the waterfront that *The Corsair* is somewhere offshore. The only thing we can do today is skulk out here." After a moment, he said, "I promised Duncan I'd teach him more knots." Something he could do in his sleep, but at least it would see him spending more hours with his son.

He was enjoying introducing Duncan to all things sailing—to the small things about it that still thrilled him—far more than he'd foreseen.

"When will we sail on down the estuary?"

"As soon as either Declan or Robert arrives. We need them to lock down the settlement before joining us at the mine, and short of seeing them, there's no way of knowing they haven't been delayed by a storm or poor winds."

"In the absence of any delay, when do you think one of them might get here?"

He looked out to sea, beyond the navy line. "I'm hoping at least *The Cormorant* will be here by midnight. If it is, we'll hand over to Declan, up anchor, and sail on. I want to reach the mine as soon as may be."

She made a sound of agreement. After a moment, she asked, "Isn't there *anything* we can do meanwhile?"

He turned his head and looked at her.

She waved dismissively. "Anything to do with the *mission*."

She was impatient by nature—and her impatience would only fuel his. He decided not to tease her further. "We can't risk a daytime visit, but it'll be helpful to learn whether there've been any relevant happenings in the settlement. When darkness falls, we can take the tender, go into the settlement, and call on Charles Babington. He'll have been keeping his ear to the ground, and he moves in the right circles to have noticed any changes that we ought to know about. Also"—he tipped his head toward the squadron—"he'll be curious about that, and we might need him to keep Macauley off Decker's back, plus we need to warn him of Declan's and Robert's impending arrivals."

She could dwell on the prospect of action until it was dark enough to risk walking the settlement's streets.

It was easier to wait when one knew there would be some prize at the end. That was, after all, what he was doing with her—waiting while she learned to trust him again not because he was naturally patient but because the prize at the end would be worth it.

As if in promise of that, she gifted him with one of her open, sincerely delighted smiles. "An excellent idea. I'll reread the relevant passages in Robert's diary." She opened her eyes wide. "So we leave at sunset?"

He grinned back. "We'll be away the instant darkness falls."

* * *

With her hand on Royd's arm, Isobel strolled beside him along what he'd informed her was the settlement's main street.

It was nearly ten o'clock, and the area was largely deserted. Even had there been people about, all they would have seen was a gentleman escorting a lady home; she was wearing a lightweight walking gown of dark-green twill with a small reticule dangling from her wrist.

They'd come ashore two hours before. Royd had directed the tender to pull in at the end of a wharf used for local trading. Even though the squadron was out of the harbor, he'd elected to give Government Wharf, and the moorings frequented not only by the navy but also by all major trading vessels, as wide a berth as possible. He and she had disembarked and, together with a small coterie of his men, had walked into the quieter, commercial side of the settlement.

Once in the narrow streets, their party had split up.

Royd's men had gone to lurk in taverns and see what they could learn. Meanwhile, driven by her curiosity, arm in arm, he and she had strolled the darkened streets into the fashionable district and all the way up to the fort on Tower Hill.

They hadn't walked into the light cast by the flares outside the fort; they'd assessed the edifice from the shadows, then turned away. They'd found the address she had for the Sherbrooks—the family with whom Katherine had lived as governess. By local standards, it was a neat house, situated well within the boundaries of the supposedly safe European quarter.

Royd had asked whether she'd wished to knock on the door and meet Mrs. Sherbrook. She'd considered, then shaken her head. "It wasn't her fault Katherine was kidnapped, and calling on her will risk advertising our presence for no real reason."

She'd sensed his approval of her decision, although he'd said nothing, just accepted it with a nod.

Subsequently, they'd gone to the small park Aileen had described. It was a pleasant spot even by moonlight; they'd sat on a bench and looked out over the estuary.

She hadn't previously journeyed anywhere more foreign than Amsterdam; while she'd been conscious of the warmth and humidity, she hadn't found the atmosphere overly oppressive. A light breeze had wafted past, dissipating the lingering heat of the day and leaving the scents of night-flowering plants to overlay the smells of surrounding humanity.

The settlement ranked as the least-civilized place she'd visited. Edwina and Aileen had told her the areas deteriorated the farther one went from Tower Hill. She was glad she was only visiting. The thought of Katherine living there… Iona wouldn't like it; Isobel didn't, either.

They'd remained in the park until Royd had deemed it time to make for Babington's apartment. As that lay close to the area Royd was keen to avoid, they exercised due caution in their approach, but they reached the stairs to Babington's door without anyone giving them a second glance.

She led the way up the stairs. Royd joined her on the small landing and rapped on the door.

No lights glimmered in any window they could see, and no one came to open the door.

Royd knocked a second time, then reached into his pocket and drew out a set of lock picks. Isobel observed without a word. There'd been times when they'd competed to see who could pick a lock the fastest. She'd usually won.

The door popped open. He pushed it wide and ushered her in.

While he shut and relocked the door, she found a lamp and tinder; a second later, flame flared. She lit the wick, turned it very low, then set the glass on the lamp. The faint light played over the furnishings enough for them to see, but left the corners of the room in deep shadow.

She moved to the sofa, sank down, and looked at him. "Now what?"

Registering the impatience in her tone, he couldn't help but smile. "Now we wait some more."

She narrowed her eyes at him, then sighed and sat back.

He took the armchair to her left, the one facing the door.

Fifteen minutes later, they heard footsteps on the stairs, then a key rattled in the lock, and the door swung open.

Babington stepped into the room. He reached to set his hat on the sideboard—and saw Isobel.

He blinked, bemused…then his gaze shifted to Royd.

Babington recognized him instantly, and relief flooded his face. "Thank God!"

Royd arched his brows, then nodded at the still-open door.

Babington turned, saw the door swinging, and shut it.

"It's nice to be appreciated," Royd murmured.

"You don't know the half of it." Babington crossed to the chairs. His gaze started to drift to Isobel, but then he grasped the back of the armchair opposite Royd's and locked his gaze on Royd's face. "Is there a rescue under way?"

"Yes. But at present, it's a covert operation. For reasons I'm sure will be obvious to you, we can't afford to tip off any of the villains or their contacts in the settlement."

Babington stepped around the armchair and sank into it. "As to that, we've had some interesting developments and unexpected visitors."

Isobel shifted to better view Babington's face—distracting Babington again.

Royd inwardly sighed, but clearly, he was going to have to get used to that. "My dear, allow me to introduce Charles Babington, of Macauley and Babington. Charles, this is Isobel Carmichael"—*Frobisher*—"a connection of Katherine Fortescue, a young lady taken from the settlement and currently a captive at the mine. Isobel is working with me."

Babington knew him of old; he wouldn't have missed that "my dear," nor the oddity of him allowing any female to travel with him, much less acknowledging her as a partner.

Babington blinked several times, then Isobel extended her hand, and Babington's well-honed manners kicked in; he smiled and shook her hand. "Enchanted, Miss Carmichael."

"I would we were meeting under less fraught circumstances, sir. I understand your intended is also in that infernal camp."

Babington's expression grew bleak. "She's been gone for months."

More gently, Isobel said, "You're likely unaware of it, but Caleb—Royd's brother—reached the mining compound. He sent word that all the captives were in good health and has remained there with a group of his men to watch over them, albeit from outside the palisade."

Babington glanced at Royd, the intensity of his hope almost painful to see, then he looked at Isobel. "Caleb mentioned Mary specifically?"

Isobel nodded. "He sent a list as well as reports from inside the compound—they confirmed that all the captives were well. The long and the short of it is that the mercenary in charge prefers to keep his workers healthy, and as he's using the women as hostages of sorts to ensure the men's compliance, the women have not been molested."

Babington took several seconds to take that in. "Along the lines of you can't threaten to damage something you've already damaged?"

"Exactly," Isobel said.

Babington's relief ran deep, easing the rigidity in his frame and the sharpness of his features. He met Isobel's gaze. "Thank you for telling me."

"You needed to know. However, when the time arrives to close down the mine, the mercenary captain will no longer need the men, and then he'll no longer need the women, so we need to get everyone rescued before matters reach that point."

Babington's gaze flicked to Royd. "Did Caleb suggest closure was imminent?"

"Not as such, but all the evidence we've amassed—the reports from those at the mine plus all we've been able to deduce about those behind the scheme—strongly suggests that the instant production starts to wane, the backers, for want of a better term, will order the mine closed. We need to get to the mine and rescue the captives before any such order can reach the mercenaries running the mine."

Babington locked his gaze with Royd's. "Anything I can do, you have only to ask. And"—he drew a deep breath—"if possible, I'd like to go with you to the mine."

"As to that, we'll need your help in securing the settlement—Robert and Declan will soon be here, and they'll be running that part of the operation. You can't come with me—I'll be making for the compound as soon as possible—but you're welcome to join them. My men will reconnoiter and prepare, but if at all possible, we'll wait until Robert and Declan's forces join us before storming the compound."

Babington nodded. "Count me in on that action. But what do you need me to do here?"

"You can start by explaining what you meant by developments and unexpected visitors."

Babington paused to gather his thoughts, then recalled his duties as host and offered them drinks.

Once they were supplied with glasses of whisky—including Isobel, whose preference for the spirit had faintly shocked Babington—he resumed his seat. He sipped, then sat forward, clasping his glass between his hands. "The first development was the disappearance, entirely without warning or subsequent trace, of the naval attaché, Mr. Silas Muldoon. He was here one day and gone the next. Holbrook huffed, and I gather Decker was none too pleased when he sailed in and found his office at sixes and sevens, but apparently Holbrook decided that Muldoon's disappearance was just another instance of men falling victim to the lure of the jungle." Babington shook his head. "I can't for the life of me understand how an otherwise reasonably sane man can be so blind."

Royd sipped, then said, "It might not be blindness so much as relying on the advice of someone who has a vested interest in Holbrook refusing to act over the disappearances. We're fairly certain someone in Holbrook's office is one of the villains—someone other than Lady Holbrook, who now appears to have been only tangentially involved, most likely by passing on information on potential kidnappees."

Babington arched his brows. "As far as I know, there are only three men in Holbrook's office who have his ear."

"So Hillsythe—one of those kidnapped—said. He was attached to Holbrook's office to investigate the disappearances, but was kidnapped before he even got a chance to assess the three."

"Well," Babington said, "no one from the governor's office has done a bunk in recent times, but about ten days ago, the assistant commissar at the fort, one William Winton, also up and vanished. In his case, along with a very large amount of army stores—supplies which shouldn't even have been brought into the settlement, let alone been lying around as surplus. The commissar, who, incidentally, is Winton's uncle, is in a complete flap. They're still trying to determine what and how much has gone, but as the assistant commissar managed all the orders..." Babington shrugged. "At this point, they have no idea how much they've lost."

"These supplies." Isobel tilted her head. "Could they be used in a mine?"

Babington nodded. "All the items I heard mentioned, yes—they'd be most useful in a mine."

"So Muldoon's vanished, and Winton's followed—we have to assume both might be at the mine." Royd considered the possibilities, then said, "Given we have someone on the governor's staff still lurking, that's not going to change our plans."

"The next piece of news might." Babington met Royd's gaze. "Those unexpected visitors." He tipped his head toward the door. "I've just come from a dinner party hastily convened by Macauley and his wife to entertain two unexpected arrivals—Lord Peter Ross-Courtney and a Mr. Frederick Neill. They arrived on a merchantman yesterday, direct from London."

Royd stilled. "Is that so?"

Babington nodded. "They don't seem to be friends but behave like business associates. The story they tried to put about was that they're merely interested in looking around the settlement, getting in some game-hunting, some fishing, that sort of thing… A poorly thought-out excuse, because if that was true, why come to a place like this? Macauley knows of both men—apparently, they're extremely well connected politically and socially and also very wealthy. Both are known as investors, although neither dabbles in anything so crude as business." Babington paused to sip, then continued, "Over the port, Macauley pressed—he wanted to know what the pair was about. After hemming and hawing, Neill said they were considering investing in a scheme to develop suitable areas for housing and were looking to get in ahead of the rush—to get agreements over the best areas before they were snapped up."

Royd frowned. "Is there any rush? This seems an unlikely region for any major expansion."

"That was where things got interesting, for Holbrook was at the dinner, too, and he hadn't heard any whisper of such a thing. Nor had Macauley or anyone else—there were several captains of local industry present. But Ross-Courtney tapped the side of his nose and murmured to Neill that he really shouldn't have told… After that, of course, everyone was falling over themselves to be helpful. However, the critical upshot was that, out of all the offers of assistance made, Ross-Courtney and Neill accepted Holbrook's offer to allow his principal aide, a Mr. Arnold Satterly, who happens to be a connection of Ross-Courtney's, leave to escort Ross-Courtney and Neill on what they described as a perambulation-cum-safari through the jungles surrounding the settlement."

Isobel straightened.

Royd exchanged a glance with her, then met Babington's gaze. "This interests me greatly. As well as rescuing the captives, I've been charged with gathering all possible evidence to expose and convict those behind the scheme."

Babington nodded. "I hoped that might be so." He drained his glass.

"So," Isobel said, "we have this Satterly person, who is Holbrook's senior aide and also a connection of this wealthy lordling, and he's to lead this pair of gentlemen, who've arrived in the settlement unheralded and with no known motive, into the jungle." She caught Royd's gaze and arched her brows. "Dare we leap to the conclusion that Satterly is the instigator from the governor's office, and Ross-Courtney and Neill are two of the London-based backers?"

Royd grimaced. "That's more than tempting. However, while I agree with your reasoning, I'm finding it difficult to credit that two such highly placed gentlemen—who, if they were backers, would surely understand the dangers of being identified as connected with such an enterprise—would take the risk of appearing at the site. If just one person—like Hillsythe—sees them and then escapes, they're done for."

"Hmm." Isobel tilted her head one way, then the other. "I don't know… If they're supremely confident that no one in authority has even noticed the enterprise, much less is focused on it—and you've all been to such pains to maintain that fiction—then I've certainly met men arrogant enough to assume all will continue to fall their way." She met Royd's eyes. "And of course, they're assuming that the captives won't live to bear witness against them."

Royd held her gaze for several seconds, then said, "What worries me is what the real reason for them arriving now might be. Are they, perhaps, getting nervous enough to want to determine for themselves how much more value might be extracted from the mine before making a decision to close it down—and as they would see it, ending all risk to themselves?"

She thought for a second, then pulled a face.

After several moments' unsettled silence, Babington set down his glass. "You were going to tell me what you need me to do. Just say and consider it done."

Royd nodded. "First, you'll no doubt have noticed the blockade of the estuary."

Babington laughed hollowly. "Noticed? Even though we have no ships in port and are not expecting any until later this week, Macauley nearly had an apoplexy. He sent messages to the Office of the Naval Attaché, but with Muldoon gone, there's no one there willing to take responsibility, and the three juniors say they've been told it's an exercise."

"That's the story Decker decided to put about. In reality, he's sealed the estuary to all shipping to ensure no messages travel between London and the settlement and mine. If possible, keep Macauley off Decker's back—not that he's going to be able to reach him. His flagship is in the line."

"Wise man." Babington thought for a moment, then shrugged. "I'll tell Macauley I've heard whispers that while the blockade is—at this point—an exercise, there might be a bigger threat in the offing, and Decker is taking potentially preemptive action." Babington threw Royd a glance. "Macauley's paranoid about pirates and other nations' privateers."

Royd grinned appreciatively. "That will do nicely. As for the rest..." He outlined the steps he expected Robert and Declan to take once they arrived in the settlement. "They would appreciate your input. I'll tell them to call on you as soon as they arrive so they don't waste time casting around in the wrong direction."

Babington nodded. "I'll post a boy on the docks to let me know when they sail in. Will they be coming in as themselves, so to speak?"

"Yes." Royd pushed out of his chair. "*The Corsair* is currently *The Pelican*, but we'll lose the disguise once we sail on. I'm expecting Declan, at least, later tonight—Robert shouldn't be far behind."

He offered his hand to Isobel; she took it, and he drew her to her feet. "We should get going."

Babington walked with them to the door and held it open. Isobel walked onto the landing. Royd stepped through the doorway—and as if Babington could no longer hold back the question, he asked, "How long do you think it'll be before the captives are freed?"

The fear in Babington's voice—fear of loss, of not succeeding in saving his Mary—rang clearly in Royd's ears. He glanced back and met Babington's eyes—haunted and hopeful at the same time—and answered conservatively, but truthfully. "My best guess is within a week."

Relief, combined with a wariness over believing, etched Babington's features.

Royd inclined his head and followed Isobel down the steps.

* * *

It was just past midnight when *The Cormorant*, currently the second-fastest ship in the Frobisher fleet, slipped through the cordon of navy vessels and, minutes later, changed tack to come alongside *The Corsair*.

Isobel hadn't gone deck to deck on a rope for more than a decade. Once again in her breeches, she bit back a squeal—not of fear but of giddy exhilaration—as she swung and dipped across the gap between the ships.

It was dangerous, but so much fun.

She landed on the deck of *The Cormorant* and, laughing, stepped out of the foot loop and released the main rope.

Declan, who'd been waiting to steady her if needed, sent her a look of resigned frustration. As she moved past him, he murmured, "You are going to be a terrible influence on Edwina."

Which made Isobel laugh again.

Edwina was waiting to greet her on the stern deck. Isobel swung up the ladder, then grinned when she saw Edwina's outfit.

The petite woman twirled. "What do you think?"

"That if the modistes in London could see you now, you would set a new fashion, at least for those ladies in an interesting condition."

Edwina sported loose-fitting breeches and well-worn

riding boots, plus a voluminous peasant shirt that did an excellent job of concealing her expanding girth, rather than calling attention to it.

"It also lets in so much more air." Edwina fanned the hem of the shirt. "I'd forgotten how hot it gets here."

Movement on the main deck caught Edwina's eye, and she leaned on the forward rail to call down to her husband, who had now been joined by Royd, "Why don't you gentlemen come up here? That way, you'll only have to tell your story once."

The hidden threat in the words wasn't lost on Royd or Declan. Isobel swallowed another laugh as they exchanged looks, then walked to the ladder.

Royd came up first. When he saw Edwina, he grinned, but immediately wiped the expression from his face and, as Declan joined them, favored her with a simple nod. "Edwina. How was the trip down?"

"Quick and easy." She smiled approvingly on Royd, then arched her brows at both him and her husband. "So what happens next?"

Royd dutifully reported what they'd learned from Babington.

Isobel cut in to say that they'd confirmed for Babington that Mary Wilson was among the captives and, as far as they knew, still well.

Edwina tsked. "The poor man must have been quite frantic."

"I don't know about frantic"—Royd glanced at Declan—"but he's keen to offer all assistance to you and Robert and to accompany you to the compound."

Declan nodded. "Another sword—especially a motivated one—won't go amiss."

"Indeed. And he knows who's who in the settlement better than any other source."

"So what else did he say?" Declan asked.

Royd had already mentioned the disappearance of Muldoon and Winton. He went on to describe the two unexpected visitors who had recently arrived—

"Good gracious!" Edwina looked stunned. "Lord Peter and Mr. Neill?"

Royd's gaze sharpened. "You know them?"

"Not personally but in a social sense. Lord Peter is one of the king's closest confidantes. He's a Gentleman of the Bedchamber and a duke's son. He moves in the highest circles, but he's a bachelor and largely keeps to his clubs and the company of his own sex. On the few occasions I've met him, he struck me as the arrogant sort who believes he's better than virtually everyone else. As for Frederick Neill, he's a scion of a noble house, but a lesser branch, obviously. Nevertheless, he's parlayed his birth into two very advantageous marriages. His current wife spends her days in the country, as did the late Mrs. Frederick Neill. Although I believe the Neills entertain in a quiet manner in county circles, they do not socialize in London." Edwina frowned, head tilting as, patently, she scoured her memory. "Both men are wealthy. Neill, especially, is known as an investor. But both are also known to spend lavishly and be…well, forever on the lookout for ways to amass more wealth."

"So they're greedy?" Royd asked.

Edwina pulled a face. "Yes, but it's well-concealed greed. Both men value their social positions exceedingly highly, so…" Her eyes widened.

"So," Isobel said, picking up Edwina's train of thought, "while they might well be the sort to finance a slave-worked diamond mine, they are also the sort to make certain that their association with said illicit and highly illegal mine remains forever concealed." She looked at

Royd. "You were right—that *is* why they're here. To assess how much longer to keep the mine operating."

"They're heading for the mine?" Declan asked.

"We can't yet be sure of that." Royd frowned, then he quickly outlined all Babington had told them about Ross-Courtney, Neill, and the interesting connection between Ross-Courtney and Holbrook's principal aide.

"Satterly," Edwina said. "I remember him. He showed us in to see Holbrook, remember?"

Declan nodded. His jaw set. "He must be the one in Holbrook's office."

"Most likely," Royd conceded. "But we still need to tread warily." He paused, his gaze unfocused as he juggled possibilities, then he looked at Declan. "Regardless of what we believe about Satterly, Ross-Courtney, and Neill, as far as I'm concerned, the captives' safety comes first."

"You'll get no argument from me." Declan glanced at Edwina and Isobel. "From any of us."

"However"—Isobel planted her hands on her hips—"I would really hate to see any of the backers slip through our fingers."

"If we can trap them at the same time as we free the captives," Edwina said, "that would be the best of all outcomes."

Royd grimaced. "I agree, but experience has taught me we rarely end with the best of all outcomes. However, let's see how far we can go in giving Satterly, Ross-Courtney, and Neill rope with which to fashion their own nooses."

"In this case, literally," Declan growled.

Royd dipped his head. "Indeed. So here's what we're going to do."

Isobel folded her arms and, along with Declan and

Edwina, listened as Royd listed the objectives he needed Robert and Declan to achieve in the settlement, while he, Isobel, and *The Corsair* sailed on up the estuary and made their way by the shortest possible route to Caleb's camp outside the mining compound. "From everything we've learned, those from the settlement don't use that north-south route to and from the mine. They come through the jungle, most likely via Kale's camp, which means we should reach the compound and join forces with Caleb at least a day before they—Satterly, Lord Peter, and Neill—can get there."

Royd paused, then went on, "When they arrive…if there's any sign they intend to close the mine immediately, we'll attack, but"—he held up a hand to stay Declan's protest—"if at all possible, we'll wait until Robert and you arrive with Babington and your crews." He met Declan's gaze. "Given all I've read about Dubois, I would infinitely prefer to go in with overwhelming numbers and preferably with some well-thought-out and certain-to-be-effective distraction in place. That's going to take time to arrange, so…unless Ross-Courtney and Neill immediately move to shut the mine, you're not going to miss the action."

Declan humphed. "All right. But I want it noted that having you and Caleb together is just asking for trouble in that regard."

Isobel pursed her lips against the impulse to grin. Declan was right, but few people knew just how reckless Royd truly was; he'd always concealed his wild streak much better than Caleb ever had.

Edwina frowned. "But if we're to cordon off the settlement from the mine…won't Satterly and the other two notice and pull back? If they see guards along the paths, won't they take fright and stay in the settlement?"

"That's the one change to our plans—the rope we're going to let them take." Royd glanced at Declan. "The first thing you and Robert need to do is to locate Satterly and the other two—my guess is that they'll be staying with Holbrook, but Babington's sure to know. Once you've found them, hang back, and give them a chance to set out for the mine. Trail them to make sure they're on their way, but once you're certain, you can notify Holbrook and the commander at the fort, and proceed with all the steps we've discussed to lock down the settlement—just in case, by all that's holy, we've missed someone."

Declan nodded. "Or we find that Muldoon and Winton have been somewhere other than at the mine, and they pop up back here."

"Precisely." Royd paused, then said, "So we're set for orders." He glanced out to sea. "Do you have any idea how far back Robert is?"

Declan grunted. "Not that far. Once you modify *The Trident* as you have *The Cormorant*, his will be the faster ship again." Royd grinned, and Declan went on, "I would expect to see him by dawn, if not before."

"Excellent. And Kit and Lachlan? Did you get any sighting of them?"

"Robert signaled that he'd seen Lachlan, and that Lachlan had confirmed that Kit was trailing him."

Royd nodded. "It looks like we're set—as far as we can be."

Edwina frowned. "Did I understand correctly that Kit will be the one to patrol off the coast to discourage any would-be blockade runners and take action should any ship try to slip out?"

Royd answered, "Her *Consort* has the best firepower of all our ships, and in such a situation, she's the most capable of any of our captains—and I include myself in that number."

Declan grumbled, "Bloodthirsty woman."

Edwina looked intrigued. She glanced at Isobel. "Kit sounds like someone I definitely should meet."

Isobel grinned. "You'll like her. She's very"—she looked at Royd and Declan, and her grin deepened—"forthright."

Declan humphed and turned to Royd. "That reminds me. Robert passed on a message from Kit for you—she's put some of her men aboard Lachlan's *Sea Dragon.* She said as *Consort* is just holding station, they can be spared."

Royd nodded. "We're going to need every well-trained and reliable hand we can muster." He looked at Isobel. "Now we all know what we're doing, we should make a start."

Isobel's eyes lit, and she turned to make her farewells to Edwina.

Royd thumped Declan's shoulder. "Today's the thirty-first. I'll expect to see you, Robert, and your crews no later than the third."

Declan thumped him back. "We'll be there."

In short order, Royd and Isobel returned to the deck of *The Corsair.* The instant everything had been settled, he'd felt an upsurge of impatience—of needing to get moving, needing to sail on.

Even before he gained the upper deck, he snapped off orders to up the anchors and set sail. Going up the ladder in Isobel's wake, he strode to the wheel.

Liam Stewart yielded with a smile. "And we're off!"

"We are, indeed." Royd called up more sail. Within minutes, *The Corsair* glided forward, leaving *The Cormorant* wallowing in her wake.

Royd steered the ship wide until they were sufficiently beyond the settlement to risk swinging into the main channel leading east, farther into the estuary.

Isobel came to stand beside him. He glanced at her, took in the way the wind twisted the loose strands of her hair, saw the excitement in her face, gilded by moonlight.

After several minutes, she leaned her shoulder briefly against his arm. “I’m going down to get some sleep.”

He nodded. “I’ll join you once I have us on the course I want. We might reach the path inland before dawn, but we won’t go ashore until it’s light.”

With a nod, she walked to the ladder and went down.

Once he had *The Corsair* gliding silently on the correct heading, he handed the wheel to Liam and followed.

Seven

Not that many hours later, Royd was dragged from sleep by a scratching at the cabin door. He gently disengaged from Isobel's embrace and silently rolled from the bed. He yanked on his breeches and confirmed with a searching glance that Isobel hadn't stirred; he debated waking her for only an instant—he suspected he knew what the question was, and she would need her sleep for the trek to come. He ran a hand through his disheveled hair as, his boots in his other hand, he walked to the door. He opened it to find Williams leaning against the corridor wall.

Royd stepped out of the cabin and closed the door.

Williams murmured, "We've spotted a ship anchored close in to shore a bit ahead. We think it's Lascelle's *Raven*, but we're not sure."

Royd nodded and bent to pull on his boots. "I'll come and take a look."

A minute later, he swung up to the stern deck and accepted the spyglass Williams offered. He walked to the corner of the deck, put the glass to his eye, and studied the vessel in question, still at some distance off the starboard bow and tucked into the lee of a small promontory.

Clouds had obscured the moon; in what light remained, it was difficult to discern the color of the hull—

was it black or some other dark color? The ship had no lights on deck; neither did *The Corsair*, but that was standard practice for any covert venture. Royd angled the glass upward and inspected the ship's masts and yards. *The Raven* ran with a distinctive angle on her upper yards…

He lowered the spyglass and handed it to Williams. "It's *The Raven*, which means we've reached our destination." He paused, then beckoned Williams to follow and walked to stand beside Kelly, who had replaced Liam Stewart at the wheel. "They can't see us any better than we can see them, and *The Corsair* is even less distinctive than *The Raven*." To Kelly, he said, "Take us in on their larboard side, but slowly." Turning to Williams, he ordered, "Light the running lights and run our flags—we need to let them know who we are before we get too close, and once we are close enough, confirm by hail." He eyed the distant bulk of the other ship. "We can't assume whoever's on watch will recognize us, or know how nervous they might be—no need to start this junket off with an unnecessary alarm."

Kelly and Williams grunted in agreement.

Royd headed back to the cabin. There were several hours yet to daybreak.

He paused in the corridor to remove his boots. On impulse, he opened the door to Duncan's room and looked in. Duncan lay sprawled in the bed, sound asleep. Smiling, Royd closed the door, then opened the door to the main cabin and, his boots in his hand, padded inside.

He stripped and crawled back into the bed, raising the covers to slide his length alongside Isobel's soft, slender limbs. The touch of her delicate skin against his tougher, rougher hide soothed something inside him. She was facing away from him. He settled his head on the pillow behind hers and spooned his body around hers.

Only then did she stir.

He lifted his head and skated a hand over her bare shoulder. “All’s well,” he whispered. “Go back to sleep.”

He saw the upper corner of her lips lift, then she took him at his word, and all tension flowed from her, and she slid back into slumber.

He studied her face, in sleep stripped of the dramatic animation that so often distracted an observing eye. Regardless of what she might think when awake, her trust in him ran bone-deep; trusting him was an all-but-unconscious act.

The realization sank in and settled in his gut. Or perhaps slightly higher.

His lips curved. He dropped his head to the pillow, settled one arm across her waist, closed his eyes, and joined her in dreams.

* * *

Over an early breakfast, Isobel listened as Royd led the necessary negotiations with Duncan over him remaining aboard. It was a novel experience to be able to sit back and consign the difficult and touchy task to one who—she had to admit—was better qualified than she to accomplish it.

There remained not the slightest doubt in her mind—or, she suspected, in Duncan’s—that Royd understood him better than anyone else possibly could. That was borne out by the tack Royd took, explaining that he and she needed to concentrate on saving the poor people held captive at the mine, and they wouldn’t be able to do that—or keep themselves safe, let alone everyone else—if they were anxious and worried about him.

It would never have occurred to her to appeal to Duncan's nascent leadership abilities. She gathered that Royd had previously described the situation to Duncan, telling him about the children and what Caleb had reported about their lives in the compound.

Given that, she wasn't all that surprised when, his expression sober, Duncan solemnly swore he would remain on board under the care of Kelly and Jolley. As Duncan had already struck up a friendship—more like an apprenticeship—with the bosun, Jolley, and was on friendly terms with Kelly, who had a son of his own of similar age, Isobel had no reason to imagine their son wouldn't be actively entertained as well as adequately supervised over the days she and Royd were away.

She was less certain about his safety. Leaving him aboard ship while said ship was in Southampton harbor was one thing; leaving her precious son aboard his father's ship on an isolated African shore was something else entirely. Or so her maternal instincts insisted.

Unfortunately, said instincts didn't offer a solution.

So she said her goodbyes to Duncan; careful to conceal any hint of her concern, she hugged him fiercely, mollified by the strength in his answering hug.

But he didn't cling; he released her, stepped back, and grinned up at her. "Papa said that while the ship is anchored here, Jolley and the others can teach me to climb the rigging—but only as far as the first yard."

Quashing her immediate thought of broken bones, reminding herself that he climbed trees much higher when at home, she shouldered a satchel containing extra clothes, a brush, and sundry other necessities and managed a creditable smile. Discarding a range of admonitions that poured through her brain, she settled for, "Be good." That, she felt, covered all possibilities.

Unable to help herself, she caught his face between

her hands, drew him to her, and planted a kiss on his forehead.

Then she released him, stepped back—looked at him for one more instant—then resolutely turned and walked to where a rope dangled over the ship's side.

He ran to steady the rope for her.

She grinned, stepped onto the rope, waved with her fingers, then slid down into the tender to be rowed ashore with a batch of Royd's men.

They massed on the beach just short of where a path led into the dense jungle. While waiting for the tender to ply back and forth, ferrying more of Royd's crew to shore, she studied the two ships now moored side by side. *The Raven* was black-hulled, a touch smaller than *The Corsair*, but she rode a fraction deeper in the water and, to Isobel's educated eye, looked to be carrying a significant number of guns.

She raised her gaze to *The Corsair*'s deck and saw Royd preparing to leave ship. The returning tender drew alongside, and more sailors eagerly slid down the ropes, almost filling the rowboat.

After giving final orders to Kelly and Jolley, who would remain with five other men as a skeleton crew, she watched Royd turn to Duncan. He ruffled Duncan's hair, then said something, and Duncan grinned and snapped off a crisp salute—which Royd returned.

Then, his pack slung over his shoulder, Royd stepped out onto the rope and slid down, dropping lightly into the waiting tender.

Immediately he sat, the tender pushed out from the ship and headed for the shore.

It beached not far from where *The Raven*'s tender also crunched on the sands. Five men waded to shore from that tender. Royd sent his men ahead and crossed to speak with the men from *The Raven.* A hand shading her eyes, Isobel watched the exchange. There'd been a short conference conducted over the ships' sides that morning, with Royd sharing their plans to march to the compound with the Frenchmen—Lascelle's crew—so that they could decide what to do.

Apparently, some had elected to join the party.

She watched as the largest of the five men greeted Royd with a broad smile and offered his hand; the pair shook heartily, friendly acquaintances at the very least. After nodding respectfully to Royd, the other four French sailors slogged through the sand to where Royd's men waited. Isobel heard the murmurs as they introduced themselves, and Royd's men reciprocated.

Bringing up the rear, Royd and the large man headed for her.

Royd halted beside her and waved to the other man. "Jacques Reynaud, Phillipe Lascelle's bosun—Isobel Carmichael."

Reynaud grinned and bobbed a bow. *"Enchanté, ma'moiselle."*

Isobel returned a smile as Royd continued, "Reynaud was in command of the group who escorted Hornby back to *The Prince* and saw Caleb's ship on its way back to London."

"Aye," Reynaud said. "I am glad *The Prince* got through, and even more glad to see *The Corsair.*"

"Reynaud and the men who walked out with him are going to return to Caleb's camp with us—they know the way."

"You have Hornby, *c'est vrai*"—Reynaud raised a hand in salute to Caleb's steward; he was standing with Royd's men and saluted Reynaud back—"but more men who know the terrain will be of help."

"Indeed." Royd cast his eye over his men. To Reynaud, he said, "Why don't you, Hornby, and Williams take the lead? Mr. Stewart and Bellamy will take center, and Miss Carmichael and I will bring up the rear."

"Very good." With a nod to Royd and another to Isobel, Reynaud crossed to where the others waited.

Seconds later, the men formed up in a line and started marching into the jungle.

Isobel fell in with Royd at the rear, but when they reached the point where sand gave way to beaten path, she paused and looked back at *The Corsair.*

Duncan stood in the bow, with Jolley nearby. Duncan waved.

Isobel waved back, but she didn't smile.

She felt Royd's gaze touch her face. Lowering his own hand, he murmured, "He'll be safer there than he would be with us. There are fourteen men aboard those two ships, and enough firepower to discourage any marauder. On top of that, *The Corsair* is *The Corsair* again—any pirate captain worth his salt will recognize both ships and steer clear."

Isobel sighed.

"*And*"—Royd closed his hand about hers and drew her around and on—"*Sea Dragon* will be mooring alongside, most likely within twenty-four hours. Trust me—no one's going to take a tilt at those ships. Any pirate will take one look and pile on sail."

She sighed again, this time resignedly. "I know you're right, but a part of me still doesn't like it."

He grinned, but said no more. She lengthened her stride and picked up her pace, and they marched into the warm dimness.

Although uneventful, the trek through the jungle proved more demanding than Royd or, he felt sure, Isobel had expected. The path led them more or less directly south, but went up and down, wound about the flanks of small hills, and dipped into gullies. Given several groups had been up and down over the past months, the path was unobstructed, but the surface rippled with tree roots, and vines snaked across, a risk for the unwary. Looking down and concentrating on where to place one's feet became a habit; they glanced up only occasionally to check their direction and keep their bearings. Not that there was much to see—the boles of trees and palms hemmed them in; rarely could they see as much as ten yards beyond the path's side.

The farther they slogged from the coolness near the shore, the more oppressive the atmosphere grew. They were all sweating freely by the time Royd called a halt for a late lunch.

After taking stock, he decreed they should rest until the sun westered and the temperatures started to ease before moving on again. No one argued—not even Isobel.

As he settled beside her on the ground sheet she'd spread over a patch of fallen leaves, he suspected that, of their company, he was the most impatient to get on. A familiar urgency was rising inside him—the impulse to go to Caleb's relief. He'd felt it often enough in the past to recognize the prodding for what it was, but this time, there was a shift in the emotion behind the prod. Previously, he'd been driven to protect his youngest brother. This time…he felt no real fear for Caleb's well-being; as far as he could tell, his little brother had matured and had run his leg of the mission with exemplary good sense. He had little doubt that Caleb was well, most likely busy plotting and planning. No, this time, his impatience had more to do with wanting to be there and take a hand in the action—similar to Declan's worry over being left out.

As he closed his eyes, Royd admitted he was looking forward to what was to come.

* * *

Hours later, when they finally made camp for the night in a hollow large enough to hold them all, while still impatient to reach Caleb's camp, Royd was feeling rather less sanguine about the time spent getting there.

At least the temperature had started to fall, and a light breeze ruffled the treetops, enough to stir the air below and make them feel they could breathe again.

Somewhat to his surprise, Isobel—who as far as he knew hadn't even tramped the moors—had managed the trek fairly well. She'd survived rather better than some of his heavier men; she was carrying much less weight.

Without anyone asking—no one would have dared—she took charge of preparing the meal. Taking charge meaning giving explicit orders, but none of his crew minded. In the state they were in, they were entirely willing to have anyone point them at something and tell them what to do. Isobel was very good at that.

Leaving her to it, he consulted with Hornby and Reynaud. They pored over Lascelle's map; it appeared they'd traveled more than half the distance to Caleb's camp. "So," Royd said, "if we wake early and walk on while it's cooler, before the temperatures rise, we should, with luck, make the camp by early afternoon."

Hornby nodded. "Aye, and we'll be climbing through this stretch." He indicated a section of the path on the map—the first stretch they would tackle the next day. "That'll be easier going in the early morning, and it'll be a touch cooler once we get onto the level of the mine."

"Good." Royd folded the map. "That's what we'll do."

They woke before dawn and were on their way before sunbeams started to slant through the canopy. The pervasive gloom of the jungle enveloped them, along with the smell of decaying leaves and rich soil, spiced here and there with heady drifts of perfume emanating from deep-throated flowers depending from various vines. As on the day before, there was little talk and no conversation; everyone saved their energy and attention for the steady upward climb.

Birdcalls cut through the silence, raucous and strident, quite unlike the genteel twitterings of home. The higher they climbed, the more often they heard rustlings in the dense growth around them. Several men tugged small crossbows from their packs, but although Hornby and Reynaud confirmed there were wild goats and probably boar in the area, no one sighted any prey.

Finally, the upward toil ended, and they stepped out along a flatter, more even stretch.

"Not far now," Hornby told Royd. "Less than a mile to the camp."

Eagerness caught them all. They picked up the pace, swinging along. Royd moved forward to take the lead, and Isobel went with him.

As he passed his men, Royd warned them to keep their voices down and their eyes peeled for Caleb's scouts.

Twenty minutes later, Reynaud, walking just behind Royd, pointed past him to their left and whispered, "That's the opening to the track that leads to the camp."

Royd halted at the entrance to the track—little more than an animal trail.

Strung out behind him, the column of men came to a shambling halt.

Standing beside Royd, Isobel saw his eyes narrow as he stared down the track as far as he could, then he looked down.

After a moment, he crouched and examined the leaves that littered the ground.

Slowly, he straightened. To Hornby and Reynaud, he murmured, "Pass the word—everyone keep their eyes peeled, but I strongly suspect Caleb and his crew are no longer in this camp."

While the order was passed down the column, Royd turned to her, a question in his eyes.

She shook her head, then jerked her chin forward—silently informing him that she wasn't about to retire to the rear of the column.

She waited to see what he would do.

He held her gaze for a second while he waged some inner debate, but then he nodded. Leaning nearer, he whispered, "Stay close."

He started down the track.

She followed. She could be as quiet as he creeping through the jungle, and if her eyesight wasn't on a par with his, her hearing and her instincts were every bit as good.

They crept down the track so very silently, she doubted anyone could have heard them. When the track cut to the left a little way ahead, Reynaud reached past her to tap Royd on the shoulder.

When Royd looked back, Reynaud signaled, indicating that, after the left turn, the path dropped through a series of steps, and then the clearing in which the camp had been would open up before them.

Royd nodded and led the way on.

In the end, their caution was wasted. There was no one there.

They filed into the clearing, turning this way and that, searching for what, she didn't know. Royd turned in a circle, surveying the clearing's floor. "No sign of any fight that I can see." He raised his head, but kept his voice low. "Anyone see anything useful?"

Negative murmurs came from all the men.

Hornby had paled; he suddenly looked haggard. "They must've got caught."

Royd clapped the old sailor on his shoulder. "Believe it or not, that might not be a bad thing."

Isobel glanced at him and wondered what he meant. He'd been sunk in thought through much of the trek there; she knew he'd been juggling this, trying out that, piecing together scenarios in his mind about what they would find, as well as how they would act and ultimately rescue the captives.

His relative calmness suggested that Caleb not being there—that Caleb and his men having been captured and taken to the mine—had featured in at least one of those scenarios.

Royd shrugged off his seabag and let it fall to the ground. "Make camp. Liam—set our pickets." He glanced around. "We need more information—we're going to find that rock shelf and see what we can see." He included Isobel with his gaze.

She promptly tossed her satchel beside his seabag. Among other weapons, she'd borrowed one of the mid-length knives from his armory chest; it rode in a scabbard belted at her hip and tied along her right thigh. She loosened the blade and stood ready.

"Hornby and Reynaud—you know the way." Hands on his hips, Royd scanned his men, then pointed to two. "Giles, Macklin—you two come as well. We'll be setting up a constant daytime watch from that shelf regardless."

That made six. They left the others sorting out the camp under Liam Stewart's eye and followed Hornby and

Reynaud into the jungle via a different path that, again, was little more than a goat track.

She'd memorized Caleb's sketch of the mining compound and its surrounds. It took her a little while to orient herself, but then they glimpsed a small lake to their left, and she knew where they were. As they climbed the narrow, rocky path up the flank of a hill, she caught tantalizing glimpses of the compound's roofs through the brush and trees to her right.

Reynaud led them unerringly on. He and Hornby looked grim; for both of them, their captains were missing, along with friends.

Eventually, they reached the rock shelf. They clambered onto it, then sat with their backs against the rock wall and avidly focused on the scene below.

The mining compound lay spread before them, a hundred feet or more below. The open gates lay almost directly opposite their position, with the mine entrance concealed beneath an overhang that was part of the rising flank of the hill on their right. The central hut that was the mercenaries' barracks lay a little to their left, a long rectangular building running right to left across the middle of the cleared and palisaded space.

A crude guard tower rose above the far end of the barracks. Beyond the tower lay several buildings they couldn't see well due to the barracks lying between.

It was midafternoon. While there was a pair of armed mercenaries ambling about, another pair propped against the posts of the open gate, and three in the hut at the top of the tower, there weren't any captives visible.

Isobel leaned forward, then pointed. "The girls who do the sorting are under that awning. If you watch, you can see them when they reach out to the piles of rocks."

Sometime later, a gaggle of rag-tag children came out

of the mine, lugging woven baskets. They tottered to the piles of ore close by the awning and upended the baskets, adding more rocks to the piles.

Isobel's gut clenched; many of the children were younger—certainly smaller and thinner—than Duncan.

She vowed then and there that she would get all the children out—and then she would turn her attention to whoever had enslaved them.

The afternoon dragged on, then Reynaud sat up. He stared down at three men, dusty and begrimed, who had come out of the mine to help themselves to water from a barrel nearby. "That's Ducasse—our quartermaster. And Fullard, but I don't know the other man."

"Good." Royd leaned back against the rock wall. "So some of them, at least, are there."

Over the next hour, with growing relief, they identified more men from Caleb's as well as Lascelle's crew, but of the two captains, there was no sign.

Isobel rarely looked away from the hut Caleb had labeled the cleaning shed. On two occasions, a woman came out, walked down the compound and around the mercenaries' barracks, and disappeared, only to return sometime later, but neither woman was Katherine.

Finally, as the afternoon was fading, the cleaning shed door swung open, and two women emerged. Isobel sat straighter. Her gaze locked on the slender woman with soft brown hair; she felt painfully certain, but didn't want to be wrong—then the woman turned to smile at her companion, and relief flooded Isobel. She nudged Royd. "That's Katherine."

He was studying the women as well. "The brown-haired one?"

"Yes." Isobel watched as her cousin crossed the beaten dirt of the compound to where the group of girls worked under the awning. "This must be the checking Caleb mentioned."

After twenty minutes or so of working with the children, Katherine and her companion turned and, carrying baskets of ore, headed back to the cleaning shed. They dumped the ore on a pile outside the door, then set the baskets down, climbed the steps, and went inside.

Isobel sat back. Katherine was alive and well and, apparently, in good spirits. Isobel breathed in, then out. Then she glanced at Royd. Now if only they could sight Caleb and his friend Lascelle, all would be well.

Instead of looking back at the compound, she continued to study Royd's face. His gaze was fixed on the activity far below. His features were rarely revealing, and they certainly weren't informative at that moment, yet still…she sensed he was curiously patient and not at all concerned over Caleb.

Given Royd's protective streak—a trait with which she was well acquainted—that seemed distinctly odd.

They were sitting at one end of the rock shelf, with a corner beyond her; the other men were far enough away to risk a quiet conversation. Leaning back against the rock wall, close enough that her shoulder brushed Royd's, she murmured, "Why are you so certain Caleb's still alive and that he's down there somewhere?"

Royd glanced sideways at her. After a moment, he murmured, "I suppose, logically speaking, I don't know, yet… I do." He looked back at the scene below, then went on, "Of the four of us, Declan's the most…rigid. The most conservative. Robert thinks he is, but he's always had another side—he's just quieter than Caleb or me. Caleb and I are cut from the same cloth. We might not be twins or anything like that, but if he was dead, I'm sure I'd… feel it. I'd just know."

She arched her brows. "I always thought you, of the three of you, rode Caleb the hardest—and I always thought that was very much the pot calling the kettle black."

He grinned. "You're right. But that's why I did it. The only difference between Caleb and me is that I learned early on to curb my wildness and direct it toward those instances when I could get away with letting it loose. So I understand the lure, the attraction he feels to that sort of behavior, but I also appreciated much better than he did—or at least, than he used to—the dangers of becoming wedded to the risks and thrills."

"Than he used to?"

He nodded toward the compound. "I've been waiting, especially over recent years, for him to bring that wild side of himself into line, under his control. To learn how to exercise that control and when to do so. His strength, like mine, lies in leading men, but to claim his true position—the position he could fill—he needed to learn how to harness his wild streak." He paused, staring down at the compound. After a moment, he went on, his voice still low so only she could hear, "Finally, with this mission, I've seen him take that bit between his teeth. Step by step, he's made the right decisions, and for the right reasons. Despite all temptation—and I'm sure there would have been plenty in a situation like this—he's held to what he needed to do and not given way to his wilder impulses."

He shifted, stretching his legs, then drawing them up again. "I've hauled him out of dangerous scrapes too often to enumerate, but this time, it's different. This time, I'm coming in to join *with* him to effectively deal with a truly difficult situation."

Her gaze still locked on his face, she tilted her head. "More like a partnership instead of older brother leading the way?"

His smile was swift. "Exactly. This time, he gets to run a part of the mission all by himself. But as to why I feel so certain he's down there…" He paused for long enough to make her look down at the compound to see if there'd been any new appearances, but there hadn't been. As she glanced back at him, he said, "The one insurmountable difficulty in safely rescuing *all* the captives was that there weren't anywhere near enough men who were effective fighters *inside* the compound."

She blinked, then looked back at the compound. "You think Caleb somehow got himself and his men taken in as captives?"

"I think that something happened, and he saw the opportunity and seized it." He lifted one shoulder. "It's what I would have done, and in action, he thinks and reacts very much as I do." He refocused on the area below. "We've seen the men who were with him—most of them are there. I'm just waiting to see if Caleb and Phillipe are, too—if Caleb managed to pull the wool over this Dubois's eyes enough for the man to allow Caleb inside his palisade. If Caleb has managed that…then he'll have removed the biggest stumbling block lying between us and a successful rescue." He shifted his shoulders against the rock. "And I cannot tell you how grateful I'm going to be if he has."

She arched her brows, but said no more. She sat back and let all he'd said sink into her mind and reshape her views—of him, of Caleb, of his relationship with his youngest brother. Royd's view that they were very alike rang true. She'd always thought he was especially harsh on Caleb, but of the four brothers, she'd known Caleb the least well. Yet as Royd had been acknowledged as the greatest seafaring hellion of his time, his criticisms of Caleb had seemed two-faced.

The sun had dropped below the hills to the west, and shadows were starting to swallow the compound.

Abruptly, Royd sat up.

Isobel looked into the compound, saw what he had, and sat up, too.

Men were streaming out of the mine—men who'd ventured out before, but also lots of men they hadn't previously seen.

Someone sent up a shout of "Food!" and the captives streamed toward one of the buildings screened by the barracks.

"Caleb's sketch put the kitchen over there," she murmured.

Royd nodded, his gaze locked on the men who were exiting the mine in small groups.

The exodus reduced to a trickle, and Isobel realized she was holding her breath.

Then Hornby nearly leapt to his feet. "There he is!" He managed to keep his voice down.

Reynaud heaved a huge sigh of relief. "And Phillipe, also."

The pair, as begrimed as any of the men, their dark hair liberally grayed with dust, were among a group of six who were last to exit the mine. Unaware of the intense scrutiny aimed at them from above, they ambled, loose-limbed and clearly free of any restricting injury, across to join the line of captives waiting to be handed their plates. The women and children had already been served and had returned to logs arranged around a fire pit to sit and consume the simple meal.

Once Caleb and Lascelle reached the front of the barracks and passed out of sight, Royd sat back, then he rocked to his feet and smoothly rose. He reached a hand down to her and smiled as he hauled her to her feet. "He's there, as is Lascelle. So now it's time to go back to the camp and rework our plan."

Eight

It took time to pick their way down the hill in the waning light. By the time they reached the camp, black night had fallen; only Reynaud's memory and the faint glow from the campsite saved them from wandering for hours.

The men had succeeded in catching a wild goat, which they'd cooked at a distance, then carried the resulting stew to the camp. Dinner was positively festive now they knew Caleb, Lascelle, and all their men were inside the compound. Captives, yes, but apparently hale and whole. That was better than most had hoped for when they'd found the camp deserted.

Isobel sat on a log. Royd sprawled beside her, and they ate with unrestrained appetite.

Royd waited until the meal was over. While his men tidied, he stared into the small lantern they'd set in the middle of the clearing, then glanced at Isobel and saw she was similarly pensive. He tapped her knee; when she looked at him, he rose and motioned her to join him by their bags at the clearing's edge. He retreated to the spot, rolled a log into place, swept it free of leaves, then waved her to it. She sat, and he sat alongside her.

"So?" she asked.

He opened his mouth—and closed it as a soft birdcall floated through the palms. He looked at Liam.

Liam's nod confirmed the sound was from one of their pickets.

A second later, they heard the tramp of marching feet, muted by the thick carpet of leaves and the soft jungle earth.

Royd rose. Isobel came to her feet beside him.

Lachlan led the way into the clearing, ducking under a low-hanging vine. He grinned. "Good evening, gents." He located Royd and saw Isobel standing alongside. "And lady." Lachlan crossed to them, his grin converting to a full-blown smile. "Isobel." He opened his eyes wide. "Fancy meeting you here."

The Carmichael Shipyards had refitted *Sea Dragon* not so long ago.

"Lachlan." Isobel bestowed a cool nod.

Royd stifled a frown. Lachlan was an acknowledged flirt. That said, he was just a flirt; measured against Royd, Lachlan was relatively harmless.

Lachlan's men filed into the clearing and exchanged greetings with Royd's crew. Hornby introduced Reynaud and the other Frenchmen to the newcomers.

Then Royd caught sight of a blond head at the back of the group. He stared, then growled at Lachlan, "What the devil is Kit doing here?"

"I suggest you ask her." Lachlan's tone suggested he refused to take responsibility for his cousin's presence.

Predictably, Isobel's expression brightened. "Where?" She went up on her toes to peer over the heads.

"Over there." Royd raised a hand, caught Kit's attention, and beckoned her over.

She wove her way between the knots of men. The setting of her features as she neared stated that, while she recognized Royd's authority, she was in no mood to have her decision to join in the action disputed.

With Isobel by his side, Royd was aware he had very little by way of leg to stand on.

Kit halted beside Isobel. "Royd." She gave him a curt, hard-faced nod, then looked at Isobel; her expression softened as she smiled. "Isobel—lovely to see you here."

Royd didn't doubt Kit's delight; while she and Isobel weren't precisely close, they knew each other well enough to instantly band together and shared a habit of ignoring boundaries they didn't wish to recognize. Still… He narrowed his eyes on Kit's face. "I specifically placed you and *Consort* on mop-up duty because"—truth being the best argument—"you outperform any of us in that role."

Kit turned her smile on him. "Why, thank you, cousin. But *Consort*'s performance isn't due to me alone—my crew is perfectly capable of functioning in that role without me. Ronsard can deal with any blockade-runners. It'll do him good to have command for a week or so."

There wasn't anything he could argue with in that; truth was, indeed, the best argument.

More, despite her gender—or perhaps because of it—Kit was an effective if unconventional fighter. She was eagle-eyed, knew how to gauge a fight, and was an experienced commander; any man in the Frobisher crews would follow her without question. All in all, she was an asset he would be unwise to attempt to turn aside—an extra commander he could rely on appearing just as he was realizing he would need more such commanders than he had. He contented himself with a disaffected humph. "As you are here…"

Kit's smile brightened by several degrees.

Royd looked at Lachlan. "We need to get working on

our plan for the actual rescue—it can't be an attempt. We'll have only one chance."

"Where's Caleb?" Lachlan had been scanning the crowd. "I thought he was here."

"He's joined the captives inside the compound."

Both Kit and Lachlan blinked, then chorused, "What?"

Royd waved them to fetch logs. He and Isobel resat. Once Kit and Lachlan had claimed logs of their own, Royd explained where Caleb, Lascelle, and their men were. He picked up a stick, drew a rough sketch of the compound in the dirt, more or less replicating Caleb's drawing, and described what they'd seen of the place thus far, then restated their goal and outlined the problems they faced in achieving it.

"Caleb, Lascelle, and their men being inside the compound gets us past the first problem—having enough fighters inside the palisade to protect the hostages during the initial phase—but we still have several hurdles to overcome. I agree with Lascelle and Caleb's assessment of the mercenaries. They may look bored beyond belief, but they're experienced and won't hesitate to seize women and children at the first sign of trouble."

"You spoke of a distraction," Isobel said. "One that looks like an innocent accident and is sufficient to capture Dubois's and his men's attention. A look-over-here type of distraction."

Royd nodded. "That's the next thing we need. I'm hoping Caleb will have some suggestions."

"The distraction will have to occur *inside* the compound, won't it?" Kit widened her eyes. "This Dubois doesn't sound like the sort to send his entire force outside to deal with anything."

"He won't, and you're right." Royd tapped the stick

to the center of his sketch. "The distraction has to be inside the palisade."

"So it's going to have to be arranged by those inside," Lachlan concluded.

"Anything we do from outside will instantly alert Dubois to our presence, and he'll immediately seize hostages. So yes, the distraction isn't something we can provide." Royd paused, then said, "Until I make contact with Caleb, let's leave the distraction to one side and focus on what we can address—namely, what should happen after the distraction pulls the mercenaries' attention away from the captives. Specifically, away from the likely hostages—the women and children. The instant the distraction hits, we need to get the women and children—all of them—out of the compound and far enough away that the mercenaries can't reseize them."

"So we need a defendable location and a protective force to escort and guard them," Kit said.

"There's plenty of jungle." Royd waved. "We can select a suitable spot and supply escorts and guards. But first, we need to work out how to get the women and children out."

Lachlan studied Royd's sketch. "Any chance of simply opening the gates and having them race out to us?"

"No." With the stick, Royd tapped the gates. "Although they're open during the day, there are two mercenaries flanking them, and whatever the distraction, they'll be the last to leave their post. Regardless, it's most likely we'll strike in the evening, once the women and children are gathered in this hut"—he pointed at the rectangle to one side of the gates—"and by then the gates will be shut with two heavy beams barring them."

Lachlan humphed. "In that case, we need to cut our way through the palisade."

"That's the only viable option, but the palisade's construction means that's not a simple thing." Royd glanced at Isobel. "You thought the tool you picked up in Southampton would do the trick. Where is it?"

"In the bottom of your seabag." When he blinked, she said, "I put it in before you packed."

He cast her a look, then reached back, snagged his seabag, and hefted it onto his thighs. He searched, working his way down. Eventually, he pulled out an oilskin-wrapped package. "This?"

"Yes." She took it and set it on her lap. She undid the bindings and folded back the oilskin, revealing a curious implement. The heavy, curved, serrated-edged, triple-blade tool had a thick wooden grip, and the teeth on the parallel blades, separated by perhaps half an inch, were set in a peculiar fashion, flaring out to both sides of the blades' spines and interdigitating. Isobel picked up the tool, angling it so the others could examine it. "It's used to saw through tarred ropes or caulked lagging. According to Caleb's report, the palisade is held together with rope made of twisted jungle vines. Cutting through them with any ordinary blade will take far too long." She brandished the tool. "This should be more effective."

Royd set aside his seabag. "I've already got an inkling of how to get our men inside the palisade once the distraction takes hold, but it'll depend on what the distraction is and where it's located in the compound." He grimaced. "We can think up ideas, but there's no point trying to finalize our plans until I've spoken with Caleb, and we know what the distraction will be. And"—he nodded at Isobel's blade—"until we know whether that will work and we'll be able to get the women and children out through the palisade."

For Kit's and Lachlan's benefit, he added, "According

to Caleb, a boy called Diccon comes out of the compound every day to collect fruit and nuts. He'll take a message to Caleb, but with Caleb in the mine until dusk, he and I won't be able to meet until tomorrow evening."

"So, until you consult with Caleb," Kit said, "all we can do is work on our options for the subsequent phases of the rescue."

"Exactly. How to get the women and children out and where to hold them." Royd listed the points on his fingers. "How to get our men into the compound in light of whatever the distraction is. How to get weapons to the men in the compound."

"Rules of engagement for dealing with the mercenaries," Kit put in.

Royd met Lachlan's gaze. "And how we deal with the others we think might be in there—Muldoon and the ex-assistant commissar, Winton."

Lachlan frowned. "You didn't see them?"

"No, but our vantage point is here." On his sketch, Royd pointed to the rock shelf. "If they're staying in the barracks, which apparently has a porch, then we won't see them unless they go strolling about the compound."

He paused, then said, "In addition to learning which of the instigators are there and confirming the number of mercenaries, I need to learn from Caleb whether there's any urgency about the rescue that we don't know about." He glanced at the others. "Given the quality of the mercenaries and the abundance of hostages, we should wait until Robert and Declan and their men reach us. Overwhelming numbers would be a good thing."

Lachlan and Kit nodded. Kit asked, "When are you expecting the others?"

"I hope by the day after tomorrow—they should make it by then." Royd grinned. "They have incentive."

Kit and Lachlan chuckled.

Royd went on, "Given I can't liaise with Caleb until tomorrow evening, then the following evening—after Robert and Declan arrive—is the earliest we could launch a properly planned rescue. I'm hoping that, tomorrow evening, Caleb's not going to tell me the captives need immediate rescue." He looked at their men, spread out in the clearing, and grimaced. "That would be significantly more difficult."

They fell silent, then Isobel reached across and filched the stick from his fingers. "Regarding where to gather the women and children"—she pointed to the round blob he'd drawn to indicate the lake at the base of the cliff that curved around the compound—"this is a small lake. The mercenaries only go to it in the morning to oversee the captives drawing water for the day. We haven't yet explored, but from glimpses, it appears to be surrounded by jungle and not easy to approach except via this path—the extension of the beaten path that runs across the front of the compound."

With Kit and Lachlan, Royd studied the sketch.

"In addition," Isobel continued, "Caleb and Lascelle buried a cache of weapons by the jetty. If the women and children are in their hut when the distraction starts, then if we use my tool and cut a gate in the palisade behind that hut—and according to Caleb, the hut has a rear door—we can remove the women and children before the fighting actually starts. Before any mercenaries might think to come after them."

"We could place a cordon of guards along that path." With his eyes, Royd traced the route around the palisade to the lake.

"And once the women and children are at the lake," Lachlan said, "if there's a position that's defendable, we'll only need a handful of men to guard the group. The rest in the cordon can regroup and come in through the gates." He glanced at Isobel. "Assuming that handy tool of yours will allow us to cut the gates open, too."

She wrinkled her nose. "I won't know until I see the gates."

Royd studied the sketch for a moment more, then glanced at the tool in Isobel's hand. Then he raised his gaze to her face. "I think it's time we tried out your tool."

Her face brightened. "Now?"

He straightened and stood. "We can't go much further until we know it works."

* * *

Naturally, Lachlan and Kit invited themselves along. Royd saw no reason to rebuff them; it would be their first sight of the compound and would give them a better feel for the position and terrain.

For himself, he was keen to get a closer look at the palisade.

The four of them took the track out of the camp, then walked quietly and cautiously up the main trail that ultimately led to the compound's gates. The instant Royd spied the top of the palisade—a different shade of black against the mottled expanse of the small mountain behind the compound—they diverted into the jungle.

He led the others in single file on a course roughly parallel to the palisade and halted when he judged they were level with the women and children's hut. He beckoned the others; once they'd gathered shoulder to shoulder, he murmured, "No guards patrol outside the compound. We don't think the guards in the tower can see anyone on the path skirting the palisade—regardless, we'll take no chances. No talking from here onward—use hand signals. And we keep under cover as far as possible."

They nodded. He turned and led them toward the palisade.

Before leaving the camp, Isobel had rewrapped the wickedly sharp triple blade and tucked the tool carefully into her breeches pocket. After following Royd into the deep shadows at the foot of the palisade, she waited until Kit and Lachlan joined them—then they waited to make sure they hadn't inadvertently raised any alarm. Nothing stirred. Finally, she drew breath and eased the blade from her pocket. She unwrapped it, handed both tool and oilskin to Royd, then, conscious of the excitement coursing through her, stepped back from the wall.

The others watched as, her hands on her hips, she widened her eyes, the better to see in the dimness, and examined the construction. Caleb's and Lascelle's descriptions had been accurate; the bindings holding each plank in place were more than solid enough for the purpose. She stepped closer, splayed her hands against two planks, and pushed, testing for any give.

As near to none as made no difference. She grimaced, then leaned close and examined the twisted vines. She tested their resilience with a fingernail, then reached for the tool, hefted it, and set the wicked teeth to the hardened vine.

She pressed in and sawed. The technique for using the blade was neither sawing nor cutting but a blend of both.

The blade shredded through the vine easily enough, quietly, too, but a minute was enough to demonstrate that it was going to take far too long to sever the bindings for the cutting to be a part of the storming of the compound. But they could get around that.

She lifted the tool, inspected the teeth, used the wrapping to wipe the blades clean, then rewrapped it and returned it to her pocket.

A preemptory tap on her shoulder had her turning her head to meet Royd's questioning gaze.

She raised a finger: *Wait.*

She stepped back again and looked up, surveying the tops of the planks—confirming that the highest bindings were some ten feet from the ground, yet still a good four feet below the top of the palisade.

She looked again at the vine she'd cut, then bent, scooped up a handful of dirt, and rubbed it over the mark. She examined her handiwork; unless someone specifically checked the bindings, no one was likely to notice the cut.

The observation led to another thought. She stepped closer to the planks and started searching for gaps—nicks, knots—any spot through which she could look and confirm that they were, in fact, at the rear of the hut.

The others realized what she was doing and started to search, too. Eventually, Lachlan reached across and tapped her shoulder. When she looked his way, he pointed at the planks and mouthed, "The hut."

She pushed to where he was standing. He pointed to the hole through which he'd looked—too high for her to look through, but that didn't matter. She placed one hand, fingers pointed toward the palisade by the edge of that plank, then she extended her other hand, similarly pointing, to her left across the planks, miming that she was trying to define the position of her "gate."

The others' expressions cleared, and they continued searching for gaps to the left of the hole Lachlan had found.

Kit found a nick in the side of a plank low to the ground. After squatting and looking through, she beckoned Isobel.

She knelt and peered through and saw the back of a

wooden hut raised a few feet off the ground. She swiveled and looked to either side; as far as she could see, the hut stretched away on either side of her position.

She rocked back, rose, grinned at Kit, and mouthed, "Perfect."

As it happened, her original cut could function as a marker for the left of her gate. She returned to the plank Lachlan had identified. Using hand signs, he indicated that the hut extended to either side of that position, too.

She took out her tool again and cut into the bindings holding that plank, then disguised the cut with dirt.

Satisfied, she looked at Royd, pointed to herself, then held up her hand and wiggled her fingers. Then she pointed along the curve of the palisade toward the gates.

His expression was hard, as impassive as ever. He stared at her for several heartbeats, but then nodded.

He flashed her a hand sign—palm parallel to the ground and moving downward—that she interpreted as an order to go slowly and quietly. She smothered a snort and fell in behind him as he led the way around the palisade.

One glance at the gates' hinges put paid to any thought of cutting through there. Instead, she examined planks to either side and selected two positions, one to the left and one to the right of the gates. She quickly marked the bindings as she had previously.

Finally, she stepped back from the palisade, looked at Royd, and tipped her head toward the jungle.

As always, he led the way. She tramped at his heels, and Kit followed her, with Lachlan bringing up the rear.

They didn't speak until they were on the main trail and nearing the animal track to the camp.

Royd fell back to walk beside her, and Kit and Lachlan

drew closer. "So it's going to take too long to cut through the vines," Royd said, "but obviously, you have a plan."

"Indeed." As they covered the remaining distance to the camp, she explained her thinking, and how her suggestions would mesh with the actions Royd had already foreseen.

Although she sensed he wasn't thrilled by the way her involvement in the rescue was evolving, he didn't argue, much less protest. Her idea would deliver the vital openings they needed to make the storming of the compound a success.

They walked into the camp to find most of the men bedded down, and all in order.

Despite feeling buoyed by the knowledge that she would be making a real and significant contribution to the rescue effort, she discovered that the long day had taken its toll. As they moved through the camp, she stifled a huge yawn.

Royd noticed, but said nothing.

Kit and Lachlan went off to find their bags.

Isobel followed Royd as he led the way to where they'd left theirs. He crouched beside his seabag, rummaged, and drew out a folded oilskin.

She unbuckled her sword belt and set it by her satchel, along with the wrapped tool.

He shook out the sheet, then spread it on the ground. With a wave, he directed her to it. "Your couch awaits, my lady."

She stifled a giggle and sat. Smiling, she shrugged off her jacket, folded it into a pillow, then, with a heartfelt sigh, slumped full length on the sheet.

She looked up at Royd as he stood over her, unbuckling his sword belt. Unable to resist, she whispered, "Where are you going to sleep?"

He gave her a look.

Seconds later, he stretched out beside her. Still smiling, she turned on her side and wriggled her back against him.

He grunted softly and turned toward her. His arm slid over her waist. She closed her eyes, then felt him lift the heavy fall of her hair and press a gentle kiss to her nape.

Still smiling, she tumbled headlong into dreams.

Nine

The men had returned to the mine after the midday break. Along with the others, Caleb was painstakingly slowly chipping away at the rock face in the second tunnel; as decreed by Muldoon, he was using a hammer and chisel to tease a diamond free of the crumbling ore—just in case that particular diamond proved to be one of the rare blues.

Muldoon's discovery of blue diamonds among the whites the mine generally produced had enabled the captives to stretch the mining out, ensuring they would live long enough for rescue to reach them.

From Caleb's perspective—and that of several like-minded males—they were now more in danger of dying of boredom than at mortal hands.

Half the time, they only pretended to chip at the rock, making up the day's production from the stockpile hidden in the first, now-abandoned tunnel. Occasionally, they drew on the stockpile the children had secreted among the piles of discarded ore. They needed to leave enough diamonds in the rock face to ensure that, through his frequent inspections, Muldoon continued to believe that there were plenty more diamonds yet to be mined.

In reality, the pipe that angled along the side of the second tunnel was now mere inches thick. Much more mining, and they would risk having no more diamonds embedded in the rock to wink and gleam and make Muldoon's eyes light up with naked avarice.

Dixon, the army engineer kidnapped to direct the opening and subsequent operation of the mine, carefully monitored their progress; today, he'd decreed they should take no more than two diamonds each from the pipe.

Caleb had interpreted that as one diamond in the morning, one in the afternoon. That left him plenty of time to think while he pretended to mine.

He was reviewing, again, the steps they'd taken to assist in their own rescue, the preparations they'd made, their assumptions, and whether those would hold up when put to the test, when the sounds of an arrival—calls from the guard tower and hails from the guards at the gates—echoed faintly through the mine.

Caleb straightened. Listened. Around him, one by one, the other men did the same. Then through their soles, they felt the reverberations of marching feet.

Caleb frowned at Phillipe Lascelle, who had been toiling with similar enthusiasm alongside him. "Who now?"

Phillipe slipped his tools into his pocket. "Muldoon's already here, and so is Winton."

As Dixon had foreseen, it was the younger Winton—the assistant commissar from the fort—who had been Muldoon's coconspirator, supplying mining tools and the like. Winton had arrived ten days ago, along with more supplies. "Arsene and Cripps haven't left to fetch stores. Perhaps it's the third man." Caleb pocketed his tools and joined the exodus of curious men. "Our elusive gentleman from the governor's office."

Phillipe's expression hardened. "If it is, we'll have to decide what that means for us. We may need to reevaluate our plans."

"God—I hope not," Caleb returned. "The rescue force must be close by now. A few days more—that's likely all we'll need."

"Don't speak too loudly," Phillipe darkly warned. "Fate might hear you."

They'd been working toward the end of the tunnel so were at the back of the pack of men who gathered under the rocky overhang protecting the mine entrance. But the men ahead noticed and stepped aside to allow Caleb and Phillipe to make their way to the front and join the other male leaders—Hillsythe, Fanshawe, Hopkins, and Dixon.

With the men at their backs, the six stood and stared across the compound at the entirely unanticipated procession that had just arrived.

A stir to their left drew Caleb's attention; he looked and saw his wife-to-be, Kate Fortescue, together with Harriet Frazier, Dixon's sweetheart—the de facto leaders of the women captives—slipping into the shade of the overhang. Her gaze fixed across the compound, Kate halted in front of Caleb—he could easily see over her head—while Harriet stopped by Dixon's side.

Caleb returned his gaze to the three gentlemen—definitely gentlemen if their clothing and mannerisms were any guide—who had walked through the compound's gates and halted halfway to the barracks. They were looking around, not with any uncertainty but with the attitude of princes surveying a minor holding.

Behind the three, a group of native bearers milled, carrying what was plainly luggage. Expensive-looking luggage.

Narrowing his eyes, Caleb studied the three gentlemen. Two were older, likely in their fifties, and wore clothes that, although not ostentatious, would have done credit to a duchess's drawing room. The cut was pure

Savile Row. The men were openly arrogant—the taller man with a shock of silver hair more overtly so than his fellow. The second gentleman was of stockier build, and his narrow-eyed survey, while no less possessive, seemed somehow colder. More calculating.

The third man was younger, possibly in his mid-thirties. He was conservatively dressed, neat and precise, but his attire lacked the style of the two older men. The younger man had had his back to the mine while he directed the bearers to set down the luggage, then paid them off. As the bearers departed, the man turned toward the barracks, and those at the mine got a clear look at his face.

Standing beside Caleb, Hillsythe swore. Through clenched teeth, he said, "That's Satterly. Mr. Arnold Satterly. He's the governor's principal aide."

Caleb glanced at Hillsythe's chillingly furious face. "Ah." He looked back at the gentleman in question—the one who had betrayed Hillsythe and had him kidnapped and brought to the mine. "It appears we've identified the third of our local villains."

"Indeed." Hillsythe's tone had grown icy. "But as for the other two, I haven't seen them before."

"Nor have I," Dixon said.

In front of Caleb, Kate shook her head. "The Sherbrooks, my employers, entertained fairly extensively. I've seen most of those in the upper levels of local society. Satterly, I've seen, but not the other two. I've never seen those gentlemen before."

The door to the barracks opened, and Muldoon, followed by Winton, appeared. They checked for a second at the sight of what awaited them; from the looks on their faces, they were taken aback, even a touch rattled.

In the next instant, the pair recovered and strode quickly to and down the porch steps. With smiles wreathing their faces, they crossed to bow effusively before the older men.

"Good God," Caleb murmured, as understanding dawned. "Those are two of the backers."

"They've come to assess their investment," Hillsythe said.

Tension, born of worry, anxiety, and underlying fear, spiked—in Caleb and all those around him. This could not possibly be a good development.

Phillipe had been right. Caleb should have known Fate wasn't finished with them yet.

Most often when standing before the mine, they couldn't hear conversations conducted by the barracks' steps, but today the breeze was coming from the west, briskly whisking across the compound; if they strained, they could make out parts of the exchange.

"Cousin." The white-haired man addressed Satterly. "Please introduce us to your colleagues."

Caleb exchanged a quick look with Hillsythe. Cousin, was it? That, presumably, was the connection between these backers and the local villains.

Satterly obliged, his voice lower, less strident—consequently less audible to the group near the mine. They missed his naming of the white-haired man, but that gentleman obliged in introducing the stockier gentleman to Muldoon and Winton as Mr. Frederick Neill.

What followed came in snatches as Neill and the white-haired man—they finally heard him referred to as Lord Ross-Courtney—quizzed the trio of younger men as to the current output and state of the mine.

Muldoon could barely contain his eagerness to explain about the blue diamonds. From their expressions of avid interest, it seemed the older two, at least, had not previously heard of Muldoon's discovery.

"They must have left London before Muldoon's information reached there," Fanshawe muttered.

Caleb felt increasingly uneasy over the unheralded arrival of the two backers. Especially as, from the snippets of conversation they overheard, it seemed that Ross-Courtney was the central figure who had organized the investors.

Most worrying was the fact that Ross-Courtney and Neill were making absolutely no attempt to conceal their identities.

Beneath his breath, Caleb muttered, "Royd better get here soon." He couldn't recall ever being so keen to see his eldest brother. With Neill and Ross-Courtney's arrival, this mission had definitely strayed—nay, galloped—into Royd-required territory.

The older men had glanced once at the group gathered before the mine, but thereafter ignored them—very much as if the captives were beneath their haughty notice.

That haughtiness was on full display when Dubois, who had followed Muldoon and Winton onto the barracks' porch, but had remained there, observing, finally stirred, descended the steps, and crossed to where Muldoon was waiting to introduce the mercenary captain to his ultimate employers.

Knowing Dubois as they now did, it was easy to see his hackles rising in response to the high-handed superiority with which Ross-Courtney especially, but Neill as well, treated him—as if he was a lackey barely worthy of their notice, and a French lackey to boot.

When Muldoon, transparently nervous, clapped his hands together and loudly proclaimed, "I'm sure you'll agree, Dubois, that the medical hut will be the most appropriate quarters for Lord Ross-Courtney and Mr. Neill," Dubois said nothing. His expression rigidly blank, he merely looked at Muldoon, until that gentleman swung to the backers and, with waves and near bows, escorted them on.

Dubois stood and watched the group—Muldoon in the lead, with Satterly and Winton solicitously flanking the two older men—as they rounded the barracks.

A flash of pale cloth by the gate had Caleb glancing that way. Diccon came rushing in past the guards, heading straight for the mine, but the sight of Dubois, his back to Diccon as Dubois watched the newcomers, pulled Diccon up short. He stared at Dubois, then looked past him at the newcomers.

Diccon visibly hauled in a breath, his skinny chest rising, then he glanced somewhat longingly at the group at the mine, before looking again at Dubois. Then the boy turned and walked quietly toward the kitchen, lugging his bulging basket.

What was that about? Caleb made a mental note to ask Diccon later.

The newcomers had passed out of Dubois's sight. He turned, saw the group before the mine, and, with a curt wave, ordered them to disperse.

They did. Caleb squeezed Kate's shoulders. She glanced at his face, returned his faint smile, then he released her, and she walked briskly with Harriet back to the cleaning shed.

Caleb followed the other men into the mine. Most returned to the second tunnel, but the six leaders gathered a little way inside the entrance.

"I don't like this," Dixon stated.

Caleb looked at the others' faces. "No one's arguing."

"So what now?" Hopkins asked. "While we're waiting for the rescue force, is there anything we can do to deflect any threat from our new arrivals?"

Fanshawe put the matter bluntly. "What can we do to ensure they don't give Dubois the order to shut down the mine?"

"The existence of the blues," Caleb stated, "which it appears the newcomers knew nothing about, remains our best defense against any immediate decision to close the mine."

"True." Hillsythe nodded. "And we almost certainly only need to hold on for a few more days—not even a week. The rescue force has to be close."

"*And*"—Phillipe pushed away from the wall against which he'd been leaning—"panic of any sort is to be guarded against. We have our plans made and all the necessary preparations in place. Just because these men have arrived today is no reason to rescript those plans."

They stood and considered. "One thing we can do," Caleb said, "is have the women make sure that when those two gentlemen go into the cleaning shed, there are a few blues for the women, or more likely Muldoon, to find and display for the gents. No reason we can't harness their greed to our advantage."

Dixon nodded. "An excellent point."

Caleb felt a tug on his sleeve. He looked down to find Diccon—who hated being in the mine—by his side. Immediately, he focused on the boy. "What is it?"

Diccon's gaze shifted to the other five men, now standing in a loose group and going over their plans once again. Diccon glanced at Caleb, then ducked his head and in a barely audible whisper said, "Can I see you privatelike? There's somethin' I have to report."

Caleb blinked, then put his hand on the boy's shoulder. They couldn't go outside; he didn't want to risk Dubois seeing Diccon speaking privately with him. "Do you mind going deeper into the tunnel?"

Diccon straightened and nodded. "I think we'd better."

Increasingly alert, Caleb snagged a lantern and, directing the beam ahead of them, followed Diccon deeper into the abandoned first tunnel. They rounded a bend, and he judged they were far enough away from the others for their purpose. He halted, and Diccon stopped and swung to face him.

In the lanternlight, the boy's face all but glowed with excitement.

"What is it?" Caleb repeated, but inside, he already knew.

"A man came up to me in the jungle—he looked just like you. Well, a touch older maybe—but he's so like you he's got to be your brother."

Royd. Caleb's pulse leapt. "What did he say?"

Diccon drew a deep breath. "He said to tell you this. Owl. Dog. Two. Eight." Diccon studied Caleb's face. "He said you'd know what that means. Do you?"

Caleb let the smile he'd been holding inside break across his face. "Oh yes. I know exactly what that means." And no one but Royd would have sent such a message.

Diccon had been searching his face with painful intensity. He cleared his throat and pitched his voice low. "Is this it, then? The rescue?"

Caleb tried to stop grinning, but failed. Nevertheless, he forced himself to think things through…but in the aftermath of the recent arrivals, this was news the others needed to hear. He refocused on Diccon. "Don't whoop—we still need to keep this quiet—but yes, this is it. The rescue force is here."

And, it seemed, not a moment too soon.

"Can I tell the other children?"

Caleb weighed that up, then said, "Keep it under your hat until I can discuss this with the other leaders. We'll probably make an announcement about the fire tonight, then you can tell your story, all right?"

Diccon nodded. After a second, he said, "P'rhaps I'll go and wash that fruit in the kitchen—that way, I won't be near the other children and I won't be tempted to open me gob."

Still grinning, Caleb clapped the boy on the shoulder. "Good lad."

Together, they walked out to where the other leaders were still gathered, still talking.

Diccon ducked his head and continued out of the mine.

Then Phillipe saw Caleb's face and broke off in the middle of saying something about fuses. "What?" Phillipe demanded.

Caleb set down the lantern. Straightening, he wiped his palms on his breeches—a habit of his just before a battle. Normally his battles were waged on the sea, but this time… He looked around the circle of faces—and beamed. "My brother Royd is here—Diccon just brought a message."

* * *

At eight o'clock that night, Caleb slouched against the back wall of the men's hut and waited to hear an owl's mournful hoot.

As young boys, they'd each chosen a different birdcall as their communication signature; being the oldest and therefore the wisest, Royd had claimed the owl's as his. Robert had chosen the raven's, Declan, a gull's, while Caleb had chosen that of the cheekiest bird—the sparrow.

Caleb shifted in the shadows, easing his long legs. Royd's message had been clear—Owl had meant it was him and to listen for his call, Dog had signified the dogwatch, Two had meant the second dogwatch, and Eight had meant eight bells on that watch.

Eight bells on the second dogwatch translated to eight o'clock. But the only functional timepiece the captives had access to was Dixon's battered watch, and they had no idea how accurately it was keeping time.

Caleb had openly walked away from the gathering about the fire pit at ten minutes to the hour—according to Dixon's watch—just to make sure he didn't miss Royd. The captives' collective spirits had dipped badly at the realization that two of the men with the power to shut down the mine and bring the captives' lives to an abrupt end had arrived. The news that the rescue force was even now outside the compound had brought a giddy rush of relief, but everyone felt rattled, very much on an emotional seesaw—down one minute, up the next. They needed some certainty; Caleb hoped tonight's meeting would give them that.

He was trying to tamp down rising anxiety over the accuracy of Dixon's watch when the hauntingly mournful call of a large owl floated over the palisade. The source was only yards away on the other side of the planks.

Caleb grinned and straightened away from the hut. He hadn't known where around the compound's perimeter Royd would choose to make contact. He'd put himself in his brother's shoes and decided, were he Royd, that he'd make for the back of the men's hut, reasoning that the latrines to one side would give Caleb an excuse to be in the vicinity. Also, the bulk of the hut screened the area at the rear and the palisade along that stretch from the guards in the tower.

Caleb put his back to the palisade near where he thought Royd was and quietly said, "I'm here."

He felt the planks at his back shift as his brother's weight settled against them; Royd was leaning his shoulder against the board behind Caleb's left shoulder blade.

"Good work on getting inside without the bastards realizing and killing you."

Blatant approval invested the words. Caleb blinked. He hadn't thought of what Royd's first words might be, but he wouldn't have expected those.

He hadn't expected outright praise…then again, while Royd was hard to please, he was also unfailingly fair.

"So," Royd continued, his voice low and matter-of-fact, "what do I need to know?"

Caleb thought rapidly. "First, where are you camped?"

"In the clearing you used—Hornby led us there."

"That's not safe. Dubois knows of the clearing—he caught us there."

A second passed, then Royd replied, "That won't matter—we're not planning a long stay."

Caleb grinned—that was his big brother all over. "All right. I take it you've found the rock shelf above the compound."

"Yes. We arrived yesterday—we've been keeping watch ever since. We've identified the buildings, and we've seen all the captives and the mercenaries and how they're deployed. Can you confirm that the two men who were already here are Muldoon and Winton, and that the three who arrived are Satterly, Lord Peter Ross-Courtney, and Mr. Frederick Neill?"

Caleb grunted. "Muldoon's the dark-haired one. Winton's the youngest, the most obviously nervous. Muldoon's been here for about a month. Winton came ten days ago. Satterly's the youngest of the three who arrived this afternoon. Hillsythe confirmed he's the governor's principal aide. As for Ross-Courtney and Neill, we know they're two of the backers, and it seems their arrival was a surprise to the three here, Satterly included. Oh, and Satterly's a connection of Ross-Courtney's."

"Supposedly a distant cousin," Royd said. "Do you have any idea if there are more in the group with Muldoon, Winton, and Satterly? Anyone left in the settlement?"

"From all we've heard, there were only the three who are here."

"Good. We've had Decker blockade the estuary—no ships are coming in or going out, so communication between the settlement and anywhere else is cut off. In addition, Robert and Declan are locking down the settlement, at least with respect to anyone heading in this direction. We hadn't expected to find Ross-Courtney and Neill in the settlement, but thanks to Babington, we learned of their presence and their rather odd plan to go on safari with Satterly as their guide. While that raised obvious suspicions, we had no proof, so we allowed them to pass out of the settlement unimpeded."

Satisfaction laced Royd's tone as he concluded, "And now they've turned up here, which is proof enough of their involvement."

"From what we've overheard, Ross-Courtney is the central organizer for the backers. Neill watches and observes like an investor, but Ross-Courtney behaves as if he owns the enterprise." Caleb folded his arms across his chest. There was something in what Royd had said that nagged at him, but the discussion of the backers highlighted the most important issue. "So, to our rescue—how many men do you have with you?"

Royd told him.

Caleb grimaced. "That's cutting it fine. Now Ross-Courtney and Neill have arrived… God knows what's in their minds, and one word from them and it might all be over inside of an hour for all of us here. They inspected the mine this evening, but both have poker faces—we've no way of telling what conclusions they're coming to. We're doing our best to support Muldoon's excitement over the blue diamonds…ah, you won't know about those."

Quickly, Caleb explained how the discovery by Muldoon that there were rare blue diamonds among the stones produced from the mine had allowed them to stretch out the mining. "Supported by, of all people, Muldoon. We're hoping he can convince Ross-Courtney and Neill that there's a windfall still to be extracted from the mine and, therefore, it's not yet time to shut it down."

Royd grunted. "It doesn't sound as if they're likely to call a halt tomorrow, and if you've got some notion for the sort of distraction you correctly identified we would need to deflect the mercenaries' attention long enough to seize the compound, then tomorrow is all we need. I'm expecting Robert and Declan and their crews by tomorrow afternoon."

"They're coming, too?"

"There's no way anyone could keep them away."

Caleb felt certainty the like of which he hadn't felt in months rise and settle in his gut. "That means—"

"That we'll have more than enough men to carry off the rescue." Royd's tone rang with rock-solid confidence. "The one issue yet to be defined is our necessary distraction."

Caleb grinned. "We have that covered and the preparations required already in place." His grin widened. "I'll tell you mine if you tell me yours."

A smothered laugh came from Royd. Then, "Go ahead."

Caleb explained what they had planned. "All that remains is for the fuse to be lit."

Royd countered with his plans.

Caleb was impressed. "That's going to dovetail perfectly with our distraction."

He was dwelling on that damn-near-perfect complementarity when Royd said, "We saw Katherine Fortescue—can you confirm she's well?"

Caleb blinked. *We.* Royd kept saying *we* instead of his usual I. That's what had earlier struck him as odd. Puzzled, he replied, "Yes, Kate's well. Why do you ask?" *About her specifically?* Royd couldn't possibly know of his and Kate's newly minted relationship.

Royd sighed. And the quality of that sigh made Caleb blink.

Then Royd said, "Isobel Carmichael's here," and completed Caleb's astonishment.

What? "Isobel's *here*?" Caleb's wits whirled as he tried to make sense of that.

"She's Katherine's cousin. The connection's through Iona Carmody, who's anxious over Katherine's fate—they only recently learned that she'd vanished from the settlement—so, of course, Isobel was all for sailing out here, tracking Katherine down, and rescuing her. So I brought her with me. It was the safer option."

Caleb knew Isobel well enough to appreciate that, but given Isobel and Royd's past history…

There was safe and not so safe.

Deciding his big brother was experienced enough to weather even a storm of Isobel's making, Caleb tried to refocus his mind on the more urgent matter at hand—but his wits were still boggling. "So Isobel's here—in the jungle?"

"Yes." That answer came more crisply. "And don't ask."

Well, well, well. Caleb shifted against the planks. He wasn't thrilled to learn that Kate was related to Iona—a dragoness of legendary fame—but as he would be marrying Kate regardless, perhaps it was as well to be warned.

"Is there anything else I should know?"

The distinctly sharper query jerked Caleb back to the here and now. He cast his mind over their exchange. "I think we've covered all that the other needs to know."

Royd grunted in agreement. "Tomorrow evening, then." Unwavering determination and ineffable command colored the statement. "Go when you're ready—once the women and children are out of the way. We'll be watching and waiting—we'll come in the instant the mercenaries look away."

Letting the certainty in those words sink in, feeling expectant excitement rising in response, Caleb remained where he was. Royd tapped the plank at Caleb's back once, then Royd's weight lifted from it. A succession of minor rustlings reached his straining ears, and he knew Royd had gone.

After a moment, he pushed away from the palisade. Hugging the shadows at the rear of the men's hut, he thrust his hands into his breeches pockets. Forcing the far-too-wide grin from his face, he sauntered back around the men's latrines and headed for the fire pit—and all those about it waiting on tenterhooks for his report.

* * *

Royd walked back into the camp to be met by a wall of expectant looks and impatient faces.

He halted by the lantern softly glowing in the center of the clearing, looked around, and grinned. "The rescue is on for tomorrow night."

They were too well trained to cheer, but the impulse was certainly there. Men clapped each other on the shoulder, then, their expressions openly eager, settled to hear the plan.

Royd started by describing the captives' planned distraction, which, given the circumstances and the limitations of what they had to hand, was impressive in its simplicity. "With any luck at all," he concluded, "that will lock the mercenaries' attention to that quarter—and that couldn't be better for us."

He proceeded to outline the plan to get their forces into the compound—the plan that he, Lachlan, Kit, and Isobel had worked on through the day. "We've made a good start on our preparations, but we need everything complete and ready for action by tomorrow afternoon. We need to be in position well in advance of the captives initiating their distraction—we have to move immediately the mercenaries' attention shifts."

He paused, then said, "As matters stand, we have three objectives. To get the women and children to safety. To deal appropriately with the mercenaries. And to capture all five of the collaborators currently in the compound." He let his gaze travel the faces of the men around him—his crew, some of Caleb's, Lachlan's, and Kit's men, and several of Lascelle's crew. "There will be groups assigned to accomplish each objective, but all of us need to be aware of all three and act accordingly as circumstances dictate. We'll need to wait until my brothers join us and we know the full extent of our forces before we assign individuals to each team. We'll do that tomorrow afternoon. Meanwhile, tomorrow morning…"

He ran through the list of preparations they'd yet to undertake, including reclaiming the weapons Caleb had buried near the lake. The devices necessary to get their forces past the palisade and into the compound were already half-made. To the men in charge of the three crews, he said, "As soon as you've finished, get yours into position, but take every precaution. We can't afford even one slip." Again, he let his gaze travel the circle. "That applies to everyone. Not one slip."

"Aye, aye, Captain," came from many throats.

With a nod of dismissal, Royd headed for the logs from which Isobel, Kit, and Lachlan had watched and listened.

As he neared, Isobel met his eyes and arched her brows. "And our little venture?"

He halted before her, held her gaze for an instant—simply appreciating the dramatic beauty of her face—then he tipped his head toward the compound. "We need to get cracking on that tonight."

Ten

The following morning, Isobel slept late, drained by the unaccustomed activity of sawing through countless twisted vines. She'd assumed the four of them would take turns at the sawing—that she'd be able to largely supervise. Instead, the other three had been hopeless; unable to ease back on their strength sufficiently to put just the *right* amount of pressure on the serrated blade, they'd constantly got the blade stuck.

Even Kit.

In the end, it had been faster and easier for Isobel to do all the sawing. The other three had helped in other ways—Royd and Lachlan taking turns in lifting her on their shoulders so she could slice through the higher bindings, and Kit pressing on the planks to tension the bindings so they were easier to cut.

By the time they'd done all they'd needed to do, Isobel's arm muscles had been screaming. But the gate she'd created behind the women and children's hut was now held in place by only two vines, both of which were half sliced through—easy to dispense with in the wink of an eye, at least for her.

The main gates had been more problematic; they couldn't risk weakening the bindings to the point where opening and closing the gates might bring them down.

She'd confirmed which planks they should cut between, one pair to the right of the gates, one pair to the left. Then, with her knowledge of structures and Royd's understanding of forces, they'd determined which particular bindings needed to remain to allow the gates to stand apparently firmly and operate normally.

Between each set of planks, they'd left a single binding vine above head level but within a man's reach, another at shoulder height, another at waist height, and a final binding a foot from the ground, all deeply scored but still holding. She'd sliced through all the other vines lashing those particular planks together, with Royd, Kit, and Lachlan constantly testing the structure to make sure it wasn't in any danger of prematurely collapsing.

When they'd finally finished, she—and the others, too—had felt reasonably confident they'd made the right decisions. The gates had still seemed as solidly fixed as ever.

Once the rescue was under way and the noise in the compound rose, sailors with machetes could hack through the remaining bindings. If all went as planned, the mercenaries would be distracted and wouldn't hear the *thunks*.

When they'd returned to the camp and she'd reached the oilskin she and Royd had been sharing, she'd collapsed in an exhausted heap and had immediately fallen asleep.

Apparently, he'd seen no reason to wake her come morning. She'd been drowsily aware when he'd left her side, but she'd been in no mood to face the day. She'd remained on the oilskin to one side of the clearing, her back to all activity, vaguely conscious of the men rattling around. Gradually, all sounds had faded, and she'd fallen deeply asleep once more.

She finally woke to the caw of a parrot in the canopy

far above. Stretching, she rolled over and saw Kit sitting on a log nearby.

Kit noticed she was awake and smiled. "Good morning, sleepyhead."

Entirely unrepentant, Isobel drawled, "Someone should have woken me."

"What? After our fearless and occasionally fearsome leader growled that you should be allowed to sleep?" Kit made a rude noise. "Not likely."

Isobel hid a pleased grin and sat up. "Well, I'm awake now. What time is it?"

Kit glanced upward and grimaced. "I've no idea. Not being able to see the sun throws me off. Breakfast was several hours ago, so make of that what you will."

Isobel glanced around the clearing; there were only three men in sight, busily plaiting rope on the far side of the area. "Where is everyone?"

"Other than those keeping watch on the rock shelf, a group went and dug up the weapons hidden by the lake, then stockpiled them there, ready to use. After that, they were ordered to join all the rest, who are slaving over those yards you and Royd thought up. They're all determined to have them ready as early in the afternoon as possible. It's going to take an hour or two to get them into position, given it has to be done so stealthily."

Isobel nodded. Although she'd slept reasonably well, she still felt enervated. It was the heat, the oppressive weight of warmth that seemed to press down on her and left her feeling as if her skin was even grimier than it was. She glanced at Kit. "The lake—don't you think we should go and acquaint ourselves with the terrain? If we're to send the women and children there, surely we need to have some notion of where to direct them."

Kit looked at her, faintly puzzled. "I suppose."

Suppressing a grin, Isobel pushed to her feet, picked up her satchel, and hunted in it until she found the linen towel she'd buried at the bottom. She pulled it out and showed it to Kit. "I believe I'll take this in case I get wet."

Kit laughed. "Excellent idea." She reached for her sea-bag. "Just wait until I get mine."

They left the clearing on the goat track that would eventually lead them up the flank of the small mountain and on to the rock shelf. But instead of going that way, before they reached the beaten path that hugged the palisade and eventually led to the lake, they selected another well-used animal track that led farther east, and in short order stepped out of thick jungle directly onto the bank of the lake.

They stood and surveyed the small lake; it was less than a hundred feet wide. From where they stood, they had a clear view of the crude jetty-cum-wharf and a relatively jungle-free area that lay past the end of the wharf opposite where the path from the compound reached it. The retrieved weapons had been cleaned and stacked ready at the end of the wharf, just before the clearing.

"Well, that's fairly obvious." Her hands on her hips, Isobel scanned the scene. "The women and children should follow the path past the compound gates and straight on to the lake, on along the wharf, then gather and wait in that area beyond it. Whichever men are assigned to protect them can form a defensive line across the wharf."

Kit nodded. "Nice and simple. And given how Royd plans to deploy our men, it's unlikely any mercenaries will make it out of the compound, much less find their way here."

The sound of rushing water was a constant background noise. Isobel tracked it to the source and, far to their left, saw water gushing over a large boulder, a stream pouring into the lake with sufficient force to throw up clouds of mist.

Cool mist.

Kit had been staring into the depths of the lake. "This looks quite deep—more than deep enough to swim in—and that also means it should be cool."

"My thoughts exactly," Isobel replied, "but I'd rather not leave my clothes in plain sight of the wharf and that path. This trail leads farther around the lake—there looks to be an inlet tucked away with a bit of bank that must face the falls."

Kit peered in the direction in which Isobel was looking, then waved her forward. "Lead on."

The animal track wended about the edge of the lake, and eventually, they found the stretch of bank Isobel had thought must be there—a cove-like indentation facing the short waterfall and entirely out of sight of the wharf.

They raced each other in stripping and slipping into the lake. Isobel had fewer blades to unbuckle. She slid into the water, felt the wet coolness—verging on coldness—slide over her clammy skin, and groaned with pleasure.

Seconds later, Kit joined her and uttered a similarly appreciative moan.

They swam to the waterfall and discovered a deep, shadowed pool behind it. It was even colder there, with the air full of mist. They dallied in the dimness until their skins felt chilled, then ventured out again into the dappled sunshine.

For the first time since walking into the jungle, Isobel felt refreshed. She looked around. There was no one bar the two of them there, and all the men were terribly busy elsewhere…on a sigh, she tipped back and floated, letting the spray from the waterfall play over her naked skin. She closed her eyes and kept herself more or less in position with an occasional flip of her hands.

How long she lay there, quietly communing, she didn't know.

Then she heard Kit say, "I'm getting out. Don't feel obliged to follow."

Without opening her eyes, Isobel smiled. "I'll stay for a few more minutes. I'm sure I can find my way back by myself."

Kit snorted, but made no reply.

The sounds of her dressing drifted to Isobel's ears, then came soft rustling and the muted tramp of boots as Kit walked away.

Isobel drifted, soothed by the coolness and enveloped by the spray, with gentle, filtered sunbeams playing over her skin—just enough to warm, not enough to burn.

Then she realized she was bobbing up and down on a series of waves.

She snapped her eyes open.

Hard hands gripped her waist—a touch she instantly recognized.

She hauled in a breath and kicked upright—

Royd dragged her under.

Then he juggled her to face him, and his lips covered hers…

She didn't bother struggling.

Countless seconds later, they broke the surface in a rush, both gasping.

She raised both hands, slicked her hair back from her face, and blinked at Royd.

He grinned. Hands locked about her waist, he started to draw her toward the waterfall, to the grotto behind it.

As, divining his intent, she glanced that way, he murmured, "I've always wanted to couple with a mermaid."

She looked at him. "Mermaid?"

In a blink, she slid her hands to his shoulders and surged up—and had just enough leverage to push him under and down.

She let go and waited.

When he resurfaced and, with a hard shake of his head, flicked water and hair from his eyes, at her most haughty, she caught his gaze and arched a brow. "I believe you should be thinking in terms of an Amazon. This is a jungle, after all."

He stared at her, then he laughed.

Then he cupped a hand behind her nape, hauled her to him and into a searing kiss. Then he kicked gently and propelled them under the waterfall.

* * *

They got back to the camp in time for a late lunch. Kit shot Isobel a knowing look, which she pointedly ignored.

Once they'd slaked their more mundane hungers, Royd sat with Lachlan, Kit, Liam Stewart, Reynaud, and the other senior officers of their combined crews—all of whom had trickled back to camp from where, deeper in the jungle, their teams were working on assembling the required yardarms—and proceeded to go through what he termed their order of battle.

Isobel sat to one side and observed. This was Royd as she'd never seen him—the commander in action.

Of an action that risked men's lives, lives he considered it his responsibility to protect. To preserve.

At first blush, the plan he'd devised sounded outrageously reckless, but as he continued detailing where this group of men would be, and that group, and how and when they would engage, the picture of the fight came clear in her mind—much like a game she'd seen army men engage in with toy soldiers on a board—and she realized how carefully thought out each move was, and how, at least in this instance, every man seemed to have another at his back.

Although the plan was Royd's, he was no dictator; there was a degree of discussion, and not just from his cousins but from Liam and some of the more junior officers, too. Royd listened to each comment, sought clarification or the opinions of others, and amended his orders in several respects. But the core of the plan remained.

And it was a good plan; judging by the expressions of the others, they thought so, too.

Ultimately, Royd addressed an issue she hadn't thought he would—what might or could go wrong. He was blunt, but his experience showed, as did that of Liam and Lachlan, as they discussed various alternatives should one of their preferred actions be blocked.

Finally, Royd rose, and everyone else came to their feet. He dismissed them, and everyone, including his cousins, snapped off salutes before tramping off into the jungle, each returning to the group of men they were to lead in the upcoming attack-cum-rescue. From the expressions on their faces, all were now concentrating on the action, on performing as required and ensuring collective success.

Isobel rose, brushing clinging leaves from her breeches.

Royd turned to her; two of the men who'd earlier been plaiting rope hovered by the opening of the track to the rock shelf. "We're going up to spell those on watch."

She nodded. "I'll come."

The trek up to the rock shelf was uneventful. They replaced the three men currently there, then settled to observe the activity in the compound a hundred feet below.

All seemed to be proceeding much as the days before, except for Ross-Courtney and Neill, who went parading around the compound, looking into this hut, then that, with Satterly and Muldoon somewhat anxiously trailing behind. At one point, Winton came out of the barracks and wandered to the mine entrance. He peered inside, as if examining what he could see, but he didn't venture in. Then he spotted Ross-Courtney and Neill nearing the hut the women worked in, and turned on his heel and strode back to the barracks.

"He, for one, doesn't want to be there," Royd murmured.

She nodded and wondered what Winton had been looking at.

Ross-Courtney climbed the steps to the cleaning shed door, Neill at his heels.

Muldoon said something—as if attempting to distract the older men—but Ross-Courtney dismissed the interruption with a supercilious flick of his hand, opened the door, and led the way inside.

Neill followed. After exchanging a glance, Satterly and Muldoon did as well.

Isobel waited to see them re-emerge. The minutes ticked past. Eventually, she stirred and murmured to Royd, "How long have they been in there?"

He glanced at the sky, then looked down at the cleaning shed. "At least half an hour." After a moment, he added, "If I was Ross-Courtney, I'd want to see the stones the mine's producing. Caleb said there were rare blue diamonds among the usual white ones. I suspect your cousin and the other women are taking the opportunity to feed Ross-Courtney's and Neill's greed, enough, at least, to ensure they don't contemplate shutting the mine down in the next few hours."

"Hmm." Isobel continued to watch the shed, only

peripherally aware of the others—mostly children and mercenaries—moving about the compound.

Finally, the door to the cleaning shed opened. Katherine, followed by two other women, led the gentlemen out. The group walked straight to the awning under which several girls crouched, sorting the rocks chipped out of the mine.

Leaning forward, her eyes locked on her cousin, Isobel saw Katherine call something to the girls as the group neared. In response, the girls scrambled to their feet and stepped out from under the awning. They congregated to one side, allowing Katherine to show the four men something beneath the awning.

"I assume she's demonstrating what the girls do," Royd said.

"That's what it looks like." Katherine was evidently explaining something. Neill and Satterly were paying close attention. Muldoon had the look of one who had seen it all before; he hung back to one side.

But as for Ross-Courtney...his attention had deflected from Katherine's demonstration. His head had turned to the side.

Isobel followed his gaze. She stiffened.

Royd glanced at her. "What?"

She stared at Ross-Courtney. After a moment, she muttered, "I don't like the way that bounder is looking at that girl—the tall one with wispy fair hair."

Royd's gaze locked on Ross-Courtney.

A moment later, Isobel elbowed him. "Look at Neill. He's seen it, too." Even viewed from this distance, Neill's expression conveyed fastidious disdain.

Then Katherine stepped out from under the awning, putting herself between Ross-Courtney and the girl. To Isobel, Katherine's subsequent performance seemed overly animated; her cousin had seen or sensed enough to feel compelled to shield the girl and deflect Ross-Courtney.

With an unctuous smile, Ross-Courtney allowed Katherine and the other women to usher him and Neill back to the cleaning shed. Isobel quietly exhaled.

Royd glanced sidelong at her. "We're going in this evening."

"Just as well." Isobel watched Katherine wave the men inside. Once they'd passed, Katherine threw a plainly worried glance back at the ore piles, then went into the cleaning shed and shut the door.

Isobel looked at the awning, but the girls had ducked under its cover. She returned her gaze to the cleaning shed. After a moment, she stated, "If that bastard so much as touches a hair on any girl's head, I will have his balls."

Royd heard, but said nothing. He knew she meant the words more or less literally. She'd styled herself an Amazon; she was perfectly capable of acting like one.

Nothing further of note happened over the next half hour. But as the sun started to slide toward the horizon, the tension steadily increased. Everyone in their company knew the time for action was drawing inexorably nearer, that the time to check weapons and make last-minute adjustments to their preparations was running out. Various officers came to the rock shelf to report on progress or discuss minor adjustments to this or that.

Then a significant stir heralded the arrival of Declan, Edwina, Robert, and Aileen. Royd suggested the two sailors who had been sharing the watch take a break, allowing his brothers and their ladies to crowd onto the rock shelf with him and Isobel.

Royd watched as all four settled, their gazes drawn to the compound below. "You made good time."

Robert, sitting next to Royd, humphed. "We left the settlement early yesterday, reached Kale's camp by early afternoon, and decided to march on. We camped in the jungle and made an early start again this morning."

"It's easier to walk in the early morning." Seated next to Robert, Aileen sent a smiling glance at Royd and Isobel. "And we wanted to be here in time to take a good look around before the excitement starts."

Royd didn't reply; he'd hoped—clearly vainly—that his brothers would succeed in convincing Aileen, and even more Edwina, to remain safely in Freetown. Just as well he'd made contingency plans; Edwina and Aileen could assist Isobel with evacuating the women and children and keeping the group corralled by the lake. He was banking on such a role appealing to the instincts all three women shared for helping and protecting those weaker than themselves.

And while they were keeping the other women and the children safe, they would remain safe, too.

"Incidentally," Robert said, "Babington joined us. He's waiting with our men."

"I thought he would come," Royd said.

Robert snorted. "We'd have had to tie him up to stop him."

Royd had a role in mind for Babington, too.

"We heard that Caleb got himself—and his men—captured."

The comment pulled Royd from his mental planning; Declan's tone suggested disapproval. Royd mildly replied, "Indeed, and by managing to get himself and his men inside the compound without anyone dying, Caleb got us over the one otherwise-insurmountable hurdle that stood in the way of us successfully rescuing *all* the captives."

Silence ensued as his brothers digested that. Robert grasped the point first. "So we now have sufficient trained fighters inside the compound to stand between the mercenaries and the likely hostages—namely the women and children."

Across Robert, Declan glanced at Royd.

Royd nodded. "Precisely. Without Caleb and his men being inside the palisade, we would have been forced to accept losing some hostages in order to free the rest. I wasn't looking forward to making that decision, so I'm grateful Caleb managed to pull off what amounts to an infiltration."

Declan snorted. "Knowing him, that was far from planned, but he's always been good at turning situations to his advantage." Declan paused, then, in a brisker, more businesslike tone, asked, "So what are your orders?"

Royd ran through his plan, outlining the actions he envisioned as necessary to take the camp while simultaneously releasing and protecting the hostages.

His brothers listened without interruption; after his earlier discussions with Lachlan, Kit, and the other officers, the plans were well honed and had no real weaknesses left to be addressed.

Edwina and Aileen listened carefully, too. Royd hoped they would be content with the roles he'd assigned them; they seemed quite pleased to have been specifically included—a reaction he prayed augured well.

When he ended his recitation, at the point where all their men were inside the palisade and engaging with the mercenaries and all beyond became speculation, Robert stated, "Everything's covered, as far as I can see." He glanced at Declan.

Declan nodded decisively. "I can't see any holes." He looked past Royd to Isobel. "Being able to get through the palisade is a critical advantage—one the mercenaries won't expect."

"They won't expect our sudden arrival, literally from out of the blue, either." Robert glanced at Declan. "We need to brief our men." He looked at Royd. "We halted in a clearing along the path from Kale's camp. How far advanced are your work parties? When do you want us to bring our men up?"

Royd glanced at the sun; the afternoon was now well advanced. "The work parties should be almost ready to shift the yardarms into position. Why don't you brief your men and Babington, then bring them through the jungle to Caleb's camp? From there, you and your men can join the work parties and help get the yardarms in place." He hesitated, then, his features hardening, added, "I'd rather be ready than not—I want every man in place, and all groups ready to go, before the light fades."

Neither Declan nor Robert argued. Both got to their feet.

Declan arched his brows at Edwina, still seated on the rock. "Coming?"

Edwina glanced at Isobel, then at Aileen, then she tipped her head back and met her husband's eyes. "I thought perhaps Isobel might show Aileen and me this lake. If we're to gather the women and children there, knowing the area—the terrain—might prove useful."

Isobel watched Declan glance at Robert, then at Royd.

Royd shrugged. "That's not a bad idea. The area's safe—none of the mercenaries ever venture that way after their morning excursion to fetch water."

Isobel leapt in. "I'm happy to show Edwina and Aileen the way." She glanced at Royd. "Then the three of us can return to our camp. Edwina and Aileen will be closer to where they need to be to help with the evacuation later."

Royd held her gaze for a second, then looked at Robert and Declan. "On your way past our camp, send two more men up to take the watch. Once I'm relieved, I'll go down to the lake and escort these three to our camp. Isobel's right—it'll be more sensible for Edwina and Aileen to wait there."

Edwina turned a sunny smile on Declan, and Aileen smiled confidently at Robert.

Both men hesitated, then Declan nodded. "We'll meet at Royd's camp." He turned and made his way off the rock shelf.

Robert followed, then the three ladies rose, and Isobel led Edwina and Aileen down the narrow path in Declan and Robert's wake.

Halfway down, they had to pause and wait by the side of the track to allow one of the work parties to haul a huge cleaned and polished tree trunk up the track.

Edwina studied the ropes and pulleys several men were carrying. "Aha. Now I understand."

Aileen nodded. "Quite ingenious. I can't imagine this Dubois will be expecting anything like what's going to happen."

"Surprise is vital for our success." With their path again clear, Isobel stepped out and picked up the pace. "Come on—I've quite a lot to tell you."

She didn't need to say anything more to have the other two hurrying at her heels.

They reached the lake. Isobel showed them the narrow wharf and the weapons that had been buried, but now lay cleaned and ready for use.

"So the women and children are funneled in here"—Aileen made a sweeping motion from the path across the wharf to the designated area beyond—"and there's a group of men delegated to protect them, and they have adequate weapons to do that." She met Isobel's eyes. "So what's the point of us being here, too?"

"My thoughts exactly." Edwina had been studying the lake. She looked at Isobel and pointed to the water. "Is it possible to swim, do you know?"

Isobel grinned. "Kit and I already have." She didn't mention Royd.

Aileen's eyes lit. "After the trek here, I would give a great deal to feel water on my skin."

"There's a tiny cove over there that's screened." Isobel pointed toward the waterfall. "It's easier to get into the water there."

She led the way around the lake.

The other two were wearing their breeches and jackets over fine shirts. As they stripped, Aileen said, "Yet another advantage of breeches over skirts—much faster to get into and out of."

Isobel perched on a flat rock. Once the other two had slid into the water and got beyond their first raptures at the coolness, she stated, "I'll be the one who cuts through the final threads and opens the gate at the rear of the women and children's hut."

Edwina nodded, sending ripples across the water's dark surface. "And we'll be right behind you—to help get the women and children out of the hut and onto the path to the lake."

"But once they're all out and have got past the main gates and are disappearing down the path"—Aileen floated on her back, hands flapping to keep her position—"with armed sailors lining the path and more at the lake itself, then..."

"Indeed," Isobel said. "So what's our plan?"

* * *

For Caleb—and he was quite sure all the captives—the day seemed to drag on interminably.

Finally—*finally!*—the break for the evening meal was called.

All the men who'd been pretending to toil in the second tunnel stepped back from the rock face. Many, he noticed, stared at the rock wall for a moment, as if recognizing that, if all went as planned—and even if the rescue effort blew up in their faces—they wouldn't be seeing the sight again.

Taking care to behave as they normally did, they trooped out of the mine. Those carrying the shovels used to clear ore from under the men's feet added the tools to the pile of shovels and picks no longer in daily use that Dixon had organized to leave just inside the mine's entrance. Close at hand.

Even better, they'd fallen into the habit of carrying the hammers and chisels they were now required to work with in their pockets; as, in the aftermath of the women's tools blunting, Dubois had declared each man responsible for the care of his own tools, not even Dubois saw anything odd in that.

He might have thought twice if he'd realized what very sharp edges the chisels now carried.

As Caleb walked out of the mine and the shadow of the overhanging rock fell behind—for the last time—he glanced around, then joined Phillipe in strolling slowly across the compound to the kitchen to fetch their meals.

He and Phillipe had already given their men their orders. When the distraction took hold and deflected the mercenaries' attention, they would rush to take position between the mercenaries and the women and children's hut; until Royd, Declan, and their men could reach them and bring proper weapons, they would be armed with chisels, hammers, and experience alone.

The women and children were already gathered about the fire pit; as he and Phillipe passed, Caleb heard Annie admonish one of the boys not to bolt his food.

Everyone was keyed up, waiting for the action to start.

Over breakfast, supported by the other leaders with whom he'd spent half the night hammering out who had to be where, doing what, and when, Caleb had spoken to the gathering around the fire pit, outlining what was expected to happen, going over the timing, and then informing every subgroup of their positions and their roles, before stressing how important it was that every single person adhered to the agreed script.

He hoped everyone did, but experience suggested that at least one if not more would think to improve on the plan.

But as far as he could manage it, every one of the captives was ready, and everything was in place.

He and Phillipe joined the line of men snaking in under the awning over the open-air kitchen. As he and Phillipe shuffled forward, they surreptitiously scanned the barracks' porch.

"We have Satterly, Muldoon, Ross-Courtney, and Neill," Caleb murmured. "All sitting at their ease and sipping from glasses of what looks like brandy or whisky."

Phillipe softly snorted. "I hope they're enjoying those drinks. If I have my way, it'll be their last luxury."

Caleb was in complete agreement. "Dubois, Arsene, Cripps, and Winton must be inside."

"Those four seem intent on giving our two superior gentlemen and their chief toadies as wide a berth as possible."

"Even curs have instinctive standards."

The comment surprised a smothered laugh from Phillipe.

Caleb faced forward. "The guards who normally watch the gate from the porch have retreated to the gate." He glanced consideringly at the pair. "I doubt it will make any difference—they'll come running once your distraction takes hold."

"Them and the other pair circulating. If all goes as planned, it'll be difficult for them to deny their instincts. They'll leave their posts to face the obvious and imminent danger."

Caleb nodded. He and Phillipe reached the surly cook, who handed them tin plates with a lump of stale bread, a square of hard cheese, and several strips of jerky. Accepting the meager fare, they returned to the logs about the fire pit and sat with the other leaders.

Caleb shared a smile with Kate as he settled on the log beside her. Talk was minimal as they ate.

As it always did in those climes, night fell with swift finality. Darkness enveloped them. One of the men built up the fire.

Caleb set his empty plate at his feet. In the uncertain light cast by the leaping flames, he swiftly scanned the faces. Everyone was tense, keen for the action to commence. Every captive knew their part; every adult was committed to their role. He met the eyes of Annie, Gemma, Ellen, and Mary, who were seated with the children; he knew he could rely on the four women, along with Harriet—seated beside Dixon—and, of course, Kate, to ensure the children, all those who slept with the women in their hut, followed the script and were in the right place at the right time to be whisked out of the compound to safety.

He, Dixon, and Jed Mathers—Annie's fiancé—had been relieved to hear that their women would be tucked safely away from the action.

Caleb shifted his gaze around the circle until it came to rest on the four older boys, who had their heads together and were talking animatedly, albeit in whispers. Caleb wasn't so sure those four could be relied on to follow orders, but he and Hillsythe had done their best to impress on the four that the best way they could assist was to stay inside the men's hut until everything quieted and someone came to fetch them. As the four slept in that hut, they couldn't be sent to join the women and other children without risking alerting Dubois or his lieutenants.

But if Caleb felt uncertain over the boys' ability to stay out of trouble when it was erupting feet away, there was no one else whose commitment to their plan he doubted.

Phillipe, on Caleb's right, grumbled, "Knowing that, after all these weeks, action is only a few hours away… it's damned hard not to pace. I need to move."

Caleb knew what Phillipe meant; he was no more immune to the ratcheting tension than anyone else.

Beyond Phillipe, Hillsythe stared at the dirt before his feet. "These last hours always seem especially critical, as if, if anything's going to go wrong, now is when it'll happen."

Bite your tongue. Caleb stirred. "We have to remain calm. We've managed so far—we just need to follow the plan step by step."

Phillipe snorted. Sotto voce, he said, "And just how is that supposed to work with you and me involved?"

Caleb ignored that. He turned to Kate and smiled encouragingly. "Is it time for the children to retire yet?"

She met his eyes, then squeezed his forearm. "Not just yet. Patience. It's going to be difficult enough to get them to tramp across as they usually do without looking back or around." She nodded to where Dixon sat with Harriet beside him. "John will tell Harriet when it's time."

Caleb pretended not to hear Phillipe's low chuckle. They'd agreed the children should retire half an hour earlier than usual to ensure that, when the time came, they were all in their hut and ready to be evacuated. Caleb prayed Royd's notion of creating a gate behind the hut went ahead without a hitch; the last thing he wanted was for the women and children to have to come out of the hut again or, potentially even worse, for them to be trapped inside.

Reining in his impatience, he turned to Phillipe. "All ready on your front?"

Phillipe and Hillsythe had devised the distraction, with technical support from Dixon. But it had fallen to Phillipe and his men to make the necessary preparations; they were the most experienced in covertly blowing things up.

Phillipe nodded. "Dixon, Fanshawe, Hopkins, and I checked the run this morning. All seemed in place and secure."

"Who have you delegated to set it off?"

Phillipe arched a brow at him. "Me. And if, for some reason, I'm prevented from doing so, Ducasse will, and if not him, Quilley. One or other of us will get the thing going. You can rest easy on that score."

"Good." Caleb was immeasurably glad they'd realized the need for such a distraction weeks ago and had devised their strategy and immediately started to put it into place. It had taken weeks of painstaking work—not because it had been physically difficult but because they hadn't dared be caught doing it, and they'd had to cross an open stretch of the compound to achieve the effect they wanted. "So everything's in place. Royd's here, and Robert and Declan will have joined him by now. Everything's on track to pull off this rescue."

He looked at Kate; when she glanced up, he met her eyes and managed a tight smile.

Everything will be all right.

He was still on edge. Increasingly so.

As if reading that in his eyes, she patted his arm, then slid her hand to his, twined their fingers, and briefly squeezed. "Harriet just signaled. It's time for us to go."

Caleb glanced around and saw the other women getting to their feet and waving the children to theirs.

When he looked back at Kate, she was waiting to catch his eyes. She tightened her hold on his hand. "Good luck. I'll see you later."

The latter sentence sounded like an order; the look in her eyes confirmed it was.

He discovered he couldn't smile. Ruthlessly quashing the urge to haul her into his arms—and not let go—he nodded.

She slid her fingers from his and rose. She gave a general wave to the men; Annie and Gemma called, "Good night."

Then the women herded the children toward their hut.

Before Caleb could, Hillsythe pinned the four older boys with a hard stare. They felt it and, reluctantly, rose, too. Dragging their heels, they slouched off toward the men's hut.

The tension gripping Caleb escalated, a vise cinching about his chest. He was sure all the other men felt the same way. The women and children withdrawing was the first step in their plan.

He forced himself to sit, apparently relaxed, and watch Kate gather the last of the children. Tilly, the oldest girl, stopped to help Kate. Between them, Kate and Tilly sent the four urchins skipping toward the hut, then fell in behind.

Watching them go, Caleb breathed, "Our rescue is officially under way."

Eleven

Keeping to her usual pace, Kate walked beside Tilly in the wake of the four over-excited children. The foursome saw the other children filing into the hut under Harriet's and Gemma's watchful eyes and pelted ahead to join their fellows.

Not exactly normal behavior at bedtime, but Dubois, Arsene, and Cripps weren't on the porch, and the four who were—Satterly, Muldoon, and the two newcomers—wouldn't know enough to grow suspicious.

"Girl. You there!"

Tilly's steps faltered.

Oh no. Kate recognized Ross-Courtney's voice. She halted beside Tilly and, with the girl, turned to face the porch steps.

Ross-Courtney stepped down to the dirt of the compound. His gaze locked on Tilly, his expression benign, yet with a far-from-avuncular gleam in his eye, he smiled as he walked toward them.

Kate might as well have been invisible.

The closer Ross-Courtney drew, the more she could read of his intent in his face; the image of a slavering satyr rose in her mind. *Oh no, no, no.*

Tilly started to tremble.

Ross-Courtney halted in front of Tilly. His pale eyes sharp, his gaze bored into her.

Kate glanced at Tilly; the girl had lost every vestige of color and looked ready to faint.

Ross-Courtney's smile deepened. "My dear girl, I believe I require your company for a few hours."

Tilly was shaking so hard, she couldn't even speak.

Kate's mind raced. They were less than an hour from rescue! They had to keep everything and everyone calm—no fuss, nothing to alert Dubois—but too much could happen to Tilly in even half an hour.

"I do believe"—Ross-Courtney's eyes gleamed more definitely, as if Tilly's fear excited him—"that you'll do very well for the nonce."

Before Kate could speak, Ross-Courtney's hand snaked out and closed about Tilly's elbow. "Come along—"

"No!" Tilly recoiled, struggling vainly to twist free.

Shocked, Kate looked at the men on the porch; they were closest—they could see and hear—but while all three found the scene distasteful, none were about to lift a finger to help.

"Let me go!" Tilly shrieked.

Kate looked back in time to see Ross-Courtney's mask fall. His features distorted; he shook Tilly and snarled, "So you like it rough, do you?" He started to drag Tilly away. "That suits me—"

Kate flew at him. "Let her go, you beast!"

Ross-Courtney yanked Tilly to one side and struck Kate a backhand blow. "You forget yourself, woman!"

Kate staggered and fell.

And a whirlwind swept past her.

Her hand to her cheek, she blinked—and saw Ross-Courtney sprawled full length on the ground, and Caleb, fists clenched, standing over him.

"Arrêté! Remain as you are!"

The bellow came from the porch. Kate glanced dazedly that way and saw Dubois, followed by Arsene and Cripps, all armed, come leaping down the steps.

Kate pushed up into a sitting position. Tilly stood nearby, gulping in great lungfuls of air between harsh, tearing sobs.

Then other hands grasped Kate, and Lascelle and Hillsythe helped her to her feet.

"Restrain him." Dubois waved at Caleb.

Arsene and Cripps stepped around Ross-Courtney. They gripped Caleb's arms and pulled him back—and Caleb let them.

He glanced across his shoulder at Kate, then his gaze lifted to Lascelle's face. "Get out of here. Go!"

The words were quiet, but they held invincible authority.

Kate glanced at Lascelle; his expression grim, he nodded once. "Come," he whispered to Kate. He led her to Tilly. Kate gathered the shaking, sobbing girl into her arms, and under Lascelle's direction, the three of them crossed to the women's hut.

Harriet and Gemma, as white-faced and as shocked as Kate, were waiting on the porch. Gemma drew Tilly into her arms and steered the girl inside. Harriet reached for Kate, but she turned toward the barracks.

Lascelle stepped into her path. "No." His dark eyes were hard. "You heard what he said. If you want to save him, you have to stay here and let me go and do what I have to do. If you want to save him, you won't detain me."

Go! Caleb had told Lascelle to start the distraction.

Kate nodded. "Yes. Go quickly."

"I intend to." Lascelle glanced at the group before the porch, then swiftly scanned all around.

Everyone's attention—including that of all the guards—was focused on the unfolding drama.

Lascelle melted into the shadows around the side of the women's hut.

* * *

Held securely between Arsene and Cripps, Caleb saw no reason to struggle. He had to let this play out; there was no other way.

Satterly and Muldoon—the cowards—had followed in Dubois and his lieutenants' wake. They crouched on either side of Ross-Courtney; as he started to regain consciousness, they helped him to sit.

Caleb viewed the blood seeping from Ross-Courtney's nose with a violent sense of satisfaction.

Ross-Courtney swiped his sleeve across his face. He looked at the blood, then he looked up at Caleb. Unadulterated hate filled Ross-Courtney's gaze.

Caleb returned the favor in full measure. He let his lip curl. "You despicable excuse for a man."

Ross-Courtney's eyes flared. His face flushed an unbecoming puce as he struggled to his feet, then he lunged at Dubois, grabbing for the mercenary's pistol.

Dubois fended off Ross-Courtney, thrusting him away. "Get back, you…" Dubois's mouth worked as he swallowed the word he'd been about to utter.

Without taking his gaze from Caleb, Ross-Courtney demanded, "Give me your pistol. I'm going to shoot this cur where he stands."

Dubois looked at Ross-Courtney. For one instant, Caleb entertained the hope that Dubois would shoot Ross-Courtney. Watching Dubois consider it, Caleb realized the enormity of what, from Dubois's perspective, Ross-Courtney had done.

He'd broken Dubois's edict.

He'd shattered Dubois's long-standing method for controlling the captives.

The captives knew rescue was less than an hour away, but Dubois didn't; all he would see was his relatively comfortable arrangement—his effective and easy control over his captives—blown to kingdom come.

Dubois would want revenge. Retribution.

Be that as it may, as Dubois slowly turned from Ross-Courtney to Caleb, Caleb understood that it wouldn't be Ross-Courtney who would pay for his transgression.

Caleb would.

Dubois looked at Caleb, and it was the monster inside who stared through Dubois's eyes. The monster who considered and weighed the prospects—the options—and chose.

Arsene, helping to hold Caleb, shifted uneasily; Arsene could see what Caleb could and wanted to be elsewhere.

Slowly, Dubois's lips curved. "I have a better idea." The words were quiet, almost serene, and directed at Ross-Courtney. "You can watch."

Ross-Courtney frowned, but even he had sufficient primal instinct not to argue with Dubois.

Focused on Caleb, Dubois mused, "I always thought you were somehow trouble."

Again, Caleb felt that wasn't the Dubois he normally met talking.

Dubois stepped back and waved toward the end of the porch closest to the mine. "String him up from the last post."

Caleb considered making that order harder for Arsene and Cripps to obey, but the distraction should break out at any moment, and once it did, he needed to be able to function, so he did nothing more than pull back against

Arsene's and Cripps's holds, making them wrestle to haul him along.

They got him to the post and backed him against it. One of the guards brought a length of rope. Arsene forced Caleb's arms down, and Cripps bound his wrists together with one end of the rope. Then Cripps tossed the rope's other end over the porch rafter at the corner, caught the rope, and hauled—stretching Caleb's arms above his head.

Cripps tied off the rope, forcing Caleb to stand on his toes with his heels against the post's base to keep his weight off his arms. He couldn't move in any direction or kick out. Cripps had even tied the rope so Caleb couldn't grip it and pull himself up.

Dubois had disappeared into the barracks. Muldoon and Satterly had remained by the steps. Ross-Courtney stood closer and glowered at Caleb. As for Neill, he'd remained in his chair on the porch throughout. His expression distant, he sipped his drink and silently observed.

Caleb could see his fellow male captives spreading between the barracks and the gates, forming a line from the fire pit to the corner of the women's hut.

Dubois emerged from the barracks. He, too, saw the men. Two mercenaries were closing in, intending to push the men back to their hut. "No!" Dubois called. "Let them come closer." He waved the men nearer and looked at Caleb. "I want them all to see what happens to those who cause me trouble." Dubois's gaze flicked to Arsene. "Tear off his shirt."

Arsene and Cripps grabbed handfuls of Caleb's shirt, yanked, and tore the flimsy material, pulling the tatters away to expose Caleb's chest and arms.

That was when Caleb glimpsed the thin knife Dubois was expertly twirling in his fingers. A flaying knife.

Instinctively, Caleb tensed, hands fisting against his bonds. *Come on, Phillipe.*

Dubois approached, a strange smile on his face, an almost euphoric look in his eyes…the monster was well and truly in control.

Caleb had finally given Dubois a chance—a reason—to allow the monster out.

Caleb's stomach felt hollow as he focused on the knife.

Flaying, he reminded himself, was a lengthy process.

Dubois halted to one side. Almost lovingly, he laid the blade just beneath Caleb's right nipple.

Then he sliced.

Caleb locked his jaw and endured. He'd be damned if he gave Dubois any satisfaction…but *damn*, the long, slanted, slicing cut stung well-nigh unbearably.

He had to hold on. It couldn't be long now.

It couldn't be.

He closed his eyes and felt his head rise, neck muscles straining as he fought against the searing agony as Dubois made another cut, this time all the way down the left side of his chest.

Pain shivered through him. His muscles quivered. How much longer—

"Fire!"

The hail came from the tower.

Dubois blinked, then spun away. "Where?" he barked.

"Supply hut!"

Every mercenary, as well as Satterly, Muldoon, and Ross-Courtney, swung toward the supply hut. Neill rose and came down the steps to look.

Pushing aside the lingering pain, Caleb craned his neck, but he couldn't see the supply hut itself—only the smoke billowing out.

A series of popping explosions sounded, and he saw flames reflected on pans in the kitchen.

Dubois cursed and swung back to Caleb.

He forced himself not to notice—to keep looking toward the hut and the guards racing toward it and not meet Dubois's gaze. He didn't need to challenge the monster.

"Bah!" Dubois tossed his bloody knife onto the porch. "You will keep." He strode for the supply hut. "Arsene! Cripps! *À moi!*"

Pandemonium ensued.

The captives hung back. Those unskilled in fighting drifted to the mine's entrance and the picks and shovels stored there. Caleb's and Lascelle's men formed a knot between the milling mercenaries and the door to the women's hut. Through the thickening smoke, Caleb thought he saw a dark figure slide out of the shadows and join the group before the women's hut. Presumably Phillipe, so that group had at least one commander.

Everyone was in their assigned position—except Caleb. He swore, gritted his teeth, and tried to loosen Cripps's knots.

* * *

At the first shout from within the compound, a section of the palisade behind the women's hut had silently fallen outward.

Isobel had led the way through, Edwina and Aileen at her heels. They'd decided the women and children would be more reassured by other women, and had delegated the sailors assigned to their enterprise to direct the captives as the ladies sent said captives out.

The first face Isobel saw when she pulled open the hut's rear door was Katherine's.

Her eyes impossibly wide, Katherine stared, then she grabbed Isobel and hauled her inside. Katherine pointed toward the barracks. "That monster has Caleb—he's strung him up, and he's *cutting him*!"

Isobel seized Katherine and pulled her to the side, out of Edwina's and Aileen's path. They rushed past and started sending the other women and children out.

After one glance to ensure all was happening as it should, Isobel turned her attention to Katherine. "Royd is here—he'll get Caleb free. Royd always gets Caleb out of trouble. Meanwhile, *we* stick to the plan."

That was one thing she'd learned through her years of running with Royd—it was always better if everyone stuck to his plan. She looked into Katherine's wide eyes. "We'll rescue Caleb, but right now, we have to get the children out and to safety."

Katherine blinked, then hauled in a breath, held it, and nodded. "Yes. You're right." She turned and joined the other women in reassuring the children and sending them out in batches, each batch with one of the women to watch over them.

The children had been ready to bolt; it was more a case of keeping them in some sort of order than having to urge them to move.

In less than three minutes, the hut was cleared. Of the captives, only Katherine remained. Isobel exchanged a glance with Edwina and Aileen.

Katherine had gone to the hut's main door. Peering out, she frowned. "There's so much smoke, I can't see..."

Her lips firming, Isobel headed for Katherine. Edwina and Aileen followed.

* * *

Caleb was swearing ever more colorfully and twisting on the post, trying to get his fingers to the knots securing the rope, when he heard footsteps coming up behind him. He froze.

Royd said, "Hold still."

Caleb heard a solid *thunk*, and the rope gave way. He slumped onto his heels, then Royd was there with a dagger, slicing through the coils binding Caleb's hands.

He shook the remnants free and massaged his wrists.

Royd glanced at his chest. "How deep are those?"

"Not deep enough to slow me down. He'd just got started."

"Dubois?"

Caleb nodded.

"Hey—squirt!"

Caleb looked up at the well-remembered hail—in time to pluck the dagger Declan tossed him out of the air.

"Stick to the plan," Royd ordered and ran forward into the developing melee.

Caleb looked around. Frobisher sailors were pouring into the compound, sliding down ropes suspended from makeshift yardarms from three different points on the cliffs above, dropping directly inside the palisade, swords in their hands and daggers between their teeth.

Robert appeared, a company of men at his back. He flicked Caleb a salute and handed him a sword. "Where are the three from the settlement and Ross-Courtney and Neill?"

Caleb tipped his head toward the barracks. "In there." He grinned. "Waiting for you."

Robert grinned back. "I'll take good care of them. Any mercenaries with them?"

"I don't think so." Caleb looked toward the cloud of smoke obscuring the supply hut. "I think they all ran toward the fire."

With a nod, Robert strode for the porch steps. An instant later, he raised a boot, smashed open the barracks' door, and, with his men at his back, plunged in.

Shouts and yells followed, but no gunshots.

Caleb looked down at his wounds. They were still bleeding, but it was more of an ooze than a stream. Dubois hadn't got to lifting the skin, so the cuts were just cuts and not anything worse. They still stung, but with his senses distracted by the mayhem around him, he had to think to feel it.

Deciding the cuts could be left until later, he raised his head and scanned the action. Declan had led his men to join the group before the women's hut; after they passed around weapons, their task was to ensure no mercenary got through and seized any hostage, or escaped through the gap in the palisade behind the hut.

Royd had marshaled his men into a cordon that was inching up behind the mercenaries, corralling them between the barracks and the supply hut, which was now aflame.

Enveloped in smoke, the mercenaries hadn't yet realized they were under attack. At ground level, the billowing clouds were thick enough to screen the advancing forces, and the lookouts in the tower were fully absorbed trying to escape the flames, which, courtesy of Phillipe's planning, were also licking higher and higher up the tower's frame.

For the first time when fighting with his brothers, Caleb had been named coordinator; Royd had ceded him the role on the grounds he was most familiar with the battleground and the enemy. He searched for weaknesses and spotted several.

Movement on the porch drew his eye. Robert's men hauled Satterly, Muldoon, and Winton out of the barracks, followed by Neill and Ross-Courtney. All five prisoners had met with rough handling. Their arms were tied behind their backs, their clothing was torn and askew, their hair disheveled. Robert's men weren't gentle as they pulled them off the porch.

Robert paused beside Caleb. "We'll keep them between the ore piles as planned."

Caleb nodded. "Keep an eye on the rear of the barracks in case any of the bastards tries to get out that way."

Robert nodded. "Will do."

Caleb thumped Robert on the shoulder, and his brother strode after his men.

Hillsythe, Dixon, Fanshawe, and Hopkins were keeping the poorly armed captives back, gathered in a body before the mine. Caleb caught Hillsythe's eye and nodded in acknowledgment.

Hillsythe raised a hand in reply.

Then came a faint creak…and a wide section of the palisade including the compound's gates fell in.

It landed with a *thump* and hadn't even settled before Lachlan and Kit led their men in.

Caleb grinned. Hefting the sword Robert had given him, the dagger from Declan in his left hand, he ran toward the gates.

Halting as he reached his cousins, he tipped his head to Kit. "You're on the gates. Can you also send some men to hold a line from the end of the barracks to the ore piles?" He pointed. "Robert will keep an eye on the corridor along the rear of the barracks, but if any mercenaries try to get out that way, he'll also need to hold his prisoners."

Kit saluted. "Consider it done."

Lachlan was scanning the increasingly smoke-fogged compound. "Where's Royd?"

"This way." Caleb couldn't suppress his reckless grin as he headed toward the impending melee.

* * *

Enveloped in smoke, Royd held his men in position and waited for the mercenaries to realize they were under attack.

He hadn't thought it would take them so long, but then neither he nor, he suspected, any of their planners had expected this density of smoke. But this was equatorial Africa; everything was damp. And setting fire to damp things invariably led to smoke—lots of it.

His men had foreseen some degree of smoke so had come prepared; all had dampened kerchiefs tied over their noses and mouths. The kerchiefs were also a reasonable badge of identification.

The mercenaries' confusion had been compounded by the tower catching alight. That had been an inspired touch. As water wasn't in ready supply, the mercenaries had grabbed hessian bags from the kitchen and attempted to beat out the flames.

By the time they'd realized that wasn't going to work, smoke was everywhere, blocking their view of the rest of the compound, then the flames on the tower had flared and roared, and they'd got caught in the mayhem…

In truth, only a few minutes had passed since the first shout of "Fire."

But Royd had felt the *thump* as—he assumed—the gates had fallen. Any minute now, Dubois was going to realize—

A bellow sounded from somewhere ahead. It took a second to decipher; Dubois or one of his lieutenants had ordered the mercenaries to fetch water.

Beneath his kerchief, Royd grinned. With one hand, he signaled his men. They gripped their weapons and slowly advanced.

The first clash came from Royd's right.

Then it was on. Steel met steel; men grunted and swore. Bodies lurched through the smoke.

While happy to engage with any mercenary, Royd was intent on hunting down Dubois. The mercenary captain needed to die. Any other enemy, he flicked to his left or right, where his men waited to take them on. Steadily, he pressed forward. His men—the most experienced fighters—were the strike force. Lachlan and his men would fall in behind, ensuring no mercenary slipped past, and Kit would hold the gate—a last line of containment.

The mercenaries would fight to the death; for them, being taken prisoner wasn't an option.

Finding well-armed sailors lurking in the smoke was a surprise the mercenaries hadn't expected; Royd's men encountered little difficulty disposing of those who came blundering into them.

The supply hut was aflame. Royd could hear the crackling roar above the shouts and the screams of those trapped in the tower. He could feel the heat, too, surging through the smoke.

A fitful breeze started to waft the smoke upward, allowing him to look around and ahead. He spotted Dubois in the instant Dubois realized there were armed men he didn't recognize in his compound.

Dubois took a bare second to assess the seriousness of the attack, then he swung and ran toward the women's hut.

The fire was burning hotter, cleaner; the smoke was thinning.

Dubois saw Declan and his men—and Caleb's and Lascelle's—all waiting with swords drawn across his path. He skidded to a halt and reversed direction.

Dubois waded into what was now a melee. Raising his sword, he bellowed, attempting to rally his men—but his forces were already greatly reduced, and those remaining were fully engaged.

His command was outmanned and about to be overrun.

Royd watched that realization sink its claws into Dubois and shake him.

His face contorting, Dubois swung out—vicious and powerful.

Royd started toward him.

The supply hut exploded, flinging everyone to the ground.

Royd coughed, confirmed nothing was broken or badly bleeding, and rolled to his feet.

His men did the same, rushing to get upright and claim any advantage—but the mercenaries were experienced and did the same.

Swords clashed anew, mercenaries and sailors re-engaged, and the fight raged on.

* * *

His hands on his hips, Robert surveyed his five prisoners. All looked distinctly the worse for wear.

He couldn't find it in his heart to care.

A cohort of his most experienced men were ranged about the five, weapons drawn and ready for anything. Any attempt to even rise would be met with inhibitory force.

From where he'd been pushed to sit on the ground, wedged with the other four between two piles of ore, Ross-Courtney glowered and fruitlessly tugged at his bonds. "You'll regret this—I promise you."

Robert looked at him. After several seconds, he advised, "You should never promise what you're helpless to deliver."

Ross-Courtney made a frustrated sound.

Beside him, Neill looked daggers—at Ross-Courtney as much as at anyone else. Neill had already tried to bribe Robert—and had inexplicably tripped and fallen. He now sported several bruises and scrapes he hadn't had before.

The three younger men remained silent—hunched, watchful, and wary. After their protestations of innocence had fallen on deaf ears, they'd given Robert and his men no real trouble. Satterly had stared at Robert enough for Robert to assume the man had recognized the resemblance to Declan, who Satterly had seen when Declan and Edwina had been in Freetown.

Robert turned to his quartermaster, Miller. "Keep them here. Make sure no one attacks them." He glanced at the mine, then looked at the five prisoners with grim disgust. "Sadly, we need them alive…for the moment."

"Aye, aye, Captain." Miller tapped his blade to his palm and stared down at the five. "We'll make sure they don't move."

Leaving Miller to impress their new station upon the prisoners, Robert directed most of his men into a two-armed defensive cordon. He positioned one group to protect against incursion along the rear of the cleaning shed and the other to cover the approach along the rear of the barracks.

If any mercenary thought to take Ross-Courtney or Neill hostage and came looking, they would come that way.

Satisfied there was no likelihood of matters getting that messy, Robert took his remaining men and went to confer with crewmen from Kit's *Consort*. They confirmed they'd been sent to prevent any mercenaries from escaping around the barracks to the compound's gates.

"Hmm." Robert considered the dark corridor along the back of the barracks. The space was fitfully illuminated by the flames licking up the guard tower. "Given none of the mercenaries have yet come this way, I suspect Royd and his men are having a good time on the other side." Robert cocked a brow at his men. "What's say we join them?"

The men grinned.

Robert smiled and led the way.

But as he rounded the barracks, a man came jogging across from the mine. The man raised his hand. "Hillsythe."

Robert nodded. "Robert Frobisher."

"Is there anywhere you need reinforcements?" Hillsythe tipped his head toward the mine. "The men have no blades, but they have picks and shovels—and a score to settle."

Robert looked toward the gates, then pointed. "You see that woman over there?"

Hillsythe peered, then blinked. "One could hardly miss her."

"That's Kit Frobisher. I suggest you take your men and merge them with hers. At some point, the mercenaries are going to try to flee. Tell her I sent you."

Hillsythe saluted and headed back to the mine.

Robert didn't wait to see what transpired. He led his men into the dissipating smoke—into the rear of an out-and-out melee.

Two paces in and he found Declan beside him. After dispatching a mercenary, Robert said, "I thought you were over at the women's hut."

"I was. But Lascelle's there, and he's more than able." Declan grinned. "I came to join the fun."

Another mercenary charged; Declan raised his sword and met the man.

Robert swung around to meet another blade. Somewhere ahead of them were Royd, Caleb, and Lachlan. And Dubois. Robert leapt back, caught a low swipe on his blade, and fought on.

* * *

Royd had plunged into the middle of the melee in pursuit of Dubois. But the coward had seen him and kept dropping back behind his men, pushing them into Royd's path.

Royd's men had noticed. They started to anticipate Dubois's next move and step in to free Royd of having to engage with yet another mercenary.

Royd had taken pains to impress on his men—and through his brothers and their officers, on all their crews—that the mercenaries would be especially desperate and would, without fail, fight to the death. He'd instructed all their forces to exercise caution; as they had superior numbers, there was no need for anyone to throw away their lives. He'd lectured them all to fight with their heads, to back each other up, to take whatever time was needed, and not get killed. That said, he strongly suspected his men were meeting the mercenaries' desperation with anger and righteous fury.

And the bulk of that anger and righteous fury was directed at Dubois.

The melee was starting to fragment and spread as the mercenaries realized they would soon be overwhelmed and that the only way out for them was to flee. As often occurred in battle, that understanding seemed to be reached collectively, and despite having no orders to do so, the mercenaries started to edge away—searching for a route away from the fight.

A mercenary backed into Royd. He caught the man and spun him away, toward another of his crew.

Between one blink and the next, he glimpsed Isobel,

fleetingly lit by the crackling flames. But when he looked again, there was no one there.

Yet some inner sense told him what he'd seen was real.

He wanted to follow her, to find out what the hell she thought she was doing, but another mercenary engaged, and he had to pay attention. Dubois was still ahead of him. He'd circled through the fighters. Unlike his men, Dubois appeared to be making for the rear of the compound.

Was there a secret gate? Some other way out? Perhaps in the relatively unused space between the supply hut and the medical hut.

Or was Dubois making for their prisoners?

Royd set his jaw and redoubled his efforts. The thought of Isobel slinking through the shadows in the same area as Dubois sent a chill down his spine.

As expected, the mercenaries were experienced fighters. Putting paid to each took time. Finally dispatching his most recent opponent, Royd whirled—and caught a glimpse of a guinea-gold head. *"Damn it!"* That was Edwina, slipping through the dark—and there was Aileen!

Royd straightened to his full height and looked for Dubois.

He saw Caleb, several paces behind him, doing the same thing.

Then Royd glimpsed Dubois sliding backward into the smoke still shrouding the supply hut.

The mercenary captain was trying to slip away.

Royd looked at Caleb and whistled.

* * *

Caleb heard the distinctive sound, searched, and spotted Royd.

Royd pointed onward, mouthed "Dubois," then pointed at Caleb and circled his finger.

Caleb nodded, turned, and charged back along the barracks. Dubois was trying to run.

While he'd been searching for Dubois, he'd seen Phillipe fighting Arsene—which meant Arsene was dead, one way or another. He'd also seen Cripps make a break for the gates, only to find Declan in his path. So Cripps was as good as down, too.

The other mercenaries were being accounted for by Royd's men and all the others. Which left Dubois. Sword in hand, Caleb rounded the end of the barracks closest to the mine, pushed through a cordon of their men, and raced on.

* * *

Royd stalked after Dubois—and sprang back as the man lunged out of the shadows.

Dubois had feinted and waited for Royd to come after him; only by deft footwork and excellent reflexes did Royd manage to get his blade into position to meet Dubois's thrust.

Royd fell back, tempting Dubois to come into the open. Out of the shadows, out of the cloaking smoke.

At Royd's back, the guard tower blazed fiercely; he broke and stepped to the side, drawing Dubois with him—away from the tower in case it collapsed or rained burning debris on top of him.

Dubois paused, then his lips drew back, and he launched a furious attack.

Royd met it, countered it, and smoothly transitioned into a series of slashes and strikes that forced Dubois to pull back and defend. The instant Royd gave him an opening, Dubois flung himself at Royd—several times—only to be driven back relatively easily.

Dubois was good. Royd was better.

Royd watched that realization sink into Dubois's mind.

Along with the fact that Royd was toying with him.

Abruptly, the mercenary captain broke and danced back, into the area between the supply hut and the medical hut. The flames still licking over the supply hut lit the scene in garish splotches, leaving pools of deep shadow untouched. Panting, Dubois crouched. His eyes gleamed white as he desperately scanned this way, then that—hoping, no doubt, for one of his men to rush in and distract Royd.

Royd didn't bother glancing behind him; he was fairly certain that any mercenary still on his feet would be making for the hole where the gates had been—and he could tell from Dubois's expression that he'd seen no sign of relief from the area before the supply hut.

Royd smiled and walked forward, twirling his sword, limbering his wrist in evident expectation.

Instinctively, Dubois backed still farther, until he reached the center of the space and halted. That would be his place to make a stand, yet his gaze still flicked sideways, along the apparently unguarded rear of the barracks...

Royd heard Caleb's stealthy footsteps. They stopped, then his brother walked out of the shadows clinging to the rear of the barracks.

Killing any hope Dubois might have entertained of escaping that way.

"No," Royd stated. "Here. Now. There is no way out."

Royd glanced at Caleb as his brother halted by his shoulder. Caleb's face was set, his gaze locked on Dubois. In that instant, Royd saw the maturity the past months had etched in Caleb's face and inwardly rejoiced. His tone mild, he asked, "Mine? Or yours?"

"Mine, I believe." Caleb's tone was decisive. Without shifting his gaze from Dubois, he gestured to his scored chest. "Definitely mine."

Wordlessly, Royd waved Caleb on. His youngest brother might not—quite—be his equal with a blade, but Caleb was no slouch—although he liked to let people think he was. Noting the sudden gleam of hope that flared in Dubois's eyes, Royd suspected Caleb had put on an act for the mercenary captain; that might have been necessary to convince Dubois that allowing Caleb—let alone Lascelle—into his compound wasn't any major threat.

As, light on his feet, Caleb glided forward to engage with Dubois, Royd stepped to the side, to a position from where he could monitor the approaches to the area. A quick glance at the space before the supply hut showed Declan and Lachlan mopping up there. As Royd swung his gaze back to the circling swordsmen, he glimpsed Robert approaching along the barracks' rear wall. Clearly, all was well with their prisoners.

Satisfied that all else was proceeding as planned—more or less—Royd settled to watch Caleb extract payment, not just for himself but for all the captives, from Dubois's hide.

* * *

By the time he got close enough to engage with Dubois, Caleb had it all planned. He circled to place his back to the supply hut—the better to have Dubois lit by the leaping flames while his own face and body remained in silhouette.

Then, quite deliberately, Caleb chuckled—derisively. He made as if to glance at Royd—

Dubois swallowed the lure and launched a frenzied attack.

Caleb defended, then caught the mercenary's blade on his own, forced it high, and leaned in. And smiled.

Dubois might be heavier, but Caleb was younger, fitter, and at least equally strong. As he fluidly disengaged and attacked, forcing Dubois back, his advantage in reach also showed.

Caleb took his time, deliberately marking the man slash by slash—the cuts increasingly deep.

There was nowhere for Dubois to run. Royd and then Caleb had backed him into the area between the side of the medical hut and the still-burning ruin of the supply hut. The mercenary captain had no option but to face Caleb—to face his fate.

Dubois's blood was dripping freely from numerous wounds when, in a last-ditch effort, he flung himself at Caleb—only to have Caleb trap his blade again. Close again.

Then Caleb heaved and threw Dubois back—and with a slashing swipe, sent his sword ripping across Dubois's gut.

Caleb cut deep enough for the wound to be fatal, but not deep enough for Dubois to die any other way than slowly.

Dubois dropped his sword and clutched both hands to his belly. He looked at Caleb, shock and disbelief in his face.

* * *

Dubois staggered back—and tripped over a lump on the ground behind him.

Royd had thought the lump just a shadow. Before he fully registered that the lump was a dead mercenary, Dubois had rolled, snatched up the dead man's pistol, and scrambled to his feet.

Royd froze, as did Caleb.

As did Robert and Declan in the shadows to either side.

Using both hands, Dubois brought the pistol to bear—on Caleb. Dubois stood with head lowered, obviously concentrating to hold the pistol steady. The click as he cocked it rang in the sudden silence.

Royd stepped forward to a position a yard or more to Caleb's right. "So," Royd asked conversationally, "who are you going to pick? Him or me?"

Dubois blinked and looked at Royd—and the pistol barrel wavered. Dubois was close to weaving, yet as he corrected his aim, this time to shoot Royd, it appeared steady enough for his purpose.

"Or what about me?" Robert came to stand on Caleb's left, again with a yard or more between them.

Dubois started and took another step back. He blinked several times; he was sweating profusely.

"Or even me." Declan appeared on Royd's right, giving Dubois a choice between four similar-looking brothers.

Confusion was gaining on Dubois; the pistol barrel swung wildly from one brother to another. Then Dubois hauled in a pained breath, held it—and brought the barrel back to point at Caleb's chest. "You." His voice was a croak. "You brought them here—it's you I choose."

"Put it down, man," Robert advised. "You're done for, and you know it."

Royd was unsurprised when Dubois tried to smile—a tortured effort—and said, "But I've got the chance to take one of you with me." Again, Dubois focused on Caleb and nodded. "Him."

"For the love of the Almighty, how stupid is that?" The words were delivered in a scathing tone only a duke's daughter could manage as Edwina marched out of the shadows on Dubois's left, like a character taking the stage in a play.

Dubois started; the pistol barrel swung wildly.

Royd heard Declan curse beneath his breath.

Halting, her hands on her hips, Edwina scowled at Dubois. "Put that gun down at once!"

Dubois's eyes had widened to saucers. He stared, but failed to comply.

"Don't be ridiculous, you horrible man."

Everyone's gaze swung to Dubois's right, where Aileen Hopkins had somehow materialized. When Dubois focused on her, she glared at him. "It's entirely pointless to shoot anyone. You could at least have the grace to die without creating any further fuss."

Dubois gaped.

Royd glanced at his brothers and found all three as grim-faced as he. What the devil did these harpies think they were doing?

Then Katherine Fortescue appeared out of the shadows even farther to Dubois's left—and Dubois jumped and stumbled back a pace, the better to face her and also keep all the rest of them in view.

Katherine eyed him coldly. "You're worse than any beast. The world will be a much better place without you—so go. Just *go*."

Dubois had been bleeding steadily throughout. His complexion was now ashen, and he looked utterly bewildered.

Then he drew in a breath that cut off on a gasp, gritted his teeth, and, once more, forced the barrel of the pistol into line with Caleb's chest.

"For heaven's sake!" A dark shadow reared behind Dubois, and Isobel brought a long-handled cast-iron frying pan down on the mercenary captain's head.

They all heard the crack; she hadn't held back.

Dubois's eyes rolled up, his hand went limp, and the pistol barrel dipped.

Quick as a flash, Isobel reached around him, swiped

the pistol from his nerveless fingers, and eased back the hammer.

Dubois slumped into an ungainly heap at her feet.

Royd looked around the circle. All the women were now smiling broadly, clearly congratulating themselves on a job well done.

He drew a long, deep breath—filling his lungs and dispelling the constriction that had clamped like a vise around his chest. He glanced at his brothers; they were doing the same. He watched as, having apparently regained some semblance of control, they each walked to join their respective ladies.

He waited for a second longer, studying Isobel as, the frying pan dangling from one hand, the pistol in the other, she looked down at Dubois very much in the vein of him being some strange insect she thought to study before she obliterated him completely.

Royd approached her and smiled easily. "Thank you." He reached for the pistol.

She glanced at him, let him take the pistol, then calmly replied, "It was entirely my pleasure. We all agreed you were taking too long to bring this"—with her chin, she indicated Dubois—"to an appropriate end."

Royd thought about that, then murmured, "Not just an Amazon but an impatient Amazon."

She grinned and looked around.

Royd looked, too. The fighting was over. The sounds of battle had been replaced by shuffles and grunts and quiet exchanges—the sounds of the living making sure of the dead.

Beside him, Isobel stirred. "Where's Ross-Courtney?"

Her tone reminded Royd of her earlier declaration.

Sure enough, she went on, "I vowed I'd have his balls if he touched that girl, much less Katherine."

Some might imagine she was speaking figuratively. He knew better. "You'll have to rein in your ferocity—at least until Ross-Courtney and Neill give us the names of their fellow backers." He glanced around, then met her dark eyes and her disaffected frown. "One thing I'm sure of is that the captives here—indeed, everyone involved—will want *all* those responsible to pay."

She sniffed, but didn't argue.

Instead, she slipped her hand into his, let him close his fingers firmly—tightly—about hers, and they walked side by side after the others to where their prisoners awaited them.

Twelve

Ross-Courtney and Neill refused to name the other backers.

Indeed, they stubbornly refused to admit that they had been at fault in any way whatsoever.

After parting from Isobel, who left with Katherine to help bring the children back to their beds, Royd joined Robert, and they approached their prisoners. Realizing Royd was the senior commander on the scene, Ross-Courtney barely waited for them to halt before launching into a tale of how he and Neill had been kidnapped by the mercenaries, presumably to be held for ransom, and despite the testimony of all the other captives, he, Neill, and Satterly, and for all Ross-Courtney knew, Muldoon and Winton as well, were entirely innocent of any wrongdoing.

Ross-Courtney pompously proclaimed, "We are victims here!" He glowered at Robert, but then his expression turned superciliously superior. "I daresay I might be prevailed on to overlook your brother's unwarranted behavior—no doubt he was carried away by the heat of battle."

Royd looked at Robert. "I can't recall the last time I saw you carried away by the heat of battle."

Robert arched his brows. "Perhaps when I was nine

and we staged that pitched battle with the Daweses on the docks."

His face turning a virulent red, Ross-Courtney glared. "See here!" He fought against his bonds. "This is an outrage! I'm a Gentleman of the King's Bedchamber. I demand—"

"Now, now, Lord Peter." Edwina halted on her way to the medical hut. "If you keep that up, you'll give yourself an apoplexy, and you'll never see London again."

Ross-Courtney goggled at her. He stared, his mouth opened and shut, then he croaked, "Lady Edwina?"

Edwina smiled brilliantly, but the expression didn't reach her eyes. "How sweet of you to remember—I'm Lady Edwina Frobisher now." She paused, then artlessly suggested, "If you would furnish us with the names of your fellow backers, I'm sure the Captains Frobisher could be prevailed on to allow you to be made more comfortable." She arched a brow and waited.

Ross-Courtney blinked. He hesitated too long to leave any credence in his eventual blustering, "Backers? I have no idea what you mean." Lips compressing, he struggled against his bonds again.

Edwina sighed. "Very well. Have it your way." She started to move off, then paused to say, "Oh—and in case you're imagining that your guilt, and that of your colleagues here, will rest solely on the testimony of the captives who were held in this compound, I assure you that will not be the case." She didn't declare her intention to bear witness against them, yet her implication was clear. And with that, she swanned off.

Although Robert and Royd asked again, in several ways, Ross-Courtney and Neill, and the other three as well, refused to say anything more—or, at least, anything Royd was interested in hearing.

After declaring that he had more important matters to deal with, he left the five trussed where they sat, watched over by three of Robert's men, and went to the barracks' porch. He'd sent men to summon all leaders—his brothers, his cousins, all officers, as well as the de facto leaders of the captives—to a conference to decide what had to be done and to delegate the necessary tasks. Although the rear wall of the barracks and the end closest to the tower had caught fire, the flames hadn't taken hold; several buckets of water had left the affected planks smoldering sullenly, but the building itself remained sound.

Royd sat on the porch. While he waited for the others to arrive, he compiled a mental list of the usual chores—treating the injured, disposing of the bodies, collecting weapons, making the perimeter at least temporarily secure again. Searching through Dubois's papers for any evidence regarding their five prisoners and the other backers. Making ready to evacuate the captives to the coast, along with the prisoners.

By the time the men gathered, along with a transparently hugely relieved Aileen, who appeared arm in arm with her brother Will, Royd had the list fixed in his mind. But before he could speak, he saw Isobel, Katherine, and the other women captives, plus Babington, striding over from the women and children's hut. Royd had put Babington in charge of the protective detail by the lake, thus allowing him to reunite with his Mary at the earliest possible moment; he now strode along with a huge smile on his face, one hand wrapped around the fingers of a sweet-faced young woman who looked as if her fondest dream had come true.

Isobel swung up to sit beside him, her breeches giving her a freedom of movement he associated with childhood days in the shipyards. "The children were so excited, they'd exhausted themselves. They're all in dreamland already."

The patter of feet heralded Edwina. She halted beside Declan. "I wanted to hear, but I'll have to get back soon—we have lots of cuts to treat and some stitching to do."

Royd nodded; he hadn't expected Edwina to busy herself with that sort of stitchery. But presumably, stitches were stitches, and he could imagine hers were small and precise. He met her gaze, then looked around the circle of faces. "First, do we have any casualties?"

Caleb, his chest covered by a shirt he'd found in the barracks, reported, "Two. One of the original captives, a navvy named Wattie Watson. He went up against a mercenary trying to escape through the gates—Wattie was armed with only a spade."

Royd knew his expression was harsh. "And did the mercenary escape?"

"No." It was Kit who answered.

Royd gave her a nod and returned his attention to Caleb. "Who else?"

Caleb grimaced. Sadly, he said, "One of the older boys—Si. The four disobeyed our orders to remain in the men's hut and thrust themselves into the fighting. The other three are bruised and cut, but nothing serious. Si took a knife to the side."

Royd thought of a young life needlessly snuffed out. They all did. Then he blew out a breath. "It could have been a lot worse."

Heads nodded reluctantly, but that was undeniably true.

Royd glanced at Edwina. "Are there any serious cases in the medical hut?"

She shook her head. "None life-threatening. Well, as long as we can stretch the salve out, but there seems to be a reasonable stock, so I expect we'll manage. But the sooner we can get everyone to Freetown and better bandages, the better."

"There'll be more supplies on board our ships," Declan reminded her.

"Next item," Royd said. "Collecting the bodies and burying the dead."

Hillsythe and Lascelle volunteered to oversee that task; as both, Royd suspected, had experience of the grisly work, he accepted without demur, and they left to gather their men.

Royd went quickly down his list. Fanshawe, Hopkins, and Dixon took on the chore of collecting all the unclaimed weapons, while Lachlan and Kit put up their hands to resecure the perimeter; as they'd been instrumental in unsecuring it, that seemed sensible.

Robert and Royd would search through Dubois's papers, aided by Babington, while Declan and two of the women—Harriet and Gemma—suggested they and Declan's crew should put the kitchen to rights and go through the stores to see what they could salvage for breakfast and the trek to the coast.

With tasks allocated, everyone dispersed. Edwina, Isobel, Aileen, Katherine, and the other three women all left for the medical hut.

Robert pushed away from the porch and gestured at the barracks' door. "Shall we?"

Royd waved him and Babington on. "You make a start—I need to show my face in the medical hut."

Robert nodded; personally checking on the wounded was a necessary aspect of command, at least as Frobishers saw it.

When he entered the medical hut, Royd found a scene that, at first glance, resembled utter chaos—then he realized it was organized chaos. As he passed down the line of the injured, bestowing encouragement and assurances, any doubts he'd harbored over the wisdom of his brothers acceding to Edwina's and Aileen's insistence to accompany them vanished beneath a wave of gratitude. In a situation such as this, the two bossiest women he knew—even more so than Isobel and Iona—were godsends. Together with Isobel, Katherine, and the other three women, they ministered to the injured with a mixture of compassion, empathy, and martinet-like command that enabled even the crustiest sailor to accept their help with good grace.

Yielding to a ministering angel was an act of wisdom, not weakness.

Something Caleb was patently learning. Royd found his youngest brother seated on a stool, being doctored by both Edwina and Katherine. Royd gathered that Caleb had committed what, in the ladies' eyes, apparently ranked as a cardinal sin by donning a shirt before having his wounds tended.

His hands on his thighs, his chest once again bare, Caleb sat and endured as the two women inspected his cuts and applied a brown salve.

Edwina frowned, then gently prodded. "Are we sure this doesn't need stitching?"

"Totally sure," Caleb responded.

Without looking up, Edwina said, "I wasn't talking to you." She glanced at Katherine. "See—just here, it's deeper."

Caleb cast Royd an anguished glance.

Grinning, Royd raised a hand in salute and left him to his fate.

He spent twenty more minutes doing the rounds of those still waiting to be seen and those already treated who'd been bedded down in one of the two large rooms.

Isobel and Katherine were both busy treating others, while Mary and the other two women were distributing cups of tea.

Isobel stopped him as he was about to leave. "You and the others"—with her head, she indicated those outside—"doubtless have scratches and shallow cuts. Katherine told me that, in this climate, we need to treat every little thing so it doesn't fester. That's why they have such a large stock of this salve." She pressed three small pots into his hands. "We're too busy here to chase you all—you and the others can anoint yourselves, then pass the pots around. Everyone needs to take care."

He nodded. "I expect we'll be gathering later, when the others return to report. I'll mention it then."

"Good." She stretched up and kissed him, squeezed his arm, then let him go and turned to the next injured man.

Royd reached the door and realized Caleb was sitting on the porch steps, his arm around the hunched shoulders of a boy sitting beside him. Two other boys of similar age were standing close by, their heads bowed, their gazes cast down.

Rather than interrupt, Royd leaned against the wall just inside the open door.

"Gerry." Briefly, Caleb hugged the lad beside him. "Si dying isn't your fault." He glanced at the other boys. "Not yours or anyone else's."

"We shoulda stayed inside like you and Mr. Hillsythe said." Gerry hiccuped. "If we had, Si'd still be alive."

"Yes, and next time you'll know that orders like that need to be obeyed." Caleb paused, then more quietly said, "It's sad that Si died, but he made his own decision to go out and join the fighting. You all made your own decisions. He was responsible for the decision that led to his death—not any of you. But you've now learned that fighting is real—that people get badly injured and die. That's an important thing to learn. If you learned that today, and you never forget it, then something useful will have come from Si's death. His dying won't have been entirely in vain."

It was hard to know what to say to striplings in such circumstances; Royd approved of Caleb's tack. The moment made Royd think of Duncan and all the learning his son had before him.

"Come on." Caleb lifted his arm from the boy and rose. "Let's get you to the hut—you should be in your hammocks. There'll be lots to do tomorrow."

Royd waited until the small band was several yards away before emerging from the hut and heading for the barracks. Lanterns had been lit and passed around to all those working, while other lanterns had been placed strategically around the compound, lighting the way for those, like Royd, moving from hut to hut.

Along the way, he passed on the three pots of salve with instructions, then joined Robert and Charles Babington inside the barracks.

They'd made a good start going through the papers and ledgers in and around Dubois's desk. Leaving them focused on that, Royd took a lamp and walked down the long, rectangular hut. At the far end, where the sidewall was blackened, he found a trundle bed set apart from the others. He set down the lamp and searched. Under the pallet, he found a small bound book. He sat on the bed, opened the book, and read.

Twenty minutes later, he walked back to Dubois's desk and showed Robert and Babington what he'd found. They'd uncovered other useful references. Babington found a satchel, and they put the papers and book inside. Royd hefted the satchel.

Robert had gone to the door. "They've built up the fire. It looks like we're gathering there."

Royd followed Robert, and Babington trailed behind. They sat on the logs around the fire pit.

Soon after, the women joined them.

Isobel slumped against Royd's side. "All those with serious wounds have been treated." She tipped her head, resting it on his shoulder. "No one needs anything more done tonight."

He turned his chin enough to drop a light kiss on her forehead.

As the warmth from the fire played over him, and the warmth of her, safe, alive, and by his side, seeped into his soul, he finally started to relax.

They'd taken the compound, rescued the captives, and lost only two in the process. They had the three local villains and two of the backers in custody. They'd succeeded amazingly well in achieving the most important of their goals.

He said as much when, drawn by the fire, the rest of the company bar the children gathered to report and learn how matters stood. In the aftermath of the action, of the excitement and fear, they were all bone-weary, but at his words, the first seeds of triumph started to bloom.

Caleb reported that their fallen had been wrapped in shrouds and their bodies placed in the cleaning shed for burial tomorrow. Hillsythe confirmed that all the mercenaries had been dispatched during the fighting. The bodies had been collected and stacked outside the gate, covered by a tarpaulin to await burial. Hillsythe's suggestion that Muldoon, Satterly, and Winton should dig all the graves was met with unanimous approval.

Lachlan's and Kit's teams had resecured the gates and closed the gap behind the women's hut. Harriet reported that they had food enough to feed everyone for several meals, as well as jerky and hard biscuits for the trek to the coast. Dixon confirmed that they'd redistributed the weapons taken from the mercenaries to those captives who knew how to use them.

The Frobisher crews, officers as well as sailors, had retreated to sleep in their already established camps in the jungle, leaving their captains and their ladies, and their injured who were resting in the medical hut, within the palisade, along with those previously held captive.

Lascelle had been one of the last to join the circle. He listened to the other reports, then said, "We have one issue yet to address." Across the fire pit, he met Caleb's gaze and smiled. "You did too excellent a job, my friend. Dubois is not yet dead." Looking at the others, Lascelle explained, "He is dying, but slowly. So very, very slowly and in agony, too, but"—he shrugged in typical Gallic fashion—"I do not think he will die within the next hours. So what do you wish to do with him?" He directed the question around the circle, to all the captives present.

They'd all suffered under Dubois; Royd waited to hear their decision.

After several less-than-feasible suggestions, Hillsythe asked Lascelle if he had any thoughts.

Lascelle's answering smile was cold. What he suggested had a similar tone and was hailed by all as eminently fitting.

As Fanshawe put it, "That will be his worst nightmare come true."

And so it was that Dubois, tied but not gagged, was carted by the captives into the mine. They tossed him on the ground at the far end of what they called the second tunnel.

Royd stood to one side and watched as Dixon, his

face like stone, tossed a pail of water over Dubois, reviving him.

Dubois blinked, then weakly shook the water from his eyes. They all waited, watching, as he looked around, as his gaze focused and he realized where he was…

"No!" The word was weak.

In a panic, eyes wide, Dubois frantically looked around, fighting his bonds. "No—you can't leave me here."

"We can," Hillsythe stated. "And we are."

Dubois started to gibber.

Isobel, her hand in Royd's, tugged, and he turned, and together, they walked out of the mine.

Declan and Edwina, Robert and Aileen, and Caleb and Katherine followed, with the rest of the adult captives trooping behind.

Dubois's wails, weak and incoherent, followed them into the night.

The ex-captives retreated to their hammocks in the huts. Robert, Aileen, Declan, Edwina, Isobel, and Royd headed for the bunk beds in the barracks. Royd hung back and let the others go in. When Isobel returned to the doorway and arched a brow at him, he said, "Choose a bed. I'm going to do a last circuit."

She held his gaze for an instant, then nodded.

He went down the steps and walked to the gate. He tested it, more out of habit than in any expectation it would fall. Then he walked around the compound in a counterclockwise direction, turning down unnecessary lanterns as he passed them. All that was left of the supply hut was a heap of charred timbers and smoldering embers. Lascelle had apologized to Caleb over how long it had taken for the fire to get going, but the Frenchman's distraction had proved more effective than anyone had imagined it would.

After glancing at the area where Caleb and Dubois had fought, Royd walked on. He paused in the open doorway of the medical hut and listened, but other than occasional snuffles and a lot of snores, all seemed settled.

Ahead lay the ore piles, with several lanterns trained on the prisoners so that the guards, sitting in relative comfort on logs in the nearby shadows, could easily keep an eye on them.

All five prisoners were awake. They shifted, unable to get comfortable against the piles of rough rock.

When they saw him walking out of the shadows toward them, they all stilled.

Halting just outside the circle of bright light, he scanned their faces. Winton would be the easiest to induce to talk. Muldoon, too, wouldn't be a hard nut to crack. Satterly... Royd knew too little of the man to judge.

As for Ross-Courtney and Neill, Royd was under no illusions; neither man was likely to speak. Unless he missed his guess, both had realized that their only hope of escaping the fate that now loomed lay in admitting nothing and saying as little as they could. Nevertheless, he fixed his gaze on the older men and arched a brow. "Well? Are you ready to change your tune?"

Ross-Courtney glared, then pointedly looked away.

Neill glanced at Ross-Courtney, and after a moment, said, "We might be forced to remain your prisoners, but we will only speak with the relevant authorities."

Royd waited, but Neill didn't look up, didn't meet his eyes.

Royd smiled; neither Neill nor Ross-Courtney had any idea of Royd's standing with the "relevant authorities."

"Very well." He turned away. "We'll see how you feel in the morning."

Did they but know it, his last sentence was directed at Satterly, Muldoon, and Winton. Digging graves and burying the dead—men who were dead because of what they had caused to happen—would shake the three more than any words.

Royd continued his circuit. He paused at the entrance to the mine; cocking his head, he listened, and from the depths heard a pitiable whimper. Dubois's penance had not yet ended.

After quitting the mine and turning down the lanterns along the front of the men's hut, Royd passed the fire pit, the fire now reduced to ashes, and finally walked up the barracks' steps.

All was quiet and still inside. He located Isobel more by instinct than sight. She was fast asleep. He considered an empty bed nearby, then looked down at her again.

Then he bent, rolled her onto her side, and slid into the bed behind her.

He closed his eyes, sighed, and his senses fell into a void.

* * *

Late the next morning, the compound's gates were swung wide, and with Kate's hand in his, Gerry beside him, and the other two older boys on Kate's other side, Caleb marched out and took the path to the lake.

At breakfast, Annie, Gemma, and Mary had nominated the spot where they'd waited with the children as the nicest around for the final resting place of Wattie Watson and Simon Finn. Hillsythe and Dixon had performed a quick survey, then Hillsythe, assisted by several of the Frobisher quartermasters who had returned to the compound, had marched Satterly, Muldoon, and Winton to the spot and handed them shovels.

When Caleb and the others reached the area beyond the wharf, the graves were neatly dug, with the bodies—wrapped in sheets taken from the mercenaries' beds and then sewn into hammocks—waiting alongside.

Enough of the men now knew how to work rock; several had toiled since dawn to shape headstones. Others had used the chisels and hammers to carve names and dates on the smoothed faces.

As the senior officer present, Royd led the service, reciting from memory all the usual passages in between the words offered by Dixon, Hillsythe, Fanshawe, Hopkins, and, unexpectedly, Kit, who had witnessed Wattie's death. No one had seen Si fall. Then the bodies were lowered into the graves. There were many willing hands to man the shovels and many silent farewells said as the pair were laid to rest.

Most lingered to see the graves completed and the headstones raised.

Three of them. Between Si's and Wattie's headstones, another stone was set. The words etched on its face read: *Daisy. Age 13. 1824. From Freetown. An angel taken before her time.*

Caleb bowed his head, as did everyone there. Someone had remembered, and all those there would never forget.

* * *

Royd returned to the compound hand in hand with Isobel.

As they walked through the gates, he saw their prisoners now clustered awkwardly around the porch post to which Caleb had been tied. Those picking over the wreck of the supply hut had unearthed, among other things, seven sets of still-useable shackles. The two blacksmiths among the ex-captives had made short work of affixing the shackles to the prisoners, thus relieving Robert's men from having to keep a close watch on the miscreants.

Royd halted and, across the compound, studied the group.

Isobel halted beside him. She followed his gaze. As if reading his mind, she murmured, "Leave them there." She glanced at the fire pit, where everyone else—ex-captive and rescuer—was now gathering. "It's time for us to eat, they're not going to be harmed by missing a few meals, and we don't have that much food that we need to waste any on them…and even more importantly, seeing them there, caught and awaiting justice, is balm to all those who were trapped in this wretched place."

She was right on all counts. With a tip of his head, he acknowledged that, and they continued to the fire pit.

The sailors who took turns in their ships' galleys had banded together to prepare a simple meal using some of what had been found in the kitchen and padding it out with ship's rations brought in from their respective camps.

Royd wouldn't have said the food provided was excessive, let alone extravagant, but watching how the ex-captives, especially the children, fell on the fare, he realized they'd all been not precisely starved but not adequately fed, either.

Caleb saw him watching and guessed his thoughts. He caught Royd's eye. "This is roughly double what we would normally get."

Seated beside Royd, Isobel looked at her plate. "Good Lord."

Royd agreed, but the ex-captives being able to fill their bellies to an extent they hadn't in months was another point that helped to establish things had changed.

That they were free.

He'd seen it before, all those years ago and several times since, when he'd rescued those who'd been held for more than a few weeks. It took time to realize that they truly were free again.

Dixon confirmed that when he said, "I keep thinking I should check my watch to see if it's time to go back into the mine."

Others nodded or murmured similar sentiments.

Royd finished his meal, laid down his plate, and looked around the circle, ultimately letting his gaze rest on Dixon, Hillsythe, and the other leaders. "We need to discuss your return to Freetown." Unsurprisingly, everyone paid attention. "I propose we walk directly to the coast along the route my party took to get here." He described the path, the likely length of the trek, then detailed the ships that would be waiting at the shore—the entire Frobisher fleet in these waters bar *Consort*, which would still be keeping watch outside the naval blockade, plus Lascelle's *The Raven*. "That makes five ships. If we divide the company, we shouldn't be too crowded, and the sailing time to Freetown isn't that long."

Robert added, "Heading to the coast and then sailing to Freetown will take the least toll on the children, the women, and the wounded."

Agreement was unanimous. Royd let the talk run unrestrained for several minutes. The children were fired with eagerness at the prospect of seeing the ships; the promise of sailing into Freetown on such vessels put stars in countless eyes.

That carrot at the end of the path would help to get them through the long trek.

Finally, he raised his voice. "Time—as in what time we should leave." He waited until calls of "Now!" and "Can't we go now?" faded. "Even if we hurry, it'll take at least until late this afternoon to get packed and ready. There's no point starting along the track only to have to halt less than an hour along." He glanced at Dixon. "I suggest we use the rest of the day to make ready, then leave at first light tomorrow—as soon as there's light enough for us to see our way."

"Yay!"

"Tomorrow!"

As the children's cheers echoed from the cliffs, the adults looked around; hearing no argument, everyone smiled.

Thereafter, the talk was of preparations and the delegation of various tasks. Katherine, Edwina, Isobel, and Aileen volunteered to pack the medical supplies. Harriet and the other women arranged to work with the sailor-cooks to gather all they could from the leftover stores—first for a celebratory meal that evening, the last the ex-captives would eat in this place, and subsequently to pack all that would be useful on the trek to the estuary. As a part of that, Diccon was delegated to take all the children who wished to go with him out into the jungle to gather enough fruit, berries, and nuts for the evening's desserts and to carry with them to the coast.

"We won't want to be stopping constantly along the way, and that's something you children can carry," Harriet said. "And I daresay the sailors wouldn't mind having some fruit and berries to keep on board, either."

The mention of fruit and berries brought Duncan forcibly to Isobel's mind. She'd thought of him often, especially when looking at the captive children. Thought of how privileged his life was compared to theirs, and how much better it yet would be once he was openly acknowledged as Royd's son and heir.

Which he would be; she accepted that, yet…she

couldn't—didn't have space in her mind—to deal with the changes that implied, not while there.

Diccon, the tow-headed lad who had acted as courier between Royd and Caleb, puffed out his chest and ordered any children who wanted to come with him to line up by the gates. Virtually all the younger children went; only the three older boys, the girl Tilly, and another bright-eyed, fair-haired girl-child refrained. Diccon dispatched several boys to the kitchen to fetch baskets, then, with three of Royd's crew ambling behind, Diccon led the procession, two by two, out through the open gates.

Watching the performance, Isobel saw Duncan in her mind's eye. She glanced at Royd and saw him watching with a similar, somewhat distant, expression.

He felt her gaze and turned his head. He read her eyes. When she whispered, "I can so easily see Duncan taking charge like that," he laughed. Squeezing her hand, he faced forward.

At breakfast, Hillsythe had quietly informed Royd that Dubois had expired sometime during the night. While the company had been burying their dead, Royd had asked two of his men to fetch Dubois's body from the mine and add it to the pile outside the gates.

Now Hillsythe and Lascelle came to crouch by Royd. When he turned to them, Hillsythe said, "As per your orders, your men had those three"—with his head, he indicated Satterly, Muldoon, and Winton—"dig a large enough hole off the path to Kale's camp to bury Dubois's not-so-little band. We were thinking that now, with the children busy elsewhere, would be a good time to take care of that."

As Royd nodded in agreement, Lascelle grinned coldly. "And now those three have rested, they can help do the carrying."

"Undoubtedly." Royd glanced at the three prisoners in question; they were sprawled on the dirt, trying to rest as comfortably as their shackles would allow. "Send as many men as you deem necessary and have them keep a sharp eye on those three—I wouldn't put it past them to try to escape."

Hillsythe and Lascelle nodded and rose, and Royd turned back to the discussions.

* * *

Seated several places from Isobel, Kate had yet to leave to pack the medical supplies, allowing Caleb to continue to hold her hand. He sat and observed the subtle changes in those he'd befriended over the past weeks as they started to think about the lives they would resume—the lives many had thought they would never return to.

When Kate leaned closer, studying his face, he met her eyes and murmured, "Second chances are precious and fragile things."

She searched his eyes, then smiled gloriously. Her hand shifted and gripped his. "I feel as if you're my second chance—my second chance at starting the next stage of my life. Successfully, this time—I was clearly not meant to be a governess."

Caleb shook his head. "Uh-uh. I'm your first chance." A second chance was what was happening between Royd and Isobel. "And look at all the smart ones about us grabbing their chance." With a tip of his head, he directed her gaze. "Annie and Jeb—and there's Mary and Babington, and Harriet and Dixon."

"And Edwina and Declan, and Robert and Aileen." Kate's gaze reached Isobel and Royd, and she paused. "But not those two."

"No." Caleb squeezed her hand. "That's a true second chance in the making."

And it was so intense and evocative in so many ways, it was almost painful to watch.

Shifting his gaze elsewhere, Caleb saw a small golden head bobbing around the circle. "Amy's still here. I wonder why she didn't go with the others."

He was destined to find out, because Amy was on her way to them. She halted near Kate and smiled winningly when Kate turned to her and asked, "Did you want me?"

Amy fixed her big blue eyes on Kate's face and, her hands clasped before her, said, "Can I please come and help you with the ointments and things? I saw you and the other ladies helping all the hurt people. I'd like to be able to help people, too, and I wondered if you might show me things."

Kate smiled. "Of course." She glanced across the circle. "We're not quite ready to go back to the medical hut yet." She patted the space on the log beside her. "Why don't you sit beside me until it's time?"

Amy beamed, stepped over the log, and sat.

Caleb returned his attention to the ongoing discussions. A moment later, Hillsythe and Phillipe, both of whom had just sent a party of men out of the gates—Caleb assumed to remove the pile of dead bodies beyond—rejoined the circle, taking places vacated by children between Royd and Caleb. When Caleb quietly inquired, Phillipe confirmed that the mercenaries' bodies were being disposed of.

At a break in the conversation, Hillsythe turned to Royd. "Lascelle and I have a suggestion to make. Our prisoners have elected not to reveal anything to you. Lascelle and I wondered if they might, perhaps, be prevailed on to share more details were he and I to ask. In our own, rather different ways."

Caleb saw the calculation in Royd's face as he looked

from Hillsythe to Lascelle. Then Royd arched a black brow. "Why not?"

"Indeed," Lascelle said, "and we have the next two days, both here and while we're tramping through the jungle to the coast. Being held at the rear of the column, surrounded by my men—French, not English, and therefore with no reason to treat the gentlemen well or be cowed by their standing—might assist in loosening their tongues."

"Well, Satterly's, Muldoon's, and Winton's tongues, at least." Hillsythe grimaced. "I don't hold much hope of getting anything out of the other two, but the younger three should be amenable to our brand of persuasion."

Royd considered for a second more, then nodded. He looked around at all the others. "Any objections?"

There were none.

"Now we've decided that, I have a suggestion to make, too." Dixon looked at his fellow ex-captives, then turned his gaze to Royd. "There are some diamonds left in the second pipe. If all the men who know how to tease those diamonds out were to work for an hour, two at the most, we'd have every diamond out—and they wouldn't really need much cleaning. On top of that, we have stockpiles hidden in the mine, at the ore piles, outside the cleaning shed, and inside it. Some would still need cleaning, but if we divided up the load, we could easily carry the whole lot out as is." Dixon paused to glance around the circle; it was to the others he spoke when he continued, "I believe that after all we've been through, restitution is in order. The authorities in the settlement might have something to say about that, but—"

"Not if the authorities behind the rescue mission have their way." Royd caught Dixon's eye. "And trust me, they will. I, too, believe a restitution scheme, funded by the diamonds you've all slaved to extract, is an excellent idea."

The notion was discussed further. Royd, backed by Robert and Declan, swore to do his best to confiscate any funds from the mine held by Ross-Courtney or realized from the sale of any stones still with the diamond merchant. When Royd called for a vote by all the ex-captives over who should be in charge of the scheme, once Caleb declined, pointing out he would be returning to England, Dixon, Hillsythe, and Babington—who had in short order earned the ex-captives' trust—were elected as executors of the fund.

Royd was pleased with that result. Hillsythe had already indicated that he would be returning to London with the Frobishers, but only to report, after which he expected to return to the settlement to oversee the governor's office for some months. He agreed to take charge of the diamonds and ensure a good price was obtained, and once back in the settlement, he would be perfectly placed to ensure the scheme achieved the desired result. With Babington's contacts to exploit, there was no reason to believe the fund wouldn't be a success and bring succor to those who had toiled in the compound for so many months, largely without hope.

Fanshawe and Hopkins suggested they would take a team of men into the mine to pull out the last of the diamonds, while others gathered up the stockpiles and brought the stones and rocks to Dixon for cataloging. Lascelle and Caleb, both of whom waived any return for them or their men on the grounds they'd not truly been captives in the same sense, offered to take the names of all those who should get a portion of the fund.

At that point, the gathering about the fire pit broke up, with virtually everyone heading off on some task or another, all intent on being ready by the time night fell so they could celebrate—and then quit the compound and not look back.

Somewhat to his surprise, Royd found himself with little to do. His men had brought his seabag and Isobel's satchel from their camp; he and she would be ready to depart without having to pack or make ready.

Declan and Robert were also at loose ends. Declan waved at the mine. "Why don't we take a look at what all the fuss has been about?"

They ambled into the mine. Lanternlight guided them to the tunnel where the men were working to remove the last of the diamonds. The three brothers got a lesson in what it took to mine diamonds from Fanshawe and Hopkins. In response to a little encouragement from Royd, the lieutenants, aided by the other men, regaled the brothers with the tale of how the captives had plotted and schemed to stretch out the mining until the rescue force reached them. It was impossible not to be impressed by how cohesive the group had grown and how inventive and dogged they'd been, how desperate and determined to survive. Equally impossible to miss was the fact that Caleb—with his indefatigable will and his uncanny knack for inspiring confidence—had played a crucial, indeed pivotal, role. With simple sincerity, Hopkins put it into words. "Without him and his leadership, we wouldn't have made it."

Royd hid a wry but self-satisfied smile. Action under pressure was what defined a man—the situations he faced, the decisions he made. Royd appreciated that better than most. Challenge cut to a man's bedrock and shaped him.

He'd been waiting for some such challenge to come along and shape Caleb. To cut away the lingering superficialities of youth, the hedonism and irresponsibility, and reveal the true core beneath.

Propping a shoulder against the rock wall, in the play of light from the lanterns, he looked at Robert and Declan, talking with Fanshawe a few yards farther down the tunnel. Each of his brothers had their special strengths, but there was no denying Caleb was the most like him. There were six years between them, and as the eldest, he'd stepped into the prime leadership role more or less from birth, so consequently, the difference in experience had been profound.

Only now, Royd judged, had Caleb finally made the transition and taken the last step, and become the leader he'd always had the potential to be. He had more to learn, of course, yet… If Royd were to put into place the plan forming in his head—that, truth be told, had been in his mind for some time, but that had gained more urgency now Isobel had come back into his life—and stepped down from his position as senior captain of Frobisher Shipping, then it was Caleb who would need to step into the role.

Royd didn't think Robert and Declan would disagree. Even more so now that they had other distractions—reasons to spend less time at sea. Like him, they would want to adjust their sailing schedules the better to accommodate their ladies—their wives. And while, if Royd correctly understood the connection between Caleb and Katherine Fortescue, Caleb would soon have a wife, too, Royd could see Katherine—Kate—maturing into a woman like their mother, Elaine, and sailing with Caleb wherever business took him.

Life was moving on, and things were falling into place.

Royd pushed away from the rock wall as Declan and Robert returned.

It was Declan who cast a slightly sheepish glance around and, in a mutter, voiced what was in all their minds. "I don't know how Caleb stood it down here—I can't see the sky. I can't feel the wind." Declan shuddered and shook his head. "Let's get out of here."

They emerged into dappled daylight. With nothing better to do, they walked to where Lascelle and Hillsythe were questioning Satterly, Muldoon, and Winton. The three must have recently returned from burying the mercenaries. They looked wretched and utterly defeated. Hillsythe and Lascelle had elected to question them away from Ross-Courtney and Neill; they'd sat the three, with wrists still shackled, on logs about the fire pit, with their backs to the barracks and the other two prisoners tethered there.

As Royd and his brothers walked up, Lascelle said, "*Bon!* So you understand that there is no way out."

Royd halted. Robert and Declan did, too, flanking him. Standing behind Lascelle and Hillsythe, the brothers folded their arms and listened.

"The evidence against you is overwhelming," Hillsythe stated. "And in your cases, you have no hope of using your positions to escape the gallows. Besides"—Hillsythe's voice lowered—"those two are already angling to throw you three to the wolves. When we spoke to them earlier, while protesting his innocence, Ross-Courtney said he really had no idea what Satterly might have been up to, and had even less notion of how law-abiding you two"—he nodded at Muldoon and Winton—"were." Hillsythe paused dramatically. "And Neill agreed."

Winton threw a furious look at Satterly. "I told you they'd give us up."

"Of course, they will." Lascelle waved contemptuously—in imitation of Ross-Courtney's superior manner. "To them, you are cannon fodder. Their lives are the only ones that matter."

Throughout, Satterly had been staring at his linked and shackled hands, but at that, he finally looked up. He stared at Lascelle and Hillsythe, then he licked his lips and said, "We may be for it, but"—he raised his gaze and looked at Royd—"if we tell all we know…" He drew in a shaky breath and rushed on, "If we bear witness against them, can you guarantee the court will change our sentence to transportation?"

Royd opted for the unvarnished truth. "I can't promise that, but it's possible." He paused, then went on, "What I can guarantee is that, for various reasons that have as much to do with politics as anything else, the Crown is far more interested in seeing the likes of Ross-Courtney and Neill brought to justice. Publicly. You three"—he skated his gaze over the three men—"are small fry. You're not the big fishes the government wants to see in its net. Were I you, I'd seize the opportunity to cooperate. If you want to survive, it's the best thing you can do."

Satterly studied Royd's face, then he glanced at Muldoon and Winton.

"I say we talk." Muldoon's voice was harsh. "He's right—we have nothing to lose."

"And, just possibly," Lascelle murmured, "another chance at living to gain."

"I'll speak." Winton looked at Hillsythe. "But I don't know much."

"You do know that Ross-Courtney and Neill are two of the backers of this illicit scheme, don't you?" Hillsythe asked.

Winton nodded. He glanced at Satterly. "Arnold introduced them as that, and by their behavior while here, they're obviously that. But I hadn't met them, or even heard their names, before they turned up here."

Lascelle looked at Muldoon. "You?"

Muldoon pressed his lips tight, then nodded. "I don't know much more, not about the backers. Arnold"—he tipped his head toward Satterly—"mentioned Lord Peter's name when we first realized we would need backers to bankroll the mine. He said Lord Peter was a second cousin who might well be interested and who would likely know others of…the right sort." Muldoon paused, then went on, "But I never heard the backers' names, not after they became backers. Until they arrived here, I had no idea if Ross-Courtney was, in fact, involved, and I'd never even heard Neill's name."

All eyes swung to Satterly. His face was pale, his expression haggard. But whatever internal battle of familial loyalty he'd been waging had ended. Without meeting anyone's eyes, he said, "Lord Peter is a second cousin, and I knew from talk within the family that he dabbled in…questionable ventures. Often, he acted as the principal organizer." Satterly lifted a shoulder. "Who better to ask to be one of our backers, especially given his position and his access to others? On my last leave, I went to London and told him of our plan. He saw the potential immediately. He was…enthused, and from that point on, he took over the financing of the project. He formed a group of investors—the backers—and everything just rolled on from there."

When Satterly fell silent, Hillsythe said, "So Lord Peter Ross-Courtney is the central figure, and he recruited the other backers, one of whom is Neill. Who else is in the group?"

Satterly frowned. He met Hillsythe's gaze. "I don't know. He—Peter—insisted we didn't need to know."

Muldoon snorted. "Didn't he say it was too *dangerous* for us to know?"

Satterly nodded. "When I pressed, that was the excuse he gave. He never mentioned the other backers by name. The first I knew of Neill was when he arrived in Freetown in Peter's train."

"So you have no idea who the other backers are?" Robert asked.

All three shook their heads. From their expressions, it was clear that, now they'd made the decision to talk, if they'd known, they would have said.

"You might not know names," Royd said, "but do you know how many backers there are? We have two here." He tipped his head toward the barracks' porch. "How many more are there?"

Satterly shook his head. "He never said."

"Four." Muldoon glanced at Satterly. "In the cleaning shed, remember? When we were showing them the blue diamonds, Ross-Courtney was gloating—and he said: 'If the other four could see these, they'd swoon.'"

Satterly's expression cleared, and he nodded. "Yes, I remember. He implied there were four more."

Hillsythe exhaled and looked at Royd.

Royd caught his gaze and nodded, then he looked at the three men. "You three are still prisoners. You'll be kept in irons, marched to the ships, placed in the brigs, and taken to London to face court there." He paused, then went on, "Between now and boarding the ships, we can, if you wish, keep you separate from the other two. Alternatively, you might continue to stick close to them, converse with them—and see if you can learn anything more to your advantage. The more information you have to offer, the better it will go for you." He gave them a second, then said, "Your choice."

Muldoon looked at Satterly. "While this might have been our idea, without them, we couldn't have done any of it. Yet they're going to deny all involvement and use their lofty positions to protect themselves while we pay the price." His features hardened. "I say we make best use of what chances come our way and see what more they might let fall in our hearing."

Winton cleared his throat. "I concur. We don't owe them anything."

Satterly looked at Muldoon, then Winton. Then he raised his head, met Royd's gaze, and nodded. "We'll remain with them and see what more we can learn."

With that decided, after a short conference with Hillsythe and Lascelle, Royd, Declan, and Robert left the three younger villains sitting by the fire pit and walked to where Ross-Courtney and Neill sat in the meager shade thrown by the end of the porch.

Both gentlemen looked very much the worse for their recent treatment, their clothes and hair dirty and disheveled.

Caleb came striding toward them; he'd been helping Dixon gather the names for the restitution fund. He noted his brothers' direction and arched a brow at Royd. "Anything?"

"I'll tell you later." Royd nodded at the two backers. "We're about to see if these two have anything to add to what we've learned."

But the instant the brothers halted before the pair, Ross-Courtney, scowling ferociously, stated, "We have nothing more to say to you beyond stating what should be obvious to the meanest intelligence. We are not and never have been involved in this scurrilous scheme. There is not a shred of credible evidence to link us to it, and once I gain the ear of those in authority, I will ensure you regret treating us in this abominable fashion. I fully intend to bring the full weight of the law and the censure of all society against you for this ludicrous attempt to besmirch my good name." Belatedly, Ross-Courtney waved at Neill. "And that of my colleagues."

"Colleagues?" Royd arched his brows. "Colleagues in what?"

"Never you mind," Ross-Courtney belligerently replied.

"Business colleagues." Neill met Royd's gaze with a flat stare. "As we explained to the governor, we are here pursuing a business venture, nothing more."

"And how many other 'colleagues' are in the group you represent?" Robert asked.

Neill's expression hardened. "That's a private matter and none of your concern."

"I believe you'll discover that's not actually the case," Declan evenly stated.

When Neill looked down, and Ross-Courtney pointedly looked away, Royd turned to Caleb. "Apparently they don't have anything worthwhile to add." He turned and led his brothers away.

Royd halted in the shade cast by the cleaning shed. The other three gathered around, waiting to hear what he had to say. He looked at the three prisoners they'd left at the fire pit, and then at the two tied to the porch. "Those two have decided to brazen this out. They assume and expect that once we reach London, they'll be questioned politely, and they'll be able to look down their noses, pull strings, and bluster their way out of any charges. Despite the government's desire for a conclusive outcome, when it comes to it, I'm fairly certain the likes of Melville will waver and, one way or another, those two will walk free. Once they do—"

"If there is any documentary evidence of their involvement in this scheme, it will turn to ashes," Robert said.

"Along with anything connecting them to the other four." Declan looked at Caleb. "We now know there are four more backers."

Caleb grimaced. "And when there is no evidence to be found, the charges will be dropped, and..."

Robert snorted. "Even if Wolverstone and his crew find enough trails to link all of the backers to the scheme, before they can be arrested, they'll take a trip to the Continent."

Declan nodded. "A long, luxurious holiday."

"Paid for by the blood, sweat, and tears—and the lives—of those who were held captive here." Caleb's jaw set. "We can't let that happen."

Royd nodded. "Obviously, we need to think more about this."

* * *

An hour later, the ex-captives and their rescuers met about the fire pit for a cup of tea and freshly made biscuits, courtesy of the small army of cooks who were engaged in assembling their best approximation of a banquet for the evening celebration.

Royd looked around the circle. "Everyone ready to leave at first light?"

"Yes!"

The chorus was deafening. Everyone grinned and exchanged glances. At last, people were smiling again.

The mood had lifted.

It lifted still further when it was revealed that several bottles of excellent brandy had been found in the barracks—bottles carried in for Ross-Courtney and Neill. A vote was taken, and brandy-punch would feature that evening.

The mention of Ross-Courtney and Neill gave Royd the opening he'd been waiting for. He raised his voice over the happy din. "There's one last issue on which I need to know your thoughts."

The noise ceased. All about the circle looked at him inquiringly.

He smiled faintly. "As commander of this mission, it's my responsibility to take our prisoners back to London, to the authorities there. As matters stand, we have evidence enough to be certain of convicting the three locals—Satterly, Muldoon, and Winton. However, when it comes to Ross-Courtney, Neill, and the four other backers without whose greed the entire scheme would never have become a reality…" Concisely, he outlined the hurdles they would face in bringing Ross-Courtney, Neill, and the four as-yet-unnamed backers to any sort of justice.

Dark murmurs sprang up. Royd held up a staying hand. "That doesn't mean they *will* escape justice. There are many in London, in positions of power, who want the backers, especially, to pay the price for their crimes. There are ways the necessary evidence might be uncovered. But in order for such evidence to be collected, several powerful people will have to go out on a limb. They'll have to allow rules to be bent." Royd looked around the circle, meeting all the adults' eyes. "I'm willing to return to London and make that case—that if rules need to be bent to bring the six backers of this heinous scheme to justice, then so be it."

A rising chorus of support came from all around.

Hillsythe had the background to understand the line Royd was taking; he raised his voice and helpfully asked, "What do you need from us? How can we help?"

Royd sent him a grateful look and, into the suddenly arrested silence, replied, "I need a clear directive from all who've been victims of these men. That what you want—that what you as free Englishmen and women *demand*—is that all six perpetrators, the six greedy backers, be brought to justice."

A clamor of agreement rose all around. There was not one dissenting voice.

Will Hopkins raised his hand. "What about a petition?" He looked around the circle. "One signed by all who were kidnapped."

Royd nodded. "An excellent idea."

"Give me the wording"—Isobel rose to her feet—"and I'll draw one up." She looked at the eager faces. "We'll have it ready on the barracks' steps by the time everyone gathers for the evening. Each of you can sign it before you sit down."

Everyone cheered.

From the corner of his eye, Royd saw Ross-Courtney and Neill scowling ferociously. He sipped his tea and smiled.

* * *

Their last evening in the compound was as celebratory as the ex-captives and their rescuers could make it. The cooks had worked to add festive touches to the meal, and the libations were sufficiently heady to put smiles on every face.

Every one of the ex-captives finally relaxed—finally truly believed that they were going home, that in the morning they would march out of the place of their captivity, never to return.

A species of giddiness took hold. People mingled, talking and laughing. Then five sailors produced hornpipes, and dancing became the order of the hour.

Reels were a favorite of young and old; the children

joined the adults, and the entire company flung themselves into joyous measure after measure.

At one point, Royd stepped out of the stream of dancers and, picking up a glass of brandy-punch, stood to one side, observing and evaluating. Reasoning that the company didn't need to see the prisoners' sour faces, he'd had the five moved into the mine for the night. Accustomed to drawing and labeling her designs, Isobel had used materials she'd found in Dubois's desk—so appropriate—to produce a beautifully lettered petition that every captive had been only too willing, even proud, to sign. Even the children; deciding that having their marks on the document would only strengthen their collective hand, Katherine, Isobel, Edwina, and Aileen had worked with each child until they could scrawl their name on the parchment.

The satisfaction the children had derived from doing so had made every minute of that effort worthwhile.

The signed petition had been carefully packed in oilskins and now rested in Isobel's satchel.

They'd done all they could here.

Royd sipped and looked to the future.

To Declan and Edwina; across the fire pit, Declan beamed with proprietorial pride as Edwina hung on his arm and gaily chatted with Harriet and Dixon. Two secure and settled matches there.

Looking farther, Royd spotted Robert with Aileen, Robert listening as Aileen animatedly talked with Will and Fanshawe.

Royd found Caleb and Kate surrounded by children, all laughing as, seated on the logs with the children forming a large circle at his feet, Caleb spun them some hilarious tale. Annie Mellows and Jed Mathers watched, arm in arm and smiling, while Babington had his arm around his Mary; the pair couldn't seem to drag their eyes from each other for longer than a minute.

Even as the intention to look for Isobel formed in his mind, he felt her arm loop around his. He looked at her.

She leaned against him and gazed into his face, searching his eyes. "What are you thinking?"

He let his eyes meet hers. It took him a moment to find the right words. "I was thinking of resilience, and that people have much more of it than they realize."

Isobel tilted her head. She watched him as, his eyes on hers, he raised his glass and sipped. She was fairly certain he wasn't talking of the recently freed captives but of her and him. Of them together.

After a second, she smiled and looked at the others, but she couldn't stop her thoughts from following his direction. He wasn't wrong; their connection—that ephemeral link that had grown between them over all the years they'd spent together—hadn't died when they'd parted. It had survived, perhaps not unchanged yet not seriously damaged and certainly not weakened—a resilience neither he nor she had appreciated.

Until this voyage.

Until now.

She could feel his gaze on her face, but she wasn't yet ready to meet it—to meet him and discuss *them*.

Them wasn't an entity she'd as yet had a chance to adequately define.

Movement to her right had her glancing that way. Harriet led what appeared to be a delegation; Annie, Gemma, Ellen, and Mary followed close behind. Annie was carrying a brown-paper-wrapped parcel in her hands.

Her expression lightening in welcome, Isobel shifted to face the other women; her movement alerted Royd, and he turned to greet them as well.

Harriet halted before them. The other women ranged around her, their expressions relaxed, yet serious. "We thought about what you said earlier," Harriet said. "About the other backers—the ones whose names we don't yet know—being very difficult to identify. That if you couldn't put names to them, and Ross-Courtney and Neill continued to keep their mouths shut, then the whole thing—our case against them—might come to naught." Harriet paused, her expression suggesting she was running through a rehearsed speech.

Isobel, along with Royd, waited patiently.

Harriet gave a small nod and continued, "When we were in the cleaning shed and Muldoon was showing Ross-Courtney and Neill the blue diamonds, Muldoon said he'd sent a letter to the diamond merchant in Amsterdam and that he'd recommended the merchant send the information about the blue diamonds on to the banker."

"The banker?" Royd frowned. Then he murmured, "Ross-Courtney isn't their banker."

"No, he ain't," Ellen said. "Because when Muldoon said that, his high-and-mighty lordship said as how that was good, and the banker would tell the others so they would know about the blue diamonds, too."

"So what we thought," Harriet said, "was that if you took some blue diamonds to London and showed them around society, then as they are very rare, those other backers might come and ask where you'd got them."

"They might think the others—Ross-Courtney and Neill, or even the three younger ones—had cut them out," Mary said. "They'd want to know, wouldn't they?"

Royd stared at the women for several seconds, then stated, "That's *brilliant*."

The five women beamed.

Annie stepped forward and held out the package.

"These are the best set of blue diamonds we could put together—enough to make a nice, big, showy necklace." She offered the package to Isobel.

She glanced at Royd, then accepted the parcel. "Why me?"

"Well, we thought as you'd be going to London with him." Gemma tipped her head at Royd. "Aren't you?"

"Yes, I am. Whatever happens, I intend to see this mission through to its end."

"Well, then." Gemma nodded at the package in Isobel's hands. "That there's what will bring the buggers out of the woodwork. We thought as you're the best one to wear it—you're so tall and striking, you just walk into a room and every man'll be looking your way."

"And then the ladies will look, too," Mary said, "and once they set eyes on those diamonds, it'll be all over town by the next day."

"And then the four we don't have names for won't be able to resist," Harriet concluded. "They'll just have to sidle up and ask where you got the stones, won't they?"

Royd could see the picture the women had painted unfurling in his mind. They were right; it might work. Possibly better than any other approach. There was, of course, an element of danger, but he knew the woman by his side.

He glanced at Isobel, waited until she raised her gaze from the paper-wrapped parcel and met his eye, then he arched a brow. "Are you in?"

She held his gaze for an instant, then replied, "Definitely." She looked at the women. "I'm honored that you've entrusted me with this. But I have one proviso. Once the necklace has played its part, and we've unmasked all the backers, and they and Ross-Courtney and Neill are on their way to the gallows, that we sell the necklace, and the proceeds be sent to your fund." Her gaze uncompromising, she stated, "No one but you and the others who slaved here should benefit from these stones."

The other women were a touch flustered; they tried to suggest Isobel keep the necklace "for her trouble," but ran headlong into the wall of her will and finally accepted her proviso.

With that settled, Royd thanked them again and suggested that the existence of the stones and the necklace to be made from them—indeed, their entire scheme to unmask the backers—would best be kept a secret to be shared only with those who needed to know. "At least until we've used the necklace and accomplished what we hope to achieve." He met the women's gazes. "You never know who in Freetown might hear and think to write to some cousin who turns out to be connected to one of the backers…" He shook his head. "The fewer who know, the better."

As he'd hoped, secrecy only added spice to the enterprise. The women readily agreed.

Smiling, Isobel offered her hand; the other women shook it, then returned to the ongoing party.

Royd watched them go, then looked at Isobel.

She was studying the package, turning it over in her hands.

"Second thoughts?" he asked.

"Oh no." She looked up and met his eyes. "I was just thinking that, in lieu of Ross-Courtney's balls, this is an appropriate alternative route to justice—one I'm happy enough to take instead."

Thirteen

They set off with dawn a mere promise in the sky. In a long column, the ex-captives and their rescuers marched out of the mining compound through the gap left by the fallen gates and headed down the path that would take them north to the estuary's coast and the ships waiting there.

One group of sailors forged ahead, clearing the path with machetes, making the trek as easy for the women and children as possible. The ex-captives followed in groups, women and children walking with the men, with sailors interspersed in threes and fours to help any who needed assistance over the occasional steep dips and climbs.

The column straggled out for nearly half a mile, with Hillsythe, Lascelle, and his men driving the prisoners along at the rear.

Initially, Ross-Courtney and Neill tried to protest being forced to walk with their wrists shackled, but they soon fell silent as the demands of the trek took hold. The three younger men could manage well enough, but the two backers would find the going increasingly hard, and Lascelle's French crew had no inclination whatsoever to lend a helping hand.

The Frobisher men and their ladies, along with Dixon,

Fanshawe, and Will Hopkins, were the last to leave the compound. They stood inside the fallen gates and looked around one last time.

Dixon stared at the dark maw of the mine. Then Fanshawe clapped Dixon on the back, and with a nod, Dixon turned and, with Fanshawe and Hopkins, walked out and away.

The Frobisher captains and their intrepid women followed. The men had their seabags, and Isobel had her satchel with the petition and the blue diamonds carefully stowed, but otherwise, they carried no luggage. Hand in hand, they walked briskly along.

They soon overtook the rearguard and the prisoners; as they came upon other groups, Dixon, Fanshawe, then Caleb and Katherine, and eventually Will Hopkins, Aileen, and Robert, slowed to join others and talk as they walked.

Many of the discussions Isobel overheard concerned the ex-captives' expectations on returning to the settlement. For most, their time in the compound had changed how they saw life and left them with a greater determination to wring more from it than they previously had, than they'd previously been content with.

By the time Liam Stewart, who Royd had deputed to lead the column, called a midmorning halt, Declan, Edwina, Royd, and Isobel had almost caught up to the column's head.

At the end of the break—twenty minutes in which to drink and rest—the column got under way again, this time with Royd in the lead. Isobel walked beside him, thinking of what lay ahead.

After an hour, she fell back to where Katherine was walking alongside Caleb. After noticing that Caleb called her cousin Kate, Isobel inquired and, when informed

Katherine preferred Kate, admitted it suited her rather better.

Kate had smiled, then asked after Iona, and their conversation turned to the Carmodys. To family.

After ten minutes, Caleb left them to it and dropped back to speak with Lascelle.

That allowed Isobel to, with a smile, ask about his and Kate's intentions. She was pleased, yet hardly surprised, to hear that Kate and Caleb planned to marry as soon as was reasonable after returning to Aberdeen. "But we want to see this business of catching and convicting the backers dealt with first."

At that point, Edwina and Aileen came bustling up—just as Kate turned to Isobel and asked, "But what about you and Royd?" Kate knew of their long-ago handfasting. "You have to formalize your…arrangement and actually get married, don't you?"

Naturally, Edwina and Aileen turned bright, inquiring gazes on Isobel, too.

She managed to keep her expression relaxed. "We haven't yet had time to discuss it." Which was true.

Edwina narrowed her eyes on Isobel's face. "But you and he *are* going to marry, yes?"

She had to answer; over the past days, she'd come to respect the other three too much to fob them off with a flippant reply. Besides, if she married Royd, these three would be her sisters-in-law. She sighed. "That, too, has to be discussed." To her surprise, she heard herself add, "But I expect we will, so yes."

She almost blinked. Had she really made that decision? Sometime over the past days, without being aware of it?

While the other three rattled on, sharing opinions about weddings, she walked beside them in something of a daze. Viewing him and her—them together—and all they'd shared over recent days and weeks, what possible reason could there be for her not to formalize their relationship?

She knew the answer. Knew it had no basis in cool rationality.

It was born of fear, pure and simple—and it still had a hold on her, albeit weakened and overwhelmed by the action and drama, and the closeness and mutual reliance they'd engaged in over recent days.

Over the past days, they'd worked as a team—not just in business but in life.

They made an excellent team—they were stronger and more powerful together than apart, more effective collectively than individually.

Over the years, they'd changed and grown—older and wiser, certainly, but also a great deal more certain of themselves. More confident in who they were—and also in what they could be together.

Could she banish that old fear? Could she believe in his love, the quality of it, the caring and understanding—the steadfastness of it—enough to trust him with her heart again?

Did she believe he loved her enough to chance it?

The question revolved in her mind.

Then Edwina asked for a description of Iona and how the Carmody matriarchy worked; relieved, Isobel pushed her still-unresolved question from her mind and returned to the conversation.

They chatted and walked and shared their hopes and dreams for their futures. Inevitably, the talk turned to the baby Edwina was carrying—supposedly the first of the next generation of Frobishers.

Except…

By late afternoon, when Royd called a halt and they made camp in a clearing the sailors had expanded to accommodate all of the company, Isobel had accepted that there was one very large confession she and Royd had to make—mostly she, for it was Edwina, Aileen, and Kate who needed to be told first.

With those three, she helped Harriet, Annie, Gemma, Ellen, and Mary settle the children—and, as usual, that made her think of Duncan, underscoring the issue. Once they reached the ships, if she knew her son at all, there would be no hiding him, and one glance would inform everyone there of his parentage—paternal and maternal.

The column had marched steadily and had covered more than two-thirds of the distance to the shore; everyone was weary. After eating a meal put together from comestibles the sailors had carried, everyone retired to their oilskins or cloaks and settled down for the night.

Sleep rolled over the camp in a wave. Conversations faded, replaced by soft snores.

After setting pickets and the watches for the night, Royd was one of the last to seek his place on the clearing's floor. He stretched out beside Isobel, his chest to her back as she lay on her side, facing into the trees.

Her eyes closed, her cheek cradled in her hand, she felt him come up on his elbow; closing his other hand on her upper arm, he leaned close and looked down at her face.

After a moment, he bent his head and pressed a kiss to her temple. "I thought you'd be asleep."

Her lips curved. "Almost." She'd been waiting to inform him, "Tomorrow morning, I'm going to tell Edwina, Aileen, and Kate about Duncan. You might want to mention him to your brothers."

"Ah."

She couldn't see his face, but she could all but hear his mind whirring, considering what had prompted her decision and—more—what her willingness to take that step meant.

She wished him luck with the latter; she wasn't sure of that herself. All she knew was that her feet were now on this path, and revealing Duncan's existence was the inevitable next step.

Eventually, he murmured, "I'll tell them."

Then he lay down and slid his arm across her waist—heavy, possessive, and reassuring.

She smiled and surrendered to sleep.

* * *

The camp rose in the pre-dawn coolness, and after a light breakfast, the column marched on.

Excitement over seeing the ships, let alone boarding them, lent wings to the children's feet, and they skipped along behind Royd and his brothers, who were following the sailors at the head of the column.

With the compound literally falling farther and farther behind them, the adults, too, seemed gripped by eagerness to forge ahead—to the shore, the ships, and back to their lives. Lives that, no matter their station, they now appreciated much more than they had.

Isobel suggested that she, Edwina, Aileen, and Kate walk behind the children, giving Annie, Mary, Gemma, Ellen, and Harriet a break from having to keep their eyes on the increasingly rambunctious brood.

When, with an undeniable air of invincible authority, Isobel called four boys back into line, Edwina remarked, "You've obviously had plenty of experience maintaining order with the brood at Carmody Place."

Isobel paused. "Yes and no." She hesitated only a second more before saying, "Actually, there's something—someone—I need to tell you about."

"Oh?" came in an interested chorus from three throats.

As simply as she could, she told them about Duncan.

"Good Lord!" Kate said. "I had no idea you'd had a child."

"Yes, well, it was over seven years ago," Isobel replied. "He's almost eight."

"And," Edwina said, her eyes alight, "he's on board *The Corsair*, so we'll shortly get to meet him."

Isobel nodded.

Aileen had been unnaturally silent; her expression suggested she was still somewhat stunned. When Isobel caught her eye and arched a brow, Aileen said, "I'm still grappling with Royd not knowing—how did he take it?"

Isobel thought back, then widened her eyes. "Quite well, actually. I was the one who fainted."

Which, of course, led to a barrage of questions; she found herself answering with more candor than she'd anticipated, yet it felt surprisingly cathartic to share her reactions with these women.

These sisters. She was accustomed to having a tribe of women about her, but these three…they were more like her.

Their men were more like Royd, so they better understood both her reactions as well as his.

It was Kate who pointed out, "Well, that makes any question over you and Royd marrying redundant." At Edwina's and Aileen's puzzled looks, she explained, "If a handfasting results in a child, then the parents must marry." Kate paused, then added, "Either that or the mother must surrender the child to the father"—she cut a glance at Isobel—"but obviously, *that's* not going to happen."

No, it isn't. But Isobel only dipped her head in agreement and let the discussion flow on to the three upcoming marriages in the Frobisher clan.

The thought of marrying Royd, of after all these years, actually walking down the aisle with him waiting for her at the end…eight years ago, she would have raced down that aisle with bright eyes and a brimming heart, but she'd left that wide-eyed, rather naive innocent behind long ago.

Now…

She was eight years older and, after the past weeks, had a much better idea of what she needed from him to make their marriage work—and what she needed to give to it, too.

Half an hour later, she saw Caleb thump Royd on the back, while Declan and Robert abruptly stopped in their tracks, then swung around and, over the intervening children's heads, stared at her.

When she returned their stunned looks with an unperturbed gaze, they blinked, shook their heads, then turned and hurried to catch up with Royd and Caleb.

Beside Isobel, Edwina laughed, and Aileen was smiling.

When Royd called a midmorning halt, they could smell the sea. The halt lasted barely ten minutes. Everyone wanted to rush on, especially the children. Only the fact that, to do so, they would have had to run past the four Frobisher captains kept the increasingly unruly mob in check.

And then, quite abruptly, they marched out of the jungle and onto the sands.

The children cheered and raced down to where waves lapped the shore, but before they reached the water, their voices suspended. Their feet halted, and jaws dropping, they stared at the six ships lying at anchor, bobbing on the blue water.

The Corsair and *The Raven* lay closest to shore, with

Sea Dragon, *The Trident*, and *The Cormorant* a length back, along with *The Prince*. Two navy sloops were standing off, presumably sent to escort the larger ships back to Freetown, although Isobel couldn't imagine anyone who knew those ships, let alone their commanders, imagining they needed any protection at all.

At the sight of his ship, Caleb let out a whoop and raced down to the shore, waving madly.

Kate laughed and followed rather more sedately.

With Edwina and Aileen, Isobel stepped to the side so that the rest of the company could walk out of the jungle and onto the sands.

Into freedom.

Many walked only so far, then sat, closed their eyes, tipped their faces up to the unrestricted sun, and simply breathed.

Isobel could empathize. She, too, closed her eyes and breathed in the fresh, salt-tinged air. The humidity of the jungle had fallen away, along with, she now realized, another weight that had rested on her shoulders.

Curious, she looked inward, but yes, it had gone.

She opened her eyes and saw a small, dark-haired figure bouncing up and down in *The Corsair*'s prow, waving madly. She felt a smile the likes of which she hadn't indulged in in recent days light her face. She waved back, saw Royd had noticed and raised his hand as well, then she turned to Edwina and Aileen and, very conscious of an upswell of maternal pride, pointed Duncan out to them.

With unfeigned eagerness, they looked. Both squinted, then Aileen commented on how tall he looked to be.

"And how energetic," Edwina said.

"He's a Frobisher, I'm afraid," Isobel replied, mock-gravely. "I don't know of any male by that name who is anything else."

That startled laughs out of both her almost-sisters-in-law.

The crunch of a rowboat's prow on the sand had the three of them looking down the beach. They laughed again, this time delightedly, as Caleb swooped on Kate, picked her up, and carried her to the tender from *The Prince*. He deposited her inside and, in between a great deal of backslapping, handshakes, and talk, managed to haul himself over the side of the boat.

But when the sailors went to push the tender out again, Caleb stopped them. Raising his head, he called something to Royd, standing on the beach, talking to Robert, Declan, Lachlan, Kit, and Lascelle.

Royd nodded and signaled Caleb to wait, then, with the others trailing him, he walked to where Dixon, Hillsythe, Fanshawe, and Hopkins had gathered, along with Harriet and the other women.

Flanked by Edwina and Aileen, Isobel watched while their men and the others divided the ex-captives into groups and then oversaw the boarding of each group onto one or other of the ships. *Sea Dragon*, *The Raven*, and *The Prince* were the first to up anchor. With sails unfurling, they glided out into the estuary's main channel, and the navy sloops came around to escort them on.

The three ladies watched as the last group to board—the prisoners—were sent off in two tenders. Isobel observed, "They're sending Ross-Courtney and Neill to the brig on Robert's ship, and the other three to the brig on Declan's." She arched her brows. "I wonder why those vessels and not *The Corsair*?"

When Declan came to fetch Edwina, she promptly put that question.

Declan glanced at Isobel. "Royd's the fastest, and he has to get to London and report. He'll make for Southampton and, from there, take a coach to London—that's the fastest route. Robert and I will be at least a day later, most likely more. We'll sail to London so we can off-load our prisoners directly into the authorities' hands. With luck, by the time we dock, Royd and Wolverstone will have worked out where best to put the bastards."

Isobel nodded.

Edwina went with Declan to board *The Cormorant*, and Robert came to fetch Aileen, and they headed for *The Trident*'s tender.

Isobel watched Royd walk up the beach toward her. Along with a few of his crew, they were the last on the sand. The tender, which had been ferrying a group of the ex-captives to *The Corsair*, was returning through the light surf, and this time, there was a slight, dark-haired figure crouched in the bow.

She started toward Royd. When she reached him, they both halted, and she nodded toward the tender. "I wondered if he would talk his way onto that."

Royd followed her gaze and chuckled. "Of course, he did." He looked back at her and met her eyes. "You would have, I would have—naturally, he did."

His gaze traveled her face. She felt it, but kept her gaze on Duncan.

"Are you ready to go on?"

A simple question loaded with layers and layers of meaning.

She drew breath and met his eyes. Father and son; the two most important beings in her life.

Sometime in the jungle, her mind had cleared, and the truth—finally—shone clearly. Through all these years, she hadn't been asking the right question. It wasn't a matter of whether *he* loved *her* enough for her to once again trust him with her heart and her future, but whether *she* loved *him* enough to take the chance.

The new perspective altered everything and brought into sharp relief the emotions she'd felt on seeing him facing Dubois's wavering pistol. The fear that had gripped her then…she had no yardstick to measure it, so great had it been. Had the pistol been pointed at her, she wouldn't have felt such impending desolation.

And if her days in the jungle had taught her anything, it was that nothing in life was assured.

She gave him the short answer. "Yes."

His eyes widened fractionally, but he was wise enough not to ask anything more. When he offered her his hand, she placed her fingers in his.

Hand in hand, they walked down to greet their precious son and forge onward into their shared future, whatever it might hold.

* * *

The return of the captives to Freetown caused nothing short of a sensation. The six ships alone, majestic, sleek, and powerful, pulling into the wharfs would have excited interest, but the tide of long-lost locals who poured from their decks and the story they had to tell brought crowds flooding out of the slums and even down from Tower Hill, all agog to learn what was going on.

Deeming the conditions within the settlement and all that had occurred, especially to the children, a lesson worth learning, Isobel, with Royd's approval, took Duncan with her when she left the ship—along with Williams and another sailor as guards. She was joined by Edwina and Aileen on the wharf; like her, they'd exchanged their breeches for walking gowns and were shadowed by sailor-guards. Isobel introduced Duncan to his soon-to-be aunts-by-marriage; it was hard to decide who was the most curious, but Duncan made his bow and shook their hands, then the three consented to let Isobel lead them on.

They headed down the main wharf. Kate had already joined the other women, and they'd marshaled the children into a large group at the eastern end.

"They all come from the slums out that way." Gemma pointed farther east, beyond the harbor.

During the trek through the jungle, the women had decided that each child should be escorted to their home by an adult able to vouch for what had happened to them, to mention the restitution fund and that the parents would be contacted in due course...and to make sure each child was appropriately welcomed back and not blamed for what had befallen them.

Several sailors from the Frobisher crews had volunteered as additional escorts for the women and children.

They divided the children into groups, but before they'd even left the wharf, word had gone out; with every step, glad cries came from the surrounding crowd as parents and siblings pushed through to reclaim one of the lost.

Isobel noted with approval and relief that, slum brats or not, every child was claimed with joy and wild affection. With obvious love.

It was soon clear that they wouldn't need to walk past the end of the wharf as more hopeful parents came running, summoned by news of what was happening at the harbor.

The sun dipped, painting the sky in a brilliant palette of cerise, vermillion, and fuchsia. Along with the other women, Isobel explained as best she could to shaken and hugely relieved parents, assuring them that other than having to work in a mine, no irreparable harm had befallen their darlings, and explaining that Captain Dixon from the fort would be calling shortly with information about money due in reparation. She invariably concluded with a recommendation to keep the children close, but in all the cases she saw, such a reminder was patently unnecessary; if any of the children managed to slip from the arms of their parents anytime soon, she would eat her best bonnet.

Throughout the exercise, she found herself touched by the vignettes that presented themselves: a teary-eyed Kate smiling bravely as she handed Diccon back to his patently doting mother and clinging siblings; Diccon recovering and puffing out his chest and telling them all how he'd acted as courier, and Kate supporting him; Aileen watching Tilly being embraced and rocked by her mother—seeing Aileen's hand steal to hover over her own stomach before she realized what she was doing and, with a small humph, lowered her hand and turned away; Edwina being Edwina and reassuring the parents of the older boys—then, when Si's mother came up, frantically asking for him, Edwina led the woman a little way away and gently broke the news, then without hesitation, she enfolded the weeping woman in a supportive embrace.

Little Amy's parents were among the last to arrive, but the expressions of desperate hope on their faces as they ran onto the wharf left their love for Amy in no doubt; the instant they saw her, Amy's mother burst into joyful tears, and her father flung himself on his knees and crushed Amy to him. Amy's excited cries of "Daddy! Mummy!" rang in Isobel's ears as, with Duncan beside her, she went to stand with Kate. Kate surreptitiously wiped tears from her cheeks, and once the parents had recovered enough to take anything in, Kate ran through their by-now well-rehearsed explanations.

Clearly, having Amy returned to them—she was the couple's only child—meant more than anything else in the world. As Kate stood and watched the small family head off the wharf, Amy riding on her father's shoulders with one hand locked in her mother's, Isobel realized that Duncan had slipped his hand into hers. She squeezed his fingers, then, as Kate sighed, Isobel murmured, "You'll have one of your own soon enough." She glanced down at Duncan and smiled. "And despite all the drama, they're definitely worth it."

Duncan grinned back.

Kate nodded, squared her shoulders, and turned to scan the area. "I can't believe they're all gone. That it's unlikely I'll ever see them again."

The other women heard Kate's comment. Annie, Gemma, Harriet, Ellen, Mary—all exchanged glances with Kate and each other as the truth of her words, that the observation applied to them, too, sank in.

And then the tears flowed.

Eventually, with hugs and promises to write, they managed to make their farewells.

Night had fallen and flares had sprung up to light the still-busy wharves as Isobel, with Duncan by her side, and Edwina, Aileen, and Kate flanking them—and all their guards hovering—strolled back along the wharf.

The long wharf jutting out into the harbor was known as Government Wharf; *The Corsair*, *The Cormorant*, and *The Trident* were moored along its length, while *The Prince* and *The Raven* had berthed at the wharf that ran along the harbor front. *Sea Dragon* had remained out in the harbor, and *Consort* had sailed in and anchored alongside.

"I assume," Aileen said, "that our gentleman-captains are busy dealing with the authorities and making ready to sail again."

"Royd is determined to sail as soon as possible," Isobel confirmed, "but given the necessary provisioning, I doubt that will be tomorrow."

Edwina looked at Aileen. "We really should call on the Hardwickes this evening." She glanced at Isobel and Kate. "We called on them briefly when we were here a week ago. They were two of the few Declan and Robert told of the rescue mission—someone had to know where we were all going. It would be polite to let them know what's happened, rather than leaving them to hear via the gossip mill."

Isobel nodded. "And Mrs. Hardwicke was instrumental in making lists of all those who went missing." She met Kate's eyes. "You were on her list. And while Reverend Hardwicke might not have been able to move Holbrook to action, at least he tried."

Aileen pointed up a street. "We can go this way."

When they reached the main street, they piled into two hackneys; with their guards clinging to the roofs, they rattled up the slope of Tower Hill to the vicarage and spent a comfortable hour in the parlor, having their first decent cup of tea in weeks while describing the rescue to the Hardwickes.

The Hardwickes were relieved that all had gone so well, and adamant in their devotion to stand ready to assist all those who'd returned to settle back into the small community. Recalling that no one had come looking for the lost Daisy, Isobel asked, and although Mrs. Hardwicke did not know which family Daisy had hailed from, she promised to inquire and tell Dixon of anything she learned.

After taking their leave of the Hardwickes, they returned in the hackneys to the main street. While walking toward the wharf, they passed a tavern with a courtyard opening onto the street—and found a largish group of men rescued from the mine gathered there, along with Dixon, Harriet, Fanshawe, Hopkins, Hillsythe, and Lascelle, and several of his crew.

The ladies joined the gathering. Seated with a still-alert Duncan on her lap, Isobel listened to the plans the others were making, storing away the details to share with Royd later. She'd known that Hillsythe had to report to London before returning to the settlement; he'd decided to take a berth on *The Trident*.

"To help oversee the prisoners." He shrugged. "Who knows? I might be able to get Neill to talk—he seems the shrewder, less outrageously arrogant of the pair."

Satterly, Muldoon, and Winton had been placed in *The Cormorant*'s brig. "They're not being allowed ashore," Lascelle said. "They'll be taken straight to London."

When asked, Lascelle confirmed that *The Raven* would be sailing from Freetown with the Frobisher fleet, but only as far as the Canary Islands. "That was where Caleb found me and asked me to join him." Lascelle grinned. "I have unfinished business there."

Fanshawe and Will Hopkins expected to return to their duties with the West Africa Squadron once the blockade—still in place—ended and their ships returned to harbor. Will promised to call on Aileen the next day; she wasn't yet ready to let him go, and for his part, Will still seemed stunned that she'd come to the settlement searching for him and then fallen in with, and assisted so crucially in, the covert rescue mission.

It seemed Will still underestimated his sister's determination. But he would learn. Aileen's immediate goal was to ensure that he returned to England for her and Robert's wedding.

Hiding a grin at Aileen's hectoring tone, Isobel caught Dixon's eye. When he came closer, she told him that Mrs. Hardwicke hadn't known who Daisy was, either.

Dixon grimaced. "I'll keep asking. Someone must know of her."

Harriet came up to join them as Isobel said, "So what are your plans? Back to the fort?"

Dixon's features hardened; he glanced at Harriet as she took his arm. "We were discussing that when you arrived. I'm not inclined to return to a command that, when I disappeared, did nothing." He nodded at the group of ex-captives. "While others had homes and, in some cases, positions to return to, these men were itinerants of one stripe or another. They worked under my supervision in the mine—they learned new skills, and I know what they're capable of. While Ross-Courtney and Neill's supposed business venture was a sham, they weren't wrong about the desperate need for new houses in the settlement and that there's next to no one building them." Dixon surveyed the group. "So I'm considering selling out and starting a business building houses in and around the settlement. Freetown is growing—Neill and Ross-Courtney were right about that—and I have a decently skilled workforce to hand."

"And I'm encouraging him," Harriet said, "along with others—Annie's Jeb and the two blacksmith's apprentices want to join, too." She looked at Dixon, pride and confidence in her eyes. "I think, all working together, we'll make a go of it."

Isobel smiled. "I'm sure you will."

Dixon asked and Isobel introduced Duncan to him—as Royd's son, Duncan Carmichael Frobisher. Duncan slipped from her lap, executed a brief bow, and then shook the hand Dixon offered him.

When Harriet and Dixon moved away, Duncan asked, "Are we going back for supper soon?"

None of them had eaten since lunchtime, and Edwina and Aileen were increasing. Isobel rose and dropped a hand on Duncan's shoulder. "You're right. It's time we returned to the ships."

She gathered the ladies, and they said their goodbyes. They'd barely started off again when a grizzled older man came running up.

"Miss Hopkins! You're back!"

Aileen spun around, then beamed. "Dave! Yes, indeed, I'm back from our adventure, and so is the captain."

Remembering hearing of the hackney driver Aileen had hired while she was investigating months earlier, Isobel resisted Duncan's surreptitious tugs and ignored his whispers of "I'm *hun-gry*!" and waited while Aileen made arrangements for Dave to come aboard *The Trident* the next morning for a quick tour and a meeting with Robert, and then for Dave to take her—and the other ladies, and Duncan if he wished—on a tour of all the places in the settlement that had featured in the investigation.

Isobel, Edwina, and Kate all added their entreaties, and Duncan stopped tugging and confirmed that he would like to go, too, please.

Dave beamed and declared he would be honored. He saluted, and they parted from him and hurried on to the wharves, finally spilling onto the weather-worn planks to discover Royd, Robert, and Declan waiting for them by *The Prince*'s gangplank. Apparently, the need for sustenance had bloomed in everyone's minds, and *The Prince* had a stateroom large enough to seat them all around its table.

The meal was decidedly celebratory. Isobel inspected the wide selection of dishes. "The cooks must have rushed ashore the instant we docked."

Declan paused to inspect the guinea fowl leg he was devouring. "They did. And all the crews are enjoying their enthusiasm, too."

Their appetites finally sated, they sat back and let the empty platters and plates get whisked away. Nursing glasses of wine, they turned their minds to the next steps. Royd let his gaze circle the table, eventually allowing it to rest on Isobel, with Duncan, his stomach now full, leaning sleepily against her side. He savored the sight for several seconds, then forced his mind to the matter at hand. "We started this mission with three goals. We've successfully achieved the first, rescuing the captives with minimal losses and returning them to the bosom of their families here in the settlement."

Everyone nodded.

He continued, "Our second goal was to dismantle the scheme, and I believe we've done all we can in that regard. There are no more diamonds in the mine, Dubois and his men are gone, Kale and his gang are gone, and we have the three locals who initiated the scheme in custody and will deliver them to the authorities in London. The only links in the chain we haven't addressed are the diamond merchant in Amsterdam and the mysterious banker, but we can leave them to Wolverstone and colleagues—they're better placed than we are to deal with such people."

Murmurs of agreement came from his brothers. The ladies simply waited to learn what came next.

He duly went on, "That brings us to our last goal—gathering evidence enough to convict the backers. That's the goal we've yet to attain. We have two of the backers in custody, but they're not going to talk. More, once back in England, they will use their positions, their connections, and their wealth to walk free."

"If we hand them over to the usual authorities," Robert said, "they *will* walk free."

"Indeed." Royd twirled his goblet between his fingers. "So what weapons, as it were, do we have to prevent that?"

"We have the petition," Isobel said. "I vote we ensure that several highly placed and influential people see it before we hand it over."

Declan nodded. "Yes, indeed. No reason to leave open the option of mislaying it."

"I take it," Caleb said, his gaze on Royd, "that you intend to use the petition as leverage to ensure Ross-Courtney and Neill aren't simply released to await possible trial—a trial that, if matters follow their usual course, will never eventuate?"

Royd nodded. "The petition will make it impossible for the authorities to immediately follow that path—and will allow Wolverstone and his cronies to push to hold the pair secretly."

"If we're to have any chance of identifying and apprehending the other four backers," Robert said, "holding Ross-Courtney and Neill in secret will be crucial. They can't be allowed to get a message to any of the other four."

"Precisely," Declan said.

"At least we know there are four others." Edwina leaned her chin on one hand. "And given Ross-Courtney's and Neill's stations, I would think it a given that the other four will be of similar ilk—members of the aristocracy or even the nobility."

"Which, perversely," Isobel added, "due to the potential political ramifications, will be a crucial point in keeping Melville and company's feet to the fire over doing whatever it takes to identify and convict them all." There were murmurs of agreement all around.

When no one advanced any further comment, Isobel said, "It comes back to the diamonds." Across the table, she met Royd's eyes; they'd already informed the others of the women's plan. "You called the women's notion brilliant, and indeed, it is inspired. If we can get Ross-Courtney and Neill held in secret, entirely incommunicado, having a blue diamond necklace being flaunted through the ton's ballrooms will almost certainly lure the other backers to at least approach and ask questions."

"Flaunted through the ballrooms by a lady unfamiliar to most," Edwina said. "And even after they learn your name, they still won't know enough to have any clue as to how you got the blue diamonds. They'll *have* to ask you—they won't be able to resist."

"And as we've just established," Aileen said, "the other four backers are almost certainly members of the haut ton."

"What's more, we'll be returning just in time for the weeks of balls and parties around the start of Parliament's autumn session." Edwina beamed. "Those other four backers will almost certainly be in town and likely to attend the major events."

Declan frowned and looked at Royd and Robert. "Surely Wolverstone and his friends will be able to trace the other four backers through the diamond merchant in Amsterdam, tracing the payments from him to the banker, and so to the backers?"

"If there was no time constraint, then eventually, yes—or so one would think. But in this case"—Royd shook his head—"I can't see the authorities resisting Ross-Courtney's and Neill's threats and holding them in complete isolation for long enough for that avenue to be a viable one. It would have been different if Muldoon had known the diamond merchant's name or direction, but his only connection was via the strongboxes sent with the captains the merchant organized, whose names he doesn't know, and regardless, I would wager those captains won't know to whom they were delivering, either."

"Muldoon thought he'd met the man, but in reality it sounds as if he merely met a few journeymen in a tavern's back room." Robert shook his head. "Whoever the diamond merchant is, he's been exceedingly careful to cover his tracks. Unearthing him won't be easy, and it definitely won't be quick."

Caleb's face hardened. "The instant Ross-Courtney or Neill gets to see anyone in their employ—from lackey to solicitor—the other backers will be notified, along with the banker and diamond merchant, and any evidence that might exist of the involvement of any of them in the scheme will mysteriously vanish. In a puff of smoke."

"I agree." Royd met Declan's, then Robert's eyes. "In order to keep faith with all those we rescued, we need to do all we can—everything we can—to bring all six backers to justice. To my mind, we're committed to achieving that as our third and final goal."

Declan shifted. "I don't disagree. But what's the best and most certain avenue to that end?"

Robert crossed his forearms on the table. "Regardless of the petition, regardless of any political pressure, the second Ross-Courtney's and Neill's feet touch British soil, a clock starts ticking on this investigation—on the time we'll have to identify and expose the other backers and secure enough evidence to convict them all." He looked at Royd. "I agree that we can't leave this as is in the hope that Wolverstone and company will turn up the required evidence in time. There are hundreds of diamond merchants in Amsterdam, and we've no information as to which one Ross-Courtney engaged. It could take months to identify the right man and induce him to give up the banker—or trace the payments if he won't. That route will turn up evidence eventually, but it will take time."

Declan grunted. He looked across the table at Edwina, who smiled sympathetically back.

Royd put what they were all thinking into words. "So we return to the blue diamond necklace. To us using the lure the women in the compound gave us." He looked around the table, meeting all the adults' eyes. "We need to start putting our minds to exactly how we're going to do that."

A tap on the door heralded Jolley. He looked at Royd. "Mr. Stewart's compliments—His Excellency, the Governor, and Vice-Admiral Decker have arrived. As per your orders, he's kept them on the main deck."

Royd nodded. "Tell Mr. Stewart I'm on my way."

Jolley snapped off a salute and left.

Royd glanced around the table. "We've done well so far, and we know where we are and what lies ahead. It's been a long day—let's table our discussions for tonight." He looked at Robert, Declan, and Caleb. "I'll call a captains' meeting for tomorrow morning to confirm our sailing plans. But now"—he pushed back his chair—"I'd better go and deal with Holbrook and Decker."

Robert slanted him a glance. "Do you need support?"

Royd thought, then shook his head. "For what I have to say to them, the fewer witnesses, the better."

Robert nodded in acceptance.

Royd looked at Isobel. She roused Duncan—drowsing, but not yet asleep—and rose.

With a nod to the others, Royd walked to the cabin's

door. He held it for Isobel, then followed her and Duncan through.

He preceded them down the gangplank, and they walked the short distance along the main wharf and onto Government Wharf where *The Corsair* was the first moored vessel.

As they neared, Isobel glanced up at *The Corsair*'s deck. "I take it you summoned Holbrook and Decker here rather than attend them in the settlement for a reason." She glanced at him. "So they're in your domain, as it were?"

He lightly shrugged. "That, and as an exercise in authority—in establishing who in this situation actually holds it." He met her gaze. "With men like them, such nuances matter."

She nodded. They reached the gangplank, and she glanced at Duncan, trailing beside her, one hand in hers, the other smothering yawns. "I would offer to help you intimidate Ralph, but quite aside from you not needing any help, I doubt having a woman present while you deliver a dressing-down will aid your cause."

He smiled. "Thank you. And you're correct on both counts."

She smiled at him and started up the plank, drawing Duncan behind her. "I'll put Duncan to bed."

She stepped onto the deck. She looked dispassionately at Holbrook and Decker and haughtily inclined her head.

Both men bowed.

With a crisp "Gentlemen. I'll leave you to your discussions," she continued toward the companionway, towing a now-wide-eyed Duncan behind her.

Decker stared at Duncan. Holbrook didn't know enough about Royd or Isobel to register the import of what he'd just seen.

Royd waited several seconds to give Isobel and Duncan time to reach Duncan's cabin, then formally said, "Welcome aboard *The Corsair*, currently sailing under marque for His Majesty's government. Thank you for attending, gentlemen." Without waiting for any response, he set off in Isobel's wake. "We can talk in private below."

He led the way down the stairs and into the stern cabin. He claimed the admiral's chair behind his captain's desk and waved Holbrook and Decker to the two straight-backed chairs angled before it. "Please be seated, gentlemen."

It was the only concession he was prepared to make; they could sit while he informed them of their incompetence. He was in no mood to pander to any delicate sensibilities.

Decker and Holbrook exchanged a glance; from their expressions, both wished to protest his assumption of command, but neither dared.

As the pair sat, Royd nodded at Bellamy, who had followed and was hovering in the doorway, to shut the door.

Then he rested his forearms on the desk, clasped his hands, and looked at the two men before him. "Let me tell you what's been happening in this settlement under your very noses over the past several months." He proceeded to outline the scheme Satterly, Muldoon, and Winton had devised and, with the financial backing of Ross-Courtney, Neill, and four as-yet-unidentified other gentlemen, put into place. He made it clear that the three instigators had seen the many weaknesses in the settlement's governance and had exploited them. He did not spare Decker and Holbrook any of the details of those kidnapped—the children and the women as well as the men—nor did he censor his description of the threats Dubois had used against the women and children, of the fate of Daisy, or of the subsequent conditions in the camp. He also told them of the attempts to kidnap Edwina and Aileen, the former instigated by Holbrook's now-absent wife. "All this, gentlemen, happened on your watch. Ultimately, the responsibility is yours, and as we are all aware, ignorance is no defense in a case such as this."

Decker looked green.

Holbrook had turned puce and seized the moment to say, "I can assure you, now we understand the situation, we will deal with those responsible—"

"Ah—no." Royd sat back. "The prisoners will remain aboard the Frobisher ships. They will be handed directly to the authorities in London."

Decker understood and, having grasped his own culpability, was only too ready to allow Royd to spare him the difficulty of dealing with Ross-Courtney and Neill.

Although far more culpable than Decker, Holbrook still failed to appreciate the seriousness of the situation, much less the precariousness of his own position. "Now see here, sir—Captain. Lord Ross-Courtney is an important man. And Neill, too. Their support for the settlement would make a huge difference—"

"They have no interest in this settlement." Royd ground out the words. He caught and held Holbrook's startled gaze. "The only business Ross-Courtney and Neill were interested in was the diamond mine. That's what they came here to see. The tale they spun you was a complete fabrication designed to deflect you, which, clearly, it did."

Holbrook deflated. Before he could rally and make a push to have at least Satterly, Muldoon, and Winton handed over so he could make examples of them in an effort to placate those who had lost loved ones while Holbrook had insisted that men, women, and children had all simply walked into the jungle in search of their fortunes, Royd crisply stated, "My orders are to take all prisoners involved in this scheme to London. Our ships are being provisioned as we speak and will depart the day after tomorrow." He looked at Decker. "The blockade needs to remain in place until the end of the day we sail."

Decker nodded. Somewhat tentatively, he ventured, "I take it you wish no word of the prisoners to get back to England?"

"Precisely." Royd met Decker's gaze, then looked at Holbrook. "All those we rescued know the importance of keeping their mouths shut about Ross-Courtney and Neill. Other than those in the rescue party—all of whom, likewise, understand the need to keep their lips shut and are committed to doing so—the two of you are the only others to know of our prisoners' identities." He paused, then, his voice quieter, said, "If there is any word that reaches England prior to their trial, any word that can be traced back to the settlement, to a comment from either of you shared where it shouldn't have been—for instance, with Macauley—or to any letter from either of you to any correspondent no matter how discreet, I can assure you the consequences for you will be dire."

He glanced at Decker, then looked back at Holbrook. "Don't test the resolve of those behind the push to bring these men to justice."

He allowed several seconds to slip past, then nodded and rose. "Good evening, gentlemen. If I have any further need of your services prior to departing, I will let you know." As they came to their feet, he rounded the desk, crossed to the door, opened it, and waved them through.

He followed them onto the deck and watched as they left his ship.

Liam Stewart appeared beside him; he, too, watched

Holbrook stump up the wharf toward the street where his carriage would be waiting. Decker went the other way, presumably to his tender to be ferried back to his flagship. "I take it that went well," Liam said. "Or at least, well enough."

"The latter." Royd grimaced. "For all his many faults, Decker's no fool. Holbrook..." He shook his head and turned back to the companionway—then remembered. "Send flags to the others—captains' meeting tomorrow at ten. Aboard *Consort*."

"Aye, aye, Captain." Liam saluted and went off to organize the signal.

Royd headed below decks.

He returned to the stern cabin. After shutting the main door, he went to the connecting door to Duncan's cabin and silently opened it.

Isobel was seated on the edge of Duncan's bed. She looked up as Royd drew near.

He looked down at Duncan's face, faintly flushed in sleep; he drank in the untrammeled innocence, the simple joy of being alive that, even in sleep, infused his son's features.

And knew he would do anything, give anything, fight any battle to be there to see his son grow and mature. To protect and guide, albeit with a light hand, and observe how this creation of his and Isobel's turned out.

He transferred his gaze to her face. She'd looked back at Duncan, and the fierceness of the love she bore him illuminated her features. He did not doubt her devotion to their son; he would always stand as Duncan's protector, but she would be there, too—an Amazon, in truth.

After a moment, he reached for her hand, grasped her fingers, and drew her to her feet. She allowed him to lead her into the main cabin.

He closed the door, smoothly twirled her, and backed her against the panel. As he stepped into her, her hands splayed on his chest, her eyes met his, and with typical challenge, she arched a brow.

He bent his head and covered her lips with his.

He kissed her, and she kissed him back. He deepened the kiss, and she slid her palms to his cheeks and held him steady as she gave him back fire for fire.

He ravaged and devoured, until she wound her arms about his neck and pushed boldly—bodily—into him, away from the panel at her back. The pressure of her body, of her long sleek limbs and luscious curves flush against his harder frame, amounted to an act of deliberate provocation.

Desire ignited. They burned hot and fast.

Reeling, in a dance of hands and touch, of greedy fingers finding laces and buttons, they waltzed across the floor to the bed.

By the time they reached the canopied expanse, they'd stripped each other of every stitch. They fell on the silk coverlet, limb to limb, skin to skin, and passion roared.

She gasped; her fingers digging into his upper arms, she rolled and pulled him over her.

But there were things he wanted to say, concepts he wanted to impress on her; with words far beyond him, he resorted to the language of lovers.

To touch and caress, to the brush of lips and the tantalizing trail of fingertips.

To long, raspy licks and hot, open-mouthed kisses.

To suckling, kneading, stroking—stoking.

He loved her, made love to her, with care and devotion and a worshipful reverence.

She wanted to—expected to—rush on, but he held

her back, held their reins in an iron grip, and held her cocooned in a web of wanting.

He let her writhe. Let her savor. Let her see and understand *this*—his surrender.

For it was that, and he knew it—had known it even eight years ago—that she was the only woman for him, hers the only arms in which he could find true succor.

Hers the only body in which he would ever find true release.

As, finally, he slid into her slick softness, and she clasped him tight, he closed his eyes and tried to hold his mind, his will, closed against the tumult of feelings and instincts. Tried desperately to hold against the temptation to plunder.

But she arched beneath him and inexorably drew him on, and the reins snapped, and he surged, and they lost their grip on reality.

The tide swept them into a familiar landscape, one of glory and wonder and inescapable togetherness.

Desperation built. Desire, passion, hunger, and need swirled in an inferno of wanting.

They rode hard and fast to a thunderous beat—rode on into reckless splendor.

Until they soared.

They clung, gasping, fingers gripping tight as ecstasy peaked and a coruscating brilliance shattered and raced through them, and scintillating glory overwhelmed their senses and swamped them.

Then passion's wheel turned one last time, and the void swirled and swallowed them.

Slowly, the thrum of ecstasy faded. They spiraled by degrees back to earth, to the here and now, to each other's arms.

Long moments later, he summoned enough strength

to disengage and roll onto his back. She followed, settling as she often did with her head pillowed on his chest.

With one arm tucked around her, he raised and bent the other and settled his hand behind his head. He looked up at the canopy and waited for his wits to re-engage.

That was familiar, too.

After several minutes, he recalled where they were and where they were going—and the questions he therefore needed to ask, that he hoped like hell she would answer.

He lowered his arm and wound one long black curl around his fingers. "We're going home. So what tack have you decided on?"

Her answer was several seconds in coming, but he knew she was awake; he could feel her breath on the heated skin of his chest, and he recognized the rhythm of her breathing in his bones. Finally, she said, "I say we follow the path we're on and see where it leads."

He considered that for nearly a minute, weighed various responses, then decided he might as well be hung for a sheep as a lamb. "This path leads to the altar. Does that mean you'll marry me?"

"Yes."

Just like that? He squinted down at her face. "So you believe I love you?"

She tipped her head up so she could meet his eyes. Hers were frowning. "Why ask that?"

"Because *that* was what us breaking apart before—you slamming that door in my face—was all about, wasn't it?" When she didn't immediately reply, he went on, "You thought because I disappeared that I didn't love you, that I'd gone into the handfasting for other reasons and I didn't truly care about you—wasn't that it?"

He might not have understood her eight years ago, but he was older and wiser, and she'd told him enough of her insecurities for him to have a reasonably good idea of what, at bedrock, had been the defining issue.

Her frown materialized. “Well, yes, but that was then, and this is now.”

And? The naked curves slumped against him were more rounded, her breasts distinctly heavier, her hips and thighs more lush…but she hadn’t changed that much. Not inside.

“Does that mean you understand and accept that I love you?” It was suddenly important—*critically* important—that her answer was yes.

But he could see in her eyes, dark though they were, that it wasn’t.

She stared at him as if he was being unnecessarily difficult. “If you must know, when we walked out of the jungle onto the beach, I realized I had had—somewhere along the way—an epiphany of sorts. I realized that it didn’t matter how much you loved me—that that was entirely the wrong question for me to ask—but rather what counted was how I felt about you.” She all but scowled at him. “So I’m staying with you, and we’re getting married.”

She slumped down again, wriggling back into her usual place.

He was getting what he wanted. And she had just, more or less, admitted she loved him.

It should have been enough.

It wasn’t.

“I love you. I always have. I need to know you believe that.” Until now, he hadn’t realized that was so, but that need burned, a bright and unwavering flame, inside him.

She sighed, pushed up on one elbow, and looked into his eyes. “I know you love me, or at least, that you believe you do. What I don’t know is whether the qualities the word 'love' embodies for me are the same as what the word means to you." She paused, then, more briskly, went on, "As far as I can see, there's no way to answer that question other than by going forward and seeing what happens. It's a risk I have to take—" She broke off, then amended, "That, I suppose, we both have to take. The only way we can find an answer is through the experience of the years."

With that, she slumped down again. Leaving him with very little room, much less reason, to argue. He wanted to argue, to wring from her some sort of admission that she recognized his love as the same as hers—as strong, as vital, as powerful, in all respects that mattered, the equivalent of hers—yet he knew her; he'd never win that argument.

He stared at the canopy for a full minute, then he closed his arms around her and dropped a kiss on her silky head. "Just as long as you accept, here and now, that I will never let you go."

Invincible resolution rang in the words.

She patted his chest. "I know. And just to be clear, I will never let you—or Duncan—go, either."

As he was never going to permit her to do so, that was irrelevant, but…

Just as there was more than one way to skin a cat, there were more ways than one to argue, even with an Amazon.

Fourteen

They set sail on the morning tide. Isobel sat in the bow with Duncan beside her. The wind plucked at her braided and pinned hair. Spray stung her face as *The Corsair* heeled and led the Frobisher ships out of the harbor.

She glanced at her son, saw the wondrous joy shining in his face, and felt her heart swell. She looked ahead, into a future she couldn't yet define.

She was a designer at heart; she liked to see things, enough, at least, to set them down on paper. Yet relationships were never that fixed; they evolved constantly.

Shifting, she looked down the ship at Royd, standing with legs braced behind the big wheel. His eyes were fixed far ahead, gauging the strength of the tide, the pull of the wind, the power of the waves.

"Mama! Look!" Duncan tugged her sleeve.

Like her, he'd looked down the ship; with the wind whipping words away, she couldn't hear orders called from the upper deck, but Duncan's sharp ears must have caught one. She followed his pointing finger up and up to where the skysails on all three masts were unfurling.

The canvas billowed, then caught the wind and snapped taut.

And their speed increased.

She leaned to the side and looked past their wake to

where the other ships followed in a staggered line. With something close to reverence, she breathed, "What a sight."

Duncan immediately scrambled to see.

She'd worked on all of those ships in recent years, implementing Royd's changes. She felt an almost proprietary glow, seeing them all under sail, majestic and uniquely beautiful, a line of graceful ladies gliding over the sea.

Looking farther back, beyond the ships, she watched Freetown and its harbor slip away. Tower Hill was the last sight to fade into the sea mist.

They were leaving the settlement, and even more its people, in a better state than they'd found them. They'd rescued those who'd needed their help and had shut down the infernal scheme. They'd all assumed the mission would be more or less over at this point—that they would be heading back to London to report and hand over their prisoners, and all would be done. While there was quiet satisfaction in what they'd achieved, they all accepted that the mission was not yet complete.

While she felt a certain cynicism over Melville and company's motives, in this, she agreed with the government. Justice needed to be served—impartially and transparently. Those they'd rescued from the mine deserved that.

The Corsair reached the wide mouth of the estuary, and spars creaked and sails snapped as Royd changed tack, swinging the bow northward.

Heading home.

Well, to England and London first—the penultimate leg of their journey. What would need to be done when they reached Aberdeen, the arrangements and decisions and all the discussions over how to merge their lives... that could wait until later.

Unbidden, her mind ranged over the past weeks and all she'd done, all she'd been a part of. She was accustomed to working with other women—that was how Carmody Place operated—but joining with Edwina, Aileen, and Kate in contributing to and achieving all they had with the rescue had been in a different league of endeavor. More demanding, more exciting—more dangerous perhaps—but also immensely more satisfying.

Edwina, Aileen, Kate—she hadn't expected them to be sisters-of-the-heart, yet given they had each chosen a Frobisher man, perhaps that wasn't so surprising.

She'd swung to face the sea; she heard Royd's footsteps stroll up behind her, then his hand lightly gripped her shoulder. She looked up—to see him looking at Duncan, who was looking up at him, an expression of eager expectation on his face, a readiness to fling himself wholeheartedly into whatever adventure his father next took him into glowing in his eyes.

That unrestrained confidence and eagerness to engage with life was a hallmark of Frobisher men, but nowhere was it stronger than in Royd.

She had her own brand of it, and while she didn't need adventures far from home to satisfy her—there were challenges aplenty not far from her door—the exotic and wild in no way frightened her. She could deal with that, too.

Being with Royd again had reminded her of that. Joining with him on this mission had reopened a side of her she'd been content to shut off, to allow to lie dormant over the past eight years.

That door had been opened again, the cobwebs dusted away.

She was whole again. She hadn't known she hadn't been before, but she recognized that now.

Iona's words on learning that Royd had agreed to allow

her to sail with him echoed in her mind. *This state you're both in—as if a part of your lives has been indefinitely suspended—cannot go on.* Had her grandmother somehow known?

And…if what Iona had said had been true about her, was it also true about Royd? Did *she* somehow complete *him*?

Searching his face, thinking of his words of the past night, she had to wonder.

Royd grinned and tousled Duncan's hair, then looked at Isobel. He swiftly scanned her face and was content enough with what he saw there. That morning, before he'd left her asleep in his bed, he'd studied her features, stripped of all screens in sleep, and decided she was right; only time and the experience it brought would convince her that he loved her in the exact same way that she loved him.

As she'd agreed they would marry, he had a lifetime to achieve that goal.

Not that he didn't want to rush, but with Isobel, perseverance often won what pressure couldn't. For her to finally lower that last fine screen of reservation—for her to love him as she once had, with an open-hearted abandon that had captured his heart—for that, he was perfectly willing to wait a lifetime.

A wave broke beneath the bow, and she faced forward. He settled his hand on her shoulder and did the same.

The sea stretched, blue and unbroken, to the horizon. Sun glinted on waves; the breeze raked briskly across their faces.

Ahead lay their future, and before he'd quit the wheel, he'd called down the moonrakers—they were flying under full sail.

"Onward," he said.

"To London." She reached up and closed her hand over his.

Duncan swung to face them. "Can I come?"

Royd met Isobel's gaze as she glanced up at him. At the question in her eyes, he shrugged. "Why not?"

She looked at Duncan.

His expression had turned pleading. "I'll be good," he promised.

Royd felt her hesitation, but then she nodded. "All right. But we'll need to make some rules."

* * *

Blessed with following winds and smooth seas, they sailed into Southampton Water eleven days later. The morning mists had already lifted, and sun glinted palely off the slate-gray waters.

Isobel stood on the stern deck and marveled at how very different the colors of England were to those they'd left behind. Along with the smells, the sharpness of the wind, and the temperatures.

Beside her, Royd swung the wheel and guided *The Corsair* toward the Frobisher wharf. Duncan hung on the rail beside the wheel, watching every move Royd made, listening to every order, seeing what was done and the effect the change had on how the ship angled as it glided along.

Isobel studied the pair, both entirely absorbed—the two men in her life.

She'd spent the days of the voyage learning how to live with Royd—Royd as he now was. Their three weeks of long ago were too far in the past to be of much help; they were both much more definite and assured—certain of what was important to them and what was not.

They were finding their way. Now they'd committed to sharing their lives henceforth, they needed to reach a working understanding, and while they were at sea and free of their respective families was the perfect opportunity.

Along the way, she'd realized how very true her epiphany had been. Love wasn't something it was possible to deny. It simply was, and her love for Royd had never so much as faded around the edges, much less died.

His attachment to her—be it love as she knew it or not—had also withstood the test of time. Whatever it was, it was very much still there, unwavering and as powerful as he.

He was also proving to be an excellent father—the relationship he and Duncan were forging, although still evolving, was already strong. She suspected Duncan recognized himself—or perhaps the self he could grow to be—in Royd, and while he still instinctively turned to her for comfort, he turned to Royd for learning and guidance on what it meant to be a man.

On what it meant to be a Frobisher.

They'd spent time talking and making plans—all three of them—but had agreed that all matters pertaining to their wedding should wait until they returned to Aberdeen. First, they had the mission's final goal in their sights—specifically the identification of all six backers and the securing of their convictions.

As Royd brought *The Corsair* into the wharf and sailors jumped down to secure the ship, Isobel stepped to the rail. "I should return that tool to the shipyards before we leave." She met Royd's gaze. "I'll go there while you sign off at the office. That way, we can be on the road to London as soon as possible."

He thought, then shook his head. "Someone from the office can return the tool with our compliments. We need to get on as fast as we can."

Duncan slid his hand into hers and smiled up at her.

She smiled back. "All right." Aside from all else, Duncan would have been torn—should he go with Royd to the office or with her to the shipyards? Somewhat to her surprise, Royd had explained to Duncan what her work at the shipyards truly entailed; subsequently, Duncan had asked to accompany her to the shipyards when next she went—which would be as soon as they returned to Aberdeen. That her son was now curious to learn about her work…perhaps there was another sort of link he and she might forge.

The instant the ship was secure, Royd handed over command to Liam. "I can't say how long we'll need to stay in London. Take your time provisioning here, then go on to the Pool and send word. Shore leave for everyone as appropriate. We'll join you as soon as we're free."

Liam saluted, then nodded to Isobel. "I hope you catch them all."

Royd met Isobel's eyes. "So do we."

They'd already packed. He directed Bellamy to dispatch their bags and trunks to the coaching inn, then escorted Isobel and Duncan down the gangplank. On the wharf, he wound Isobel's arm with his, and with Duncan skipping alongside, they walked briskly into town to the Frobisher Shipping Company office.

Higginson, the head clerk, had met Duncan and Isobel when they were in Southampton earlier; while Higginson asked and Duncan poured out a remarkably detailed description of the estuary and Freetown harbor, Royd signed off on *The Corsair*'s voyage, authorizing payments to his officers and crew. He set down the pen and pushed the ledger back to Higginson. "Mr. Stewart will sail on to the Pool once he's taken on supplies. From there, we'll be heading home."

"Very good, Captain Frobisher." Higginson nodded to Isobel. "It's been a pleasure to meet you, Miss Carmichael."

Mrs. Frobisher. Royd bit back the words. Such a declaration might be construed by some as being a little too pushy.

Isobel smiled and inclined her head graciously. "Until next time, Mr. Higginson."

Somewhat appeased by that statement, Royd ushered Isobel and Duncan out of the office and turned their steps toward the nearby coaching inn.

Fifteen minutes later, they were rattling out on the road to London.

* * *

They met with Wolverstone and Melville early that evening. Royd's message had been terse and to the point. When he and Isobel walked into the Wolverstone House drawing room, he wasn't, therefore, all that surprised to find the company Wolverstone had assembled to hear his—their—report.

Minerva rose to greet them. She made the introductions. Royd knew some of those there; like him, they had, at one time or another, worked with Wolverstone. Royd had crossed professional paths with Christian Allardyce, Marquess of Dearne, in the days Dearne had been one of Wolverstone's most trusted agents, and he knew Jack, Lord Hendon, owner of Hendon Shipping, from commercial shipping circles.

"Don't tell me," he said to Hendon, "that you have a covert side to the business, too."

Hendon humphed. "Sadly, no. There's only one company that still sails under marque, and that's yours. My connection comes through my days in the army."

It was Jack who introduced him to Major Rafe Carstairs.

Royd recalled the name. "You were involved in the Black Cobra incident."

"Indeed. Which is why I have such an interest in this latest scheme." Carstairs nodded at Wolverstone, now talking to Isobel. "I'm still active, but at headquarters here. As you've got prisoners, I suspect I might have a role to play."

Carstairs looked pleased at the prospect.

Isobel chose her moment and presented Wolverstone with the captives' petition for justice. Minerva and Dearne flanked the duke as he read the statement, then flicked through the signatures. It was Minerva who pointed out the children's scrawls, and Isobel confirmed they had put their names to it, too.

Wolverstone passed the petition to Carstairs and Hendon, and nodded at Royd. "That will help. I'll have a few others look it over before I hand it to the Prime Minister. No need to further rattle Melville at this point."

On the heels of that comment, a tap fell on the door, then it opened, and the butler announced Melville. The First Lord of the Admiralty came walking in, his demeanor suggesting wary resignation.

Wolverstone reclaimed the petition and set it on a sideboard. "I believe you know everyone."

After a quick glance around, Melville nodded.

"Excellent." Wolverstone waved the gathering to the grouping of chairs and sofas. "Let's get started. From Royd's note, I gather there's a degree of urgency above any pressure from closer to home."

The last words were accompanied by a glance at Melville, who humphed and sat in one of the armchairs.

Royd sat beside Isobel on one of the long sofas. Once everyone was settled, he commenced a dry and strictly factual account of all that had happened, and all they'd discovered, from the time *The Corsair* reached the estuary north of Freetown.

During the voyage back, he and Isobel had had plenty of time to decide what to reveal, and to rehearse and refine what to actually say. He paused to allow her to describe the condition of the women and children, and also to detail the killing of the girl Daisy; Isobel had insisted that the horror of that crime would have more impact if she related it, and by the looks on the men's faces, her assessment had been correct.

He resumed his recitation of events. The identities and positions of Satterly, Muldoon, and Winton made Melville uneasy, but that they were now in custody and on their way to London brought him some relief.

When Royd revealed that, in seizing the compound, they had also captured two of the financial backers of the enterprise and had established that there were four more they had yet to identify, the attention of those listening sharpened to a knife's edge.

"The two you captured—I take it they're on their way here?" Wolverstone asked.

"Yes. We've kept them separate from the other three." Royd went on to detail what they'd learned about the enterprise from Satterly, Muldoon, and Winton. "There was no prospect that the scheme would ever have become a reality without the greed and the lack of morals of the six backers."

Wolverstone nodded. "Very well—you've set the stage and strung us along long enough. Who are the two backers you've captured?"

Royd told them the names.

Melville paled. He opened his mouth, shut it, then managed to croak, "Good God!"

"Indeed." His expression harsh, his fingers steepled

before his face, Wolverstone arched his brows. "That does put rather a different complexion on things."

Dearne had been studying Melville. Now he switched his gaze to Wolverstone. "If Neill is an example of those Ross-Courtney recruited to this scheme, the other four are certain to be of similar ilk."

In obvious agitation, Melville waved his pudgy hands. "But this is dreadful! Bad enough that we must—absolutely *must*—pull down whoever these backers are, and publicly, too, but to be reaching so high and then not have sufficient evidence to be sure of our case!"

"We'll get the necessary evidence." Wolverstone's tone was deceptively mild. There was nothing mild about the hard glint in his eyes.

Melville shot to his feet and started to pace—two short steps one way, two back—as he chewed on one nail. "I tell you, the government won't stand unless we show resolve in this matter." He shot a look at Carstairs. "Not after the Black Cobra business. And all the unrest." He waved as if the "unrest" was both general and obvious.

Royd paid precious little attention to politics, but from the looks on the other men's faces, Melville's "unrest" was, indeed, well understood.

"We've already got two of them in our hands," Dearne said. "Even if they continue to deny all wrongdoing, you may be sure we'll find some trace."

"Some trail that will lead us to the other four." Rafe Carstairs watched Melville pace. "You and the rest in the government knew this was going to involve persons of standing—that was the reason you've been so keen to see the mission, and the case against those involved, prosecuted, because you are all aware it's the only way to save your political skins. And"—he held up a hand to stay Melville's ire—"I agree that's the only possible avenue to stave off what might otherwise be...a situation none of us would welcome."

Wolverstone murmured, "Well said." His comment drew Melville's increasingly agitated gaze. "Melville—I suggest you prepare your colleagues in the government. No matter what they wish, there is no going back—no way to sweep this under some rug and hope no one notices. Too many people already know of Ross-Courtney's and Neill's involvement. No matter their denials, they will need to be brought before the courts and tried under the same laws that apply to every man. There can be no special leniency shown."

Melville grimaced, but nodded. "I—we—know and accept that. But without sufficient evidence, how are you even going to hold Ross-Courtney, let alone Neill?"

Wolverstone's smile was all hard edges. "Leave that to us. We can and will hold them—and yes, it will be in secret, so as far as you or anyone in government will know, they will not even have reached England's shores. Meanwhile, we will follow the obvious trails—the diamond merchant in Amsterdam, and from him to the banker, and so to our as-yet-unidentified four, along the way implicating all six in initiating and deriving monetary benefit from a heinous crime."

"There's also the connection between Ross-Courtney and Neill." Minerva spoke for the first time. She caught her husband's eye. "They are not friends. They might have known *of* each other, but they don't move in the same circles."

"So they will have met somewhere, several times, along with others." Dearne nodded. "Almost certainly at some club, so that, too, might assist us in identifying the other four."

"And in proving conspiracy," Jack Hendon put in.

Wolverstone looked at Melville. "We will get the evidence—you can rest assured of that."

Melville grimaced. "But all that will take time, won't it? I accept that you can arrange to hold Ross-Courtney and Neill incommunicado, but for how long? One slip, and the whole incident will blow up in the government's face. For pity's sake, Ross-Courtney is one of the king's closest confidantes!"

"As to that," Royd said, "there may be another way." He considered Melville; he and Isobel had agreed not to mention the plan involving the blue diamonds until they understood more about the situation. He'd heard enough to know they definitely needed to put the plan into action. For all his fussy ways, Melville was not a fool; he wouldn't be this agitated without reason. Royd continued, "A faster way to learn who else is involved and—with luck—get one of them to talk, and so gain the solid evidence we need to"—*send all six to the gallows*—"bring the six backers to justice."

"Assuming the other four are of the same social stratum as Ross-Courtney and Neill, then the best evidence we could get is for one of them to confess and so implicate the others." Wolverstone held Melville's gaze. "That would be the cleanest and neatest solution for everyone."

Melville drew in a tight breath, then nodded. "Yes. All right." He paused, then said, "You've told me that Ross-Courtney and Neill are two of those involved, but they're not yet on English soil, are they?"

"No." Royd gave Melville the statement he was angling for. "At present, they're in transit between Freetown and London."

"They are not, therefore, currently under English jurisdiction and are not in a position to make any demands to see their solicitors or anyone else." Wolverstone smiled coldly at Melville. "So at present, there is no chance of any…public difficulties from that quarter."

Melville was calming. He nodded. "Very well." He looked at Royd. "So what is this faster plan?"

Royd studied the First Lord. He and Isobel had studiously avoided any mention of blue diamonds. "With all due respect, my lord, I suspect you would rather not know."

Melville blinked, then he stared at Royd in some consternation. "Nothing illegal or untoward, I hope?"

Royd smiled. "No. But if we do need to…bend a few rules, then perhaps…?"

"Oh, indeed." Melville held up his hands as if to ward off the notion. "You are absolutely correct—I do not need to know." He looked around at all those present, then tugged down his waistcoat. "I realize that this sort of business is not my forte. I accept that in this matter, I must place my trust in you—in all of you." With an unexpectedly dignified bow, he stated, "I will therefore take my leave and allow you to continue your deliberations. Ladies. Gentlemen."

Minerva rose; the men came to their feet as she tugged the bellpull. She walked with Melville to the door and handed him into the care of the butler. The men waited until the duchess returned and resumed her seat, then sat again.

"Well?" Wolverstone arched an imperious brow at Royd. "You've teased us enough. What is this plan?"

Royd told them.

Isobel noted that, when Royd finished detailing how they imagined the plan would work, it was to his wife that Wolverstone turned for an initial assessment.

Minerva's nod was enthusiastic. "It will work. A necklace of blue diamonds? The entire ton will be agog." She paused, then said, "The most difficult part will be getting the necklace made in time, but"—her eyes narrowed—"with the right sort of enticement delivered in the correct way, I believe we should be able to arrange it."

"So..." Wolverstone looked from Minerva to Isobel. "The ton and society is your battleground. How do you see this playing out?"

Royd sat forward so he could watch their faces as Isobel and Minerva batted ideas back and forth.

Minerva was adamant that a major ton ball was the venue of choice during which to dangle the necklace in the hopes of enticing the four unidentified backers to present themselves. She promptly volunteered to hold such a ball ten days hence, and to persuade her fellow duchess and good friend, Honoria, Duchess of St. Ives, to hold another several days later. "We need two events scheduled, because it's entirely possible that not all four will attend my function, but they will hear about the necklace and will attend Honoria's—I really can't see them not wanting to set eyes on it, at least."

"How can you be sure to have invited them?" Jack Hendon asked.

Minerva smiled. "We don't need to bother our heads over that. If the four elusive backers are gentlemen of the same stripe as Ross-Courtney and Neill, once they hear about the necklace, they'll arrive in our ballrooms, invitation or not. They'll just arrive later, once the receiving line is done with."

When Dearne asked who would be best to display such a necklace, Minerva blinked, then, as if the answer should have been obvious, gestured at Isobel. "There is no one better than Miss Carmichael. We need a lady who is going to attract the eye, who can carry off such a piece with aplomb, and that Isobel is so tall is simply an added blessing. But more, she must not be anyone well known about town, yet at the same time, it needs to be obvious from her bearing and manner that she belongs within the upper echelon."

When all the men looked puzzled, Minerva sighed. "It's really quite simple. If the lady our elusive but intensely curious gentlemen see at our ball is someone they know, they will wait for some other, more private time to approach her. They won't approach her openly but will arrange some other, incidental meeting. As for her belonging to our circles, anyone who doesn't will immediately make our gentlemen suspicious, and they might well not approach at all but watch from a distance."

Minerva fixed her spouse with an interrogatory look. "Am I correct in thinking that you will wish to ensure that, should anyone approach Isobel and ask about the necklace, we have several witnesses to the interaction, so it will not simply be Isobel's word against theirs that they approached her at all?"

Wolverstone nodded. "As we're talking of one of yours or Honoria's balls, then given the usual crush, we should be able to have at least one if not two others close enough to overhear any exchange."

Rafe Carstairs held up a hand. "I have a quibble. Won't every lady at the ball demand to be told where Isobel got such a fabulous necklace? And once she answers...well, our gentlemen won't need to ask themselves, will they?"

Minerva looked at Rafe pityingly. "Really, Rafe—how long have you been on the town? I can guarantee that no lady—certainly no lady present at my or Honoria's balls, anyway—would ever be so gauche as to actually *ask* Isobel where she got the necklace. You're correct in thinking that every single lady will want to know, but not one will ask. Instead, they'll speculate and whisper—which is precisely what we want."

Isobel glanced around; the men were still mulling, but there seemed to be no further questions.

"Right, then." Wolverstone swept his gaze over their faces. "We have three avenues to pursue. One—identifying the diamond merchant and following the trail from him to the banker, and thence to the six backers. I'll pursue that avenue"—he cocked a brow at Hendon—"and perhaps you can assist with any information from your shipping contacts in Amsterdam. Someone must know of stones coming from Freetown."

Jack nodded. "I'll put the word out."

"As for our second avenue—identifying where Ross-Courtney and Neill met, and who else attended the meetings…" Wolverstone looked at Dearne.

The marquess nodded. "I'll take that on and call in a few others from the club to assist."

Isobel wondered what club he referred to, but the duke seemed content.

"Our third avenue—the lure of the necklace—we'll leave in the hands of the ladies." Wolverstone inclined his head to them both. "No doubt you'll inform us as to when and where we will need to present ourselves as guards."

"Indeed," Minerva said. "We won't require your assistance until the night of the events, although I might contact your wives in the interim, should we require any help in the social sphere."

Wolverstone's lips lifted in a faint smile, then he sobered and looked at Royd. "That leaves us to address our most pressing concern. When will Ross-Courtney and Neill arrive?"

"They're with Robert on *The Trident*," Royd said. "And Declan has the other three on board *The Cormo-*

rant. I don't expect either ship to reach the Pool for at least three, possibly four or even five days."

"Good." Wolverstone looked at Carstairs. "That gives us—or more specifically, you—time to arrange suitable accommodations." To Isobel and Royd, he explained, "Rafe has access to army property and personnel."

Carstairs smiled. "Access that won't be questioned, at least not in the short term."

Royd nodded his understanding. "Theoretically, we could put Satterly, Muldoon, and Winton into any of the main jails to be held pending charges and trial. However, I would suggest we shouldn't give them any scope for changing their minds and attempting to curry favor with Ross-Courtney and Neill and their powerful friends by sending word to Ross-Courtney's agents as to what has befallen their employer."

"Indeed." Wolverstone looked back at Carstairs. "Any suggestions for them?"

Carstairs considered, then said, "I wouldn't suggest keeping them in London—one never knows where a connection of Satterly's, or even Winton's, might pop up. But there are holding cells in Cardiff that might do. Out of the way, and also unlikely to have many Englishmen or Irish nearby."

Wolverstone looked at Royd, who nodded. "We can discuss transporting them later—by sea might be best."

Carstairs inclined his head. "As for the backers… again, not in London, yet we don't want them too far away. There's an old barracks in Essex Forest with a skeleton staff. The place has holding cells. I could give the usual staff a holiday and send in a select troop to guard our precious pair—and any others we catch—until charges are laid and we can transfer them to a civilian prison."

That suggestion found immediate favor. The men fell to discussing how best to move the prisoners from the Pool of London to their selected destinations.

Minerva glanced at Isobel. "What say we leave them to it, retire to my private parlor, and put our minds to the question of getting this fabulous necklace made?"

Isobel agreed. She rose with Minerva, who waved the gentlemen back to their seats. "When you've finished, we'll be in my parlor."

With that, the duchess looped her arm in Isobel's and steered her out of the room. As they started up the stairs, Minerva said, "I have to admit that I wasn't looking forward to the next few weeks—ton events can be such a bore, yet it's expected we host at least one in this season." She glanced at Isobel and smiled. "I can't tell you how happy I am to be able to turn a ball of mine to such a good cause." She arched her brows. "And, of course, there are the blue diamonds."

Isobel laughed.

By the time she and Royd departed the ducal residence, she'd been inducted into the circle of Wolverstone's duchess—one of the most influential hostesses in the haut ton.

Fifteen

After spending her morning at Wolverstone House writing and addressing invitations, early the following afternoon, Isobel pushed open the door to Rundell, Bridge, and Rundell, jewelers to the ton and favorites of the Crown. Located on Ludgate Hill not far from St. Paul's Cathedral, the store was a fashionable oasis of soft light, discreet murmurs, and display cases loaded with sparkling gem-studded pieces, any of which would be suitable to grace the throat, wrist, or finger of a queen.

Her head high, Isobel glided confidently forward. Minerva and Honoria, Duchess of St. Ives and Minerva's friend, followed close behind. In such august company, Isobel needed no introduction. Long before she'd reached the wide counter at the rear of the shop, one of the younger assistants had spotted them. The young man's eyes had flown wide, then he'd turned and dived behind a long black curtain concealing an archway in the rear wall.

Isobel reached the counter just as a gentleman of middle years and discreetly elegant style emerged from behind the curtain. His smile already in place, he bowed low to the duchesses. "Your Graces. We are delighted to receive you." As he straightened, his smile included Isobel. "Might we help you with something?" He spread his hands. "As ever, we are entirely at your service."

"Good afternoon, Mr. Bridge." Minerva stepped to the counter beside Isobel. From the corner of her eye, Isobel saw the duchess glance around, confirming no one else was close. Turning back to the gentleman—presumably one of the owners—Minerva lowered her voice to a conspiratorial level. "My good friend Miss Carmichael has a very special commission. We wondered if we might discuss it with you in more private surrounds."

Bridge was intrigued. His nose all but quivered. "But of course, Your Grace." He gestured to a small antechamber. "If you will come this way, we may be entirely private."

He led them into the antechamber and through a door cleverly disguised in the paneling. The room beyond was of a decent size and luxuriously appointed. Bridge held the door for them. "His Majesty was here just last week—a new snuffbox."

"He does seem quite partial to the things." Honoria paused on the threshold of the room and said to Bridge, "It would be helpful if you would summon Mr. Rundell to attend us as well. The commission in question will require his particular skills."

Bridge bowed low. "Indeed, Your Grace." He followed Honoria into the room and shut the door. "If you will be seated, I will ask Mr. Rundell to join us." With another bow, Bridge departed through a second door.

A highly polished oval table sat in the center of the room, with six straight-backed chairs with rose-velvet-covered seats arranged around it. The room had no windows; it was certainly private. Light fell on the table from an elegantly ornate gold-and-crystal chandelier. The ladies sank onto the chairs, Isobel at one end of the table, with Minerva to her left and Honoria on her right.

They'd barely settled when the door through which

Bridge had departed opened again, this time to admit a heavyset man of acerbic mien. He shut the door, then bowed, but there was nothing of servility in his manner. "Your Graces. Miss Carmichael." He came forward. "I regret Mr. Bridge has been called to the counter. The Marchioness of Dearne and Lady Clarice Warnefleet have arrived, and they're insisting they'll see no one else." His hand on the chair at the other end of the table, Rundell—from the duchesses' descriptions, Isobel knew it was he—paused and studied them through shrewd blue eyes overhung by shaggy brows. "You wouldn't know anything about that, I suppose?" When Minerva and Honoria widened their eyes in all innocence, Rundell humphed and drew out the chair. "It's just that I recall they're friends of yours."

"They are, indeed. Be that as it may," Minerva said, "Miss Carmichael has something to show you, and then we, collectively, have a request we would like you to consider."

Rundell set his large hands on the table and waited—a man of few words.

From her reticule, Isobel drew out the brown-paper-wrapped parcel the women had given her in the mining compound. She hadn't even unwrapped it; she was no expert on uncut stones. She placed the parcel on the table. "This contains raw gems from a mine. I have no idea of their state."

She pushed the parcel down the table.

Rundell reached out and, a frown on his face, accepted it. He turned the parcel over, then drew a pocket knife from one capacious pocket. He held up the knife. "May I?"

"By all means." Isobel watched as he cut the thin string securing the packet, then carefully unfolded the paper.

What lay revealed when he smoothed the paper flat were about twenty-five gray-, brown-, and black-streaked pebble-sized rocks. Their surfaces were chipped, all angles. They looked like unpretentious gravel except that, here and there, the light from the chandelier struck sparks—flares of intense blue-white light—from the otherwise unremarkable stones.

Phillip Rundell, reputed to be the best judge of gemstones in England, stared down at the stones, then he sucked in an audible breath. He cast a piercing glance up the table. "Where did you get these?"

Isobel replied, "From a mine in Africa."

Rundell studied the stones for a moment more, then pulled a loupe from his pocket. He fitted the magnifier to his eye, picked up the largest stone, and examined it. After setting it down, he examined three more stones before removing the loupe.

He stared at the stones. Isobel could read nothing from the severe expression on his craggy face. Eventually, he said, "Are these for sale?"

"No." When Rundell looked up at her, she added, "At least, not yet. The intention is to sell them after they've served their purpose."

"Purpose?"

Minerva held up a hand. "Before we go further, we need to tell you what we require, and you need to tell us whether you can do what we need."

Rundell nodded.

Between them, they described the necklace they needed made and the time constraints. "And," Isobel concluded, "we need a guarantee of absolute secrecy." She held Rundell's gaze. "This mission is of importance to the entire country and, even more, the government and the king."

Rundell held her gaze, then humphed. He looked down at the stones his fingers had been constantly playing over. After a moment, he grimaced. "How can I turn away a commission like this? Stones like this?" From under his shaggy brows, he sent a look approaching a glare at Minerva and Honoria. "But Your Graces knew that, I'm sure."

Again, Minerva and Honoria attempted to look innocent.

"All right." Rundell pushed away from the table. "I'll—we'll—do it. When did you say you needed it by?"

"By the night of my ball." Minerva rose. "Wednesday the twenty-ninth."

Rundell pulled a face as he got to his feet. "We'll need to work all hours, but we'll do it. It won't be ready until that afternoon, mind."

"That's quite acceptable," Honoria informed him. She patted his shoulder as she passed him. "Now get to work—we'll see ourselves out."

Rundell grunted and turned back to the table. As she left the room in the duchesses' wake, Isobel saw him reverently wrapping up the stones in the plain brown paper.

* * *

Six evenings later, all four Frobisher brothers and their ladies strolled into the drawing room of the Stanhope Street house, which had become their de facto headquarters. They had dined well and were now intent on catching up with each other's news.

Declan and Edwina had sailed into the Pool of London three days after Royd and Isobel had reported to Wolverstone. Declan had sent a messenger to inform Royd of their arrival, and Royd had subsequently alerted Rafe Carstairs as well as Wolverstone.

Carstairs had accompanied a troop of experienced soldiers to the docks and taken charge of Declan's prisoners.

"They're apparently to be held in Cardiff." Edwina settled on the sofa beside Isobel. Duncan, loath to miss anything, scrambled up to sit between the two ladies. Edwina smiled and patted his arm.

Royd pulled up a straight-backed chair. "We decided that, while it might have been less difficult to transport them by sea, fewer were likely to know of their final destination if we used a single carriage. Carstairs was sure he could spirit them out of London without anyone being the wiser."

"It helped that *The Cormorant* didn't actually dock." Declan set a chair beside Edwina. He looked at Robert, who had settled in an armchair beside Aileen, who was seated on the second sofa opposite Edwina. "Where did you leave *The Trident*?"

Robert and Aileen had sailed into London thirty-six hours after Declan and Edwina. "She's alongside *The Cormorant* now, but as we'd discussed, I initially dropped anchor off Limehouse." Robert looked at Royd. "After I sent you word, Carstairs appeared and came aboard, and we docked at Limehouse long enough to off-load our prisoners. Carstairs had a troop of older soldiers waiting with a small closed carriage—he said they were taking the precious pair into Essex."

"Did you have any trouble from Ross-Courtney and Neill?" Isobel asked.

"They gave up shouting and trying to suborn the crew after the first day at sea." Aileen shuddered. "Dreadful men."

Robert reached across and squeezed her hand. "Carstairs tied their hands and gagged them before dragging them off the ship. And they did have to be dragged.

I seriously doubt Carstairs untied and ungagged them until he had them safely secured in Essex."

Royd briefly explained the reasoning behind their prisoners being held in out-of-the-way military prisons, then all eyes turned to Caleb and Kate. They'd arrived just that morning.

"I didn't see any reason to hurry." Caleb grinned. "You lot had everything in hand. So we laid over for a day in Las Palmas with Phillipe. Kit and Lachlan sailed on for Bristol. Then we came on to Southampton." He looked at Royd. "*The Corsair* was still there, but Stewart said he was leaving tomorrow for London." When Royd nodded, Caleb asked, "Do you want *The Prince* here or in Southampton?"

"Send orders to reprovision there, then sail up to the Pool." Royd glanced around. "I suspect we'll all be headed to Aberdeen once this is over."

When Declan looked at Edwina and arched a brow, she brightly replied, "Well, we do have *weddings*—plural—to arrange."

Declan chuckled and looked at the other couples; each pair was looking at each other. "So when is the grand finale?"

Isobel drew her eyes from Royd's and briefly described the plan to flush out the remaining backers, including the involvement of the two duchesses and her trip to the jeweler.

Robert looked at Royd. "So we're running this exercise in a crowded ton ballroom. How do you see the action panning out?"

Royd didn't really want to think about what might happen in Minerva's ballroom; whenever he did, he saw holes the size of galleons in any protective net they might place around Isobel. And there was a very large part of him that didn't like that.

Having just got her back, more or less in his keeping, to risk her, and their future, and his heart, again…

No, he didn't like their plan at all.

But it was the only viable plan for rapidly luring the other four backers into the open, so he put aside his concerns and anxieties and ran through the various gentlemen and ladies who had volunteered to be a part of the protective crew revolving around Isobel as she swanned about the Wolverstone House ballroom four nights from then.

"And if we still haven't learned all four names, the Duchess of St. Ives's ball on Friday will give us a second chance." Isobel glanced down at Duncan. The talk of prisoners, army troops, and ships had held his interest, but when the talk had turned to jewelry and balls, his head had started to loll. "Come along. Let's get you to bed." She eased him up. As she rose to leave with him, she glanced at the others. "At the moment, everything's in hand, and we have a few days of peace and calm."

Royd got to his feet. "There's nothing we need do until Wednesday." He looked around at the others. "Until then, we're free."

* * *

They might have been temporarily free of the mission, but there were other demands they'd overlooked.

The following afternoon, Edwina, Isobel, Aileen, Kate, and Duncan were in the upstairs parlor playing a rowdy game of spillikins. On hearing heavy carriage wheels halt before her door, Edwina got to her feet and went to peer out of the window.

She frowned. "How odd."

"What?" Isobel went to join her. She looked down on

a large, ponderous traveling carriage drawn up before the house and caught a glimpse of a footman climbing the steps to the house's front door. "I take it you aren't expecting more guests."

"No," Edwina replied. "And I don't recognize that carriage or the coachman."

The others had come to look, too, peering over Edwina's shoulders.

Duncan pushed his way in front of Isobel. He leaned his forehead on the glass and stared down. "That's Great-Grandmama's carriage."

"Iona?" Kate said.

"Oh, my heavens. He's right." Isobel stared. "That's her John Coachman on the box."

Duncan cheered and dashed for the door.

In a flurry of skirts, all four ladies rushed after him.

They reached the front hall and, as one, paused to draw breath, smooth down their skirts, and then raise their heads.

Duncan had dashed outside, followed more circumspectly by Humphrey.

Royd—presumably alerted by the thunder of feet on the stairs—looked out of the library where he and his brothers were lurking. "What's happening?" He looked at Isobel.

"Iona's here." Isobel paused only long enough to say, "Tell Caleb he can't run and hide," before sweeping forward.

She and Edwina reached the open front door—and discovered Iona wasn't the only unexpected guest Humphrey, a footman, and Duncan were helping to the pavement.

Edwina turned to call back into the house, "Frobishers—your parents are here!"

Isobel looked down on the scene below; Duncan had

already greeted Iona. As Royd joined her, she watched their son and his grandfather meet for the first time.

Fergus was smiling. He offered his hand, and Duncan bowed, then placed his hand in his grandfather's. Duncan's smile was bright, his usual confidence shining, while the smile wreathing Fergus's face held joy, delight, satisfaction, and not a little pride.

"Iona's already told them about Duncan," Isobel whispered.

Royd grunted in agreement as his mother, Elaine, descended from the carriage, her eyes, for once, not searching for her sons but fixed in nothing short of wonder on her grandson.

Iona stumped up the steps on Humphrey's arm. She halted on the porch and looked at them—first at Royd and Isobel, standing to one side of the entrance, then at Declan and Edwina, just behind them. Then her gaze traveled to Robert and Aileen, before finally coming to rest on Kate and Caleb. "Well," Iona said, "it appears several of you have interesting things to tell me."

Isobel stepped forward. "Grandmama." She bent to kiss Iona's cheek. "We weren't expecting you."

Iona humphed.

Released from her shock by Isobel's action, Kate came forward to kiss Iona's other cheek. "Great-aunt Iona."

Isobel took charge before Iona could. She took her grandmother's arm. "Come in." She waved at the others. "You know all the Frobishers, and this is Lady Edwina, Declan's wife." She paused while Edwina brightly welcomed Iona. "And this"—Isobel gestured to Aileen as she drew Iona on—"is Miss Aileen Hopkins. She's to marry Robert."

With Kate, Isobel guided Iona into the drawing room, cravenly leaving Royd to deal with his parents. Then again, he had his brothers, and Edwina and Aileen, not to mention Duncan, to help distract them.

Iona allowed herself to be settled in an armchair. When Isobel inquired, Iona explained that, on reading Duncan's note and realizing what had happened, and what would therefore inevitably occur, she'd decided to speak with the elder Frobishers and break the happy news that they had a nearly eight-year-old grandson they'd known nothing about. "They took it well, I must say." But when Iona had told them of Isobel's quest to find Kate, Fergus had revealed that Royd had departed for Freetown on the last leg of some mission. "When we put two and two together and still ended with two, we decided to inquire further. Fergus interrogated the London office and learned of so many Frobisher ships being diverted to Freetown that we came down here to see what's going on."

Movement at the door had Isobel straightening. Elaine Frobisher came in on Royd's arm.

Of average height, Elaine had a wealth of red hair, now faded to a copper brown, and soft hazel eyes. Her face was alight; it was obvious that, despite the circumstances, meeting her grandson had been a moment of joy.

"Isobel." Elaine released Royd's arm and held out both hands.

Isobel responded to the gesture and the unvoiced plea in Elaine's eyes. Royd was Elaine's firstborn and very close to her heart. Elaine didn't want any difficulty between them—and neither did she. She gripped Elaine's fingers and, leaning down, bussed her cheek. "I'm sorry I never told you," she whispered, "but I couldn't—not then."

Elaine drew back; her eyes searched Isobel's face. "But now?"

Isobel smiled. "Now I think everything's going to be all right."

Elaine beamed. "Lovely!" She squeezed Isobel's hands, then set her free to greet Fergus.

Over the years, Isobel had had more to do with Fergus than she had Elaine; his bluff geniality covered a certain hurt, but he appeared to direct that equally at Royd. After she'd kissed his whiskery cheek, and he'd grumped his usual "Well, miss" at her, he clapped her lightly on the shoulder. "Just give me another grandson-baby, and we'll say no more about it."

She laughed, and the last of the tension dissolved.

Duncan appeared delighted to have two new grandparents to add to his supporters. He wriggled into the corner of the chaise between Elaine and Iona in her armchair. Fergus sat beside Elaine. As the younger ladies sank onto the other armchairs and the opposite sofa, Fergus directed a piercing look at his sons. "We haven't made the journey from Aberdeen to be kept in the dark. So cut line and tell us what you've been about."

"It wasn't just the four of us." Royd took a straight-backed chair from a footman and set it between the ends of the sofas. As he sat, he waved at the ladies. "We were all involved."

Both Fergus and Iona rapped their canes on the floor at the same time. They exchanged a swift glance, then Fergus said, "So tell us."

"From the beginning, mind," Iona said. "None of your general summaries that leave out all the dangerous bits."

As his brothers settled in chairs alongside his, Royd inwardly sighed and complied. He knew better than to do otherwise, not in this company. But he'd be damned if he would do it all alone—he passed the baton to Declan, and Edwina helped by painting their first visit to Freetown in significantly more vivid colors. Then Robert took up the tale, aided by Aileen, while Edwina arranged rooms, and refreshments were served. Caleb started his story by somewhat sheepishly admitting that he'd seized the mission before anyone else could be sent because he'd wanted to test himself and show his true colors.

Royd promptly informed Fergus in advance that Caleb had more than proved himself in the jungle.

Caleb colored, but plowed on, relating his first deeds on reaching the settlement, then he passed the limelight to Kate. Hesitantly at first, then with increasing confidence, she related what life had been like for the captives in the compound, ending with the capture of Caleb and his men—something she plainly considered her fault.

Caleb closed one hand over hers in her lap and explained how that capture and the consequent assimilation of him and his men into the compound's workforce had proved a critical advantage when the rescue force arrived.

That brought the story back to Royd. Concisely, he described the action, from their first meeting with Decker on his flagship to the final meeting aboard *The Corsair*. Robert and Declan added the precautions they'd instituted in the settlement before joining Royd in taking the compound.

With his gaze on his son, Royd skipped over the details of the fighting, saying only that the mercenaries had been appropriately dealt with; his parents and Iona knew enough of the world to correctly interpret those words.

He concluded with the avenues currently being pursued by Wolverstone and his colleagues to collect evidence against the backers.

"Ross-Courtney, heh?" Iona sniffed. "Can't say I'm surprised. He always was a nasty little toad, forever giving himself airs."

"I've crossed paths with Neill," Fergus said. "Not the sort of man I'd care to do business with."

Elaine was frowning. "If you haven't already got sufficient evidence against them…well, you won't be able to hold men like that for long, will you?"

Royd looked at Isobel. He'd omitted any mention of the necklace.

"That's why," Isobel said, accepting the inevitable, "we've set up a lure of sorts in the hope we'll entice the other backers to step forward, and hopefully, one of them will lead us to more readily obtainable evidence we can use to convict all six."

"What sort of lure?" Iona asked.

Isobel outlined the plan for using the necklace of blue diamonds and showing off the creation at two major ton balls.

Somewhat to Royd's surprise, Iona and his parents seemed to think the ploy had every chance of success.

At that point, the clock chimed, and Edwina pushed to her feet; her pregnancy was becoming more evident by the day. "I've asked for dinner to be moved forward a trifle—you must be tired by the jolting and rattling and will be keen to get a good night's sleep. The first ball isn't for several days, so we'll have time to talk and organize tomorrow."

Her apparent inclusion of everyone—including Duncan and the elder three—in what was to come left everyone perfectly ready to rise and head upstairs to rest, wash, and change.

Isobel encouraged Duncan to show Fergus to his room. She found herself walking with Elaine out of the drawing room and into the front hall. Most of the others were ahead of them; Isobel saw Kate on the stairs and halted—they'd left Iona in the drawing room.

She was about to turn back when Elaine put a hand on her arm.

"I wonder, my dear, if I could have a word in private." Elaine's gentle eyes were smiling. "Perhaps you might show me the garden? I wouldn't mind stretching my legs in the fresh air—or at least what passes for fresh air down here."

"Yes, of course." Isobel realized Royd hadn't gone past them; he could deal with Iona, she hoped. "The garden's this way."

The rear garden of the town house was a pleasant oasis of shrubbery and gravel paths. They stepped outside, and the September evening fell, cool and oddly serene, about them.

Elaine set out along the path, her gaze on the gravel.

Isobel fell in beside her and waited.

She didn't have to wait long before Elaine said, "I know I speak for Fergus as well as myself on this. We want you to know that, despite all that happened, despite the years since, you've been the only woman we could ever imagine Royd marrying. It was always you and only you. His mind—and even more importantly, his heart—never wavered." Elaine raised her head, and Isobel saw a small, wry smile on her lips. "Never shifted in even the smallest degree—and that wasn't because we didn't try to steer him elsewhere." Her smile bloomed more definitely. "Shifting Royd from any goal he's set his heart on is well-nigh impossible, but I daresay you're aware of that."

Isobel snorted softly.

"Indeed, but that wasn't all I wanted to say. Back then, we all made mistakes—and that includes Fergus and me. When Royd left and didn't return, I knew Fergus should have told you where he'd gone."

"Fergus knew?" That was news to Isobel; she'd never imagined Fergus had lied.

"*Not* as to the place, but he—and I—knew Royd had sailed on a mission for the Crown. That only duty to his country, or being honor bound, could have kept him from returning to you." Elaine paused, then went on, "I knew you'd visited the office, trying to contact Royd. Duncan told me his age. You were pregnant and trying to reach Royd to tell him—we didn't bend the rules and help you. That was our mistake. What happened after Royd came back—that was your and his mistakes. And Iona—if she hadn't insisted on a handfasting in the first place…" Elaine sighed and looked down.

After a moment, she went on, "What I'm trying to say is that, back then, we all contributed—we all played our parts in what happened. We all owe apologies and forgiveness." She glanced at Isobel and caught her eyes. "It's all water under the bridge, and if we're wise, we'll let the past go and move forward from here."

Isobel halted; she felt as if a weight she hadn't realized was there had lifted from her shoulders. She smiled at Elaine. "Thank you for telling me. And I agree—we should take the wiser course."

Elaine's face lit with her trademark glorious smile. "Excellent." Then she paused. A second ticked past, then she refocused on Isobel's face. "Am I allowed to ask… you and Royd are getting married, aren't you?"

Isobel laughed. "Oh yes. As soon as this mission is over, and we return to Aberdeen."

She said it, meant it, and felt the certainty in her soul; marrying Royd was the right path for her.

Elaine beamed. "Lovely!" She turned back to the house. "We'd better go and change."

"Indeed." Isobel started back through the greenery

with an appreciably lighter step. "Edwina's a despot—she will not be pleased if we're late."

* * *

Royd deliberately hung back in the drawing room to ensure it was left to him to escort Iona up the stairs.

For her part, Isobel's irascible grandmother made no attempt to rise from her armchair. The instant Caleb's back cleared the doorway, Iona pointed her cane at Royd and then at the door. "For goodness' sake, shut the damned thing and come and sit down."

Lips twisting—in his experience, grinning at Iona was rarely a good idea—he went to obey. As he shut the door, he heard her mutter, "I'm not going to glare up at you—all that will get me is a crick in the neck."

His brows rose fleetingly; had she just admitted she knew she couldn't sway him? At least, not with her glares?

He returned and sat on the opposite sofa, directly in Iona's line of sight.

She nodded approvingly. "Well, here we are—as anyone with a grain of sense could have foretold."

He couldn't keep his surprise from his face.

"Pfft!" Iona waved dismissively. "Neither of you have ever changed your mind about anything—not once you've made a decision. Be that as it may…" She studied him for several seconds.

He bore the scrutiny with untrammeled ease.

Iona's eyes narrowed. "It's no secret that I've never believed you worthy of her—and I still don't. That said, I've never thought any man worthy of her—she has depths, and layers, and is so much more than your average young lady."

"I know."

"Hmm…perhaps you do. Now." Iona shifted, leaning

on her cane. "But as she's chosen you—again and still—and there's Duncan as well to think of, I won't be opposing a marriage between you." Her eyes bored into him. "Assuming, of course, that's the direction you're taking?"

He nodded. "Definitely. We'll be marrying as soon as this business is dealt with and we return to Aberdeen."

Iona nodded in turn. "Very well. But hear me well." She trapped Royd's gaze. "If you hurt her again, I will have your guts for garters." She paused, then added, "Believe it."

Royd had always known where Isobel got her bloodthirsty streak. But whether he believed Iona or not… "You have my word that you will never have cause to regret giving your blessing to our marriage. I know it will mean a great deal to Isobel."

"Yes, well." Iona heaved herself to her feet. "She never would see sense—not when it came to you."

Royd rose and ventured a smile, one Iona did not take badly. She motioned for him to lend her his arm, which he dutifully did, and they left the room and climbed the stairs in greater harmony than he'd ever anticipated sharing with Isobel's formidable grandmama.

Sixteen

Royd escorted Isobel through the ornate doorway of the Wolverstone House ballroom. Even though, in ton terms, it was relatively early, the room was crowded, and the stairs and front hall were jammed with guests making their way to the receiving line. That line currently snaked from Wolverstone and Minerva, standing just ahead, across the foyer, and down the stairs.

Regardless of everyone's preoccupation, the lady gliding beside him drew all eyes. She'd already been responsible for four different people tripping and nearly falling down the stairs. He set his jaw and pretended not to notice the stares, let alone the speculation that immediately sprang to life in so many eyes—male as well as female.

And then there were the whispers.

Although far removed from London society, the women in the compound had chosen correctly in giving the diamonds to Isobel. The gown she wore tonight had been created to showcase Rundell, Bridge, and Rundell's most fabulous creation. Somewhat to his surprise, it had been Iona who had insisted Isobel needed "the right" gown. Even more surprisingly, his mother had joined the chorus, and the entire female above-stairs contingent of Stanhope Street had rolled away in carriages to visit warehouses and modistes.

If he'd known what the result of their efforts would be, he would have found some way to stop them. When Isobel had walked down the stairs this evening, his tongue had stuck to the roof of his mouth, and he'd been literally unable to speak. Even Duncan, darting about examining all the nattily dressed gentlemen and ladies, had stopped and stared.

Royd had known Isobel for most of his life, had grown accustomed to having her beside him; apparently, he'd forgotten how magnificent she truly was—his Amazon.

She looked every inch a regal warrior-queen, in sleek silk the color of the late evening sky in those moments before it turned black. Against the alabaster skin of her bosom shone the blue diamonds, set in plain gold with nothing to detract from the stones' fire. The result was austere yet dazzlingly gorgeous—the stones blazed with a stark blue radiance that was literally riveting.

Once seen, it was difficult to look away, and that wasn't simply a matter of expensive silk and stones. It was Isobel herself; she possessed both the grace and the ineffable confidence to carry the moment—and the gown and the necklace—off. On most other ladies, the same gown and necklace simply wouldn't have had the same, almost shocking impact.

About them, conversations stuttered, then halted, before starting up again even more avidly.

They reached Minerva, whose face lit as the guest she'd just welcomed moved off and she finally saw them.

Isobel curtsied. Royd bowed, and they murmured the usual pleasantries.

Minerva nodded meaningfully. "Excellent!" Her eyes alight, she passed them on to Wolverstone, standing beside her.

Wolverstone arched his brows. They went through the

motions, but as the duke straightened from bowing over Isobel's hand, he murmured, "If *that* doesn't lure them out, nothing will."

Royd managed not to grunt.

He led Isobel to a group of friends, a predetermined next step. All those involved in the effort to identify the backers and collect the necessary evidence to convict them had met at St. Ives House at the—for the ton—unholy hour of ten o'clock that morning. Devil Cynster, Duke of St. Ives, and his duchess, Honoria, would be hosting the second ball, should it be necessary, but they were all working on the assumption that they would need two nights to draw at least two more of the backers into their net. Honoria had suggested using their house for the meeting, so that anyone happening to notice the people coming and going would think it more to do with their event and not the Wolverstone House affair.

The meeting had, in essence, been a foregathering of their troops—an opportunity for all those willing to be involved to meet Isobel, and for her to meet them. As well as St. Ives and Honoria, three of his cousins and their wives had joined the group, as had several other couples Dearne and his marchioness, Letitia, had recruited. Carstairs had been there, with his wife, Loretta, and three other couples he introduced as those involved in bringing down the fabled Black Cobra. Wolverstone and Minerva, and Jack Hendon and his wife, Katherine—another Kit—had been there, as well as all the Frobishers and their ladies, and Iona, who, it transpired, was well known to both Minerva and Honoria, as well as Letitia and several other ladies.

The Carmody matriarch's reach was greater than Royd had appreciated.

As usual, it had been Wolverstone who had called the

meeting to order; he'd explained their strategy and the tactics they intended to employ. Because this was a ball and there were so many uninvolved and unaware sharing their stage, of necessity, those tactics had to be fluid, able to respond to situations as they evolved.

The critical point, one Wolverstone had stressed, was that Isobel should never be out of sight of at least two of their number, and if anyone, male or female, approached and asked her about the necklace, at least two of them should converge to a distance close enough to overhear the exchange.

As for how they would know to close in, if Isobel was asked outright as to where she'd got the necklace, she would raise her hand to the stones and fiddle with the links.

Their preparations had been made, and everyone was in place, eager to put their plan into action.

He and Isobel chatted, smiled, and moved through the crowd, in reality shifting from one group of protectors to another. They circled the room once, giving all those there the opportunity to notice and stare at the diamonds—which everyone did. Royd hadn't been certain that the prediction that no lady would boldly walk up and ask where Isobel had found the stones would hold true, but it seemed Minerva had been correct; although any number of ladies ogled the diamonds, not one asked specifically about them.

That Isobel wasn't widely known among London's ton undoubtedly helped; people couldn't place her, but as she was plainly acquainted with a select group among the upper echelon, no one dared patronize her, either.

"Everyone—simply *everyone*—is talking about the diamonds," Edwina softly crowed as she swanned past on Declan's arm.

Then the musicians started up, and Royd claimed the first waltz. As it was the only waltz he was allowed that evening, he was determined to enjoy it.

As he drew Isobel into his arms and stepped onto the clearing floor, he realized it had been a very long time since they'd shared a dance in a ballroom, let alone a waltz. Yet she moved with him instinctively, her steps mirroring his; as they were both so tall, it was easy to tighten his hold and step out. She matched him; on a gurgle of laughter, she met his eyes. "If I haven't already become the cynosure of all eyes, this will surely achieve that."

He dipped his head and, his eyes on hers, murmured, "I live to serve." *You. Only you.*

She held his gaze as if she'd heard the unspoken words. They drowned in each other's eyes, navigating the crowded floor more by instinct than design, lost for those moments in the other's presence, in the reality they now shared.

Unfortunately, the measure wound to a close.

As he whirled her to a halt, her gaze still on his face, as if sensing the battle he waged to allow her out of his arms, she murmured, "This will work—you know it will."

He met her eyes. "It better."

She knew he wasn't speaking of luring the backers to show themselves but of her being adequately protected through the night.

As arranged, as he led her off the floor, Caleb stepped forward to, with an insouciant grin, filch her hand from his.

Royd released her. As he stalked through the crowd, he reminded himself not to scowl, and that it was infinitely better his youngest brother was first in the long line of gentleman-protectors scheduled to step in; any of the others and he might not have been able to play his part and let her go.

He gritted his teeth and tried not to let it show. He'd known he wouldn't enjoy the evening, but until that moment, he hadn't appreciated just how onerous his role would be.

* * *

Isobel smiled and joked with Caleb, who spent most of their dance extracting as many facts about Kate and her family as he could. He handed her off to Dearne, who smiled kindly, waltzed extremely well, and, she learned, had been one of Wolverstone's operatives in France during the last war.

When the dance ended, Dearne conducted her to a group including his wife and several other couples. They chatted and waited to see if any gentleman not of their number approached, but none did.

That became the pattern of her evening; she would dance with several of her protectors, then chat with them and their wives while waiting in vain for a backer to appear.

But they'd foreseen that the backers might not be so easily tempted into openly approaching her—not in full sight of a goodly portion of the ton—and had planned accordingly. Consequently, after dancing the supper waltz with Rupert Cynster, one of the duke's cousins, she prettily declined his offer to escort her into the supper room. After sending him to look for his wife, she turned and, unhurriedly, strolled down the ballroom and into a short corridor. She opened the door at the end and walked into the mansion's conservatory.

She closed the door behind her, paused for a second to listen, then, choosing the central path of the three leading into the moonlit shadows, walked down the avenue of densely packed palms and ferns.

Anyone watching her would think she had gone there to meet with some gentleman, which, as it happened, was true. According to the plan, several gentlemen of her acquaintance, Royd among them, would be concealed among the profusion of palms. She strolled, making no attempt to mute her footfalls. Now to see if any other gentleman sought to follow her and have a word in what appeared to be a private setting.

The conservatory's walls as well as its roof were made of glass. Moonlight slanted in, gilding leaves and laying a silvery sheen over the tiled floor. At the far end, all three paths converged on a circular space hosting a small fountain. The tinkle of water, the smell of rich loam, and the scents of night-flowering plants brought the jungle the diamonds had come from vividly to Isobel's mind.

"How appropriate," she murmured sotto voce.

Immediately, she heard the click of the conservatory door closing. After the briefest of pauses, heavy footsteps started following her down the path. Subterfuge was clearly not the gentleman's intent. She reached the fountain and turned, head rising, to see who had walked into their trap.

A large, florid-faced gentleman, no more than an inch taller than she but three times as wide, came stumping down the path. He'd pulled out a white handkerchief and was already mopping his brow. "Dashed warm in here." His tone was complaining.

Isobel studied him. "It is rather humid."

He stuffed the handkerchief in his pocket and sketched her an excuse for a bow. "Sir Reginald Cummins. Miss Carmichael, is it not?"

Isobel barely inclined her head. "Indeed, sir." In contrast to the room, her tone was chilly.

Sir Reginald didn't notice. His gaze had locked on the necklace.

Even in the moonlight, Isobel was fairly certain it would be winking and blinking, casting its invisible net.

Sir Reginald certainly seemed caught. He moistened his lips and, without shifting his eyes from the stones, said, "I wonder, my dear, if you would tell me where you got that necklace."

"This?" Isobel raised her fingers to the diamonds. She paused, then said, "From an admirer. Quite recently. It's the first time I've worn it."

Sir Reginald forced his gaze to her face. His expression was no longer the least bit friendly. "Frobisher?" The word was a demand.

Isobel arched her brows, then let a small smile play about her lips. "Sadly, no—not him. Someone else."

Sir Reginald's hand shot out and locked about her wrist. "Who?"

"Why, sir—"

"Dammit, woman—don't play games with me! Those are blue diamonds, as anyone with a half-trained eye could see. That many stones could only have come from one place, and I supposedly have an interest in that venture. Yet I've heard nothing about this damned necklace. So tell me, you minx—who gave it to you?"

Three large male bodies materialized from the shrubbery and surrounded Sir Reginald.

Another—Royd—appeared beside Isobel. Before Sir Reginald got his mouth closed, Royd gripped Sir Reginald's wrist.

Sir Reginald's eyes popped wide. A sound of pain escaped him, and he released Isobel's wrist as if he'd been burned. He hauled in a breath. "See here!" Even in the moonlight, his face had reddened. "What is this, heh?"

One of the shadowy figures leaned closer. "I believe, Sir Reginald, that you had better come with me." It was Dearne who spoke. "There are several gentlemen waiting to speak with you, Wolverstone among them."

"What?" The panic in Sir Reginald's face echoed in his voice.

A chirp sounded from close by the door.

Dearne seized Sir Reginald's wrists and bound them; one of the other figures stuffed a handkerchief into Sir Reginald's mouth when he opened it to shout, while the other promptly wrapped a scarf around the man's head, effectively and efficiently gagging him.

The three bodily lifted the shocked baronet aside, into a darker pool of shadows. How they planned to immobilize him, Isobel didn't know, but she trusted they would.

Royd melted away, back into the shadows from which he'd come. Isobel blinked. Even though she knew he was there, she couldn't see him.

Footsteps approached, not down the central path but along one of the side paths. And this time, they were quiet—not quite stealthy but careful.

Isobel waited to see who would arrive. Once she was certain from which direction they were coming, she shifted to look into the bowl of the fountain; the position allowed her to watch the side path from the corner of her eye.

She hadn't carried a reticule, but a fan dangled from her wrist. She flicked it open and idly waved it before her face.

A tall, rather cadaverous gentleman, exceedingly well dressed yet projecting an aura of ennui and overt dissipation, stepped from the shadows. "There you are, my dear. I've been looking for you."

She ceased her waving and widened her eyes at him. "You have? Yet I don't believe we're acquainted, sir."

"Lord Hugh Deveny." He gave her a nod rather than a bow. "And I've been looking for you to reclaim my property—I believe that lovely necklace is mine. If you would be so good as to hand it over?"

Isobel nearly laughed, but even on less than a minute's acquaintance, she realized Lord Hugh actually believed she would comply. "Yours, sir?" She infused enough shocked amazement into her voice to be convincing. "There must be some mistake. I received this necklace from my papa—he, in turn, had it from a gentleman acquaintance in Africa. It's only been in the country for a very short time—I fail to see how it could possibly be yours."

Lord Hugh's expression darkened. His lips compressed, then he contemptuously spat, "It's simple, you silly girl! That gentleman from Africa was some bounder who sold your father stolen goods. Those are blue diamonds and come from a mine I've invested in, so I'm right—those diamonds belong to me, and I suggest you hand the damned necklace over immediately!"

Lord Hugh reached for the necklace.

Royd caught his hand.

Lord Hugh jumped, then blinked, dumbfounded, at Royd.

Wolverstone walked out from the shadows. "Good evening, Deveny. In case you're wondering, I was here all along and heard every fascinating word you let fall."

Lord Hugh opened and shut his mouth several times without emitting any sound. Unlike that of Cummins, Lord Hugh's complexion had turned deathly pale.

"I don't know..." With a visible effort, Lord Hugh pulled himself together. "See here, Wolverstone. I don't know what game you're playing—"

"More to the point, Deveny, is what game you"—Wolverstone glanced aside as the other three gentlemen appeared, pushing Sir Reginald, bound and gagged, before them—"and Sir Reginald here have been involved in."

At the sight of Sir Reginald, every vestige of color drained from Lord Hugh's face.

"Cat got your tongue, Deveny?" When Lord Hugh didn't respond, Wolverstone glanced at the trio behind Sir Reginald. "Ungag him."

When they'd complied, as Sir Reginald moistened his lips, Wolverstone stated, "Now would be a good time to start talking, gentlemen. Leniency can be extended only to those who cooperate, and we only need one of you to do so to complete our investigations."

Lord Hugh stared helplessly at Sir Reginald.

Sir Reginald stared back, then he set his jaw pugnaciously and glared at Lord Hugh. "You'll get nothing out of me, sirrah! Whatever fabrications and wild accusations you might make, there's not a shred of evidence to say we've been involved in anything underhanded." He switched his now-belligerent gaze to Wolverstone. "We're innocent. You have to let us go."

Wolverstone arched a dark brow. After a moment, in a quiet voice, he said, "Not yet, Cummins. Not yet."

Lord Hugh tried to wrench free of Royd's hold—to no avail; Royd simply held him. "I've no notion of what you're talking about, Wolverstone." To Royd, he hissed, "Let go, damn it!" Straightening, trying to ignore Royd, he addressed Wolverstone. "If you will instruct this gentleman to release me, Your Grace, I believe I will return to the ball."

Wolverstone's smile flashed sharklike in the moonlight. "Sadly, I'm not so inclined." He turned to the other three. "Take them away—you know where."

One of the other men—Isobel saw it was Lord Trentham—moved to Deveny's side and took his arm in a hard grip.

Wolverstone looked at Deveny, then at Sir Reginald. "Let's see if we can't find some lever to loosen their tongues."

* * *

They hadn't expected to snare two of the backers on their first attempt.

"Sadly," Carstairs reported, "even though we now have four of them, and we've taken care to keep them separate from each other, none of the bloody blighters will talk."

It was early in the afternoon of the next day, and all those who'd been involved in the attempt to capture the backers had gathered in the Wolverstone House drawing room to learn of the end result.

Wolverstone arched a cynical brow. "It appears there's honor among thieves, even of this ilk."

Jack Hendon snorted. "No honor there." Along with Carstairs and several others of the company, Hendon had been involved in the subsequent interrogations. "They're as guilty as sin—you can see it in their eyes. Cummins and Deveny haven't even denied involvement. They've simply shut up."

"I got the impression they'd discussed what to do in the event of any interference from the authorities," the Earl of Lostwithiel put in.

Wolverstone nodded. "That does, indeed, seem likely."

"What we have got from them"—Carstairs's tone was redolent with frustration—"is that they're utterly convinced they are beyond the law—effectively untouchable. That if they just hold the line and admit nothing, they will, in the end, walk free."

A dissatisfied silence fell, then Dearne stirred. "On a more positive note, we might have got a bead on where the six met. Apparently, Ross-Courtney favors the Albany for his more discreet meetings. We're working on getting information from the staff there, and knowing four of the six names will expedite that." He paused, then added, "But, at most, all that will give us is the other two names and evidence that the six met in private—possibly frequently over the crucial period. It won't give us anything to link them to the mine."

"That's the critical link our lure has delivered," Wolverstone said, "at least with respect to Cummins and Deveny. By their own words, they implicated themselves with a venture producing blue diamonds—ergo, the mine."

"Ross-Courtney and Neill implicated themselves by their presence and actions at the mine," Caleb said.

"True." Looking across the crowded room, Wolverstone met Caleb's gaze. "However, sad to say, I doubt that's going to be enough to convict Ross-Courtney. Not with his connections. He'll fabricate some ridiculous tale of being captured and held for ransom, and because many will prefer to believe him, they will."

"And if Ross-Courtney walks free, the others will, too." Robert looked at Royd.

Royd met his brother's gaze, then directed his own at Wolverstone. "So how long do we have before our weakest link fails?"

Wolverstone softly snorted. "You mean Melville." It wasn't a question. "He was bad enough about Ross-

Courtney and Neill. Now we've added Lord Hugh plus Cummins, Melville is all but having conniptions. Lord Hugh's father is a strong supporter of the government. That we've more or less kidnapped the duke's son, more or less under Melville's aegis, is making Melville exceedingly nervous." He paused, then added, "I can't, regrettably, order Melville on no account to tell anyone we have the four in custody, but I have cautioned him over the extreme inadvisability of doing so, and asked him to inform me before he shares the information with anyone at all—including his wife." Wolverstone faintly shrugged. "We'll see."

"In other words"—Trentham's tone was cynical—"in spite of the government's exceedingly desperate desire to convict in this case, we won't have all that long." To the room at large, he reported, "We've men trawling through the diamond merchants in Amsterdam, but it's slow going, and we haven't had even a glimmer of a possibility so far."

"We've started making inquiries via the banks," Rupert—better known as Gabriel—Cynster put in. "We're trying to identify our mysterious banker by attempting to find payments made to both Ross-Courtney and Neill from the same source. Now we can include Cummins and Deveny as well, that might go faster." He paused, then grimaced. "Fast being a relative term. Given the degree of discretion we're having to employ so as not to alert the men's agents…it's going to take at least a week, possibly more."

Devil Cynster caught Wolverstone's eye. "We might not have a week."

When Wolverstone didn't respond, Lostwithiel shifted. "Loath as I am to suggest it, perhaps employing other methods of persuasion, not just words, might be in order."

Wolverstone hesitated, then shook his head. "Were this war, that would be justified. But this isn't war, and engaging in such practices would lower us to their level." He paused, then more decisively went on, "With respect to the four backers in our custody, our best tack will be to continue to interrogate them while seizing every opportunity to undermine their confidence—to convince them we're certain we'll be able to hold them incommunicado long enough to get the evidence we need."

"The best way to do that," Dearne said, "is to tell them of the avenues we're pursuing—perhaps lead them to think that the staff at the Albany are not quite as deaf as Ross-Courtney imagined."

Trentham nodded. "And that the diamond merchant guild in Amsterdam is proving most helpful. In fact, it's the opposite, but our backers won't know that."

"Their banker is a key weakness for them," Gabriel Cynster said. "He most likely knows their names and that the money he or his institution is funneling to them comes from a particular diamond merchant." Cynster looked at Hendon and Lostwithiel. "You might mention we're closing in on the banker."

Lostwithiel nodded. He looked at Wolverstone. "My only concern in going that route is that if they do, in fact, succeed in walking free, even for a short time, the first thing they'll do is move to obliterate all potential evidence—and we know they're of the ilk to order men killed without a blink."

Wolverstone grimaced fleetingly, then, slowly, he arched his brows. "It's almost like a challenge—with time running out, can we hold our nerve better than they can?"

Seated beside Royd, Isobel stirred. "It's a risk and reward situation. If we don't take the risk, we'll lose the prize."

Heads nodded all around the room.

Once again, silence fell, this time with everyone wracking their brains, trying to define any lever or other avenue to move forward with speed.

Eventually, Wolverstone said, "We've come so far. We've rescued the captives, shut down the illegal enterprise, and have the three local villains in our hands, ready to talk and accept their punishment. Unlike the six backers—and it's the backers we want, and that the government truly needs to convict. We have four backers in our hands, and the prospect of evidence enough to convict them given several weeks...but to get those weeks, we're relying on no one alerting their families, agents, or supporters, who will then start asking questions." Wolverstone looked at his wife. "Neill and Cummins are married. Are their wives likely to start agitating over their disappearances?"

Minerva shook her head. "I wouldn't think so." She glanced at Honoria.

Honoria stated, "Neill's wife lives permanently in the country, and as far as she or anyone in his household would know, he's still in Africa."

"As for Cummins," Minerva said, "his wife hasn't come up for the season, and he keeps no house here, merely lodgings. So only his staff would know he hasn't returned home. I suspect it will be days, possibly even a week, before Cummins's manservant might think to notify his mistress of his master's non-return...in short, it's unlikely anyone will come looking for Cummins for a few weeks at least, and even then, only if Lady Cummins bestirs herself."

"It seems," Devil Cynster somewhat grimly said, "that the more immediate threat is the other two backers. They'll have no idea Ross-Courtney and Neill have been seized, but they'll notice Lord Hugh and Cummins have mysteriously vanished, most likely within a few days. And then they'll raise hell with the authorities."

Dearne nodded. "Especially if they've discussed what to do in the event official interest is shown."

"I suspect you won't have even two days," Lady Clarice Warnefleet dryly opined. "Not with the tales sweeping through the ton of a fabulous blue diamond necklace appearing at the Wolverstone House ball." She regarded the gathering with a steady gaze. "Assuming they weren't at the ball last night, the other two backers will have heard about the necklace by now. The first thing they'll do is contact each other—including Cummins and Lord Hugh. When they don't hear back from Cummins and Lord Hugh within a day or so..."

Honoria nodded. "They'll start asking questions."

"And given their ilk," a gentleman by the name of Delborough put in, "they'll be clever enough to raise those questions via avenues that disguise their involvement. We won't be able to identify the backers by tracing the questions back to the source."

"We need to identify the remaining backers as a matter of urgency." Wolverstone spoke decisively. "Without getting the last two into our hands as well, the odds stacked against us are too high, and we're unlikely to be able to pull this off." He looked at Isobel, seated beside Minerva. "My dear, are you willing to act as lure again?"

"Yes—of course." Isobel glanced at Honoria. "I assume we're speaking of the St. Ives ball?"

Royd clenched his jaw and forced down the protest that, instinctively, had risen to his lips. The smoothness of their operation at last night's ball should have been reassuring, yet his instincts—those prickling feelings he'd long ago learned not to ignore—were stirring, unhappily fermenting.

As discussions over repeating their ploy the following evening rolled on, he listened with half an ear while trying to identify the specific source of his unease. Yet he couldn't see any reason Isobel behaving tomorrow evening as she had last night, surrounded—as it seemed she would be—by an even larger contingent of "guards," should pose any greater danger than had been the case last night.

The only excuse he could advance for his lack of enthusiasm was a craven quibble that trying the same tack twice was akin to tempting Fate that critical one step too far.

As he listened to Isobel and heard her resolution—her determination to do all she could to ensure the backers were brought to justice—ring clearly in her tone, and saw his brothers and their ladies equally committed, then looked further and saw so many others ready and willing to stand with them, he could do nothing other than, by his silence, agree.

And so it was decided. As a group, they would attempt one last throw of the dice.

Isobel would wear the blue diamond necklace at what was expected to be the biggest crush of the season—the St. Ives' ball tomorrow night. If they succeeded in identifying the remaining two backers, no further hurdle would stand in the way of, one way or another, seeing justice done.

If they failed to reel in the last two backers…they would be no worse off than they were now, but their ability to secure what had become the ultimate goal of the mission would remain under threat, their grasp on success uncertain, and likely to grow more tenuous with every passing day.

* * *

Royd and Isobel strolled back to Stanhope Street with the other three Frobisher couples.

They arrived to discover that Duncan had been taken out for a drive in the park by his grandmother and great-grandmother. Fergus, however, was waiting and insisted on being told the state of play. Edwina ordered tea and cakes, and the eight of them sat with the patriarch of the family and ran through the recent deliberations leading to their latest tack.

Edwina fixed her gaze measuringly on Isobel. "The second of your new gowns should have been delivered while we were at the meeting. We should go up and check that it will look as well with the diamonds as we'd thought."

"That it will show them off as spectacularly as we'd hoped." Aileen rose, bringing the others to their feet.

"Indeed." Isobel threw an inviting glance at Kate.

Kate smiled and joined the exodus.

The instant the door shut behind the ladies, Declan stated, "These days, quiet moments have to be seized. I'm for the library."

"I'll come with you." Robert followed Declan to the door.

Caleb looked at Royd. "You've heard of this picnic the ladies are organizing for next Monday?" When Royd nodded, Caleb went on, "I've been deputed to take the official invitation to the office for dissemination to our crews." He pulled out a folded sheet and held it out. "If you approve, I'll take it around there now—it'll need one of us to authorize it."

Royd took the sheet, opened it, and swiftly scanned the lines; Fergus read over his shoulder, snorted, and grinned. Royd handed the "invitation" back to Caleb. "It reads more like a summons, but I have no inclination to tamper."

Caleb grinned, tucked the sheet away, saluted, and headed for the door.

Fergus tapped Royd's arm. "Join me in the garden. I wouldn't mind a stroll."

Royd followed his father out into the rear garden. They ambled down the path, with him shortening his stride to match his father's gait.

To Royd's surprise, Fergus made no move to initiate a conversation; his father simply walked down the path, apparently noting and approving the greenery.

Eventually, entirely of its own accord, a question rose to his tongue. "How did you manage it with Mama?" He waved widely. "Letting her swan into danger? I assume she did so several times over the years she sailed with you."

Fergus laughed. "Oh, indeed. Many times more than several. How did I cope?" His father turned his piercing gray gaze—a gaze Royd had inherited—on him. "Much as you are, I warrant." Looking forward, Fergus added, "It's not easy, but you have to hold it all in and just stand ready in case your fears come true. It's the price we pay to have them by our sides, in our lives."

Royd pulled a face and kept walking.

"Actually," Fergus said a moment later, "I would think you, of us all, would have the easiest road. You've known Isobel for so long, and she always was fearless."

"That was then," he grumped. "This is now."

"Unarguably, but the quality of fearlessness doesn't

change. Any more than her intellect, and that's never been in doubt. No ninnyhammer there."

"No." After a moment more of studying the gravel, Royd sighed. "I know it's me and not her—that it's *my* reaction and I have to deal with it."

Fergus chuckled. "If you understand that, you're at the head of this class. Unless I miss my guess, Edwina is still bludgeoning that lesson into Declan's hard head and will be for some time. If I understand what happened on his leg of the mission, Robert wasn't given much choice, but he'll still try to resist if he thinks he can get away with it—not that he will. Aileen will set him straight. As for Caleb…it appears he's going to get off lightest. His Kate is much more amenable to being protected, but even there, as I take it she plans to sail with him often, I foresee he'll be tested, too, but as we both know, and he's so recently proved, Caleb can adjust to damn near anything and thrive."

"Hmm. Speaking of which, I wanted to discuss a change in our roles." Royd explained what he had in mind.

Fergus asked several pertinent questions, then gave his blessing. He halted and waved toward the house. "Let's seize the chance while Caleb's out to run this past Robert and Declan. Not that I think they'll argue, but then we—you and I—can make the announcement at this picnic the ladies are planning."

Royd returned with his father to the library and spent the next hours discussing the shipping business and, when Caleb returned, breaking the news of his new position to him.

"His reaction," Royd told Isobel as, after a restful and reassuring evening, they walked down the corridor to the room they now shared, "was something to see. His legs literally gave out, and he collapsed in a chair."

"He still thinks of himself as so much the youngest—the baby none of you realize has grown up."

"I think what shocked him most was Declan's and Robert's patently sincere agreement."

Isobel smiled. "This mission opened their eyes. Until then, I think only your parents and you—and me—saw Caleb as he truly could be. I don't think even he truly comprehended his abilities, his strengths, not until this latest adventure."

They reached the room two doors before theirs. Isobel opened the door and looked in. Royd looked over her shoulder.

Moonlight poured in, striking the carpet and shedding enough diffused light for them to make out the lump that was Duncan curled up in the big bed.

Still smiling, she closed the door. "Your mother and Iona wore him out. They took him to the Serpentine to feed the ducks, and they're both perfectly content to encourage him to talk and question nonstop."

Royd followed her into their room. "He's learned a lot since leaving Aberdeen."

As have I.

One of his major realizations was that secrets between them never ended well.

She walked to the dressing table and started unpinning her hair.

He shrugged off his coat and waistcoat, laid both aside, and started unraveling his cravat. Thinking.

"Help me with these laces."

He dragged the cravat loose and glanced her way. Hands on her hips, her back to him, she stood before the dressing table. When he didn't reply, she glanced over her shoulder.

That look—half sultry siren, half expectant innocent—would draw him until he died. He tossed the cravat to join his coat and walked to her.

She faced forward again. He set his fingers to her laces and tugged. He kept his eyes on the task.

"What is it?" Her tone suggested she was perfectly aware he was harboring some…inner turmoil.

As usual, she waited—teasing answers from him was one of the few occasions when her patience seemed limitless.

He dragged the last lace loose, and her gown gaped all the way down her slender back. He slipped his hands inside the garment; his fingers and palms against her silken skin, he slid his hands around to the front of her waist and drew her against him.

In the mirror, over her shoulder, he met her eyes.

He wanted to tell her, but getting the words out wasn't easy. Closing his eyes, he drew in a breath, his chest swelling against the curves of her back. "I feel as if, after eight years of emptiness, I've only just got you back, just long enough to glimpse heaven again—my version of it, at least—and here I am happily or, as it happens, not at all happily risking you and everything between us, and all hope for our future, again." He let his chin drop to her shoulder; from beneath his lashes, he watched her face in the mirror. "I know it's what needs to be—that you need to do it, and all the reasons why—and yet…" He closed his eyes, fractionally shook his head.

Isobel heard the words he didn't say; she felt the tension in him, through his body at her back, in his hands as they held her.

She slid her arms free of her sleeves and turned in

his hold. Instantly, he straightened, raising his head and opening his eyes. She met his gaze, searched, and saw what he allowed her to see in the roiling gray. "What do you think I felt knowing you would lead the attack in the compound? That you would be the first of our men to drop inside an enemy-held perimeter? And that I could be nowhere near—not even within sight of you, let alone close enough to step in should anything unexpected occur…" Her eyes on his, she tilted her head. "Isn't that the same thing?"

He held her gaze, then bluntly said, "It might be, but you're a woman—you handle it better."

She battled a laugh—as he'd intended; having brought up the subject and said his piece, he was intent on distracting her. When he tried to draw her in, she put a hand on his shirt-clad chest and held him back. "That might be so, but that wasn't what I meant." She waited until he stilled, until she could capture his gaze again. "What I meant was that you don't need to hide this side of yourself from me—I understand what you feel because I feel the same. But doing the sorts of things we do—going into danger perhaps, but as far as possible with control in our hands—that's a big part of us. Of both of us. It's who we are and what we do—and that's one of the links in the chains that bind us."

She paused, trying to read his face, but seeing only that he was listening. "We shouldn't—we can't—limit ourselves, can't turn aside from doing what we might when there's a need. We can't cut this out of ourselves—we'll always be like this. But now we both can see it"—she tilted her head, her eyes still on his—"perhaps we can manage things better. Or, at the very least, with greater experience, the moments will become less…fraught."

He studied her face for several heartbeats. "You're saying we have to get used to this?"

When she nodded, he sighed. "That's what I said—you're better at that than I am."

She laughed and reached for his face to draw his lips to hers.

He obliged and bent his head, but before their lashes lowered, he murmured, "Just for my record, tell me plainly—you're not just willing but you actively *want* to play the lure again."

His face framed between her palms, she held his gaze. "I want to do this. For the captives we freed, for those we didn't, for all who helped us, for Kate, and yes, I want to do this for you and me. Tomorrow is our last roll of the dice—we need to let the wind fill our sails and see where chance takes us."

When he sighed and fractionally nodded, curious now, she asked, "What if I'd said I wasn't truly willing?"

His lids rose, and his eyes searched hers.

"I'm just curious. Would you have backed me then—supported me if I'd cravenly said no? Even if it meant we might fail to catch the backers?"

His gaze hardened; he frowned as if her question was close to idiotic. "If you didn't want to do it, I'd whisk you away so fast your head would spin. Catching the backers is important to you, me, my family, an army of friends, the captives, and if Wolverstone and Melville have it right, the government and the country—but *you*, your safety, transcends all of that, at least for me. To me, *you* are paramount—keeping you safe…for me, there is no higher imperative."

She wasn't sure her heart, swelling so dramatically, would remain in her chest.

Any lingering niggle over setting aside her concerns

over the quality of his love and instead letting herself be guided by hers for him had just cindered and blown away.

She smiled radiantly and knew her heart was in her eyes.

"What?" He was still frowning at her. "Did you think—"

She kissed him. Held his face firmly between her palms, planted her lips on his, and kissed him with an intent and a determination that flowed from her soul.

Enough of words; actions spoke louder.

Tonight, she wanted to be in charge—to take the reins and show him all he meant to her. To ensure he understood she valued all he was—all and everything that came with his love, even his bouts of overbearing overprotectiveness.

He, of course, had his own notion of who should script their play.

The result was an intimate wrestling match the likes of which neither had indulged in before.

Clothes flew, hands seized and grasped, palms caressed, and lips lingered hot and wet.

They finally reached the bed—and she won by tripping him and toppling him backward onto the coverlet, then diving atop him and quickly scrambling to sit astride…

Only to discover he'd sneakily led her on. That he'd plotted to be in this position all along, so he could see her and send his hands searing over every square inch of her skin, caressing, tantalizing, kneading. Possessing.

She tried to cling to supremacy, to return the favor at least, but in this sphere, he knew her far too well; he reduced her to gasping, throbbing need—to that state where her wits had flown and her senses whirled to a giddy beat and her pulse thundered in her veins.

Until passion roared, and desire raked her, and she sobbed with wanting.

And there was only one source of relief.

She rose up and, in one long gliding slide, took him in—and her world contracted to this. To him and her, joined physically and linked in every other way, together, naked on the fine sheets.

Eyes closed, her fingers linked with his, she used his support to rise up, and then slide slowly down again, repetitively impaling herself on him. Desire flicked, whiplike, and she shuddered. She used her inner muscles to hold and caress him, and felt every muscle in his long body harden in response.

She smiled. She kept her eyes closed, her fingers locked with his, and gave herself over to satisfying the demands of her body and his.

To taking them both up—refusing to let him hold back and observe, but demanding and commanding that he journey with her. In that, she'd learned how to get her way—how to sinuously sway and tense just there, slow and hold, and compel.

In the end, he surrendered, and they rode on together, both absorbed and caught, immersed in sensation, in the rhythmic, undulating slide of her body over and around his, only to pause here, then there, struck helpless by exquisite, excruciating pleasure, holding tight and still as they savored…until they breathed again and rode on.

Up, ever upward. Letting the tension coil steadily tighter, higher, until they were moving rapidly, fluidly, their breaths coming in pants, their skins flushed, slick and burning, their bodies striving as one in their desperate race for the peak, for the completion that beckoned, just out of reach.

The coil snapped, and they soared—high, higher—

into the fire of their inner sun, a supernova of their senses.

Ecstasy hit them and stole their breaths. Had them both arching and tightening, gripping and clinging in desperation.

The rearing wave broke, roared over and into them. Filling them, easing them, flowing through them.

They sank back to earth, to the mortal plane.

To their thudding hearts, to the glory in their veins.

With pleasure, bone-deep, wreathing their souls, they eased apart just enough to find the sheets and settle themselves in each other's arms.

She listened to the slowing thud of his heart. Sensed their mutual slide into oblivion.

Before they slid over the edge into that most blissful of seas, she found strength enough to say clearly, "You can never lose me because I'll never let you go."

His arms tightened about her. He raised his head and dropped a kiss on her forehead.

As sleep stole across her mind, she heard him say, "You're mine, and I'm yours. And nothing in this world will ever change that."

Seventeen

To describe the Cynster ball as an unrelenting crush would be a massive understatement.

At eleven o'clock the following evening, Isobel stood beside Declan at the side of the huge ballroom and, over the intervening heads, watched the drama unfolding in the rear corner of the room.

Edwina had just joined them. "I can't see—tell me what's happening!"

"I'd just finished dancing with Harry Cynster," Isobel explained, "and he was leading me from the floor when a large gentleman came up, bold as you please, and asked—no, that's too weak a word—he *demanded* to be told where I'd got the necklace."

"And?" Leaning on Declan's arm, Edwina stood on her toes and craned her neck to see, but was defeated.

"I was so surprised that I stared at him—and before I'd collected my wits, he started to bluster and said the diamonds were his, that he knew where they came from, and there'd been some mistake, and if I didn't hand them over then and there, he'd have me taken up..." Isobel shook her head. "He went on and on. It was the most idiotically blatant attempt to get the necklace. Harry and I could barely believe it. Then, to cap it all, when Harry asked him how the necklace could be his, the man—Harry later told me he was the Marquis of Risdale—realized he'd said too much. He swung around, intent on making off—but Dearne was there along with two of the others. They'd come up behind Risdale and had heard all he'd said. Risdale put his head down and tried to plow through them, but they caught him and held him—and now Devil Cynster's there, and they're trying to get Risdale out of the ballroom without too much fuss."

Declan said, "Wolverstone's just walked up, along with Minerva. She's talking rather severely to Risdale—it looks like she's telling him to behave himself."

Edwina grinned. "I'm quite sure she is…*oof*!"

Isobel and Declan looked around in alarm.

Edwina was pressing a hand to the side of her belly and doing her best to wipe the grimace from her face.

"What's wrong?" Declan looked ready to panic.

"It's just a twinge." When he didn't look convinced, Edwina lowered her voice and said, "If you must know, your dratted offspring kicked me. Hard."

Declan didn't look relieved. "Is that normal?"

"Quite normal," Isobel assured him. "But why don't you take Edwina to those windows over there. It'll be a touch quieter, and your offspring might settle again."

Edwina frowned. "We can't leave you alone. You have to have two people with you at all times."

Isobel glanced around and spotted Letitia, Dearne's wife, talking with Lady Clarice. "I'll go and join the marchioness and Lady Clarice. The musicians are resting, but they'll start up again soon, and my scheduled partners will find me. Who knows?" She edged toward the marchioness. "Our luck seems to be in. We might actually succeed in luring the last of the backers out tonight."

Declan glanced at Edwina.

She met his gaze, then looked at Isobel uncertainly.

"I would prefer to retreat to the window—it'll be cooler over there. If you're sure?"

"Quite sure." Isobel waved them away. "It's a matter of…what? Five yards?" With a smile, she gave Edwina and Declan her back and slid into the crowd.

Her gown tonight was fashioned from a rich, almost iridescent peacock silk, an intense blue-green hue that brought out the deeper shades in the blue fire of the necklace as it lay against her white skin. If anything, the diamonds made an even more striking display than they had two nights before.

She smiled and nodded, easing past shoulders clad in silk and superfine. It was much like tacking through a crowded harbor—this way, then that.

She was still several yards short of her goal when a youthful dandy stepped into her path.

"I say—are you Miss Carmichael?"

She halted; the gentleman—given he was a guest, he had to be that—looked barely twenty. "Yes. I am."

"Capital! I told the butler I'd find you—he's trying to be everywhere at once at the moment. But there's a messenger in the foyer asking for you. Seems in quite a state—he said something about a search for some boy."

Boy? "Oh no." Every other thought fled her head. Had Duncan somehow slipped past his grandparents? Iona was here, somewhere in the crowd. Was Duncan headed here, or would he make for the docks? Or…?

Frantic panic unlike any she'd ever known clutched her throat and made it difficult to breathe. She swung toward the ballroom doors; they weren't too far away. "The foyer, you said?" She sounded breathless.

"Yes—at the bottom of the stairs. Here. Let me help you get through." The young man didn't presume to take her arm, but by walking beside her, he helped clear their path through the throng.

They finally reached the ballroom doors. The area about the top of the stairs was crowded, but the young gentleman pointed to the entrance hall below. With a weak smile, she edged past various guests and, barely restraining herself from running, started down the stairs.

The entrance hall was full of guests, both arriving and departing. The exchange of coats and cloaks, hats and canes, some being handed over, others retrieved, created a shifting morass of bodies. She halted on the landing and scanned the crowd, searching for one of Edwina's footmen.

The young dandy halted beside her. "He was over there… Ah! There he is." Half crouching, he pointed out of the open door. "He's waiting outside on the pavement."

Isobel picked up her skirts and, dispensing with caution, hurried down the stairs. She pushed through the people clogging the front hall and rushed onto the porch.

"He's over there." The dandy pointed to the right.

As often happened at major balls in Mayfair, a crowd of onlookers—maids, bootboys, footmen, and milliners' and modistes' apprentices—had gathered on either side of the red carpet to observe and ooh and aah at the guests' clothes, jewelry, and hairstyles. Isobel saw several footmen who might be from Stanhope Street, but the night's shadows were rendered blacker by the flares burning so brightly around the mansion's entrance; she hurried down the steps and turned right.

The dandy gripped her elbow and stepped close, pushing into the crowd, who glanced at them curiously but readily gave way, their gazes refastening on the open doorway at the top of the steps.

"Just a trifle farther…"

She registered the odd tension in the dandy's voice. Her instincts flared. She halted—but the dandy pushed her on.

He was stronger than she'd expected; she took several more steps before she locked her legs, wrenched her arm free, and, fury igniting, rounded on him.

Black cloth fell over her head.

In the same instant, her hands were caught and swiftly tied in front of her, even as she was jostled farther down the pavement, away from St. Ives House.

The black material of the hood was impenetrable. She sensed two men, burly and strong, closing tight on either side, then the weight of a heavy cloak settled on her shoulders. She hauled in a breath—

"If you value your son's life, don't scream," one rough voice told her.

She shut her lips. Stunned realization bloomed. They—whoever they were—had succeeded in getting her out of the house. Had any of her protectors seen her leave?

The burly pair herded her on, but they were keeping to the pavement. Where was the dandy?

Hell—this was Grosvenor Square, the heart of fashionable London. Where was everyone?

Watching the distraction provided by the guests going in and out of St. Ives House.

On the thought, the men, each of whom had grasped one of her arms, halted. Straining her ears, she heard the familiar rasp of a door latch, then the men were lifting her up—into a carriage. They bundled her inside. She was too tall to stand upright; she twisted and, with her legs tangling in her skirts and the cloak, collapsed inelegantly onto the seat—the one facing St. Ives House.

Her knees brushed those of a man sitting opposite. He immediately—politely—moved his legs away.

The door shut. She shifted and wriggled and managed to sit upright.

"Good evening, Miss Carmichael. I regret the inconvenience, but if you value your life and wish to see your son again, you will remain still and answer my questions." The voice was not merely cool but cold, utterly devoid of inflection. "I merely wish to speak with you away from that infernal crush and the oh-so-watchful eyes of your friends." The man—a gentleman by his precise diction and choice of words—paused, then said, "Pray excuse me for a moment."

She waited, but he didn't leave the carriage. Instead, he lowered the window and spoke to someone on the pavement. The dandy, she realized. She thought of lifting the hood enough to see, but the cloak was wrapped about her; it would take too long to free her hands of the folds, and the man would surely notice. She listened instead, but they used no names. Nevertheless, it was clear that the dandy had been paid to lure her out of the house.

Chagrin coursed through her. She'd been playing the lure, but had been lured out instead.

Surreptitiously, she tested the bindings about her hands, but they gave not at all. Foiled on that front, she started cataloging everything she could—all her senses could tell her. The man in the carriage was patently the one in charge—he had to be their sixth and last backer. He was, she judged, of middle years—probably much the same age as the other backers.

The man dismissed the dandy. The window scraped as he raised it.

She gathered her wits and, her bound hands in her lap, her limbs restricted by the heavy cloak, prepared to do verbal battle.

"To reassure you, Miss Carmichael, we aren't going

anywhere. As I said, I merely wish to question you—oh, and to retrieve that lovely necklace, which, as it happens, belongs, at least in part, to me."

She heard him shift, sensed him leaning nearer. She locked her jaw and forced herself to remain still as she felt the edges of the hood shift.

Then the man's cold fingertips brushed her skin as he searched for the necklace's catch; she suppressed a shiver.

He found the catch, released it, and the weight of the fabulous necklace fell away.

He sat back; she sensed he was holding the necklace up, admiring the stones in the weak light.

They were still at the curb in Grosvenor Square. She had to admire his sangfroid.

But surely she would have been missed by now. Her protectors would be searching.

Royd would be furious and…he didn't really grow frantic, except perhaps inside. Panic wasn't something a man as experienced as he indulged in.

He would come for her. She just needed to buy him, and the others, time.

"Quite exquisite." The man shifted on the seat; she imagined him tucking the necklace into his pocket. "Now, to our discussion. No matter the temptation, I most strongly advise you to leave that hood in place. That way, I won't have to kill you once our conversation is over. However, in case you doubt the sincerity of that threat…"

She heard the telltale click of a pistol being cocked, the sound loud in the enclosed space. She stopped breathing.

The man leaned forward. Then she felt the end of the pistol's barrel press gently between her breasts.

"That's where I'm aiming, and at this range, I can hardly miss." His tone was still cold, but the cadence of his words verged on the conversational. He drew back, and the pressure of the pistol barrel vanished.

Her chest felt tight. She managed to draw in a shallow breath.

"So, Miss Carmichael, please tell me from where you got the necklace. And don't think to fob me off with some nonsense that you don't know where it came from—you're Iona Carmody's granddaughter, and by all reports, your apple didn't fall far from her tree. You know all the pertinent details, so if you please, share them with me—I want to hear all you know about these lovely blue diamonds."

She'd been thinking furiously about how best to stretch out their exchange. Her heart thudding, she hesitated just long enough to give the impression of consternation, then said, "*All* I know of the stones will make for a very long story. I could ramble for hours, but that won't help either of us." It was easier to manage men if they thought they were in charge. "Perhaps if you ask me what you wish to know, we might be done with this sooner, and you can let me go."

Silence greeted her suggestion, then she heard what she took to be a rather dry laugh.

"I had heard you were a refreshing change from the usual gently bred miss." He paused, then said, "Very well. Here's my first question. What do you know of a gentleman by the name of Lord Peter Ross-Courtney?"

She drew in a breath and prepared to tell all.

* * *

Finally!

Inside the ballroom, Royd stood by one wall and, with Wolverstone by his side, watched the Marquis of Risdale, mute at last but still looking murderous, be led away by Trentham, Carstairs, and Hendon. A carriage with an escort was waiting by a rear door to whisk the marquis into Essex.

Dismissing Risdale, Royd raised his gaze and looked around the room, searching for Isobel's dark head…

He forced himself to complete two visual circuits before he turned to Wolverstone. "Isobel—I can't see her. I don't think she's here."

Wolverstone was already frowning; he'd been searching, too. "I can't see her, either." The words were clipped.

"She wouldn't have left—not unless she had good cause."

"Even if she had," Wolverstone replied, "someone should have seen and alerted us."

In seconds, they, and all the others of their company they came across, were quartering the crowd. The congestion was at its height; just fighting one's way through the bodies was an effort. The musicians were playing, and the dance floor was packed; Royd scanned the dancers, as did others, but Isobel wasn't among the circling couples. Jack Warnefleet, her scheduled partner for this dance, hadn't been able to find her.

Royd searched to the far end of the room, but he knew she wasn't there. His instincts were in full flight, pressing and urging.

He met up with Wolverstone and Devil Cynster in the space beneath the musicians' gallery.

Grimly, Wolverstone shook his head.

Devil Cynster swore.

Then the duke turned and took the stairs to the gallery three at a time. Abruptly, the musicians stopped playing.

As the dancers noticed, slowed, and looked up, Devil leaned on the gallery railing and roared, "Silence!"

All conversations ceased. Silks shushed as everyone swung to face the gallery.

Into the shocked silence, Devil said, “This is vitally important. We’re searching for a lady—the one with the necklace. Tall, black-haired, striking, in a blue-green gown. Most of you have seen her. Look around you now—can anyone see her?”

Rustles filled the room as people obeyed, but no one spoke up.

Then a pudgy beringed hand waved from the end of the room, and an older lady called, “That gel went out a few minutes ago—the Strickland pup was with her.”

Royd strode for the main doors, Wolverstone beside him. The crowd parted, clearing a path up the center of the room. Others of their company fell in behind them as, from above, Devil called, “Strickland!” When no answer came, Devil said, “Look around again—is *he* here?”

This time, no one answered.

Royd swore beneath his breath. The ballroom doors lay just ahead. He asked Wolverstone, “Do you know Strickland by sight?”

Wolverstone shook his head.

“I do.” Dearne was just behind them.

“You stick with Royd.” Wolverstone nodded ahead. “We’ll split up—you go downstairs. I’ll set people searching up here, then join you.”

They strode into the area at the head of the stairs. Leaving Wolverstone there—he was immediately joined by Honoria, and they started sending pairs of searchers down various corridors—Royd and Dearne, with several others falling in behind them, hurried down the grand staircase.

Royd paused on the landing, Dearne by his side; the position gave them an excellent view of the entrance hall. “Can you see Strickland?”

Dearne and several others searched, then Dearne

pointed to a stripling leaning against the wall of the corridor running beside the stairs. "There." The youth's head was down, his attention on the notes he was counting.

"You're on interference," Royd ground out.

He all but leapt down the remaining flight and swung around the newel post. Two strides and he filled his fist with Strickland's neckcloth, lifted the youth, and slammed him bodily against the wall.

He snarled into the boy's stunned face. "Where is she?"

Strickland swallowed, then babbled, "She's in the carriage outside." His gaze darted to the wall of aggressive men closing at Royd's back. His eyes widened to saucers. "It was just a lark! He said he just wanted to talk to her. I just had to get her outside—it was the others, his men, who took her and put her in the carriage, but he swore he'd let her go once they'd talked!"

The last word came out on a squeak as Royd flung him aside and raced for the door.

Behind him, he heard Dearne order, "Hold him!"

Royd heard the thunder of feet at his back, but didn't turn to see who was following. He shouldered his way through the press of bodies and stepped onto the front porch. Carriage, the boy had said.

A chaos of carriages lay before him.

The thoroughfare was clogged with vehicles setting down arrivals and others summoned to take their owners up.

"Not those." Royd looked farther afield. "If he wants to talk…"

Veiled by shadows, the small black town carriage drawn up by the curb some way to the right, well outside the light thrown by the street flares, was almost indiscernible.

Royd was moving again before he'd even thought. He reached the pavement, pushed through the crowd of onlookers, and raced for the carriage.

* * *

"So, you see," Isobel said, "I haven't actually spoken to Ross-Courtney or Neill at all. Indeed, I haven't set eyes on them since we left the jungle."

"But you're sure they're still in custody?" the gentleman pressed.

"I really can't say, but I assume they are as I've heard nothing to the contrary."

"And you don't know where?"

"No." She caught the sound of rushing footsteps and hurriedly went on, "But I do know they're not being held in any usual jail or by the police—"

The door was wrenched open.

"He has a gun!" she screamed.

"Frobisher!" the man snarled.

The carriage tipped as a large, heavy body came through the door.

Royd was going to get himself killed!

She couldn't do much, but her legs weren't tied; she raised one foot, shod in her ballroom pump, and drove the thick heel as hard and as deeply as she could into where she judged the man was sitting.

Flesh squashed beneath her heel, and the pistol went off.

The sound was deafening in the enclosed space.

The carriage rocked; grunts and curses filled the air.

Obviously, Royd wasn't dead.

Then came a hideous *thwack* of fist forcefully meeting flesh, and the rocking eased.

An instant later, Royd's hands closed on hers. "Hold still—let me get the hood off."

She'd fainted for the first time not so long ago; now she was hyperventilating. She'd come within a whisker of losing him. The stupid man had flung himself at a villain with a pistol! Admittedly, to save her, but still!

Then the hood was lifted away, and she looked up, into Royd's face. He was standing bent over her. In the poor light, she could barely make out his expression; he looked grim, but not in pain.

After one searching, comprehensive glance at her face, he looked down and picked at the knots in the rope about her wrists. "Are you hurt?" The words were a deep growl.

"No. Not at all." Her heart was still galloping. "You?"

"I'm fine."

She hauled in a breath, then another. The dizziness faded. Peering around him, she saw the man who had captured her sprawled in an ungainly heap across the seat. He didn't look particularly notable in any way—a rather conservative gentleman of no great physical distinction.

The man stirred, then groaned.

Wolverstone and Dearne stood by the open carriage door, with others behind them.

She quickly said, "He threatened me, but other than that, he asked about Ross-Courtney and Neill. About what they'd said and where they'd been, and where they are now. And he took the necklace—it's in his pocket."

She paused to draw in another huge breath.

Royd drew away the rope; awkwardly, he crouched and massaged her wrists. Beneath his fingertips, he felt her racing pulse. "Everything's all right."

The words brought her gaze back to his face; her dark eyes were huge. "He knew about Duncan—knew I had a son." Her fingers clutched his. "Oh, God—do you think—"

"No." So that was why she'd left the ballroom. He

wished he could hit the man—whoever he was—again. "No one will have got to Duncan."

But he could see from her eyes that she wouldn't calm until she knew for certain. He rose and helped her up. "We'll send a footman to make sure."

"Yes. Right now!"

He climbed down from the carriage, then turned to lift her down. She all but fell into his arms.

Her hand landed on his left shoulder—right on the spot where the pistol ball had scored a furrow—and he bit back a hiss.

He stepped back from the carriage, giving the others room to go in and haul the still-insensible blackguard out. With a house railing at his back, he set Isobel on her feet.

She looked down at her palm, then at his shoulder. Then her lips set, and she jabbed him in the chest. "Damn it, Royd—you *are* hurt! You've been shot, for heaven's sake!"

"It's just a flesh wound. It'll stop bleeding in a minute."

"How can you know? There's barely any light." She bobbed on her toes, studying the bloody scrape.

Royd saw one of Wolverstone's footmen and beckoned. He gave the man orders to go to Stanhope Street and inquire as to the location of one Duncan Frobisher.

The footman looked to his master. After one glance at Isobel, Wolverstone nodded. "As fast as you can."

Isobel barely seemed to notice. She was still muttering over his wound. "I told you there was a pistol. Are you sure it doesn't sting? Did you really have to just leap straight in—"

He hauled her to him and kissed her.

Let free all the pent-up anguish of the past fraught minutes, reveled in—let both of them revel in—the fact they were both still there, both alive, relatively unscathed…

After the first heartbeat, she grabbed his head and gave as good as she got.

When he raised his head, she opened her eyes, looked into his—and he knew she was back. That she was with him, focused again.

He released her, but caught her hand. She turned, and they watched as the barely conscious man was dragged from the carriage. Royd caught Wolverstone's eye. "Who is he?"

"Clunes-Forsythe. An exceedingly wealthy man of excellent birth—something of a powerbroker. Keeps to the shadows. I've heard he has no interest in any enterprise unless it promises some personal advantage." Wolverstone joined them. They watched as several others, under Dearne's direction, bound the still-groggy Clunes-Forsythe's hands and commenced lugging him, hunched over and apparently unable to stand upright, along the pavement in full view of a now-goggling throng. The onlookers had deserted the St. Ives' guests in favor of more action and drama.

Wolverstone gestured, and they followed the others, the three of them bringing up the rear.

"This may be the breakthrough we've been angling for." Glancing at Royd, Wolverstone nodded at his shoulder. "How's that?"

"Flesh wound. It's nothing." Of course, Isobel shot him a glare and humphed. He decided he owed her the truth. "It would have been much worse except Isobel kicked the blackguard where it hurts the most at just the right moment—his shot went high."

Isobel swung to stare at him. Her gaze tracked down from the furrow in his shoulder, and her eyes widened…

He squeezed her hand—and kept squeezing until she dragged her gaze up and met his eyes. He grinned. "We make an excellent team."

A muffled sound escaped Wolverstone, who was studiously looking ahead.

Isobel wasn't appeased. She glared again, then muttered, "Later," and faced forward.

Two paces on, Wolverstone inquired, "I take it they used some threat against your son to lure you from the ballroom?"

"Yes." Isobel explained. In conclusion, she shrugged. "As soon as Duncan entered into the calculations, I forgot about everything else."

"Entirely understandable," Wolverstone returned. "That was what Clunes-Forsythe was counting on."

They'd reached the St. Ives' steps when pounding footsteps and a hail of "Your Grace" gave them pause.

Wolverstone looked back. "Yes?"

The footman they'd sent to Stanhope Street pulled up with a grin. Although breathless, he managed to get out, "All's well with the boy—he's apparently fast asleep in his bed."

"Thank God!" Isobel felt a lingering weight slide from her shoulders; she'd been *almost* sure Duncan was safe and sound, but when it came to her son, almost would never be good enough. She smiled at the footman. "And thank you."

The footman, still grinning, bowed. "A pleasure, miss."

"Right, then." Wolverstone started up the steps with renewed vigor.

Arm in arm, Isobel and Royd followed.

Wolverstone paused just inside the mansion's doors.

They were joined by Devil Cynster. "Dearne said you wanted to have a go at Clunes-Forsythe here and now.

Honoria suggested the ground floor drawing room—it'll fit all of us who want to watch."

Wolverstone nodded. He glanced at Isobel and Royd. "I've a feeling that, thanks to a mother's overriding instinct to save her child, we've just been handed the lever we've been searching for. In kidnapping Isobel, stealing the necklace, and shooting Royd, Clunes-Forsythe committed three capital crimes—ones we can easily prove—and all before witnesses of unimpeachable standing."

"As to that," Devil said, "Strickland's fallen apart. He'll testify as to Clunes-Forsythe's instructions. Strickland's an idiot, but his family is sound—they'll hold him to it."

"Excellent." Wolverstone waved them all forward. "Let's see about bringing this oh-so-lengthy mission to a comprehensively satisfying end."

* * *

"Let's endeavor to make this easy on all of us." Wolverstone stood before the huge fireplace in the St. Ives' downstairs drawing room.

Clunes-Forsythe, his hands still bound, had been placed on a straight-backed chair at the end of the Aubusson rug, facing Wolverstone. To either side, the room was packed with all those who had assisted in his capture. The ladies filled all the available seats, and the men ranged about the walls.

Clunes-Forsythe's face showed little expression, little by way of reaction to Wolverstone's words, but the man was listening.

"Our position is this." Wolverstone drew the blue diamond necklace from his pocket. Walking forward, he handed it to Isobel, seated in the middle of one of the long sofas; Clunes-Forsythe's eyes tracked the winking stones. "These diamonds represent the products of an illicit mine operating in West Africa, a few days out of Freetown. The area in question is part of the British colony of West Africa. The mine could have been set up legitimately, but those behind it elected to improve their profits by keeping the enterprise a secret and, most relevantly, using slave labor—British men, women, and children seized from the settlement of Freetown. Through various efforts, a mission was dispatched with the aim of rescuing those held captive, closing the mine, identifying those responsible, and securing evidence sufficient to convict those behind the scheme." Wolverstone paused to incline his head to Clunes-Forsythe. "Courtesy of your intervention tonight, we now know the identity of all six backers—and we have all six in custody."

Clunes-Forsythe blinked.

Wolverstone's smile took on a sharp edge. "Indeed. We already have Ross-Courtney, Neill, Deveny, Cummins, and Risdale secreted away. We realize that the rationale behind what you all believed to be a very safe investment was the assumption that your positions—especially that of Ross-Courtney as one of the king's closest confidantes—guaranteed that, even if the scheme was uncovered, even if your involvement was discovered, ultimately no charges would be laid."

His dark gaze resting on Clunes-Forsythe, Wolverstone paused, then, in a conversational tone, went on, "Five—or even three—years ago, that might well have been the case. But thanks to some of those here"—a wave indicated those watching and listening—"the Black Cobra was brought down last year. Together with unrest over the courts' perceived reluctance to hear charges against the upper echelon—those with political, monetary, and social clout—the incident of the Black Cobra and the ramifications flowing from it have forced the government to take a stand." Wolverstone leveled a steady gaze on their prisoner. "The government has already decreed that those behind schemes such as this diamond mine will be treated as any other men and bear the full consequences of their actions. Publicly."

Clunes-Forsythe twitched; he was now listening avidly.

"As the investigating force, we currently have all six backers in custody. The other five are being held incommunicado—there will be no chance for any of them to alert any supporters to their incarceration. No chance for Ross-Courtney's friends, or any others, to attempt to interfere. You will shortly be joining the other five. None of you will be freed again—the next time you appear in public will be at your trial. As for the evidence we either already hold, or are in the process of gathering, we have the three local managers of the scheme in custody as well, and all three have agreed to turn king's evidence. Their testimony, linked with the personal evidence of the agents who freed those at the mine and of several officers who were among the captives, will prove conclusively the criminal nature of the mining operation. In addition, Ross-Courtney and Neill had already reached the mine and demonstrated their involvement beyond doubt to said agents and officers before the rescue was carried out and Ross-Courtney and Neill were captured. Further, we now have documentary evidence of the money Ross-Courtney sent Satterly to fund the mine. Now we know the identities involved, we will be able to access evidence showing where that money came from—namely, the six backers. We also know of the existence of the diamond merchant and expect to learn his identity any day. He will lead us to the banker, and that will close the circle, giving us evidence of the six backers profiting from the sale of the diamonds taken from the mine they paid to establish."

Wolverstone sent a congratulatory glance around the room, at all those gathered. "All in all, we've managed to construct a strong and inescapable case." He returned his gaze to Clunes-Forsythe. "We expect to have the last pieces in place within days."

Clunes-Forsythe met Wolverstone's gaze. "Why are you telling me this?"

In an even tone, Wolverstone replied, "In order to expedite the gathering of evidence to the point that any trial will be cut and dried—for obvious reasons, the government does not wish such a spectacle to be prolonged—I've been authorized to offer leniency to one of the six backers. Just one, for we don't require more than one of you to give us the few pieces of information we're still waiting on. To be clear, the crimes involved in the establishment and operation of the mine and profiting from it are hanging offences. The Crown's leniency will extend only to commuting one sentence from hanging to transportation for life. That is the offer currently on the table. However"—Wolverstone paused in a histrionic manner Isobel, for one, appreciated—"once we have all the required evidence in our hands—which will be within a week, if not days—then the need for cooperation will vanish, and the offer of leniency will be withdrawn."

Clunes-Forsythe was patently following every word. A moment elapsed, then he asked, "Have you made this offer to the other five?"

"To four of them. Risdale was picked up this evening—we haven't yet spent time talking with him."

Clunes-Forsythe arched his brows. "And none of the others took up the offer?"

"No." Wolverstone smiled. "But none of them know

about the investigations—all the rest I just shared with you."

A touch of wariness seeped into Clunes-Forsythe's expression. "Why did you share that information with me?"

"Because at this point, you, of the six, are the one who stands to gain most by cooperating. Consider—if, by some misbegotten chance, Ross-Courtney managed to get word out, and the king stepped in before we have the necessary evidence, and our ability to prosecute vanished, then the other backers might well walk free—but you won't. You're facing the gallows come what may. Tonight, your pursuit of the products of the mine led you to commit three major crimes. First, you kidnapped a lady from a ton ball. Second, you lifted a necklace worth a king's ransom from about her neck and placed that necklace in your pocket."

Clunes-Forsythe's black gaze swung to Royd. "Frobisher could have done that."

"No, he couldn't have." Dearne spoke from his position by the wall. "I was on his heels. You'd put a hood over Miss Carmichael's head. Frobisher didn't have time to lift the hood, retrieve the necklace, and put it in your pocket before I was there."

Wolverstone caught Clunes-Forsythe's eyes. "You see? And your third crime was to shoot Frobisher, at point blank range, in front of me, Dearne, Lostwithiel, and several others. Your chances of talking your way free of any of those charges are nil."

Clunes-Forsythe stared up the room.

No one said anything; Isobel found it amazing that even though there were close to fifty people in the room, no one fidgeted, let alone moved. Not even Iona, who had insisted on attending and was seated beside her. They were all waiting to see which way this would go. Wolverstone had made their position out to be much stronger—much more immediate—than it actually was. But he'd been convincing, and Clunes-Forsythe appeared to have followed Wolverstone's careful direction.

Eventually, Clunes-Forsythe straightened and drew a deeper breath. "If—I say *if*—I were to…expedite your investigations, would the commutation of sentence extend to the charges arising from my actions tonight?"

He was going to accept the offer. Isobel felt triumph well and tamped it down. He hadn't accepted yet.

"That," Wolverstone said, "would depend on those involved in those charges." He arched a brow at Royd, to his right. "Frobisher?"

Royd had been standing with arms crossed, legs braced, his eyes rarely leaving Clunes-Forsythe's face. His gaze still on the man, he nodded curtly.

Wolverstone turned to Isobel. "Miss Carmichael?"

Her gaze also on Clunes-Forsythe, she, too, nodded.

"St. Ives?"

Isobel glanced around.

His arms crossed over his chest, Devil Cynster was leaning against the edge of the fireplace. "I'm not delighted at the prospect." The expression on his harsh-featured face made that obvious. "However, if agreeing means he'll never darken England's shores again and, instead, will slave away in a penal colony at the ends of the earth for the rest of his natural life…" Devil shrugged. "I suppose I can accept that."

Wolverstone looked back at Clunes-Forsythe. "You have your answer."

"In that case"—Clunes-Forsythe drew in a long breath—"you may consider your investigations complete." He smiled, a thin-lipped gesture. "I never trust anyone and men like Ross-Courtney least of all. I've kept records of everything. All the details you might wish for. Far more than Ross-Courtney ever had an inkling I knew." He raised his bound wrists and reached inside his coat. He struggled, but no one rose to help him. Eventually, hc drew forth a chain from which dangled a key. "If you will send someone to my house, to my study, this key opens the safe behind my grandmother's portrait to the left of the desk. Inside, you'll find ledgers with all the details you might need."

Wolverstone walked to Clunes-Forsythe and took the key.

"I have one question." It was Caleb who spoke. "Pure curiosity. You just made a choice between hanging or what Cynster said. Why choose what many, especially of your age, would consider a fate worse than death?"

Clunes-Forsythe's brows rose. After a moment, he replied, "Ironically enough, I daresay it was the same choice those I condemned to slavery made. Where there's life, there's hope."

Wolverstone studied Clunes-Forsythe for a moment, then said, "Purely as a formality, we allege that you—along with Risdale, Neill, Lord Hugh Deveny, and Sir Reginald Cummins—were recruited by Lord Peter Ross-Courtney to fund an illegal diamond mine to be worked by slave labor in the West Africa Colony. The local management of the mine was provided by Arnold Satterly—a connection of Ross-Courtney's and principal aide to the colony's governor—along with Muldoon, the resident naval attaché, and William Winton, the assistant commissar at Fort Thornton. Can you confirm those details are correct?"

Clunes-Forsythe leaned back in the chair and met Wolverstone's gaze. "Your summation is correct in every respect."

Isobel smiled. She looked across at Royd as he looked at her.

"Done." They mouthed the word simultaneously.

Then they laughed.

* * *

Triumph buoyed all those who'd been a part of the effort to capture the backers.

Wolverstone dispatched Clunes-Forsythe to Essex, then returned to congratulate everyone. During her husband's absence, Minerva had arranged for champagne to be served in the drawing room. The company toasted themselves. They toasted the captives. They toasted Royd and Isobel and all the Frobisher captains and their ladies, who, as Wolverstone put it, "had been critically instrumental in bringing an ugly chapter in British colonial rule to an end."

Isobel kept a satisfied smile fixed on her face; she felt the triumph as much as anyone, but she also had trouble ignoring the dark stain marring the left shoulder of Royd's coat.

When he bent to whisper in her ear, suggesting they use his injury as an excuse to leave, she dallied only long enough to place Iona under Kate's wing. Along with all the others, Iona had returned to the ballroom, where fully half the ton waited, agog to learn what had transpired. Rather than dally in the front hall, stationary prey for all those intent on speaking with them, admiring the necklace—once again gracing her throat—and asking all sorts of prying questions, they left the carriages for the others, slipped out of the mansion's side door, and, arm in arm, set off at a brisk pace.

Away from the bustle about the St. Ives' steps, the night was cool, the sky overcast, the streets relatively empty of pedestrians. They skirted two other residences hosting parties. Their long legs ate the distance, and soon, Humphrey was admitting them into the quiet of Declan and Edwina's front hall.

After reassuring Humphrey that all was well with his master and mistress, and that they and the others would be along shortly, Isobel pointed to Royd's wound and requested hot water to be delivered to their room.

Humphrey bowed. "At once, ma'am."

She turned and led the way up the stairs. Humphrey had consistently referred to her as "ma'am," not "miss"; she hadn't bothered to correct him, reasoning that, in truth, his choice of honorific was more accurate than not.

Royd climbed the stairs in Isobel's wake. Inside him, a morass of emotions were swirling, welling, and churning, surging toward breaking loose. He'd managed to keep them suppressed, managed to maintain a civilized façade, but even as they reached the top of the stairs, he could feel his control eroding.

The wound on his shoulder stung, but getting shot had been a relief. Once the pistol had discharged, it had no longer been a threat to Isobel. Seeing her as he had in the instant in which he'd wrenched open the door—hooded and tied, with an unknown gentleman holding a pistol trained on her…he never wanted to face such a horrifying sight again.

Capping the sequence of realizing she was missing, then grasping the fact that she'd been lured away, that moment had shaken him to his foundation, to a depth and a degree that, until then, he hadn't realized was possible.

To have secured her again, only to lose her… That couldn't ever happen.

She stopped outside Duncan's door, eased it open, and tiptoed inside.

Royd followed. He couldn't understand why she tiptoed; their son slept as heavily as he did.

Halting just inside the darkened room, lit only by a small night-light on the dresser, he watched as she gently tucked Duncan's arm beneath the sheet, then she brushed back his hair and dropped a kiss on his temple.

From where Royd stood, he could see Duncan's face, in sleep more like Isobel's than his.

He could see her face, too—see the unconditional love that transformed her features from Amazon to madonna.

Something inside him swelled, overwhelming all other emotions.

When she stepped back from the bed, he reached out, caught her hand, and towed her out of the room. He shut the door, then drew her on to theirs; he opened it, swung her through, then followed and shut the panel.

He'd forgotten just how much, emotionally, they mirrored each other. As he turned, intending to haul her to him, she flung herself at him, and he caught her.

At the first touch of their lips, all restraint cindered. There was no argument about who was in charge; tonight, neither of them were.

Neither of them could control *this*—this maelstrom of need.

Passion was there, pulsing and strong, while desire raged, a fiery torrent in their veins, but it was need, raw and ungovernable, that drove them, a near-violent craving for reassurance.

For the most elemental affirmation that they had weathered the challenge, that they were hale, whole, and oh-so-intensely alive.

He loosened her laces just enough to drag her bodice down, then he feasted on her breasts. Her head tipped back, and she moaned, her nails biting into his upper arms through coat and shirt.

Then her grip eased, and her hands went a-wandering—over his chest and down to, through his trousers, cup and caress him. Then her busy fingers found the buttons at his waist and slid them free.

Her hand dove inside, and she found him. Held him, claimed him.

Chest swelling, he raised his head, pivoted, and pushed her back against the door, then he bent his head and ravaged her mouth again.

She met him, matched him, challenged and defied him every step of the way.

His Amazon.

He couldn't wait. Neither could she.

She kicked off her pumps.

He rucked her silken skirts up to her waist, slid an arm beneath her hips, and hoisted her against the door.

"Your shoulder," she gasped, even as she wrapped her long legs about his hips.

"Later." He positioned his erection at her entrance, sucked in a breath at her slickly heated welcome, then thrust in, deep, into the indescribable wonder of her body.

She wrapped him in warmth and welcome, in passion-slicked delight, held him tight and caressed…then he withdrew and thrust in again, deeper, farther, and she gasped and held him even tighter.

They fell into the rhythm they knew so well, one that caught them, trapped them, built, then drove them.

On, ever on.

Into the waiting glory.

Into the joy, the wonder, the scintillating pleasure neither could reach without the other.

This was theirs.

Forever and always.

This joining at a depth that linked their souls.

Where, beyond the senses-numbing, wit-shattering tumult of a shockingly glorious climax, love waited, a blessed benediction, to soothe their forever-yearning hearts.

To reassure, to renew, to reaffirm what was, and what would always be.

Them, together.

For eternity.

* * *

Hours later, long after they'd heard the others come in and the house had settled for the remainder of the night, Royd surrendered to Isobel's insistent prodding and consented to sit on the edge of the bed so she could tend his wound—bathe it enough to remove his ruined coat, waistcoat, and shirt, and then dab some ointment Humphrey had provided over the raw red groove.

He set his teeth and endured, but when she stared at the ointment-daubed spot and said, "Should we bandage it, do you think?" he'd had enough.

"No." The word was categorical. He fell back on the bed and used the opportunity to wriggle out of his trousers. "Come back to bed."

"Hmm." Through the shadows, she studied him, then she turned and set the pot of ointment aside.

He shuffled higher on the bed to recline against the pillows and watch as she removed the necklace, stripped off her exceedingly crushed gown, then shed her stockings and garters, and finally, her chemise.

Naked—an Amazon in truth—she walked through the shadows to the end of the bed, then, with an almost feline grace, she crawled up until she could sit straddling his waist.

Her gaze had locked on his latest wound.

Then, as if noticing them for the first time—which he knew wasn't the case—she let her fingers trace old scars. "Was it true," she asked, "what you said on the pavement—that if I hadn't kicked that bastard, his shot would have gone lower? Or was that just you gilding the lily?"

He hesitated—he had no idea what tortuous path her mind was taking—but…no secrets. "It was true. In such a situation, he could hardly have missed, and I didn't reach him in time to deflect his aim."

Her gaze rose to his eyes. Her eyes were so dark, he had no hope of reading their expression, let alone her emotions, and even less her mind.

"If it hadn't been you… I don't think I would have thought to kick him. I was so…" She paused, clearly thinking back. "I was going to say *frightened* for you, but that isn't accurate—I was so far beyond frightened, even beyond desperate."

"You were where I was when I hauled open the carriage door and saw him holding the pistol on you." He paused, then more quietly said, "I'd reached the point where nothing else mattered but keeping you safe."

Her gaze on his face, on his eyes, she nodded. "Yes. That's it exactly. I don't matter if I can't have you—me living doesn't matter if you're not there to share my life."

He let a moment go by, then confessed, "That's the way I've always felt about you."

She drew in a breath, then replied, "And that might be the way I've always felt about you, too, but when we handfasted, I hadn't had a chance to find out—hadn't had a chance to experience that moment, that instant of utter selflessness. That instant when you realize that, even though we're two people, in reality we're effectively one." Her gaze dropped to the long scar beneath her fingertips.

And in an instant of blessed insight, he caught her train of thought. "I mentioned that I was thinking of re-arranging roles in the company. I talked to my father yesterday, and he agreed. When we get back, I'll be retiring as Principal Captain of Frobisher Shipping—the operational head of the company. We've all agreed that hat will pass to Caleb."

She considered that. "So what will you do?"

"I intend devoting all my time to building and improving ships. With you."

She studied him, one finger beating a tattoo on his chest. "Won't you get bored?"

He shook his head. "Now I have you in my life again, now I've been reminded of how precious what we have between us is, now I have Duncan to care for, too, I don't need missions to give my life purpose. I'll have you, Duncan, and the ships we'll build together. And the rest."

"What rest?"

"A home. And Duncan's nearly eight—don't you think it's past time he had some siblings?"

"You just want him to have more brothers so you'll have more sons to teach to sail."

He grinned. "Not true. A girl or two, or even three, would keep my life interesting equally well."

She laughed, but then she looked at him and sobered. After a moment, she said, "What truly frightened me—not just tonight, but in the attack on the compound, too—was the extent I would go to save you. Love might be a strength, but it's a vulnerability, too, isn't it? We both feel it that way."

"Yes, but there's responsibility to counter that—a responsibility in being the one loved, in not taking silly, unnecessary risks. In not risking what we have unless we must." He captured her fingers, drew them to his lips, and pressed a kiss to the slender digits. "And we both understand that, too."

Slowly, she nodded. Then she asked, "So in the future? No risks?"

"That I can't promise—and neither can you. But as we proved tonight, if there are risks we deem must be taken, then we'll take them together, and we'll win through."

She smiled, then tipped sideways onto the bed and stretched out alongside him, her legs tangling with his, her head resting just below his uninjured shoulder, her hand splayed over his heart. He heard the smile in her voice as she said, "Because we're an excellent team."

"Indeed." He settled his arms around her, then raised his head to press a kiss to her forehead. "Because we're bound by unbreakable chains that will never release us, that will draw us together even if we try to stay apart."

"Together," she murmured. "Together for the rest of our lives."

He wasn't about to argue. Instead, he held her close as, together, they slid into dreams of their joint future—a future built of, built on, and built around their love.

Epilogue

Three days later, the Frobisher ladies hosted a picnic in the grounds of the Royal Observatory at Greenwich. The crews of all the Frobisher ships currently anchored in the Pool of London were summoned to attend. As well as *The Trident* and *The Cormorant*, that number included *The Corsair* and *The Prince*, which had arrived two days before; the combined crews formed a rowdy crowd, ready to toast their recent adventures and exchange already embellished tales of their parts in the action.

Royd had several announcements to make, the first of which related to the mission. He stood under the spreading branches of a tree and addressed the surrounding horde. "In deference to His Majesty's distress on learning of the culpability of his longtime confidante Lord Peter Ross-Courtney in such a heinous crime, a trial was held in camera yesterday. Due to the wealth of evidence unearthed in Clunes-Forsythe's study, combined with the testimony of Clunes-Forsythe, Satterly, Muldoon, and Winton, the judges reached a swift and unanimous verdict. Although the trial was conducted behind closed doors, all agreed that the sentencing would take place publicly in a few days' time. However, it has already been decreed that Satterly, Muldoon, Winton, and

Clunes-Forsythe will be transported for life, while the remaining five backers will hang."

Cheers erupted on all sides. Royd waited until they'd quietened, then added, "The latter sentence will be carried out publicly, too. The news-sheets are going to have a field day, and for once, that will be to everyone's benefit." He looked around at all the eager faces, smiled, and somewhat wryly said, "Thanks to all here, and to all who assisted in the success of this mission, the government is breathing much easier today."

Everyone laughed.

Royd continued, "The diamond merchant and the banker involved have been identified and various monies recovered. The collective weight of several members of the nobility was brought to bear, and the Crown agreed to surrender the money to the restitution fund already established for the ex-captives in Freetown."

Another round of cheering greeted that news.

Kate broke in, "A toast!" She raised her glass high. "To Daisy, Si, and Wattie Watson, as well as all the friends we left behind in Freetown." The roar as the company raised their tankards high startled several passersby.

Royd waited, patiently, until all eyes returned, expectantly, to him. "My other news is of a change at the company's helm. As of today, I'm stepping aside as captain of the fleet. That role will henceforth be filled by Caleb."

Shocked surprise filled many faces.

From among the crowd, Williams called out, "Surely you're not giving up sailing, Captain?"

Royd grinned. "No. *The Corsair* will remain under my captaincy, and we'll still be taking our usual voyages, although not as many as previously. Instead, I—and the crew of *The Corsair*, all old hands as we are—will be spending more time working in partnership with the

Carmichael Shipyards in building and testing the next generation of Frobisher ships."

That news pleased everyone—not least Duncan, who was sitting on the grass before Royd, his legs drawn up, his gaze fixed with rapt attention on Royd's face.

"One other change," Royd continued, "is that the government missions that Robert, Declan, and I have been responsible for running will now devolve to Caleb and, although they don't as yet know it, Lachlan and Kit, at Caleb's direction."

So he, Robert, and Declan would now be spending more time in port, and when they sailed—almost certainly with their wives by their sides—it would be on voyages inherently less dangerous. The decision for Robert and Declan to pull back from such missions had been theirs, one Royd understood and supported. The responsibility of being loved and the need to keep those they loved safe were not issues they could deal with from half a world away.

Royd glanced around. Everyone was talking, discussing the changes and what they would mean. Isobel came up and looped her arm with his.

Briefly, he met her gaze, then he looked back at the gathering and raised his tankard high; the crews noticed and immediately looked his way.

"To absent friends. To the Frobishers."

It was a traditional family toast, and the men knew it well. They raised their voices in chorus.

"May the skies remain clear, the wind fill our sails, and the seas run smooth and swift beneath our hulls. *To the horizon and on!*"

The final roar rose to the skies, and everyone drank.

Royd had heard Isobel's low, sultry voice repeating the words. He lowered his tankard, turned from the men, and met her eyes. Saw love, unshielded, shining in the rich brown and smiled.

She smiled back. "Come and walk with us—Duncan wants to go down to the river to see the boats and ships."

Duncan stood waiting, trying to hide his impatience.

Royd grinned and handed his empty tankard to one of the men. "In that case, let's go."

Duncan cheered and led the way.

"Not too far ahead," Isobel called.

The other Frobisher couples fell in behind them. Declan supported an increasingly bulky yet still pluckily and determinedly mobile Edwina. Aileen leaned on Robert's arm, a wide smile on her face. Kate and Caleb followed, but not before Iona, stumping along with Elaine and Fergus in the rear, had acerbically remarked that Kate could forget any notion of returning to work in Freetown. "I'd rather see another Carmody married to a Frobisher than that!"

"I take it," Royd murmured, "that that's Iona's way of saying she approves of both my and Caleb's suits?"

Isobel tipped her head in thought, then said, "I think approval might be stretching the truth. Resignation is nearer the mark."

Royd chuckled and shook his head.

They ambled on, ahead of the others, with Duncan skipping before them.

Royd realized Isobel was studying him. He caught her eye and arched a brow.

"I was just thinking of what you said before—how much sailing for the company do you think you'll do?"

"Not much for the foreseeable future. There's not just the new fleet to design and work on, but I plan on spending time with Duncan." He let his gaze slide down her svelte figure to her still-flat stomach. "And with that one, too. I missed all that with Duncan—I'm not going to miss a minute this time around."

"Ah." She looked ahead. "You noticed."

"I run a business and engineer your designs—I can count."

The smile that lit her face was more madonna than Amazon. "I intended to tell you when we were back at sea and free of all the others."

He considered, then agreed, "We don't need to tell them yet." He thought, then added, "Duncan, Declan's firstborn, Robert's firstborn, and now our second. We've made a good start on begetting the Frobisher captains to sail our new fleet."

"We'd better start on those new designs."

"As soon as we get back to Aberdeen." He glanced back, then seized her hand and, in three long strides, whisked them off the path and around the large trunk of a nearby tree.

A soft laugh was on her lips as he backed her against the bole; he kissed it from the luscious curves, then deepened the exchange and savored.

Isobel leaned against the tree, wound her arms about his neck, and gave herself up to the kiss—to him, to them. To the knowledge that, with the end of this voyage, they'd finally found their way back to each other, and together, they'd found their way home.

* * *

They sailed into Aberdeen five days later. Through breaks in the thick clouds, the morning sun beamed on their backs, and a blustery wind filled their sails.

The Corsair led the way, with the rest of the small fleet strung out behind them. Fergus and Elaine had elected to sail with Declan and Edwina on *The Cormorant*, while Iona was on *The Prince* with Caleb and Kate.

They crested a wave, and from her position at the stern deck's forward rail alongside Royd as he steered his ship, Isobel saw the roofs of Aberdeen ahead. She laughed and pointed. "Home!"

Beside her, Duncan jigged and cheered.

Isobel glanced down at him. *Home.* For her, for Royd, and for Duncan, too, the word had taken on new meaning.

The mouth of the Dee came into view, and Royd swung the wheel and called the required sail changes to angle *The Corsair* in past the pier. Isobel looked back at the procession of sails following in their wake. With the sun lighting the swollen canvas, the sight was both majestic and evocative.

They'd sailed far away; they'd taken on villains and accepted risks. They'd triumphed and won through to a right and just reward, and now they were returning with the wind at their backs and the sun on their sails.

Smiling, she faced forward.

People on the pier had spotted them. More came running; it wasn't that often that such a grand sight came sailing in. And these were locals—even more reason to cheer and wave.

Duncan rushed to the side and waved back. "Africa," he yelled. "We've been to Africa! And London, too."

Royd heard and laughed. He met her eyes. "He has his priorities in the right order."

She smiled and pressed a hand to his arm.

He turned to her and, when she looked up, pressed a fleeting kiss on her lips. "How are you feeling?"

She widened her eyes. "Surprisingly well." She hadn't sailed when she was carrying Duncan. She'd expected to feel at least queasy. "Apparently, this babe is a Frobisher through and through—born to sail."

He grinned and turned back to the task of easing down the river and through the narrows into the docks.

Finally, all sails were down, and the hull glided the last yards to gently bump against the Frobisher wharf.

Sailors leapt to secure the ship. Royd handed over command to Liam, then turned to Isobel.

She met his gaze and saw their future in his gray eyes.

He held out a hand. "Are you ready?"

He wasn't referring solely to disembarking. Smiling, she put her fingers into his, felt his grip, and returned the pressure. "For our future?"

Royd held her gaze. "For our wedding and all the years to come."

Her smile grew radiant. "Yes."

He pulled her in for a quick, passionate kiss, then, with the entire crew grinning and Duncan impatiently leading the way, they made for the lower deck, the gangplank, and the wharf—and the future they'd decided to claim.

* * *

Practicalities dictated the order of the weddings. Robert and Aileen fronted the altar in the Church of St. Mary, just below Scarborough Castle, in late October.

Aileen's parents were delighted with the match, with the prospect of a grandchild when they'd given up hope, and they felt even more blessed when all three of Aileen's brothers managed to get shore leave and make it home in time to attend.

Robert's brothers stood as his groomsmen. With no sisters and not even any close female cousins, Aileen had elected to ask her three soon-to-be sisters-in-law to be her attendants.

Kit and Lachlan raced across country from their home port of Bristol for the event, arriving just in time to beat the bride into the church. They joined Robert's officers and most of his crew, who had traveled from Aberdeen to see their captain tie the knot with a lady who had won their respect and affection.

Needless to say, although the company was select, the wedding breakfast was a riotous affair, with toasts and tales and laughter and happiness lasting long into the afternoon.

No one was surprised when Kate caught the bride's bouquet.

Edwina's only comment was that it was a sign they needed to hurry up—she was determined not to miss a single wedding, and she was only weeks away from not being able to travel… No one was inclined to attempt to argue with a heavily pregnant daughter of a duke.

* * *

Consequently, Caleb and Kate were married in the Dunnottar Parish Church in the woods outside Stonehaven in early November. Although Iona had argued for an Aberdeen location, Kate had insisted; her parents were buried in the graveyard at Dunnottar, and that was the congregation she had always been a part of.

As Royd and Isobel's upcoming nuptials would be celebrated in Aberdeen, Iona had given way with reasonable grace.

Kate had also put her foot down—strongly supported by Isobel—over Iona's suggestion of a handfasting rather than a wedding. Faced with Isobel, a testament to the advisability of such a route when a Frobisher was involved, Iona had accepted Kate's position without even a quibble.

Once again, the same four gentlemen and the same four ladies made up the bridal party; only the identities of the groom and bride had changed.

Kate and Caleb made their vows in clear, strong voices, and the sun broke through the clouds and shone through the stained-glass windows to bathe them in a golden glow.

Despite the season, the setting was idyllic. The well-wishers thronged the small church and later flowed onto the grounds, waiting to congratulate the newlyweds as they did the rounds. To Kate's surprise, many of the locals who had known her mother, and her, too, came to wish her well, along with more members of her father's family than she'd expected.

Caleb's crew were all there—and in a delightful surprise, Phillipe Lascelle had sailed into Aberdeen that morning. He made it to the church in time and brought Ducasse and several of his crew who Caleb knew of old and Kate had grown to know in the jungle. Most surprising of all, Phillipe brought Hillsythe, who, theoretically, was on his way back to Freetown to reorganize the governor's office.

With such a crew assembled, the wedding breakfast, held in a nearby inn under Iona's aegis, was a rollicking event. When Kate came down the stairs, changed and ready to leave with Caleb and his crew for a short honeymoon trip to Copenhagen, she paused on the landing, looked down at the unmarried ladies who had been herded into position by a ring of laughing gentlemen, took careful aim, and threw her bouquet.

Isobel caught it—to the raucous cheers of all around—but she'd had no option. Kate, her innocent young cousin, had flung the flowers directly at her face.

* * *

On an overcast day in late November, in the Cathedral Church of St. Machar in Old Aberdeen, Isobel Carmody Carmichael finally walked down the aisle to meet Royd Frobisher.

Her father, James, gave her away, his pride etched in his face for all to see.

In her usual unique fashion, Isobel had chosen to be married in a watered silk gown in tones of blue that recalled the colors of the sea. A delicate lace veil lay over her black hair and floated about her shoulders, and around her throat, the cerulean fire of the blue diamond necklace blazed. Royd had bought the necklace anonymously at the public auction conducted by Rundell, Bridge, and Rundell, the proceeds of which had been added to the restitution fund in Freetown. He'd presented the fabulous memento to Isobel as his wedding gift; as he'd said, the necklace would always mean more to him and her than to anyone else.

In turn, she'd given him her heart, her soul, one son, with another child on the way.

Both considered themselves well and truly blessed.

Isobel's three attendants wore silk gowns in a range of paler sea greens and sea blues. They lined up beside her at the altar, the medley of colors reminding everyone of the central role the sea played in the lives of those involved.

The service wasn't short; all those who had waited so long for this day had been determined to extract their due. When the bride and groom exchanged their vows, lace handkerchiefs fluttered, and tears gleamed in many an eye.

The bridal party lined up before the altar was familiar to many, with one notable addition. Duncan popped up between his parents to offer his father a shining gold band on a red velvet cushion; with a thoroughly joyful expression, he watched as Royd picked up the band, took Isobel's hand, and slid the ring into place.

Duncan stepped back only when, after the minister pronounced Royd and Isobel man and wife, Royd drew

Isobel into his arms and they kissed—before God and their families and the massive congregation gathered to witness the joining of two families who had for so long been a part of the town and, with this union, looked set to take Aberdeen ships and shipping onto ever more challenging seas.

With the groomsmen and attendants, Isobel and Royd retired to sign the register, then they returned from the vestry to stand hand in hand with their heads bowed for the benediction.

Finally, they raised their heads, turned, and, with joy in their hearts and happiness lighting their eyes and faces, with ever quickening strides, led the bridal party up the aisle.

A burst of unseasonal sunshine greeted them as they emerged onto the church's front steps. Royd dragged his gaze from Isobel's face, looked ahead, and laughed.

Isobel followed his gaze and discovered a long avenue of uniformed figures with swords raised in honor. "Good Lord!"

There were army, navy, and merchantman uniforms, along with others she didn't recognize. And in between, she spied many young cousins—both hers and Royd's—skulking.

She looked at Royd.

He arched a brow at her. "Shall we?"

She laughed. "Yes—but let's run."

She hiked up her skirts, and they ran, weathering a storm of rice and flowers to emerge, still laughing, at the end of the long line.

Their groomsmen and attendants, now all married, followed. Caleb and Kate had returned from their honeymoon in time for Kate to be fitted for her gown.

The church was mere yards from Carmody Place, and

the entire congregation had been invited to a wedding breakfast destined to feature in the annals of Aberdeen.

Royd and Isobel circulated among their guests, accepting congratulations and thanking those who had traveled, some from considerable distance, to attend.

The company sat in the great hall for a sumptuous meal, then the toasts began. While there were tales, jokes, and laughter aplenty, ultimately, Iona had the last word. Isobel's cantankerous grandmother rose to her feet, recommended everyone charge their glasses, then raised hers and, with startling brevity, declared, "About time."

Everyone cheered and drank to that, Royd and Isobel included.

Then the music began, and Isobel rose, her hand in Royd's. They whirled down the floor to unstinting applause.

Once the bridal party, and then all others so inclined, had joined them on the floor, she smiled, let Royd draw her nearer, and rested her head on his shoulder. "About time," she murmured.

"At last," he replied.

Later, when she returned from changing out of her silk gown, and the ritual of tossing the wedding bouquet was upon them, instead of taking aim, she held to tradition, turned her back to the expectant crowd, and flung her bouquet—somewhat exuberantly—over her shoulder.

The force of her throw had the bouquet clearing the heads of all the eager cousins and young ladies vying to catch it. It sailed on, then abruptly descended, hitting one outstretched hand, then another, before Kit Frobisher reflexively caught it. Her laughing expression transformed to one of horror. She stared at the bouquet as if it were a snake. She shook her head. "Oh no. No, no, no."

She looked up, and Isobel, who had turned to see, caught her eyes and smiled widely.

Kit narrowed her eyes. She looked around wildly. "Here." She thrust the bouquet at the nearest young lady.

Who, grinning, held up her hands. "Oh no—I couldn't possibly."

No matter who Kit approached, no one would take the bouquet from her.

Isobel walked up; although she managed not to laugh, she was smiling. "It's no use. What's done is done, and I should warn you it's a family tradition that's never failed to deliver."

"*Your* family." Kit frowned at the offending bouquet. "Not the Frobishers."

"Ah, but the Carmodys are now inextricably linked to the Frobishers." Isobel leaned close and lowered her voice. "Were I you, I'd keep my eyes peeled. Someone is coming your way."

Kit met her gaze through narrowed eyes. "That someone had better keep his distance if he has any notion of what's good for him."

Isobel laughed and allowed Royd to draw her away.

They circled the room again. Isobel was content to chat, but Royd had other plans—plans he'd shared with no one but their son.

Very aware of the shenanigans that, especially in the circumstances, were likely to be played on him and his bride, he'd arranged a decoy. A smart phaeton and pair presently sat in the drive; various items were, even then, being attached to its axles and rear.

He bided his time. Carmody Place was a very old house. From Duncan, he'd learned of the secret routes leading from the great hall; he chose his moment and whisked Isobel through a hidden door. Surprised, she looked at him.

"Come on." He took her hand and led her quickly through a maze of minor corridors to the rear of the huge house—where Duncan sat in a plain gig, concentrating as he held the reins.

Jeb, the old head groom, laconically holding the horse's head, was the only other soul around. He grinned and tipped his hat to them as Royd helped Isobel up to the seat. "Good luck to ye, both."

"Thank you, Jeb." Isobel waited until Royd climbed in on Duncan's other side and started the horse trotting down the rear drive before asking, "Where are we going?"

Over Duncan's head, Royd met her gaze. "Home."

He drove them to the manor at Banchory-Devenick.

When he drew the horses to a halt before the weathered gray stone façade, Duncan jumped down and ran to the front door. Isobel waited for Royd to hand her down. He left the gig in the care of a young groom and steered her inside.

She'd been there before, but only as a visitor. Now… felt different. For a start, the house was curiously quiet. "Where is everyone?"

"Papa decided now would be a good time to pay a visit to the Bristol office. He and Mama will sail with Kit on *Consort*—they'll be leaving on this evening's tide. As I assume Aileen mentioned, she and Robert are heading to New York on a belated wedding cruise, while Declan, unsurprisingly, wants to have Edwina back in London as soon as possible—her mother will be staying with them in Stanhope Street until after the baby's born. So *The Trident* and *The Cormorant* will also sail tonight." Royd arched his brows. "Believe it or not, Caleb and Kate have decided to live at Carmody Place, at least for the moment. Kate said that with you and Duncan gone, Iona will feel lonely, and Caleb pointed out that Carmody Place is closer to the office and the docks than the manor."

Royd halted at the bottom of the stairs and faced her. "We haven't discussed where we should live." He glanced around. "If you'd rather be in town—"

"No." She shook her head. "This is where we should be." She'd known that the instant she'd walked in the door—a sensation as if the house had embraced her. "But I've never been beyond the drawing room." She looked at him. "Show me."

He took her over the entire house. It was larger than she'd imagined, a solid structure built of local gray stone that had been added to and added to over the generations.

He halted in a large first-floor room at the end of one wing. "This is the wing I thought we should have." He nodded to the view of lawns bordered by woods. "It's the most private, and there are rooms aplenty for Duncan and a nursery, and studies for us, as well as a private parlor should we feel the need to escape the bustle that sometimes overtakes the rest of the house."

"It's perfect." She stood before the window. It was perfect in so many ways, not least because he would be there, Duncan would be, too, and they would be part of a larger family. It was what she was used to and also what she needed. But…

When he came to stand beside her and look out of the window, too, she glanced at his face, briefly studied it, then asked, "Will it be enough, do you think—the inventing and designing and commissioning, along with the occasional trip?"

Outside, Duncan was running in circles on the lawn, chasing a puppy Isobel hadn't seen before.

Royd turned his head, met her eyes, and smiled—an

expression far softer than he usually let show. “One thing I’ve learned through all our years—life is for living, and family is life. Nothing can or ever will take me away from this, because nothing can or ever will matter more.”

She saw the truth of his words in his eyes. She smiled a touch mistily. “Iona has a saying that, until today, didn’t apply to me. She’s always insisted that home is where the heart is.” She raised a hand and placed it over his heart. “Over all our years, my heart has never been anywhere else but here.”

He raised his hand and placed it over hers. “As I’ve said repeatedly, Mrs. Frobisher, we make an excellent team.”

* * * * *

Dear Reader,

I hope you've enjoyed the adventure and the romances of The Adventurers Quartet. In many ways, the series name said it all—it wasn't just the heroes who were adventurers, but their respective ladies, too!

As most of you will know, my works are usually set in Britain, mostly in England or Scotland, but when your heroes and their ladies are of swashbuckling ilk—those who will boldly go wherever life's challenges take them—then remaining in Britain simply wouldn't have worked. These characters needed a broader and less civilized stage on which to make their marks, and bigger, wilder challenges to test them and reveal their true strengths. I chose West Africa and the town of Freetown as the setting for this series because it was a place where the British were already established, yet at the relevant time, it was, indeed, very much a frontier, with all the dangers and associated lawlessness. I hope you had fun walking on the wild side—through dusty streets and jungles, and pacing on the decks of ships racing before the wind—rather than down Pall Mall.

Using such a very different setting to my usual circles of the British haut ton was also intended to provide a refreshing break for both you and me before I return with more tales of the Cynster Next Generation, namely the Devil's Brood Trilogy—*The Lady By His Side*, *An Irresistible Alliance*, and *The Greatest Challenge of Them All*—three connected stories of romance and intrigue coming to you later in 2017.

Until then, happy reading!

Stephanie Laurens

For alerts as new books are released,
plus information on upcoming books, sign up
for Stephanie's Private Email Newsletter,
either on her website or at:
http://eepurl.com/gLgPj
Or if you're a member of Goodreads,
join the discussion of Stephanie's books at
the Fans of Stephanie Laurens group.
You can email Stephanie at
stephanie@stephanielaurens.com
Or find her on Facebook at
http://www.facebook.com/AuthorStephanieLaurens
You can find detailed information on
all Stephanie's published books,
including covers, descriptions, and excerpts,
on her website at
http://www.stephanielaurens.com

STEPHANIE LAURENS

31896	THE DAREDEVIL SNARED	___$7.99 U.S.	___$9.99 CAN.
31878	A BUCCANEER AT HEART	___$7.99 U.S.	___$9.99 CAN.
31861	THE LADY'S COMMAND	___$7.99 U.S.	___$9.99 CAN.
31834	A MATCH FOR MARCUS CYNSTER	___$7.99 U.S.	___$8.99 CAN.
31782	THE TEMPTING OF THOMAS CARRICK	___$7.99 U.S.	___$8.99 CAN.
31765	BY WINTER'S LIGHT	___$7.99 U.S.	___$9.99 CAN.

(limited quantities available)

TOTAL AMOUNT	$________
POSTAGE & HANDLING	$________
($1.00 for 1 book, 50¢ for each additional)	
APPLICABLE TAXES*	$________
TOTAL PAYABLE	$________

(check or money order—please do not send cash)

To order, complete this form and send it, along with a check or money order for the total above, payable to MIRA Books, to: **In the U.S.:** 3010 Walden Avenue, P.O. Box 9077, Buffalo, NY 14269-9077; **In Canada:** P.O. Box 636, Fort Erie, Ontario, L2A 5X3.

Name: ______________________________
Address: ____________________ City: ____________
State/Prov.: ________________ Zip/Postal Code: __________
Account Number (if applicable): ______________________
075 CSAS

*New York residents remit applicable sales taxes.
*Canadian residents remit applicable GST and provincial taxes.

www.MIRABooks.com

MSL0117BL